SPLINTERED

BOOK TWO OF THE ASUNDER TRILOGY

Gloria —
Very best wishes.
Curt Locklear

CURT LOCKLEAR

We invite you to download your complimentary MP3 album of Americana music insipired by *Splintered* at:
www.reverbnation.com/splinteredsongsofthecivilwar

PRAISE FOR
CURT LOCKLEAR AND THE
ASUNDER SERIES

*Asunder is a book full of passion... for a
good story, for history and for the Civil War.*

– ROBERT HICKS, NEW YORK TIMES BEST-SELLING AUTHOR
OF THE *WIDOW OF THE SOUTH* AND *THE ORPHAN MOTHER*

*Mr. Locklear has a particular talent for stringing
words together, which makes for very lovely prose.
And his word pictures are exquisite. As a researcher
myself, I also enjoyed the detail used in creating this
historical world — especially during the heavy battle scenes.
Extremely engaging. Overall, a very rewarding read.*

– MICHELLE ISENHOFF, BEST-SELLING AUTHOR

*Cyntha's ability to spin a fine story when she's stopped by
soldiers on the road, the efforts made by siblings parted —
sometimes forever — by the war... and the decisions made by a
host of characters operating well outside of their comfort zones
makes Splintered a riveting saga that's hard to put down.*

– D. DONOVAN, SR. REVIEWER MIDWEST BOOK REVIEWS

Splintered
ISBN: 978-1-943258-46-8 (soft cover)
978-1-943258-49-9 (hard cover)

Warren Publishing
www.warrenpublishing.net

Printed in the United States of America

To my father who loved to tell stories
and passed this attribute down to his children.

To my mother who gave me
a love for reading and creativity.

ACKNOWLEDGEMENTS

I wish to thank these dynamic, talented people who have made *Splintered* and the accompanying music CD and mp3 a reality. Most importantly, I wish to thank Sandra Timm, whose support and guidance have been beyond measure and is deeply appreciated. Her heart is pure gold.

Further, I wish to acknowledge Dick and Allyson Meacham, Eddie Medina, Katherine Glinka, Allen Haines, Marlys Boettner, Lorrie Reid, and Betty Schroeder — all of them excellent musicians. I also wish to acknowledge the wonderful support of Bobbie Carlton-Hess, Jody Townsley Morse, Daniel Umbehr, and the entire Woodlands Writers Group.

I appreciate excellent, insightful editors, Tracy Crow and Becki Kinch, and my patient book cover artist, Karen Phillips. Of course, praise goes to my publisher, Mindy Kuhn of Warren Publishing.

Lastly, I am deeply grateful to my son, Nathan Locklear, who filmed and edited the stunning *Splintered* book trailer. He was assisted by the ever-caring, Eva Busch.

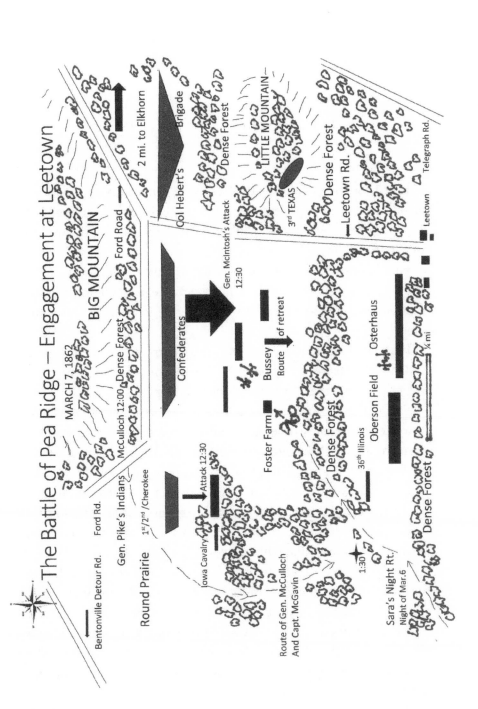

The Battle of Pea Ridge – Engagement at Leetown

MARCH 7, 1862

BIG MOUNTAIN

Bentonville Detour Rd.

Ford Rd.

Gen. Pike's Indians

1st/2nd /Cherokee

Round Prairie

Route of Gen. McCulloch
And Capt. McGavin

Iowa Cavalry

Attack 12:30

Confederates

McCulloch 12:00

Dense Forest

Ford Road

2 mi. to Elkhorn

Col Hebert's

Brigade

Gen. McIntosh's Attack
12:30

Dense Forest

LITTLE MOUNTAIN

3rd TEXAS

Dense Forest

Leetown Rd.

Leetown

Telegraph Rd.

Bussey

Route   of retreat

Foster Farm

Dense Forest

36th Illinois

Oberson Field

Osterhaus

¾ mi

1:30

Sara's Night Rt.

Night of Mar.6

Dense Forest

HISTORICAL FACTS

Fact 1: Before and during the Civil War, rumors abounded, often encouraged by newspapers. For example, before the war, many in the South believed that a Northern army was being prepared to invade the South.

Fact 2: Disease was the major killer of soldiers during the Civil War by a two-to-one ratio. Dysentery was the most common killer. Typhoid, malaria, and measles were other deadly diseases, to name a few.

Fact 3: Just before the war, Southern General Benjamin McCulloch was ironically part of a "peace commission" who went to Utah to keep the Mormons from seceding.

Fact 4: Previous to the war, during the 1600's, tens of thousands of white Irish men, women and children were "expelled forcibly" from the British Isles into servitude in the Americas, most often, the West Indies. Though not true chattel, they were sold to wealthy land owners who forced them to work under arduous conditions.

In most cases, these Indentured Servants earned freedom in seven years, although, often, the owners abused the servants, treating them more like white slaves.

Fact 5: Native Americans had Negro slaves before and during the war. They also made slaves of other tribes and often kidnapped whites. Even a few Negroes had Negro slaves before the war, one of the more notable ones was a Negro woman named Coincoin who inherited the plantation from her white husband. Before she died, she made sure her own children were free, but did not free her slaves.

Fact 6: Native Americans living in the Oklahoma territory took sides in the Civil War and often traded allegiances during its course. When removed from the south by President Andrew Jackson's order, they brought their slaves with them.

Fact 7: General Sterling Price of the Confederacy had been the governor of Missouri.

Fact 8: Mary Todd Lincoln, after she moved into the White House, had rudimentary plumbing installed. The water came from the Potomac and other rancid water sources, which may have been the cause of her sons contracting typhoid. Many of the words in the preface are the exact words recalled by witnesses that Mary and Abraham Lincoln spoke at the event of Willie's death.

Fact 9: Mary Todd Lincoln was mentally imbalanced. There were many instances where Mary Todd Lincoln exhibited evidence of insanity. Her wild mood swings became even more pronounced after the death of their son, Willie. Oddly, even though Willie was quite ill with typhus, Mary put on a grand ball in the White House.

Fact 9: Marauders, or loosely organized criminal gangs, ranged throughout Missouri during the war. Marauders who generally aligned with the North were often referred to as Jayhawkers. Marauders who favored the South were called Bushwhackers.

Fact 10: In October of 1861, Colonel Greer's Third Texas cavalry were tasked with gathering information (spying) about movements and plans of the Union army under General Freemont who had re-captured Springfield, Missouri.

Fact 11: Spiritualism, or the belief that some individuals could talk to the dead, was believed to be true by as much as one-fifth of the population. The most prominent seers, or mediums, were the Fox Sisters of New York state.

PROLOGUE

∞

The glum surgeon patted the hand of the deceased child and announced, "He's passed."

"No! That can't be!" Mary Lincoln shrieked. "Willie cannot have died. See to his pulse again! I can hear his heartbeat." Her words turned into a growl. "Again, I tell you." She leaned from her ladder-back chair that was shoved up to her son's bedside, and then cradled her son's head in her arm and stroked his cheek.

Abraham Lincoln leaned against a wall, eyes raised, hands clasped. He whispered prayers.

While Mrs. Lincoln watched expectantly, the surgeon traced his wooden monaural stethoscope across the dead child's chest for well over a minute. A handful of White House maids and close friends, including Senator Orville Browning, bowed their heads.

Next, the surgeon held a small mirror to the boy's nostrils. No vapor formed on its surface. He shook his head and placed the instruments in his medical bag.

"No, no, no! This can't be." Mary Lincoln sprang from her chair, sending it skittering across the floor. "Willie can't die. He's only eleven years old." She stormed about the room, pointing her finger at every individual. "You!" she called, then to the next in the circle,

"You! You could've done something. You could've warned me."
Tears flooded from her eyes, her expressions flashing from anger to
sorrow and back to anger, all the time, her voice like a banshee's.

She arrived at her Negro seamstress and calmed herself.
"Elizabeth, did you know about Willie catching the fever? Did
you know?"

"No, ma'am, I sure 'nuff didn't." The maid's face was screwed
up in sorrow. She cried, her spare frame heaving.

"Of course, you didn't." Mary Lincoln, her voice softening,
patted Elizabeth's shoulder. "You are too sweet and dote on my
children so. You would've said something."

Senator Browning tried to console Mary with a hug, but she
shook his embrace away.

Mary turned and walked to her husband who stood solemnly,
his arms at his side, his cheeks already moist from tears. Mary
changed her demeanor, taking Abraham's arm in both hands, and
looking up. "My dear husband, our beloved Willie is no longer on
this earth."

The president turned his head slightly toward Mary, though
he did not look right at her, then patted her hand. "My poor boy,
he was too good for this earth. God has called him home. I know
that he is much better off in heaven, but then we loved him so. It
is hard... hard to watch him die!" With that, he slowly removed
his wife's hand and strode wearily down to his secretary's office.
Behind him, Mary wailed, falling to the floor, then rising to her
knees to hug her deceased son's body. The president hoped the
surgeon would sedate her, but he could not deal with her now. His
own grief was too intense.

He opened the door and trudged into the office, awakening his
drowsing, youthful secretary, John Nicolay, who looked up bleary-
eyed, a hopeful expression on his face. "Well, Nicolay," Lincoln
said, "my son is dead."

Nicolay nodded. He bent slowly to his knees, bowed his head,
and began to pray silently.

For a long while Lincoln stood looking out the west window at the sun subsiding in a gray mess of muddy, slogged hills. Not a blade of grass, nor even a tree. Just tall mounds of mud, some blue-gray hills beyond that. Below the window, a sergeant in a heavy coat, rifle to his shoulder, paced vigorously. In front of the wrought iron fence that surrounded the lawn, a band of soldiers warmed themselves by a meager fire. Beyond the fence, a platoon of cobalt blue marched drearily to somewhere. The war had taken its toll on Lincoln. He admitted as much to himself, but this typhoid fever that took his son plunged like a saber into the depth of his being. *What is more, little Tad has just beaten the disease. I'm sure he will fear for his own life now. I'll visit him as soon as I can clear my head.* Lincoln sank into a leather chair, extending his legs toward the window. He buried his head in his hands and wept softly.

Nicolay was back on his feet. "Mr. President," he whispered. "Shall I enlist the service of an embalmer? It's best not to wait, and...."

"Have Senator Browning secure the embalmer. And if his wife is here, have her see to Mary, please." He put his hand to his chest.

"Yes, sir. Shall I have the doctor administer laudanum to Mrs. Lincoln?"

Lincoln did not gather Nicolay's question. He looked back at Nicolay, and, for just a fleeting moment, he could have sworn he saw a dark, cloven-hoofed shadow pass by in the hall. He had barely slept for days while keeping vigil at Willie's bedside and still attending to the affairs of his office. He realized the vision was the result of his exhausted mind.

He rubbed his eyes and stood abruptly, striding to the doorway. A maid was lighting a lamp in the next room. Another carried black drapes. Beyond her, a third maid was hanging the mourning crepes over the windows. "Has Willie's soul left so quickly," he asked the maids politely, "that we must be about that task now?"

The maids shook their heads no and exited quickly downstairs.

Lincoln dabbed his face with a kerchief. Down the hall in the guest room, Mary's wailing had turned to weeping. The president paused in the hall to listen to her.

"Get me a medium," she begged. "I want to speak to my little boy before his soul is completely gone. Get me the Fox sisters, or anyone who speaks to the dead. Do it now." Her trembling voice faded into sobs.

Lincoln knew her entreaties fell on deaf ears. "Yes, Nicolay," he said over his shoulder "See to Senator Browning for an embalmer. And remove Willie's body to the Green Room downstairs with as much haste as is appropriate. Have the surgeon do what needs be done for Mary." He left to sit in another room with his youngest, Tad, free from the fever, but still weak.

ONE

∞

ESCAPE

In her boarding house room, Cyntha Favor rose in total darkness at the slight knock on her door. She had slept in her dress, her dreams filled with dread. Her crinoline hoop, shoved in the corner, would be left behind. This was an escape, not a time for propriety.

She tip-toed to the closed door. "Just a moment," she whispered, shivering. The shock of cold within the room took her breath away. Though she had lived through snowstorms in Iowa, this cold was like a knife of ice. She was shivering not just from the cold but from the trepidation at what she was about to do. To her recollection, she had never made such a reckless decision.

Her mind swam back and forth. *I must escape! They will surely catch us! I must escape.*

She believed with no doubt that she had no other recourse than to flee Springfield and the clutch of the Union army to rescue Joseph's tormented soul. Joseph was dead, that much she had been informed of by the colonel of his Iowa regiment after the battle of Wilson Creek.

Mrs. Grunewald, the convincing spiritualist with the Tarot cards whom she had consulted but a few days previously, had assured her that his soul was trapped and that Cyntha needed to speak to his soul through a medium who had the capacity to speak to those beyond the grave. She believed without a doubt that only she could dissuade him of his fears and free his soul.

A further pressing reason to rush headlong into certain danger was she felt driven to find her brother who was accused of stealing from his bank. *Please, dear Lord, give me strength*. Her prayers spilled in whispered intensity.

Her breaths were short, and her heart beat erratically like loose shutters, battered by a gale.

She fumbled for the matches on the dresser, found them, and lit the oil lamp, turning the flame low. She sat before the crazed and speckled mirror of the dark dresser, lacing her high-topped shoes. Tying her long black hair tight in a bun was an ordeal with her hands shaking so, and pinning a snood to hold it in place seemed to take interminably long.

For a moment, she looked at her face in the mirror, admiring it but a little — her smooth white complexion, her green eyes and slim, pert nose. She never thought herself a beauty, though many beaus offered her the title.

If she were caught, perhaps her appearance might earn some mercy. She had never tried to use what some called womanly wiles to gain special treatment. It would have been beneath her. She knew that comely women seldom were held as accountable as homely ones. Could a cheery smile divert imprisonment?

She deeply desired the Union army to vanquish the Rebels, and thus free the slaves, for slavery wore so heavily on her heart. She realized the irony that she could be imprisoned by the very army she supported. She had been warned by the officious captain and townsfolk that travel on roads out of Springfield was forbidden.

Donning her hooded cape and folding a heavy blanket over her arm, she turned out the lamp and took a deep breath. *I don't care if General Curtis has restricted all civilians from the roads beyond Springfield, I will prevail.*

She opened the door.

In the hallway, Constance Carver, dressed in a shaggy buffalo hide coat over her coal black dress with the starched white collar, stood beside two Negro maids of the boarding house, each holding candles. Constance held a doctor's kit filled not with medicine but with her few clothes and sundry items. At Constance's direction, the maids entered the room and hoisted Cyntha's clothes chest. The four quietly descended the stairs, Constance shushing the maids often. A guard dozed on the boarding house parlor sofa. The clock glimmering in the candlelight indicated just past three.

They tip-toed to the door and slipped out into the frigid night. The sharp-toothed wind bit at Cyntha's cheeks, and all their breath rose in white plumes. A shallow bowl of a moon perched on the horizon. In the still street before them, Reynolds, the tall freeman and her loyal friend, stood shivering in his long coat and holding the bridle of a horse hitched to their carriage. The gig was covered with a layer of ice. The horse snorted and stamped its feet. A second horse, to be used to trade out in pulling the carriage, was tied behind.

The maids loaded the chest onto the rear of the gig atop heavy blankets, ropes, and a canvas tent that Cyntha had purchased at an exorbitant price from a sutler. Though she knew of a boarding house in Rolla where they could stay, the long journey to St. Louis would require that they camp, and she was determined not to freeze to death by the side of the road.

The maids hugged Constance and crept back to the porch.

"Don't go gettin' caught by dem soldiers, y'hear, Miss Constance," the maid named Abagail whispered. "You dark enough, they think you a colored woman like us." The maids sneaked inside the boarding house.

Reflecting on Abagail's remark, Cyntha remembered that her new companion was half Cherokee. Constance and she climbed into the carriage.

"Mr. Reynolds," Constance whispered. "you best let me stow your pistol. If the army catches us, you won't want them to find that pistol on you."

The stout Negro slipped the gun from under his coat and handed it to her. She placed it deep in the medicine bag.

Reynolds led the shivering horse, his hand on the harness. In his other hand, he held a lantern with only one pane shedding a sliver of light. They continued at a tedious pace down an alley, followed by another alley, then into a field that had been trodden by soldiers into a grassless, muddy plot. To their left, they witnessed a few paltry campfires among hundreds of tents, most of which had been walled around with logs and boards. The tents, turned into shanties, sported chimneys, and from them, lazy smoke drifted out into the stars.

Here and there outside the tents, they saw several glowing lanterns swinging on tall staffs, and near them, shadowy figures of soldiers on guard duty.

"Are you sure the army can't hear us?" Cyntha asked in a whisper.

"No, I ain't sure," Constance replied, "but if you listen, you can hear all sorts of commotions. Our noises just mix with the others."

Just as Constance explained, Cyntha became aware of a multitude of jangles and thuds — horses stamping in a nearby corral, guards talking in subdued voices, a horse trotting down the street behind them and going away, and dogs barking. Wooden houses and barns and trees creaked in the stiff wind.

Out in the open, the wind shrieked a phantom wail. Cyntha did not feel any safer, for, in crossing the field, they were completely visible.

"Move like a dead man, Reynolds," Constance whispered.

Reynolds had closed the window of the lantern, and they proceeded in almost complete darkness. Beyond the meadow, a forest loomed, a massif of deeper black. Reynolds had slowed the forward movement to a few feet at a time, negotiating the hardpan soil.

Listening to the clip clop of the hooves, Cyntha could barely see the coffee-toned horse pulling. She drew the blanket around her shoulders. She could not remember feeling so cold. She shook involuntarily. Suddenly, the horse stopped moving, and Cyntha heard Reynolds carefully removing fence rails to the ground. The horse whickered and shook its mane, the ice on its hairs tinkling.

Cyntha thought she heard the cessation of the guards' talk in the camp. Then she heard a chorus of laughs, and she sighed in relief.

In a moment, the horse and carriage jerked forward, and they were soon passing along a narrow foot trail. Though many of the trees had been removed by the soldiers to build their enclosures, the tall bushes stood so close that the limbs brushed and bent against the side of the carriage. Stray, thin branches reached into the carriage, snatching at Cyntha's hair and slapping her face.

"I's sorry about those branches, Miss Cyntha," Reynolds whispered in the dark.

"Never you mind, old man," Constance whispered back harshly. "Just keep moving. There may be a sentry about."

No sooner had she spoken than a loud furor broke from somewhere to their right. None of the three could make out what the many voices were saying, but they were using fierce, combative words. Then they heard running and crashing in the woods and the sounds of a row with dozens of men fighting with fists and clubs. More sounds erupted behind them and in front of them. Reynolds slowed the horse to a stop.

Cyntha held her breath. She could tell Constance was doing as much. Suddenly, four armed soldiers raced through the trees from their left and across their path not ten feet in front of where Reynolds stood. The one in front held a lantern. The four continued in haste deeper into the trees towards the commotion. Ultimately, all the sounds came from their far right.

"Proceed, please, Reynolds," Cyntha whispered.

Slowly, slowly, Reynolds led the carriage into the bitter night. The path often veered in a sharp turn, then twisted again. They seemed to be crawling. Her anxiety growing, Cyntha felt as if she could jump from the carriage and just run. *Oh, why did I agree to this plan of escape? There is no way we can flee an army. Why did I listen to Constance? I just hope I can reach my brother in St. Louis. I know he could not have stolen from the bank. Oh, Anthony, surely you didn't steal.*

Cyntha closed her eyes and tried to pray. Her mind jumped between cross and anxious thoughts.

After an hour, the trail opened and she could see a smoother terrain a few yards ahead.

"Reynolds," she called in a murmur. "Bring the light so I may check the time." Reynolds opened the lantern door a slight amount. Cyntha pulled out her pocket watch. It read almost four.

"We should be nearing that back road," Constance said aloud.

"Yes'm." Reynolds returned to leading the horse. Suddenly, they arrived at what could marginally be called a road. Mostly overgrown with grass, weeds and brambles, the old cart path stretched north and south.

Cyntha hugged Constance. "Thank you."

"Don't be thankin' me," Constance retorted. "We ain't in St. Louis yet."

"You're right. Reynolds, turn the horse left and climb in with us. Let's get as far from Springfield as we can."

Reynolds settled in between the women and shook the reins. The horse trotted along the road for the better part of an hour. Reynolds often had to draw up the horse and remove brush from the seldom-used road. Nearing the top of a hill, the three could see light like a burgeoning sunrise emanating from the valley below. Reynolds reined the horse. Cyntha left the carriage in haste and jogged to the hill's edge.

What she saw caused her to draw back. The road no longer existed. The ground plummeted away into a dry creek bed.

Before them was a chasm that sloped upward on the opposite side into a field in which hundreds of tents and hundreds of campfires stretched, disappearing into the forest. Cyntha stumbled back to the carriage. She stopped at the horse's head, took hold of the harness, and pulled on it, turning the horse and carriage around.

"What in the good Lord's name is goin' on, Cyntha?" Constance was bewildered.

Cyntha shook her head wearily. "We can't go that way. There's no more road, and at least a thousand men are camped in every direction."

"How about we go around them through the trees?" Reynolds offered.

"And run right into a picket or a cavalry troop? No. We're too close to them already."

"So, it ain't just the army in Springfield, then," Constance said moodily. "Them's reinforcements for Curtis's army. What'll we do? I can't stay in Springfield. I ain't no colored folks' mistress." Her tone changed to emphatic. "I ain't going back."

"Well, maybe you and me could go back to Springfield?" Reynolds said.

"No," Cyntha said, her head down, staring at her dusty shoes. "If we try to sneak back into town, they'll lock me up for sure and take you away for a work detail. Constance, how far does this road go south?"

"Why you askin'?"

"Well, you said you wanted to get back to your home."

"That's right. Guvnor Price's army's done went south anyway. I need to get back to my farm. I only told you I was going to St. Louis with you to get you to agree to my plan. Actually, come sunup I'd planned to ditch you and head south. Sorry for the lie."

Cyntha felt no desire to respond to Constance's admission of deception. "So, how far does this road go south? I have cousins living south of Springfield at a tavern on the Butterfield Stage Road."

"Well, if I remember rightly, this here road ends up at the Butterfield."

"Will that get you closer to your home, Constance?"

"Yes, ma'am. This is a far better plan. Maybe I'll find my husband who ran off and left me high and dry. Home would be fine, too."

"This will have to do, until all this fighting ceases," Cyntha said. "Reynolds and I will wait it out. At least we'll be with family in Arkansas. And if you don't find your husband in the Missouri Guard, you can head home any time."

"It's too cold to figure anything else out. Let's get goin'."

Cyntha climbed into the carriage.

Reynolds shook the reins. "These here cousins of yours, will they be understandin' of me bein' a freeman?"

"They'll have to be," Cyntha said.

"What's the name of that tavern you mentioned, the one where your cousins live?"

"They call it Elkhorn Tavern. Their names are Jesse and Polly Cox."

TWO

∽

THE DYING TENT

FIVE MONTHS EARLIER, SEPTEMBER 16, 1861, 3 PM
TEN MILES SOUTH OF CARTHAGE, MISSOURI

J oseph Favor felt dizzy and extremely hot. But each time the
nip of an autumn breeze whipped up, he felt punitively chilled.
He rode a roan mare in the middle of the two companies
of the Third Texas Cavalry.

He knew he had a fever. His eyes burned, the inside of his
nose burned, and his skin itched like he had fallen in a patch of
bull nettle, but he was resolute to keep up an outward façade of
strength. After all, he was the newest recruit. For all he knew, this
had always been his regiment.

His memory had been stolen from him in battle. His few recent
memories of the kind Reeder family who had nursed him back to
health and of the beautiful, young, blond woman, Sara, seldom left
his thoughts. He generally felt a deep confusion because a memory
of another woman often plied its way into his brain, but he knew
not who she was.

Original orders for the companies had changed, and now they
were headed to join Colonel Greer's regiment at a new encampment
near Carthage, Missouri. They had been traveling for a week. Ten
mule-drawn wagons loaded with provisions trailed ponderously
behind them.

One rider was tootling a tin whistle, and many cavalrymen were singing a new, raucous tune called "Dixie." Though Joseph found the tune catchy, he did not sing. He felt shaky throughout his entire dimensions.

"So, anyway," the soldier riding beside him in the column rambled on, "right after that battle of Wilson Creek, we done fetched up the body of the Yank General Lyon what was killed on the bloody hill, and him all wrapped up in that Mrs. Ray's bed cover. I'm sure she hated to see that go. And we hauled his body in a wagon all the way to Rolla and gave it to them ungrateful Yanks. Pitiful. They didn't even say thanks or nothin'.

And besides..."

Joseph tugged at the man's jacket.

"I feel sick."

The gray-bearded soldier gaped at Joseph. "Son, you are sick. Your face is covered with the red spots."

No sooner had the man finished his pronouncement than Joseph swooned and began sliding from his saddle. He landed hard on his side, then stood, wobbling. In short order, his fellow cavalrymen hoisted him into a wagon amid barrels, crates and burlap sacks, then heaped blankets on him. For the rest of the day, he endured a foggy, disordered complaint, a hybrid of fitful wakefulness and unsettled sleep.

In the evening, he awoke on a cot in a large, dark tent with one heavy blanket across his shivering body and a wet cloth on his forehead.

"Where am I?" he asked through chattering teeth.

A solicitous attendant in a blood-smeared apron spoke a sentence he could not understand. The man spoke more odd words, and Joseph surmised the nurse was not speaking English. He looked about the shadowy tent and saw about fifteen cots, most of them with men lying on them. One man choked a hacking cough.

"Where am I?" Joseph tried to yell. His voice squeaked like a door needing oiling. His face burned, while his chest felt like it heaved under a sheath of ice. His wavy blond hair was wringing wet, and his feet felt prickly, like he had been treading on stiff grass stubble.

A second nurse, a man with a misshapen nose and a cauliflower ear, seemed to drift up to his cot. Joseph looked down to see if the man had any feet. In his fevered state, he saw the man distorted, ballooning out, then collapsing.

"You're in the *dying* tent outside Carthage, Missouri. You and a bunch of your company have the spots. This is where you get to die with some measure of peace. If you weren't so infirmed, you'd be up at the courthouse. It's the hospital now." The man seemed bothered. He turned and, by Joseph's estimation, floated into a haze.

"I thought we were going to Arkansas." But the man was gone.

A young Negro, clean-shaven and thin as a fence rail, came to his cot and draped another damp cloth on his head. He leaned over and whispered, "General McCulloch done ordered the Third Texas to establish itself here near Carthage. And you ain't at the gates of death yet."

Daylight flashed. The tent flap opened, and a stout man with a peppered beard burst in like a runaway train. He wore a black velvet coat and a wide-brimmed hat. "Is this one dead yet?" He pointed at Joseph.

"No, General McCulloch," a string bean of a man in a dirty apron said. He began to push the general's chest, attempting to shove him out of the tent. "But he has the spots, and you could catch it and die."

General Benjamin McCulloch grabbed the man's arms and twisted them in a crisscross sort of knot. "I know he has the measles. I already had measles long time ago. Can't' catch 'em again."

He released the nurse who rubbed his sore wrists and backed away.

"If it'd hadn't been for the measles, I'd a been with Crockett at the Alamo and been planted in the ground a long time ago. The measles did me a favor." He gave a wry smile. The attendants smiled, and Joseph attempted to grin, weak as he was.

"I'm going to all the men with the measles. Seeing if they're going to make it." He paused. "You nurses, give 'em all as much water and as much lemonade as you can make. Give 'em applesauce, whatever they'll eat. I need this army healthy. And especially this one." General McCulloch approached the cot where Joseph lay. "Do you remember me, son?"

"Yes, I do, sir," Joseph whispered, his throat hoarse. "You came to the Reeder farm for that party, and you saw the marauders in the forest before anyone else noticed them. You're a friend of Lucas Reeder."

"And you're a friend of his daughter, Sara. If Lucas Reeder puts as much stock in you as he says, you need to stay alive and go back to that little sprite." He gave a broad grin and patted Joseph's shoulder. "Get well now." He exited the tent. When the tent flap opened, the sunlight burned Joseph's face like hell. He put his hand over his eyes.

"He called her a sprite," Joseph whispered to himself and smiled. He licked his lips wishing he could feel the warm smoothness of her kiss. "That would make me better," he said aloud.

"What would make you better?" the nurse with the misshapen nose asked. He handed Joseph a tin of lemonade. He guzzled the tart liquid, and fell immediately asleep.

At the middle of the day, he awoke to a loud clang. The skinny Negro had dropped a basin and spilled the water on the neighboring cot's occupant. The man rose on one arm and slapped the Negro full in the face. "When I get better, I'm gonna whip your hide, you worthless piece of flesh. I'm sorry I ever bought you." The ailing man fell back on his pillow.

The slave had no sooner risen, rubbing his jaw, when the bent-nosed nurse began kneeing him in the stomach and drove him into a corner.

Joseph was astonished and almost outraged. His memories of how Lucas Reeder and his slave, Abram, had been friends, laughing together, playing checkers, and sharing chores, then meals at the same table; all that stood at odds with the treatment of this slave. Slowly, ever so slowly, his memories of what had molded his opinion against slavery began returning to him.

He remembered a drawing in a newspaper of a slave with huge scars on his back, and of a pamphlet detailing lurid treatment of slaves, and a book, *Uncle Tom's Cabin*. He asked for water. When the Negro poured a tin of water from a decanter, Joseph's weary mind tried to reconcile these remembered matters with what he had read in Southern newspapers: stories of the expressed necessity of slavery and how one article said it benefitted the *lower* race. What his own eyes had just seen told a different narrative.

His fever was too much for him to concentrate, and he slumped into deep sleep.

That evening, his temperature spiked.

THREE

⚭

NO ROOM FOR MIRTH, ONLY TEARS

Three Weeks Later, October 9, 1861, Early Afternoon
The Boston Mountains, Arkansas

Sara Reeder was lost. She winced at the dire nature of her predicament. Further, her food had been wasted two days previous. She glanced at her hands intertwined with the reins of her mare, Esther, and they were shaking.

Having fared well for over a week in balmy weather riding along the Butterfield Stage Road, known by many as the Telegraph Road, she now had become a wayfarer in a treacherous land of mountain knobs, gullies, and vales.

In the days previous on the road, she had passed several foot travelers, galloped past a man with a cartload of manure, and said "Hey" to folks in wagons and carriages. It seemed that all the war that had inundated her life in August and September had subsided. Hearing no word to the contrary from the people she passed, maybe the war *had ended* in only three months like everyone had been saying it would. Perhaps there was now a lovely peace.

Then she met a man just shy of twenty-years-old carrying a rusty musket who told her he was enlisting in any army as soon as he could find one. He did not care which side. Sara rolled her eyes and rode on.

Seeing so many people on the road, she almost forgot about B. Franks Richards, the man who had nearly raped her. The first thoughts coursing through her head when she departed her burned out home had been of her father, Lucas, and of her love, Joseph.

After the initial day of her journey, she became acutely aware that Richards could have followed her. She remained wary and skittish, jumping at noises in the brush.

She had slept once in an abandoned house, once under a rock overhang, though she knew that to be unwise because snakes preferred such a place, and four times under quickly made lean-tos of gathered branches. If the soldiers saw it fit to do so, she figured she could also.

She had spent an evening at Elkhorn Tavern. She paid a nickel for a mat on the kitchen floor and gave a penny for a boiled egg and a piece of bacon for breakfast.

The next morning, she encountered the aged peddler, his hair standing out on his scalp like sprung wire. Pushing his barrow of pots, pans, and what-nots, he sported a crafty smile. He offered her the trade of an ointment that he assured her would cure any malignancy in exchange for one of her books. Instead, she proffered him a newspaper she had marshalled from a portly woman who was using the paper to swat flies, and he gave her the brown bottle. She uncorked it. It smelled of liniment, a good muscle ease for her or for her horse, and she considered the trade a good one.

In what appeared to be a friendly gesture, the peddler told her of a sure-fire shortcut to the Confederate encampment, her destination where she hoped to find Joseph. The bespectacled codger explained that a slight veer to the left off the Butterfield Stage Road would have her at the cantonment in no time.

The desultory byway, in a mile or so, became sometimes a cow path, sometimes a hunting trail, and oftentimes an overgrown meadow. It was switchbacks and dead ends, and it ended at an impassable, swift-flowing creek.

Sara tried back-tracking to the road, but became even more vexed and disoriented.

Her sojourn thus complicated beyond her imaginings, she endeavored to continue over the hardscrabble terrain, sometimes on steep grades up, then on perilous downward slopes. She kept the sinking, burnished sun on her right, trying to maintain a southwesterly course.

She endeavored to exculpate her naiveté about pathfinding by blaming the old man and cursing him under her breath. Wild Ozark Mountains were nothing like the low hills of southern Missouri. Seldom did any signs of life appear, save an occasional songbird or lizard or a circling buzzard. One lone dwelling along the way was abandoned; no plowed fields or cow patties were there to indicate anyone had lived there for years.

She wondered if she had ventured into an unholy desolation and if the peddler was a demon from hell.

On the first day of being lost, against any proper judgement at all, she had crossed a deep stream and wetted her store of cornmeal and lard. She had held her satchel of books and cartridge bag above the water, the horse's reins in her teeth, but now she had nothing to eat. Her apples were gone, the dried venison eaten days ago. Her five attempts to shoot game or fowl came to no fruition, each time missing her mark.

Dining on only handfuls of wild blackberries for the two days, her stomach grumbled often. She kept some string and a hook in her saddlebag and vowed to fish for whatever was worth catching at the next stream.

Sleeping each night on a bed made of thresh, the threat of wild beasts made sleep daunting. The last morning, she awoke to find bear scat a few paces from where she slept. She pondered how delightful it would be to sleep on a bed of hay with a shingled roof over her head and the barn door closed.

On this, the ninth day traveling, she hungered for some of Abram's fried fish and hush puppies. She thought of their old slave's tender eyes on his brown, gray-bearded face with freckles like sprinkles of stars. A lump rose in her throat.

She so missed him and her father, Lucas, even more. His strong arms and guiding words were like gold.

Where are they? Somewhere on the way to Richmond. She felt like they were an eternity away, and the tears trickled down her face. *Why did I ever part ways with my pa?*

Alone in a boundless wilderness, the overwhelming solitude and deeper silence of the woods pounded her eardrums. She felt as though God, who she knew in her heart was everywhere, had for some reason evacuated from this corner of the world, leaving her to manage by her own wits.

If only she could arrive in the Confederate camp and fall into the arms of her love. "You are my heart, Joseph," she whispered into the hushed forest. The salt from her tears touched her lips and, for a moment, she sensed the sweet taste of his mouth when he had kissed her at the creek on that summer day that seemed eons ago.

Now, in the late afternoon, Sara's forward motion became a mindless ambling; her horse, Esther, pursuing a haphazard route. A cloister of cicadas spun up their whizzing burr. Sara wondered what it would be like to be unable to hear anything save that constant whooshing. Remembering her father's diminished hearing, she prayed, *Dear Lord, please take care of Pa.*

All of a sudden, Sara smelled intensely acrid smoke. She leaned forward over Esther's withers, peering through the foliage to see the cause, wondering if the forest was ablaze.

Traces of smoke filtered through the trees.

The odor was not that of roasting meat, nor of a boiling stew, but an ugly vile scent like eggs burned on the stove, a mixture of burning wood and manure.

Riding further, rocky soil met a scant roadway where wagons had passed, and the course led into a quiet, golden meadow. Opposite the lea was a sparse parcel of plowed field.

Then she saw the source of the smoke — the burnt remnants of a farmhouse, a few support columns and interior walls standing like shadowy, unholy pillars. The rock chimney squatted like a throne of a dark knight in his black tower. Smoke still drifted from the rubble and portions of boards held glowing embers.

Drawing closer, she stopped short. Two bodies lay before the house, burned to charcoal, one lying prostrate in the front yard, the other hung up on the picket fence.

She was appalled at the abhorrent sight. The odious stench was more repugnant now that she knew the cause was charred flesh. The memories of her own torched home flooded her mind and took her breath from her. She clutched her throat.

Beyond the house, a swaybacked horse stood munching at a hayrick in a corral abutted to a spacious barn. Chickens strutted about the back yard.

She shook the reins and trotted Esther up to the picket fence. She stood in the stirrups, looking for anyone still alive.

The sounds of grunting and snorting caught her ear. About thirty yards in the opposite direction, in the shade of trees lining a shallow creek, three wild hogs tugged at the remains of a human body in a recently dug, shallow grave. A big black and white sow wrenched at a mauled hand, the shirt sleeve tattered. The two smaller hogs snuffled and dug with snout and hooves at the mound, grunting and growling.

Sara quickly slid her rifle from its saddle holster and dismounted in one smooth motion. She jammed her hand into the ammunition box of the saddle bag and removed a paper capsule of gunpowder, some cotton wadding and a bullet. She tore open the capsule with her teeth and poured the contents into the gun barrel, all the while keeping an eye on the enormous hogs. Their tusks could shred muscle and bone. The beasts set to squealing, ripping at the dead body's clothes and flesh.

Then, the sow looked up, straight at her.

Esther stutter-stepped.

"Steady, Esther." Sara stroked the mare's neck. She placed the cotton in the barrel, then the ball on top of the cotton, then withdrew the ramrod and shoved the load home. She removed the ramrod and stuck it in the ground like a pike and placed a firing cap under the gun's hammer. Kneeling just under the mare's neck and wrapping the reins around her forward hand, she took aim. The kick of the gun would hurt her shoulder. It always did.

She fired. The sow that had been gnawing on the corpse's hand fell with a thud, the bullet through its eye, blood pooling around its body. Its legs quivered a little and went still. The other hogs flinched when the sow fell, but continued pulling at the corpse's body.

Sara stood, waved her arms, and yelled, "Get out!" She feigned a run at the hogs. They gave her no heed.

Again, she waved her arms and screamed her loudest. The hogs went about their gnawing.

She drew another round from the saddlebag. Before she could load the rifle, one of the hogs jumped away from the grave. Then the second one leapt high in the air, almost comically, and trotted off a few feet. Sara wondered what was happening. In a moment, she saw some sort of missile hurtle through the air hitting the first hog straight in the snout. The hog squealed in pain and scampered into the woods. The last hog sauntered off a little slower, but was soon gone into the underbrush.

Sara stood bewildered.

The brush near the creek parted, and a tall brown-skinned man of about thirty, wearing a flowing tan robe that was tied about his waist with a cord, came forth. He wore a tattered straw hat and held in one hand what Sara immediately knew was a Bible.

When he strode to a stop at the grave, she saw he held a slingshot in his other hand. The man knelt and made the sign of the cross, folded his hands together, and bowed his head. Sara knew the movement of signing from reading her many tomes of European knights. She had never actually seen a Catholic. Him wearing a robe, she surmised he was a priest.

"Hello," Sara interrupted.

The man looked up, made another sign of the cross and walked toward her. "Are you all right, señorita?" he asked. Though he spoke perfect English, Sara recognized the tenor of Spanish.

"I am fine...uh, bien, Señor."

Her attempt at Spanish brought a smile to his face. He bore chiseled facial features. Sharp chin, straight nose, and high cheekbones. There was fire in his dark eyes.

Turning, he pointed to the demolished grave. "It is most dreadful what those hogs were doing to that poor man's body," he said.

"Madre mia. Mother of Mercy."

"You're a priest, aren't you?"

"Sí, es verdad. That is true. I am Father Antonio. Mucho gusto. Pleased to meet you."

"I am Sara Reeder, late of just outside of Springfield, Missouri. My house was burned down just like this one just days ago." She pointed at the charred bodies. "And you can pray for that fellow in the dirt, but you best pray for those poor people, too."

"Yes." He made another sign of the cross. "I was just coming up the road with my companions, and we smelled the fire. We ran up and saw the hogs, and... I guess we arrived at a propitious time to stop the degrading of that man's body. Sadly, too late for these two souls in the yard."

Sara was struck with the silvery tone of his words, surely to be the tongue of nobility. She wondered if he was of regal lineage, a prince who had forsaken his crest and taken a vow of poverty like the parsons and friars in her esteemed novels. Lost in the musing, she caught herself. "Ahem. You say you're with some companions."

"Sí, they are local Indians. Cherokees. We were looking for a new place for them to live. The Confederates have taken over the whole valley."

"Confederates? Near here?" Sara hoped.

"Yes, let me call my companions." Father Antonio walked into the brush, whistled, then came forth, followed by several Cherokees, three women and four children from toddlers to teens. They each carried lumpish cloth bags on their backs. Their soiled clothing was a combination of bright blue shirts, brilliant red skirts, patched trousers, and ragged shawls.

For what they lacked in their clothing, there was no paucity in their jewelry. Women and boys and girls alike wore gaudy necklaces and bracelets of colored gems amid strings of river shells. The oldest boy, being about thirteen, wore a striped turban.

A gray-haired squaw had a wattled neck and was as round as a rain barrel. She bore a fierce face, her wide nose over grim, tight lips. A ladder-back chair was strapped on her back.

The other women were much younger and thinner and walked with a sort of aloof bearing unbefitting their dress. The youngest squaw carried a two-year-old child, and, though evincing a handsome face, her left eye was white, like it had been stabbed out. They were a tawdry lot, but all smiled upon seeing Sara.

She had seen many Indians in her life, generally walking the Telegraph Road near her home. They were usually dressed in clothes like those of the white folks of her valley, not at all like the draped apparel of the Plains Indians she had seen in magazine drawings. She had met and talked with a Cherokee chief at their neighbors' house, the Rays.

John Ray served as postmaster for Wilson Creek Valley. The chief had written a letter to President Buchanan in Washington. He spoke formal English, more pleasant sounding than some of her neighbors, and was as affable as a store clerk.

The Indians came up to Sara, treating her like a bosom friend, speaking in English, all except the old squaw. Sara shook their hands, then turned to the priest. "You're pretty precise with that slingshot. Is that how you're feeding them? I see no other weapon; neither bow, nor rifle."

"The slingshot serves its purpose for small game, rabbits and such. I don't think I need a big weapon. Was it not David who brought down Goliath with a sling and a rock?" He smiled, holding up his weapon of choice.

The Indians beamed cheerfully. The tall boy reached in a leather pouch and pulled out a brace of rabbits. "There, you see," Father Antonio said, "we already have a dinner for tonight."

"You've done better than I have. I haven't hit a thing with my rifle in three days."

"Not for want of skill. You reduced that sow to a feast with a single shot."

"I was lucky."

"We will skin and boil the rabbits, but perhaps we can skin that hog and dry the meat for a fortnight of sustenance. My companions know so much more than I about how to make food last a long while."

"So, are they Catholic, too?"

"I do not believe they have a Christian belief. Perhaps one day they will accept the Lord. For now, their husbands died of measles caught from the Confederate army. The army moved in and took over their cabins and their land. I was passing through at the time, so I helped them bury their husbands and offered to accompany them to their ancestral home in Alabama, so we must find a new place for them to live. A fine place where they can farm. Then I must be on my way."

"Where are you headed?"

"East to serve the Lord and his people in whatever way I can."

"Why did you leave your home, your, uh, monastery?"

"I felt called. I am originally from San Antonio, Tejas. Muy bonita ciudad. A very pretty city, but there are already many

Catholics there. I must go where, perhaps, people have not met the Lord."

"I wish you well. I'll pray for you and your Indian friends. Now, you said the Confederates took over their valley. Are we near?"

"Which camp of all the many Confederate camps? I would wager we are a few rods from the camps, but the army is thousands, and their camps cover several miles. Is there someone for whom you are looking?"

"Yes. My future husband. He's a corporal in the Third Texas Cavalry. Might you have met him?"

"I'm quite sure I have not. Where these families dwelled, there was only infantry, thrown together like a swarm of bees. And I would not know one regiment from another. Lo siento. I am sorry."

"Can you give me directions? Someone must know where he is."

The trim, clean-shaven priest looked consolingly at his new friend. "I will assure your safe arrival at the Confederate cantonment. But night will soon be upon us. I will not be leaving you out alone in these woods at night. I will tell you why later. For now, let us be about burying these poor souls and preparing a dinner, and I will send you straight to your destination in the morning."

Sara nodded, but her heart had plummeted. She had not foreseen the possibility of a melee of soldiers in camps spread over miles.

FOUR

∞

TWO SOULS
CARVED APART

THE SAME DAY, OCTOBER 9, 1861, MID-MORNING
EASTERN MISSOURI

A top a verdant hill, Dred Workman tossed the last shovelful of dirt on Private Chamberlin's grave and tamped it down. "Wish he could've hung on a little longer." He blew through his bushy mustache. His lanky frame was too long for his Confederate uniform, the jacket collar chafing his neck at his bulbous Adam's apple. "He's the only one I lost. Maybe if I hadn't taken so long constructin' that confounded saddle for him, he'd a made it."

"You're a good nurse, Dred," Lucas said. "It was beyond our means to save him. Sad. I think we may be close to his home. Couldn't have been much farther." Lucas recalled for a moment his days as an officer in the War with Mexico when he was tasked with burying a boon companion. He buried that friend the night before the attack when the cannon exploded, destroying most of his hearing.

They laid the shovels in the back of the wagon, then looked down at the valley with trees painted gold, rust, and scarlet. "If his spirit looks out from here," Workman said, "he'll appreciate the view."

"Yes, it's a pleasant spot. There's a little town down below. We'll go there first and inquire after his family. Maybe someone knows them. If not, we'll spend a couple days inspecting the farms 'round there"

Lucas walked over to Abram, who was sitting on a rock near their wagon laden with the last of their belongings, saved from their burned home at Wilson Creek Valley. The old slave looked downtrodden and weary. "Abram, join us, please," Lucas said. "Let's say some prayers over the body."

Abram rose slowly. He refused to look at Lucas and had barely said a word to him in their nine days of journeying.

Lucas opened his worn Bible, flipped the pages, and then read the twenty-third Psalm. He finished, "And I shall dwell in the house of the Lord for years to come. Dear Lord, this brave man saved my daughter. He suffered much in this life, losing his leg and arm. I believe that he is now whole again with you in your mansions. Bless him. Bless us all."

They each said, "Amen."

Lucas pulled Workman aside and whispered, "I want you to know that I plan to give Abram to my family friend, Julia Dent, and her father, Colonel Dent. I can't keep a slave any more. He's past his prime, and I don't have the means to look after him. It'll be better for him that he not be with me, considering what I plan to do back east anyway. He wouldn't understand."

Workman bent his tall, lanky frame down to whisper in Lucas's ear trumpet. "I get your need to get rid of the feeble fella."

"He is feeble, but he's like family. I take that back. He *is* family. For years, he's been my best friend. He helped me deal with the deaths of my wife and boys like no other friend ever could. He did more to raise Sara than many a good mama." Lucas sighed. "But, more importantly, I can't have him along when I carry out my plan that I am determined to do. That is where I need your help. It will take two to...."

"I hear you talkin' over there, Lucas," Abram called. "Or should I call you Massa Reeder?"

Lucas whirled around, taken aback by Abram's harsh tone, which he had never once heard before this moment.

Lucas whispered to Workman, "I'll explain later. I think you'll approve of the plan." He walked back to where Abram stood by the wagon. "We were just saying, Abram, that I plan to spend just a little time to hopefully locate his family, then head to Julia Dent's farm."

"She ain't a Dent no more," Abram said angrily. "You shoulda paid more attention to that letter we got years ago."

"Well, I didn't pay much attention. I just know her by her maiden name."

"Well, I read the letter, too. She was so complimentary of you. A fine lady. She misses your dear wife. They used to correspond regular-like. Or didn't you notice that either? She's married now. Got kids. Her husband works the farm." Abram coughed several times. His face flushed.

"What's the matter, Abram? I've not seen you upset like this."

"Never you mind. You never cared a whit about important things. When you was a young man, you loved my daughter. I could tell. There you were, tryin' not to let on, but you loved her. Then you let her die. Never sent for the surgeon. Never came by the house when she was dyin' not even to say a kind word. She mighta lived if you'da come by."

Lucas blanched, his secret revealed to Workman. "How'd you know? I...I..." He turned away from Workman's aghast stare and looked at his worn boots. He had the compunction to run, but he stayed. Speaking to the ground, he said, "Abram. I couldn't. My pa was strict. He'd a beat me like...." He paused, shaking his head. "Like he beat a slave if he ever found out I cared so for your daughter. I'm truly sorry."

"You don't think a man sees when another man fancies his daughter? You were a heartless scoundrel then, but you always treated me right. And your dear wife and the boys and Sara treated me like family, too. So, I forgave you a long time ago."

"Thank you, Abram."

"And I know you plans to leave me with your wife's friend. Live out my last days there as a real slave. Not like family like I was with you and Sara, but *as a slave*."

"Sara's gone. I have no means to... can't you see? It's for your own good."

"Is it?" Abram felt out of place like he never had in his life. He had not once said a cross word to the family. And he knew down in his bones that despite their many considerations of him, he always had been a slave. Not equal to Lucas, no matter how he was treated. The way for him now was clear. "You know how you tol me once you wanted to let me go free."

"Yes, it's been on my mind a long time."

"Well, do it now. You're a former military officer. Write me a letter givin' me my freedom. Right now. Workman can sign as the witness. Make it official, and I'll ride away like the wind. Chamberlin don't need his horse no more. It ain't really yours. I'll take that horse now." He broke into a steady fit of coughing.

Lucas dipped a ladle of water from the crock under the wagon seat and gave it to him. He drank and regained his voice. "Go on, now. Give me my freedom. I'm ready." Abram's cataract white eyes shone brilliant and fierce.

"Give me a moment." Lucas gazed for a long time at the face of his old friend. Abram did not flinch. Giving a sigh, Lucas opened his Bible. "I've got a passage here. Let's see." He thumbed through the tattered pages. "Ah, here. Paul's letter to Philemon. Paul's asking Philemon to free his slave, Onesimus."

"I know the passage." Abram's tone lightened.

"Paul writes, 'that you might possess him forever, no longer as a slave, but as more than a slave, a beloved brother.' Very well. You are no longer a slave to me, but a beloved brother. I will free you now." He lifted Sara's small writing desk from the wagon, drew out paper, pen, and ink, and in a few strokes, had written the letter granting Abram his freedom. During that time, Workman took it upon himself to saddle Chamberlin's horse. He hung a canteen, a sack of cornmeal, a small pot, and a second sack of dried venison on the saddle horn.

Workman signed at the bottom of the release paper as witness. Lucas let a new breeze dry the ink. He looked about him, marking the location in his mind. He realized that this was the last time he would lay eyes on Abram. Sara was gone seeking Joseph, probably never to be seen again, and shortly, his dearest friend, who had helped him deal with the grief of losing four of his family members and who had raised Sara from childhood, would be gone. He reflected how, in his early years, the idea of ever being friends with a slave seemed obnoxiously inane. "Abram, my heart is breaking. My family is forever gone."

Abram stared out into the valley, stone-faced.

Finally, Lucas folded the page and handed it slowly to Abram. They stood there for many minutes, avoiding eye contact and saying nothing. A bitter breeze swept up from the valley. Abram, now satisfied with his declamation finished, and his late-fulfilled dream in his possession, looked down at his bent hands, so crooked and stiff they could barely hold the paper. He stuffed the parchment in his shirt pocket. "You can keep my banja. My old hands can't play it no more."

Lucas, in the most awkward fashion, moved forward so as to hug the old man, but the gesture just did not play out, and he found himself with his arms outstretched, then ultimately falling to his sides.

Abram put on his jacket and hat and, with some help from Workman, mounted the horse. The horse side-stepped and whirled in a circle, but Abram finally brought it under control.

Lucas shaded his eyes from the sun, looking up at Abram. "Goodbye, old friend. God be with you."

"If I ever own a slave," Workman proclaimed, "I hope he's one like you."

Abram did not respond to either man, though he nodded at them. The wind had grown blustery and a gust lifted Lucas' hat off and sent it rolling along the ground. He chased after it before it went off the side of the hill.

When he caught up with the hat some many feet away, Abram called, "Goodbye, Lucas. Give my best to Sara if you see her again."

"But where are you going?"

"Makes no never mind. I'm free," he fairly chanted. "I'm free!" He galloped away, then turned the steed and came back a way. "Julia's husband is the name of Grant," he called. "Ulysses Simpson Grant. Just thought you'd like to know." His summation completed, he trotted down the road. Lucas and Workman watched him make his way through the village in the valley and out the other side into the forest. In another moment, Lucas could not see him anymore.

"I feel I made a horrible error," he said. "I feel I must go after him. After all, he's the best friend I ever had."

"What about your plan? The big plan to save the Union?"

"We can still do that. Right now, I must regain my friend."

FIVE

∞

THE TWILIGHT
OF SORROW

THE SAME DAY, OCTOBER 9, 1861, 2 PM
THE BOSTON MOUNTAINS, ARKANSAS

Sara, staring at the burned-out cabin where she had shot the wild hog, was steeped in her disappointment. She was closer to the Confederates, but had no guarantee that she was nearer to Joseph. The entire scene of death at the farmer's burned out home, the dead parents and children, was too visceral, too familiar.

"Come," Father Antonio leaned over and looked at her crestfallen face. "We will talk more at dinner. The sun is setting soon. We must find tools and give these people a better final resting place. Come, everyone, we should look for any tool to dig with. The barn is a likely place."

"You all go ahead," Sara said. "I want to look around the house. This is too much like what befell my own home. This poor family."

The Indians followed the priest at a rapid pace. Their language sounded to Sara like chittering magpies.

Sara let Esther's reins hang on the ground. Stepping around charred boards and shattered glass in the yard, she covered her nose passing the black, crusted form that she took to be that of a woman.

Portions of the skin had flaked off, revealing pink inner flesh. The blackened remnants of a U.S. flag lay clutched in her hand.

Many of the boards and floor planks exuded heat, so Sara stepped gingerly into the remains of the home. She made her way across the porch, past a still-standing portion of wall where the remains of a pie, now charcoal, sat in a tin on the windowsill.

She walked into the main room with its destroyed furniture, then into what must have been a bedroom. Two blackened iron bedsteads leaned against a scorched wall, the only wall still standing. Shards of pottery were strewn on the floor. Burned picture frames lay about with remnants of pictures, curled and black. Metal toys were tossed here and there. A cloth doll, untouched by the fire, save for gray smudges, sat on the floor. *The children's room.* Sara nudged the doll with her foot, but chose not to pick it up.

"Where are the children?" Sara whispered.

When she went around a tenuously standing wall and into the parents' bedroom, the floor was solid and the rug unsullied by the fire. There she discovered the bodies of the children. Two young ones of about ten and eight, at Sara's guess, lay huddled, their faces toward the floor, in a corner by the parents' bed frame. Not burned, but no less dead, their little bodies sadly clinging together with the anguished faces of final breaths. Looking up to heaven, she asked, "Who does this, dear God? These little children were of no harm to anyone."

She thought to call to Father Antonio and the Indians, but they were inside the barn. She considered an inexplicable desire to look closer at the dead children's faces but could not bring herself to do it. She turned instead to a chest bound by metal bands positioned at the end of the bed beside a tiny cradle. The exterior of the trunk was severely scorched, and the latch was sprung. *Maybe I can find some evidence of who this family was, perhaps some correspondence, and inform their next-of-kin.*

Kneeling on the woven rug, she gathered a singed dress from the floor and used it as a hot pad to lift the lid. The inside was replete with hooks and boxes and drawers, all untouched by the fire. She deftly opened each box. The first one held a stack of letters bound with ribbon. She set those beside her. In the other nooks, she found a tortoise shell comb, a garnet amulet, a pair of spectacles in a decorated case, a damask tablecloth, two intricately painted fans, and some books written in a language she could not read. Clutching the objects in her arms, she stood and started for the front yard.

Her eye caught a glint from the mantle of the fireplace. Picking her way through burnt furniture and fallen posts, she reached the hearth. A bellows sat by iron kettles and pots. The rocks of the fireplace emanated intense heat that made Sara's eyes water.

She set her bundle of heirlooms on an unburned chair and inched closer to the mantle. Atop the mantle sat a music box, the paint worn off, the ivory turned brown. She tapped the box. Its exterior was cool. Carefully, she opened the lid. A cheery tune immediately played. Inside it, she found a small sliver of parchment. She drew it out and read it. "To my dear grandchild. May your life be filled with music." The music box continued to plink the melody. Sara stared at the note, her eyes brimming with tears, contemplating such a profoundly ironic message.

Her thoughts were interrupted by the tittering of the two youngest Cherokees. She wheeled around and saw them leaping in turns over the legs of the burnt body in the yard. Gathering the music box and other family belongings, she hurried toward the children to get them to cease their game. Reaching the porch, the old squaw came from seemingly nowhere and wagged a finger at the children and hissed like a snake. The youngsters immediately stopped and hung their heads.

Behind the old woman, the young squaws, the teen Indian boy, and Father Antonio came carrying spades, hoes, a plow blade, and picks to begin digging graves. Father Antonio carried two horse blankets, as well, that he threw over the burned couple's bodies.

Sara stopped Father Antonio and whispered in his ear about the deceased children. He nodded his head.

With the old squaw sitting in her chair giving orders in her language, the Cherokees and the priest set about digging graves. Sara carried the family articles out beyond the yard and spread them onto a wide tree stump. She untied the ribbon of the letters and discovered that many of the letters were written in an unfamiliar tongue. Though the addresses on the envelopes were easily read, she felt at a loss. How could she correspond to these people in any manner they would understand? She resolved to sleep on it.

She stuffed the family's belongings in a saddlebag, except for the music box. Pacing quickly to help the diggers, she wound the music box, set it on the ground and opened the lid. She took a shovel and began digging, tears flowing down her cheeks while the tinkling tune played.

Halfway through the digging, the matron squaw appeared before Sara with a damp cloth. She gently bathed Sara's face, removing the gunpowder stain around her mouth from when she tore the gun's powder cartridges with her teeth and the grimed tear stains.

"Thank you," Sara said.

The old woman nodded.

Dusk bled into night which wrapped around the laborers like a dark tourniquet, ever-tightening against the dim single lantern's glow. The still-drifting smoke from the fire rendered a changing array of phantasmagorias that floated like troops of the dead across the meadow. Bullfrogs from the creek grumbled. A waxing moon hovered, silvering the trees.

By the time five graves were dug, crude stick crosses erected, and Father Antonio had led a final prayer, the night had wound its way past midnight, and the weary grave diggers retired to the barn.

One of the young squaws had skinned the rabbits, built a small fire, and boiled the hares with some carrots, cornmeal, mushrooms, and wild onions. The old squaw produced some flatbread from her parflech. Sara marveled at the intricate designs on the Indian travel pouch. The stew was served up on the pieces of fried bread as though on a plate. Sara, at first not hungry from having witnessed so much unwarranted death, found her appetite to be more than she expected, and she asked for seconds. The squaw with a single eye took bits of meat and carrots, chewed the pieces until they were pithy and well-masticated, and fed them to the youngest child.

The entire party, horses included, settled inside the barn. Sara took the saddle and reins from Esther, combed and brushed the mare's hide a few strokes, and then tossed some hay for the redoubtable animal. The Indians managed to drag the dead sow inside.

While the Indians settled to sleep on piles of hay, Father Antonio secured the barn door with a bar, then took Sara aside.

"I will tell you now," he began, "why I would not let you go to the Confederate camps tonight. There is a marauding band, criminals of the worst sort, nearby. We saw them twice just today. The mother squaw, White Owl, is very wise. She can read nature and signs. She saw the many hoof prints and pistol shell casings around the house. She told me some Rebel Bushwhackers had an old score to settle with this family. Before they could burn the barn and take the horse, someone scared them away.

"The body attacked by the hogs was a marauder. Perhaps shot by a family member and buried by the other Bushwhackers. They may have been chased off by an army patrol. If these marauders are who I think they are, they are ruthless. Muy malo. Very bad. I heard talk about them even before today. I will keep watch in the hayloft. But keep your rifle loaded."

Sara knew well what marauders could do. She had faced one in her own home who had been intent on raping her, only to be saved by Private Chamberlin. She hated the lawlessness that had hatched like a nest of snakes upon Missouri. She loaded her rifle, but her hands trembled. *If only I could be with Joseph, I would be safe. We'll marry and I'll be Mrs. Favor.*

When at last Sara lay down to sleep, she heard the whimpering of a whippoorwill.

SIX

⚭

FORTUNE FROM PLIGHT

TWO-AND-A-HALF MONTHS LATER, DECEMBER 30, 1861
ALMOST NOON, FAYETTEVILLE, ARKANSAS

Anthony Atkinson dodged a runaway mule-drawn caisson careening through the streets and vaulted onto the boardwalk, skidding to his knees. Dusting off a new suit and adjusting a broad-brimmed hat, he stood up and faced the telegraph office on the main street of Fayetteville, Arkansas.

His week long journey by carriage from St. Louis after the sinking of the Aurelia had been an arduous one. First, he skirted Union lines and then piecemealed a route through the Confederate camps around Springfield, down the Telegraph Road, and finally into Fayetteville.

He had brought with him what he considered his most precious cargo, Jeanette Bennett and her daughter, Clara.

Setting down a rope-tied sack, he wrenched his lambs-wool-padded wooden leg back into position on his knee, took up the sack, and strolled as upright and smoothly as he could into the telegraph office and up to an untidy clerk sitting next to a Confederate lieutenant. "I'm Anthony Atkinson. I'm here to see General Benjamin McCulloch."

"Hello, Anthony." General McCulloch sauntered forth from the shadows at the back of the edifice and vigorously shook

Anthony's hand. He pulled a pipe from his mouth and stroked his beard, taking a long look at his old friend's son. "I received your telegram. I'm glad you're here. I'm especially glad you're alive. When I heard about the sinking of the Aurelia in the Mississippi, I wondered how you'd fared."

The two departed to a back room.

"Well, Benjamin, or rather, General McCulloch, it was a fearsome adventure, but a fortunate one for me. After the ship sank, a handful of us survivors were taken prisoner by river pirates on an island. We got the better of them, but I'm afraid I lost an entire valise full of gold when the steamboat went down. I have a few coins of my own I saved. Here they are."

He laid a small, clinking pouch of gold coins on the table.

"That is a shame," General McCulloch said, lifting the small bag. "The South could have used that gold a lot more than some bank in Minnesota. Anyway, that was a big chance you took, stealing the gold."

"They have enough money. All the northern banks do. Besides, when I heard that my home state of Tennessee had seceded, I couldn't see not trying to help the cause. I've always felt the states should be able to decide a lot more for themselves without Washington dictating to them. It's about time the south set its own course. Not that I abide with the slavery that riles up so many...I just think the south would be better off without slaves. The south needs to learn commerce like the northern states. That's where the real money is."

General McCulloch raised an eyebrow. "Perhaps you're right. But the pressing matter is our need of gold and silver to buy arms from England and France. We need silver to disburse to the Indian tribes to fight for us. But I'm glad my old friendship with your father back in Tennessee has at least garnered us this happy meeting and even this small amount of gold coin."

"And it is happier still. Though I lost the valise in the river, our hostility with the pirates afforded me, shall I call it, their treasure. I

took a fair amount of their booty from their hideout. And here it is."
He untied the sack and dumped out the contents onto McCulloch's
desk — hundreds of gold and silver coins, rings, jewelry, silverware,
a silver candelabra, and a gold-plated cup and saucer.

General McCulloch's eyes widened. "You did well, Anthony.
With this, we can purchase guns from England. Your father would
be proud. And I am indebted. What can I do to repay you?"

"I'm not done, yet. I want you to meet a Negro I've come to know
well." Anthony's powerful voice echoed out into the street. "Owen!"
In a moment, the Aurelia's Captain's top hand strutted in from the
street. He wore a spanking new ditto suit and a collared shirt, and
had no trouble brushing off the soldiers grabbing at his arms to stop
him. He carried two heavy satchels. Arriving beside Anthony's chair,
he hoisted the load atop the table.

"That, General McCulloch, is over two hundred silver pieces,
courtesy of the Mississippi river pirates."

Owen beamed. General McCulloch waved off the two soldiers
trying to drag Owen from the room.

"General McCulloch. Let me introduce Owen Pilgrim. He saved my
life and just about everyone else's with his quick, courageous actions."

"I'm honored to meet you, General McCulloch," Owen said.

General McCulloch nodded at Owen. His curiosity was too
strong. He opened the satchels and peered inside. "Well done,
Anthony. You, too, Owen Pilgrim."

"General, you said you wanted to repay me. There are two
things I want you to do. First, how about you join me for the noon
meal. We could do some catching up on old stories. And... you
could meet my new bride and her daughter. They'd be honored to
meet you."

"Your new bride?'

"Yes, the steamboat's sinking was more gladsome than I could
have imagined. Had it not sunk, I would've never met the widow
who is my new bride, Jeanette, and her lovely daughter, Clara. We
were married yesterday right here in Fayetteville."

"Congratulations, my friend. That was indeed a lucky turn."

"I must warn you, though. She's from the north and is not quite sure what to make of this whole war. However, when I mentioned that she might be able to meet a general, she could barely contain her delight."

"Very well, then. Tis noon already. Let's join your wife and step-daughter. I hope I don't disappoint her. I'm not cut from the same cloth as a West Point graduate."

"She will be pleased. It's in her nature. Now for the second thing." Anthony dropped his gaze and drummed on the table.

"Yes," the general asked, "what would that be?"

Anthony stared straight into the eyes of the General McCulloch. "Because of Owen's bravery and fortitude, I would ask you to grant him his freedom. I believe you have the authority."

General McCulloch sat back in his chair. He glanced back and forth at Anthony and Owen several times. Finally, he leaned forward, ducking his head and folding his hands. Anthony thought he detected the murmur of a prayer.

"Colonel Armstrong! Fetch me my letterhead," the general called.

A tall, pleasant-faced young colonel with long sideburns ending at his neck entered, his uniform immaculate, his demeanor officious. "Yes, sir." He handed General McCulloch fine parchment, a pen, and an inkwell.

General McCulloch signed his signature with a flourish and handed the paper to the colonel. "Frank, prepare a letter granting this Negro here...."

"Owen Pilgrim," Owen piped, smiling. He was rocking on his heels, adjusting the collar of his new shirt, then brushing the sleeves of his jacket.

"Owen Pilgrim his freedom," the general continued. "Use some flowery language. Talk about his bravery and support of the cause, et cetera, et cetera, and you sign it as a witness." He turned to Owen, "All right, young hero, you tail the colonel, and he'll prepare your freedom document."

Owen fell in step with Colonel Armstrong to the outer office.

"Oh, and Owen!" Anthony called after him. "When you finish, hurry to the café and save a seat for us and Jeanette and Clara."

"Yes, suh."

General McCulloch lowered his voice and leaned in toward Anthony. "But what will *you* do next? You can't go back north. There's a price on your head."

"I know I must disappear. I have cousins not far from here at a wayside tavern on the Butterfield Stage Road. I'm hoping my family and I can stay there through the winter, then come spring, we'll build a new life out west in Texas."

"Good plan, and I know the tavern you speak of. Elkhorn."

Anthony leaned forward "What news of the army? I know of the victory at Oak Hill, or Wilson Creek as the St. Louis papers called it."

"We were fortunate to carry the day, and it was the last time General Price ever did anything I could stomach. For now, he has his Missouri Guard wintering in Springfield and probably has done nothing to fortify. He's an idiot. I cannot endure the man." General McCulloch's face turned momentarily red.

"My own soldiers," the general continued, "are in cantonment stretching from just north of here at Cross Hollows to some grazing meadows for our cavalry along the Arkansas River. Fort Smith is our primary recruiting and training post. The army's in good spirits. Tomorrow, I'm heading to Richmond. That dastard, General Price, has stirred up a journalistic hornet's nest with the newspapers. His remarks make me out as incompetent for not pursuing the Yanks after Wilson Creek. It wasn't enough that we drove them clean out of the territory."

"I'm sorry to hear that, sir."

"Also, I need to speak directly with President Davis to convince him we need more clothing, shoes, and arms. We are woefully lacking guns and ammunition. At least we do have some chemists making gunpowder for us."

"Gunpowder? Is there a plant or foundry?" Anthony's face showed amazement.

"Yes, working out of ordinary houses." General McCulloch flashed a smile of pride. "Ingenious sort of men, these Arkansans and Texans. They extract saltpeter from bat guano, add sulfur, then charcoal from burned logs, and they make usable gunpowder."

"If we don't win this war by the bravery of our Southern boys, we'll win it on ingenuity."

"Indeed." General McCulloch smirked.

"I wish you the best on your trip to Richmond."

"I do hope my visit with President Davis will garner our needed weaponry. Else we can't fight. And we can't win."

Anthony nodded, understanding the gravity of having an army with no supplies to fight.

"But for now, let's go meet your new Yankee wife and step-daughter and recall old times. On the way, I'll tell you my best news." General McCulloch took off his hat and ran his fingers through his dark, graying hair. "I finally have some decent scouts. I went for months without a single soul who could reconnoiter and give me usable information. I almost lost the battle of Wilson Creek because of it. But now I have the best I've seen. The McGavin brothers from Texas."

⚬⚬

SEVEN

THE HISTORY OF MANKIND IS CARRIED ON THE BACK OF A HORSE

FOUR MONTHS EARLIER
TEN DAYS AFTER THE BATTLE OF WILSON CREEK

D allas baked in the mid-morning summer heat. The dust churned up from a many horses and wagons hesitated in a constant dry wind and would not settle, generating a chalky haze. Asa McGavin trotted his sleek, black horse along the main street.

He noticed how the town had grown in the decade since he had last traveled its streets. A healthy mercantile lined the main street including two general stores, two saloons, a hat shop, a barber and tonsorial parlor, two harness maker shops, numerous boarding houses, and three blacksmiths with liveries.

A portion of the downtown businesses that had been burned by a large fire of a year previous remained unrepaired, a collection of charred remnants of several families' livelihoods.

Languid slaves drove wagons and carriages for their masters and did their bidding. Asa knew this was the one area of Texas where slavery was hoisted like a shining flag demanding allegiance.

A gallows looked as if it was planted like a hideous tree in the center of the street, creaking in the stiff summer breeze with three snake-like hangman's nooses dangling and twisting about with each gust of wind. Carriages, carts, and wagons had to veer around it.

The Battle of Wilson Creek was now ten days past, and word of the Confederate victory had toiled its way to Dallas. Asa watched a gaggle of newsboys, clutching the Dallas Herald newspapers under their arms, rush from customer to customer hawking their astounding news. "Read all about it. General McCulloch Triumphs Over Yankee Invaders!"

Nary a single adult failed to dig into a purse or pocket and render up the penny for the four-page diatribe and commentary. Men and women alike, flushed with excitement, gathered in small circles to read and discuss the grand Confederate victory.

Two lads of a dozen years each raced down the center of the thoroughfare, waving the papers in their hands, shouting, "Huzzah! Huzzah for the Confederacy and for Texas!" They stopped momentarily in mid-street and feigned a sword fight with sticks, then cavorted up to a church and into a crowd who swatted at them and sent mild curses toward the boys. The waifs danced away, laughing and thumbing their noses. Asa halted his horse to avoid plowing into the youths, and then rode to a general store halfway down the block from the gallows.

A sandy-haired man, twenty years old, stood on the porch of a general store, loading sundry sacks of flour, cornmeal, beans, onions, turnips, jerky, coffee, and peanuts onto a buckboard wagon. He took off his straw hat and wiped his brow. His shirt under a leather vest was soggy with sweat. When Asa rode up beside him, he complained, "I think that mare is getting ready to foal, and I need to be there when she does, Asa,"

"Don't you be worrying about the herd, Ben. Just keep loading those sacks of victuals. We've got to have enough food for the drive to Arkansas. Last thing I need is a bunch of hungry wranglers." Asa, sitting on a massive, seventeen-hand, charcoal-colored stallion, swatted a fly, knocking it to the ground. He was a huge man a few years over forty, barrel-chested with coal black hair and bushy mutton chops. He wore a black jacket, black pants and a broad-brimmed hat with a rattlesnake skin band. A brace of matching colt revolvers protruded from his belt. Reaching into his yellow silk vest, he pulled forth a silver watch on a chain and checked the time.

"Why do I have to do all the loadin'?" Ben asked. "Why ain't you doin' some?" He brushed his long mop of sandy hair from his hazel eyes. His sinewy biceps bulged against his sleeves. He was bow-legged from constant horseback riding, but he moved with a graceful force.

"Little brother, you just keep doing as you're told. If some heavy lifting comes along, I'll help you."

Ben hoisted another sack of flour from the porch of the general store. "You at least could have had Paul or one of the other wranglers come with us to help."

"Ben," Asa answered tersely, "your older brother and the wranglers have other chores with the herd, and you complain too much. You got two hands, don't you?" Asa was the only brother who bore a semblance of the Scottish brogue from their parents who had landed in South Carolina, marshalled their way to Tennessee, and then to Texas where they died.

"Yes, I do, and I got two eyes and...." The uproar of a boisterous crowd gathered in front of a church broke his tirade. He and Asa turned toward the *hurrahs*.

"This town has sure grown from the puddle in the road it was when I was little," Ben said. "There's actually enough people livin' here now to have a crowd. What d'ya suppose they're all worked up about?"

Asa bit the end off a cigar, spit out the piece, and then lit the cigar. "Stay here." He trotted his horse to the back of the throng who faced a tall, gray-bearded man in a black suit with a white pastor's collar. His ruddy cheeks shone with beads of sweat, and silver hair spilled from under a stovepipe hat to flow to his shoulders. He stood on the high porch of a white-washed church, raising himself on his tiptoes at dramatic points of his message and waving one arm in broad gestures while his other hand held pages of a sermon. His resonant voice rolled out into the air like the peal of a large bell. Almost every two sentences brought cheers from the flock of believers — men, women, and children.

Asa extended his boot from his stirrup and nudged a narrow man standing in the back. The man wheeled, an indignant expression on his face, and was taken aback as he looked up at the man dressed all in black atop a black mountain of a horse. "Who's he?" Asa asked, as if the thin stranger owed him the favor.

The man turned his back to Asa and answered over his shoulder, "*He* is Reverend W. H. Stokes, shepherd of this church. He has been speaking of the South's recent victory at Oak Hill, near Wilson Creek in Missouri. He is one of our city's most distinguished leaders."

Asa booted the man again, "What's he want?"

"Well, though I have no idea who you are, our Reverend Stokes is repeating a portion of his moving sermon of Sunday last. It was so well-conceived that many, including myself, have asked him to repeat it, and, he, being the gracious man that he is, has endeavored to speak again this rousing testimony on behalf of God and the cause of the Confederacy. Now, leave me be." He stepped away, deeper into the crowd.

Reverend Stokes elevated his voice to a strident pitch, "Who, my countrymen and women, opposed the war of 1812? Was it not the Yankees? Who threatened to leave the Union if Texas was annexed? Why, of course, it was the Yankees! Why did they not leave the Union for the Union's good? No tears would have been shed upon the occasion — no swords unsheathed to force them back again."

The crowd murmured agreement and nodded their heads.

Asa shifted in his saddle. "Yes, but the Yanks *didn't* leave the Union," he muttered.

The reverend continued reading from his sermon, speaking in the most enthusiastic fashion. "The political history of our country of the last portion of this century has been nothing less than a battle *for* the constitution by the South and *against* it by the North. Suffice it to say that every single vote by our national Congress has been to enrich the shipbuilders and manufacturers of the North while undermining Southern agriculture. All interference by the Northern, traitorous demagogues has been in violation not only of the Constitution but of the solemn pledges of our Northern neighbors." The crowd cheered.

Asa turned his horse. "I've heard about enough of this lunacy."

Some in the crowd turned to look at him. The preacher continued his admonitions. Asa loped his horse back to the buckboard.

Ben loaded the last sack on the wagon. "Who was he?" He scuffed mud from his boot on the boardwalk.

"Just another blowhard trying to drum up support for this infernal war." Asa dismounted and pulled two silver dollars from his pants pocket. He and Ben strode into the store, spurs jingling. Asa dropped the coins in the grateful shopkeeper's hands. "Shopkeep, what is the purpose of the gallows standing in the center of the street? Somebody due to be hung?"

The diminutive shopkeeper, dressed in an oversized apron that draped to the top of his shoes, had a round, jovial face with many wrinkles about his smiling eyes. "That, sir, stands as a reminder to the niggers that they should not even think of rebellion. They's the ones what set the terrible fire last year that nearly destroyed our town. So, we hung three of 'em and rode two foul-mouthed abolitionists out on a rail." He did not wait for a response from his audience, but continued in his garrulous fashion. "Yes, sir, it were a terrible thing — the fire and all. But we got it in hand pretty quick. The mayor ordered every slave be whipped, and that's what we all did. I whipped mine. You see, besides runnin' this here store,

I have a cotton farm outside of town. And my slaves are workin' a great deal harder now. Keep their eyes down. Yes, sir."

Asa grimaced. "And you say the whole town and any white man living nearby whipped their slaves even though they had nothing to do with the fire."

"Well, since we didn't know for sure which niggers were the criminals, we hung three and whipped the rest."

"And you're sure the Negroes started the fire?"

"Sure as we can be." The jovial man chuckled, seeing no contradiction in his or any of the white citizens' actions.

"So, you had a trial for these Negroes?" Asa's question was pointed.

The loquacious shopkeeper was wholly befuddled by this question and stammered a moment. Regaining his composure, and in a somewhat vehement tone, he said, "Of course, we did *not*. If ordinary chattel, like a horse, steps on your foot, do you give it a trial? No, you take a stick and beat its backside. These niggers will only dodge work and snicker behind your back unless you make it clear who's in charge." He once again smiled broadly, sure that he had made perfect sense.

"Thank you for the vittles, Shopkeep." Asa turned. Under his breath, he said, "I sure hope that when the Yanks come down here and plough under the South that they don't whip us all for what *you folks* done."

Ben, following on his heels, asked, "What do you mean, Asa? Aren't you in favor of us beatin' the Yanks?"

"I'm in favor of whoever pays us in silver for the mustangs we round up," Asa barked. "Right now, that's the Confederates' General McCulloch. If the Yankees want to pay more, I'll round up horses for them."

"But the Yanks were plannin' to invade Texas even before this war. You heard the rumors."

"And that's all it was — rumors. Those Yanks have no more idea why they're fighting this war than that stultified blophus of a parson over there trying to separate these good people from their money every Sunday... and steal their sons to go to war."

On the front porch, Ben grabbed Asa's sleeve. "But if Abe Lincoln wins this war, he'll take away the slaves. The state's livelihood will collapse. Texas and all the Southern states will go bankrupt. You bein' a former state representative should know that."

Asa rolled his eyes, tossing his cigar in the street. "And Texas seceding is why I resigned. Same as Governor Houston. Besides, the Confederates didn't even have to start this war. I showed you the newspaper story about Senator Crittenden of Kentucky. He had already got the Senate close to ratifying an amendment to the Constitution that would have guaranteed slavery for all time. These all-fired secessionists could see that it would've been better to stay in the Union and work things out. But no, they aren't about saving anything. They just wanted a fight. Just like Abe Lincoln. Everybody's lying. Everybody wants to fight."

"That ain't it, at all."

"That *is* it! Why do you care if some rich planter gets to keep his slaves or not? Last time I checked, you didn't own a slave."

Ben sputtered, lost for words. Finally, he said, "Well, maybe one day I'd like to own one. As soon as we deliver this herd to Fort Smith, I'm joinin' up. I aim to whip at least a dozen Yanks and send 'em high-tailin' back to Abe Lincoln's cellar."

"You do that, Ben. Go ahead and die for some useless cause for the sake of some rich plantation owner in Georgia. And while you're at it, why don't you spit on Ma and Pa's graves."

"I would never do that," Ben fumed. "Besides, I don't even remember Ma and Pa. I was too young when they died."

"And I'm the one that had to raise you. I wish I'd a done a better job."

EIGHT

∞

AN UNCLOUDED BROW

Asa McGavin rode his stallion alongside his youngest brother, Ben, who drove the supply wagon. A short distance east of Dallas, they arrived at the herd of new-broke horses, grazing in a bowl-shaped, shallow valley. Three other wranglers on their mounts stood watch along the periphery of the herd and waved a hello.

Paul McGavin, the middle brother and the tallest and thinnest of the three, limped around a campfire, tending a boiling pot of beans on a spit. He was clean-shaven, with a receding hairline and black hair, trimmed short. Absentmindedly, he ran a finger over a ragged scar on his neck and watched his brothers approach. The steam from the cookpot rose and fogged his spectacles. He removed them and cleaned them with a kerchief. His untethered mount, a dapple gray, nibbled grass behind the buckboard wagon.

When Ben and Asa arrived, Paul called to them, "Saw some Comanches, maybe Kiowas, on the ridge earlier."

"Did they seem interested in the herd?" Asa asked.

"Hard to tell. There were only five of them. They had a string of horses already. Maybe they think they need some more."

"We're going to have to be more vigilant. This is their territory. I was talking to the shopkeep in Dallas, and he told me some

Comanches attacked a family farm north of here and burned them out, stole the horses and killed one of the boys."

Ben jumped from the wagon and tightened down the tarp over the supplies. "Let's get going. I worked too hard to round up these horses."

"Yeah." Paul chuckled. "And we appreciate you doing all the work by yourself."

"I know you worked hard, too. I just meant..."

Asa interrupted, "Ben, go bring in the wranglers. We need a meeting to plan what to do with the Indians."

Ben flung his hands in the air, "All right. I'll get 'em. Don't bother listenin' to me."

In a few minutes, the three brothers and their hired wranglers stood in circle around the fire, eating pinto beans and biscuits, kicking dirt on the dying fire, and listening to Asa's remonstrations to be "extra cautious."

Paul stood off to the side, rubbing his right leg that often ached deep at the bone.

Standing next to Asa, the Mexican wrangler named Manuel Juarez chewed his beans with gusto. He sometimes struggled with speaking the English language and understanding his companions' words. "Say again. What you mean?" he said repeatedly. He wore a red and yellow striped sombrero and a ragged serape, and his upper lip was draped by a dense, black mustache. Around his tight belly hung a wide belt, and he wore two navy Colt pistols strapped down into holsters on his hips. His boots were decorated with red and green filigree.

Across from Juarez stood the stout French Canadian, Gustav d'Orleans. He wore a stovetop hat and an amber neckerchief with lace embroidery. His mustache was pencil thin, and he had a habit of twisting the ends into small curls. "My uncle fought in the French and Indian War, and I think the Iroquois were a much finer, more civilized tribe. I think these Comanches are...."

"Loco. Estan muy loco. They are very crazy." Juarez laughed heartily. Then he frowned in his big mustache. "And they are mean."

The third wrangler, Stew Ingdoll, merely nodded. He was short, a little over four feet tall, with squatty legs. His back was crooked and he had to stand on a stump or the wagon gate to mount his horse. When he rode, his legs generally splayed straight out in the stirrups. He regularly smiled, even under duress.

Asa finished his directions and turned to mount his big black stallion.

"But, Amigo," Juarez said, in between bites of his beans, "If they are solamente cinco," He held up five fingers. "We are six. Do we need to worry?"

"If they raise a commotion," Asa said, "the horses will scatter. If we chase after the horses going in all directions, it could be one of us against five of them. Stay sharp! Don't let your brow be clouded."

"Es verdad," Juarez said. "That's right. They would pick us off uno by uno." Seeing the other's sour faces, he dropped his smile and began drawing in the dirt with his boot.

"I will ride in the lead," Gustav said. "If the horses break, I will turn them. I have the fastest horse." He nodded at his appaloosa stallion and twirled his mustache tighter.

"No, Señor," retorted Juarez, sticking out his chest, "you do not have the fastest caballo. He could not win a race with hes self."

Ben said, "I have the fastest horse and the smartest. And my roan's a durn sight smarter than you, Juarez." He laughed and kicked dirt in Juarez's direction.

Juarez laughed and feigned a jump at Ben, who pretended to run from him. Soon, all were laughing, save Asa, his dark eyes with little gold specks squinting at the midday sun.

"Mount up," he said.

With little effort, the six men got the herd of thirty horses moving across the north Texas prairie. The wind was blustery and whipped the knee-high grasses in an undulation like ocean waves for miles and miles. Save for a spare oak or elm with tough bark that thwarted wildfire rage, their branches filled with flocks of sparrows or murders of crows holding noisy court, the endless grassland stretched to the horizon and blended into the cloudless sky, golden amber to blue.

Behind the herd, Ben drove the buckboard wagon with their grub, tarps, and tack. His roan was tethered to the buckboard tailgate.

Asa rode before the carefully clustered herd, sometimes pointing a new direction for his wranglers, but generally heading the herd northeast. He knew that herding horses would have difficulties, and he hoped the Comanches would not be one of them. He had enough concerns about losing horses on their sojourn, but he fervently worried about his two brothers being killed.

The three of them were a family adrift, forced to sever roots again and again. For years, the boys had rounded up horses and sold them, but the job was grueling and dangerous. When Ben was barely fourteen and almost killed by a bucking mustang, Asa retired them all from wrangling, and they bent their backs to the plow, farming corn. Somewhat successfully, Asa ran for the Texas legislature, but the cost of buying whiskey to entice the voters set back his savings.

When Texas severed ties with the Union, he resigned his seat. The last thing he expected was for their corn crop to crumble with blight. He pulled up stakes, sold the farm in July of 1861, and convinced his brothers to go back to rounding up and breaking wild horses, a task they knew well, but not what he wanted. Deep down, he felt he had failed his brothers. *We need a place to settle, Lord*, he prayed. *We ain't no Saharan nomads.*

The wranglers drove the herd along for miles across the interminable prairie. The dry summer weather left the creeks barely filled, and they traversed them with ease.

Topping a rise, they encountered a herd of bison, their number extending beyond the low hills and mesas, and in no mood to move out of the way of the horse herd. Despite the wranglers' best efforts at yelling, whistling and waving, the bison were intransigent.

"Do *not* fire your guns," Asa admonished. "You'll spook the horses."

"Move on, you silly beasts!" Gustav waved his lariat. A handful of bison took a step or two, but continued grazing. He turned to Asa. "We must go around. They are as stubborn as my former wife. Ah, mon cheri." He doffed his stovepipe hat and held it to his heart.

"Head 'em to the right," Asa said.

The horse herd flowed around the bison like a river around a mountain.

Toward mid-afternoon, Asa sighted Ben driving the wagon pell-mell up from the rear.

Ben shouted, "The Indians are back!" He drew the wagon up beside Asa and pointed at the five Indians, about half a mile behind the herd, riding slowly. They did not have the string of horses they had earlier and were following at a measured pace.

"Go tell the others," Asa said to Ben, "if the Comanches come in, we concentrate on fighting them. We can gather the horses later. And, Ben, tell them that if the horses stampede, we need to travel in pairs. No one's alone. When you get done, drive the buckboard beside me and bring Stew with you."

Ben's heart sprinted in his chest. He had never fought Indians, and tales of the Comanches taking pleasure in torturing a man fetched immediate apprehension in him. He hurried to each wrangler and repeated Asa's instructions. Ultimately, Ben arrived beside Asa at the front of the herd. Asa did not acknowledge him, but his eyes scanned the hills around them.

A dark thunderhead towered in the distant sky. When Ben looked back again, the Commanches were circling at a gallop to the right and towards a line of low mesas.

NINE

∞

THE GRAY TWILIGHT

OCTOBER 3, 1861, EARLY MORNING
THIRD CAVALRY CAMP OUTSIDE CARTHAGE, MISSOURI

J oseph awoke at the itchy tap of a fly's feet on his cheek. Begging strength to his arm, he flapped weakly at the fly and opened his eyes. He immediately noticed the burning sensation had gone from his eyes and nose, and his skin had ceased to itch. His chest no longer ached. He felt clammy, for his clothes were sweat-soaked. His fever had finally broken.

He could not remember feeling so weak, not even when he awakened from the coma in the Reeder home and discovering he was bereft of his memory.

He was no longer bound up with constant coughing. Pneumonia, the nurse called it. In his weeks in the "dying tent," two bodies had been carried out for burial.

He closed his eyes, and someone put a damp cloth over his forehead and eyes. He was too weary to remove the rag. He tried to speak, but a gurgling sound was all that came from his throat. He lay on the cot in this state for what seemed like hours, his breath shallow as a mouse's.

All of a sudden, a loud voice racketed in his ears. "Get these dead bodies out of here!" A moment later, "And bury 'em!"

Through the crevice under the rag, he observed a wiry, gray-haired man wearing a shabby coat, hung open.

"But, Doc," another voice said, "if we take 'em out to bury 'em, who's gonna take care of the sick 'uns?"

"Never you mind. Take this one out and this one... and do it quick or we'll have a disease crisis on our hands to equal the plagues of Egypt!"

Joseph could catch glimpses of the doctor wading through the crowded infirmary tent, pointing at bodies on cots. A cadre of attendants followed him. The Negro attendant stood to the side. Joseph became aware of the tromp of feet approaching the front of the tent where he lay. "And take this one, too. Look at it. Body's as gray as a wasp nest."

"But, Doc," came the voice, "Shouldn't you ought to check his pulse?"

Joseph felt a calloused hand flap at different points on his chest. A gurgling sound was all he could muster.

Then, the doctor yelled, "There. You satisfied? Look at 'em. No color left. The reaper has come for him."

Joseph heard the doctor's heavy tread pass by his cot and felt the sunshine bleed through the tent flap. He felt good he was alive. He agreed with the doctor to remove the dead bodies immediately. No sense in contracting a worse disease. He was so weary; a ponderous sleep overtook him.

He awoke, jostled, and became aware he was being carried, wrapped up in the blanket that had covered him. He felt relieved he had survived the measles, but the bouncing around was uncomfortable. Opening his eyes, he realized the blanket was wrapped entirely around him. Someone had his feet. Four others held the blanket closed around his torso, carrying him. His head bobbed along with their every step. He could see nothing, felt the rough wool scratching his face and hands. He tried to call out but discovered someone had tied a cloth around his head and chin, binding his jaw shut.

Just then, he felt his body laid roughly down on soft earth. He knew the smell of fresh, cool soil. He brought his fatigued arms up to his face and pulled the bindings from around his jaw. No sooner had he done that than a pile of dirt, for he knew it was such, landed on his chest, followed by another. He was being buried alive.

With all his might, he struggled up to a sitting position and moaned, "I'm alive."

Another spade's load of dirt hit him in his blanket-covered face. "I'm alive," he screamed, though it sounded like a frog's croak. "I'm not dead."

"Look!" the voice sounded like it was from a cavern. "This one ain't gone. Get 'im out. Get 'im out."

Many hands grabbed his body, pulled the blanket from around him. Five smiling faces in diverse caps and hats looked at him, including the bent nose nurse. "Well, I'll be." The nurse reached a hand to Joseph's and pulled him up to standing in the grave. The rest of the men, their noses and mouths covered with cloths, helped him climb out.

With support from the nurse, Joseph stood beside the grave. He had the desire to curse the would-be murderers to hell, but could not bring forth the words. His nose was filled with the foulest odor he had ever smelled. He looked around. Stretching into the trees were a dozen graves and a dray with swollen bodies. Workers were digging more holes, and the stench was like rotten swill.

"What is happening?" he choked out. "Is the whole army dying?"

No one answered him.

With two men holding his elbows, he shuffled toward a wagon. They laid him in the wagon bed. In a moment, the wagon trundled away up a slight hill toward the town of Carthage. At one point, Joseph heard the rumbling of charging horses and a considerable measure of cheering. He raised his head to look out into a long field where a dozen horses raced. *I'd like to do that, now that I'm well.*

At length, the wagon stopped and the driver ushered Joseph inside the Carthage courthouse among rows of sick and injured soldiers. "Is the whole army sick?" he asked an attendant at the door.

"Nope," the man said. "Some have broken arms and cracked skulls from racing horses and brawling. Others got the trots or some other malady."

"Oh."

"You take that mat over there. Keep the blanket on you. I'll check you directly. Surgeon'll be by later. I guess you wasn't ready for the gray twilight. So, don't you relapse on me. I done lost two just today that was well, then died of the croup."

Joseph squatted on the thin mat. His clothes were still wet, and he shivered.

TEN

∞

BRAVE ENOUGH, WEAK ENOUGH

OCTOBER 10, 1861, PRE-DAWN
THREE MILES EAST OF THE CONFEDERATE CANTONMENT, ARKANSAS

S ara awoke with a start. The barn was a halcyon chamber. The Cherokees slept, making no sound. A few flies buzzed the sow's corpse. *Too quiet*, she thought.

She lifted her rifle and stood. In so doing, she bumped the music box, and it tinkled a few notes. Using her free hand, she brushed hay straws from her dress. She had traveled over a week on dusty roads and rugged terrain with no chance to bathe. Then she had helped to bury the five bodies at the fire-destroyed home and now felt wretchedly filthy. Her long blond hair was tangled and laden with scratching hay chaffs.

Bare strands of sunlight seeped through cracks in the barn walls. Dust motes glimmered in the shafts of light.

She whispered up to the loft, "Father Antonio."

No answer.

"Father Antonio, are you there?"

When the priest gave no response, she carefully climbed the ladder to the loft and stepped onto the creaking board floor. The loft window was open a crack, bleeding in sparse light. She could see where the priest had lain, his haversack and straw hat left beside an indention in the hay pile. She bent down to it and felt the warm hay, his body heat retained there. Feeling the warmth left by the man aroused in her a deep desire, a need akin to what she had felt when she had touched the sheets where Joseph had lain when he was recovering from his head wound.

Her heart raced.

For a moment, she was back at the creek on that scorching summer day, and Joseph and she were in each other's arms. She remembered the power in his biceps that embraced her, and recalled how his shoulder bones felt under his skin, the hardness beneath the supple flesh. In her fingertips, she could almost feel again the curls of his hair, then on her lips the whisper of a kiss.

A rooster crowed in the barnyard. Sara hastened to the loft window and shoved open the shutter. The sun was not yet visible, hidden by a bluish-white fog that filled the forest corridors. She heard what sounded like distant thunder rumbling. In the barn, the Indians began stirring and grumbling. The smallest child began mewling, followed by shushing from the mother. They spoke in the Cherokee tongue.

Sara hurried down the ladder, her rifle slung on her back. The Indians were already munching on their dry bread.

"Good morning," Sara said to the Indians.

They mumbled spare greetings.

Sara strode to the barn door, pushed it open and emerged into the almost viscous fog. The rooster, perched on a post, crowed an unbroken chant, and the chickens pecked at the remains of scratch around the barnyard. The shroud of mist seemed to both silence and amplify sound. The bird call of the night before seemed louder.

The distant rumbling she had barely perceived earlier was growing louder.

A rustling in the brush snatched her attention. Then she heard a whistle. To her right, Father Antonio was holding his slingshot in one hand and motioning for her to go back in the barn.

No sooner had he done that than the cause of the rumbling became evident. Three riders sprang from behind the trees at the path. They wore no uniforms. Revolvers were aimed. Looking square in the eye of the lead rider, she dove to the ground. Shots chipped off pieces of barn above her head. She scrambled inside and secured the door with a heavy crossbar. Peering through cracks in the slatted wall, she could see fleeting glimpses of the trio of Bushwhackers. One of the men was striding toward the barn door, his revolver drawn.

"Hide! Quick!" Sara called to the Cherokees while ascending the ladder two steps at a time. She raced to the open window and peeked out. The two men still in their saddles shot at her, the bullets piercing the wall by her throat and chest. She dropped down and shifted her rifle around from her back.

Below, the first man was yanking and kicking on the barred door and hollering vile curses, followed by, "Come out, you sorry Yank filth. Traitor. We need that horse, and we want to teach you and them Indians a lesson."

Sara knew there was no use in saying she was not a Yankee, for now she needed to defend the unarmed Cherokees.

Sara brought her rifle parallel with her body on the floor, then shouldered the weapon, and cocked the hammer. She took aim at one of the Bushwhackers. A thought, deep and painful, entered her mind. She had never killed a man. The shot would be easy. She closed her eyes, her head barely above the floor, trying to slow her breathing.

Both men, their steeds swirling, fired again at her, the shots plugging the wall inches above her.

Sara held her breath, took careful aim. An easy shot. She pulled the trigger. The gun misfired. She cocked the hammer again, and still it misfired. Her ammunition satchel was below. Leaping up, she raced to the ladder, climbed down, falling the last steps. She regained her footing and looked out the cracks in the wall. All three men were off their horses and had lit dry, leave-laden branches like torches.

She gathered her satchel and pulled out a fresh firing cap and clamped it on the nipple at the hammer. The unarmed Cherokees huddled in the rear of the barn. Esther and the farm horse jigged left and right in their stalls, stamping. When Sara looked again through the wall gaps, smoke was permeating the air. The marauders had lit the piles of hay around the barn. It would be mere minutes before the blaze spread.

Sara sped once more up the ladder. *Where is Father Antonio?* From her vantage point at the window, she witnessed flame and smoke broadening and rising. She coughed. The marauders were backing up, their revolvers drawn, watching the barn door.

Before she could take aim, one of their horses bucked and took off at a gallop into the forest, followed by a second horse. Just before the third horse fled, Sara watched a projectile fly from the thicket hitting it in the rump, followed by a speedily-fired second stone, hitting the horse's flank. The horses were out of sight into the fog in seconds.

When the men turned to see their horses racing away, Sara took aim at the tallest marauder who bore a mangy beard.

She ached in her heart. Her fingers trembled. She pulled the trigger, but flinched when firing. The bullet grazed the top of his scalp, peeling his hat from his head. Blood flowed down his face in a bubbling stream, and he howled. Holding his head, he raced away after the horses, followed by the other two. One of the marauders kept trying to stop him, pushing a kerchief down on the wound, but to not avail. Soon, they had disappeared into the fog.

The smoke intensified, and flames licked up the sides of the barn. Sara let the gun slide to the floor. She had not killed a man, but she felt proud that he would be aggrieved for his travesty for a good while. She picked up her gun and satchel and leaped to a haystack below, tumbling. She untied the horses and led them out. The Cherokees sprinted out the door, White Owl carrying her chair.

Father Antonio sped from his brushy refuge. He hugged each of his Cherokee friends, tousled the hair of the baby, then patted Sara on the shoulder and smiled. Keeping their eyes peeled should the Bushwhackers return, the group moved into the thicket away from the flaming barn. It eventually collapsed on itself, and the fire played out.

When late morning arrived, the fire had dwindled to nothing. Father Antonio excused himself from the group and returned into the copse of bushes where he had been when the Bushwhackers attacked. In a moment, Sara heard the priest intoning a chant.

Curious as to his enterprise, she sneaked closer and spied on him. Atop a broad tree stump, he had spread a white cloth; atop sat a small gold plate, a silver cup and a crucifix. He held in his hands a wafer of bread and was gazing up to heaven pronouncing words Sara did not know. He lowered the bread and ate it, and then genuflected. He next took the tiny silver chalice, elevated it, again speaking the Latin. Lowering the chalice, he quaffed the contents. Though Father Antonio continued the spiritual celebration, Sara considered it best to leave him be.

When she returned to the Cherokees, the young mother with the white eye said, "He does his Mass every day. He is a man of the Great Spirit. Though we do not know his ways, we admire him."

All of a sudden, Sara again heard the whimpering sound that she mistook for a bird call, but it was evident this time the sound was of a baby screaming in pain.

She vaulted across the broken land into the trees behind where the barn had stood, down a steep grade, and sped far from the farm.

In a moment, she discovered a sobbing baby girl lying in a small basket under a blanket. Sara realized the child had been hidden by the farm family when the Bushwhackers attacked. Ants crawled over the girl. Sara grabbed the child, swept the ants away and threaded her way back to the Cherokees, now joined by Father Antonio. The baby bawled.

The young Cherokee mother immediately took the little girl, stripped the wet cloth diaper, opened her shirt and began suckling the child at her bosom. The baby calmed.

Sara beamed, knowing one of the family members had survived. Her mood dropped when she thought about her own future. It seemed that finding Joseph had become near impossible.

By midday, the group had moved well away from the burned-out farm, deeper into the forest. Sara said, "I need to go."

Father Antonio nodded. "I've drawn you a map. This path becomes quickly a road into the Cross Hollows encampment. It's nearly three miles by my estimation. For a while you will go due west, then curve south. You'll hear the place before you see it."

Sara gave him a quizzical look. She took the map. "If this is correct, then I should see my Joseph today." Her excitement grew. Folding the paper and placing it in her skirt pocket, she asked, "What about you, Father, what will you and the Cherokees do? You can't stay here. The marauders may return."

"Well, we have the farmer's horse. The young ones can ride. We will make better time. I must help them reach their homeland. We will travel the side paths through these mountains."

"Why not just make your way to the Stage Road and then make your way to Alabama?"

"We cannot go on that road. White Owl will not allow it. She says it is Nunna daul Isunyi. It means 'the trail where they cried.' She won't walk on it. Nor will she allow the others to walk it. When she was a child, President Jackson ordered all Indian tribes be removed from their homes, and many died from disease and exposure on that road."

"I see."

"So, we will find a better path. Send us your prayers."

"I will." She looked once more at the little group. She would not forget them. She felt a tinge of remorse that she was not caring for the baby, but did not have the means to nurse the child. She was glad for the Cherokee mother who had already secured the child with a cloth against her chest.

She mounted Esther, waved, and headed toward the encampment, hoping.

ELEVEN

⚭

THE PLACE WHERE
LIGHTNING IS DISPENSED
— BOOK OF JOB

ONE WEEK LATER, OCTOBER 19, 1861, 4 PM
SOUTH OF IRONTON, MISSOURI

Lucas and Workman saw the measureless storm closing rapidly on them like a black mountain erupting from the earth. It rose above the southeastern Missouri hills and was racing toward them. Fingers of lightning crackled and leaped across the clouds.

"I'm hopin' we find some shelter soon," Workman announced, "else we'll be no better than the soggy fish."

"Or burnt to ashes by that lightning," Lucas added.

They had driven the wagon along a waggling course, skirting the Union soldiers at Rolla and hoping to catch up with Abram. Lucas continually mulled over his hasty response to Abram's request for freedom, giving it to him out of guilt and remorse and a longing to not lose his best friend. But Abram had ridden away.

In their search, Lucas had halted the wagon at every homestead and village and asked about the old Negro, with no luck.

Their current road was pitted with holes, and the going was rough enough without a storm imminent. Rounding a curve that was more hole than road they came upon an aged drover, herding a half-dozen hogs at fast as he could prod them, though the hogs took their own time. A blue-eyed hound trotted alongside the swineherd. Just before they passed through the marginal excuse for a road, they caught up with the man who abruptly sat down spraddle-legged in the road, plumb in their way.

He was gray-haired, as tanned brown as an Indian, and possessed numerous lesions on his arms and neck, like he had a sort of pox. The hound took to licking the man's wounds. Lucas drew the wagon to the halt and called, "You're about to lose your hogs!"

The man never looked up from under his tattered straw hat, and the hogs ambled down the road. Directly, the man removed his shoe from a sockless foot and pinched a blister so large that Lucas and Workman could see it from their seats on the wagon.

"I've had enough of this." Workman descended from the wagon and walked directly in front of the man.

The old codger looked up, surprised. "Hello," he said.

Workman watched the man scan the length of him, and then he whistled. "Did you not hear the wagon and the horses? Did you hear us yellin'?"

The man batted at his ears and shook his head.

"He's deaf!" Workman, pointed to his own ears and called to Lucas.

Though Lucas's own hearing was drastically marginalized, he caught Workman's meaning.

Workman helped the man up, who immediately thumbed his chest and said in blurred deaf person speech, "Caleb."

Workman mouthed his own name and pointed to Lucas. "We need to get by." He used a concoction of gestures.

Caleb indicated understanding, gathered his shoe and his prodding staff, and hurried after the hogs that milled about in waist-deep grasses near a single rail fence by the roadside. He herded them out of the trench, and lifting the fence rail, nudged the hogs through the opening and out into the field. He turned and waved, hobbling along, walking backward. He smiled warmly and turned his attention to the hogs. His dog barked once and tagged along behind him.

Workman climbed back up in the wagon seat. "If that don't beat all." He spoke into Lucas's ear trumpet.

Lucas nodded. "I guess if you're born deaf, you may just feel good to be alive, even if nothing seems to be going your way."

The storm was drawing closer; lightning lashed out and snapped the ground a mile in the distance. The thunder arrived almost instantly.

"We need shelter soon," Workman said. "I can stand a lot of things, but I don't care none for being sopping wet."

They turned another corner, and a stout slave woman with heavy arms and a broad chest was strolling toward them. Lucas drew up the horses. Workman called, "Is there a place to lodge near here?"

"Why? You ain't scared of a little rain, are you?" Already, the wind had picked up and slapped against the woman's thin skirt, making it flap about like a sheet on a line. She pushed her skirt down, and her heavy bosom almost hung out from the low-slung blouse.

The first raindrops flew sideways, pelting them.

"No," Workman replied, "we just have things in the back that need to be stowed so as not to get wet." The wind grabbed at his hat, and he barely got a hand up to catch it.

The slave woman nodded. "I'm headed to St. Louis," the woman said. "Are you Yankee or Confederate?" She cocked her head at them.

"Right now, neither," Workman said.

"Well, good. Den I can tell you I done walked off my master's place. The army in St. Louis is takin' in de colored folks, and when I get to St. Louis, I be a free woman." She glowed.

Lucas, who had been doing the best he could despite the wind, and using his hearing device to capture the conversation, caught the last of her comments. "Well, you best turn around. St. Louis is the other way. You're headed south."

The woman gave a befuddled look, then stamped her foot. After a moment of looking up and down the road, she closed one eye and cocked the other at the two men. "You be lyin' to me?"

"No, we're not lyin'," Workman said. "We're tryin' to go northeast ourselves."

The woman hemmed and hawed and almost seemed to be humming a tune. "Hmmm, mmm. Hmmmm, mmm." Finally, she said, "If you be headin' the way I was a comin', den I show you a place to stay if you gim me a ride in dat wagon." She pointed to the back.

"Climb on and show us the way, and be quick about it," Lucas said.

When the large woman swayed toward the back of the wagon, Workman noted, "She looks like she's hidin' two piglets in her backside."

Lucas stifled a laugh and shook his head, grinning.

The rain plunged from the sky.

After the woman attempted several times without success to climb into the bed of the wagon, Workman got down and helped the slave climb onto the wagon seat. She spread her ample backside across the short bench, so that Workman, when he got aboard, barely had a few inches of the seat on which to balance.

True to her word, Elisheba, named by her owner for Old Testament's Aaron's wife, directed them to a short side-road, and then to a lightless dwelling with but one window. The building's walls leaned, the porch roof sagged, and the porch floor was woefully lacking boards. An immense barn with half its roof burned away stood beside the edifice. Lucas wondered who would have ever needed such a large barn.

The three drenched travelers stood on the wobbly porch, and Elisheba banged on the door.

TWELVE

SURPRISE UPON SURPRISE

Two Months Earlier, August 20, 1861, Late Afternoon
Northeast of Dallas, Texas

The Comanches were perched on a craggy mesa, some hundred yards to the right of the herd. The cowboys, fully aware of the Indians' presence, were heading the horses toward a creek nestled just beyond two mesas that angled together like a funnel, with high, steep limestone and clay walls. On the other side of the tree-lined creek, the land sloped gently upward to a plush meadow.

"I do not like this," the Mexican rode up from the rear to Gustav, riding on the herd's flank.

"What is it, Juarez, that you do not like?" Gustav wiped his brow with his amber scarf.

"I do not like that we go into this hole in mountains, and Comanches jump us muy facil. Easy." Urging the herd ahead of them, the two rode among verdant bushes, mesquite, and primrose. Lush grass grew in the shade of the steep canyon walls.

"I see," said Gustav. "I think that is exactly what Asa wants them to think. As you may have noticed, he and Paul have gone on ahead." He pointed toward the cleft of the mesas.

"Oh, so thees is the trap we lay for them. I no comprendo Señor Asa when he splain earlier. Muy bien." Juarez smiled broadly.

"Next time, if you don't understand, ask."

"Sí, I will."

At that, the two waved their coiled lariats, clucked their tongues and whistled at the horses to move them quicker into the cut. "Hey, Gustav, where is the little one, Stew?" Juarez asked.

"He's part of the plan. You best get on the other side of this herd, so they all keep going the same direction if those Indians start shooting." Gustav pulled his rifle from his saddle holster. Juarez followed suit and galloped around the herd to the opposite flank.

The walls of the canyon drew closer, and shade enveloped the herd. The two men could no longer see the Comanches.

To the rear, Ben maneuvered the buckboard. Two saddled horses were tied to the back.

Gustav rode close to one wall of the canyon. Without warning, a shot ricocheted off the rock ledge just above Gustav's head. His horse reared and spun, and he barely held on. The herd, frightened by the gunshot, lurched forward, crowding into the narrow split between the mesas.

Juarez looked up. He caught sight of a lone Comanche slipping from bush to bush on the ledge above. He fired in that direction, but found no mark. Gustav grappled with controlling his mount until finally he could chase the fleeing herd.

Immediately, three more Comanches appeared, riding hard after Ben's wagon.

He shook the reins and hollered at the team. The buckboard racketed over large stones and prickly pear. He glanced over his shoulder at the rapidly closing Comanches. All of a sudden, one of them pitched off his horse, struck by a bullet. Stew, who had been hiding in the back of the buckboard, threw off the canvas that had covered him and hurried to reload his rifle.

The other Comanches rode faster in pursuit. An arrow struck the buckboard seat just below Ben's back. He felt the arrow hit his seat, but did not look behind him. He kept thrashing the reins and rushing the team toward the cut in the mesa walls. "Hurry, Stew! Shoot them!" he called. "They're gaining!"

Passing through the split, the herd broke apart and splashed across the shallow creek, spreading in all directions up a sloping embankment. On the opposite side of the creek, Paul, who had been waiting, bent low to his saddle and raced at a full gallop alongside the larger portion of the herd, waving his free hand trying to keep them together.

Asa, on foot, darted along the creek bed and took a position behind a boulder that protruded over the creek. He knelt, waiting for the last of the herd to come through and kept an eye on the lone Comanche on the ledge above. He was too far away for a clean shot, but Asa was mostly concerned with keeping his younger brother and Stew alive.

The buckboard burst through the gap. Ben turned his team sharply to the right, the wheels skidding in the sandy soil until he pulled hard on the reins, bringing them to a halt a dozen yards from the creek.

The Comanches swept through the gap, their bows drawn. Asa fired and hit the lead Comanche. The second one drew up and attempted to turn back. At the opening, Gustav and Juarez blocked his escape. The Comanche raised his bow, but Juarez felled him with a single shot from his revolver.

The Comanche tumbled from his horse, grimacing and holding his stomach.

A bullet pierced Juarez's horse. Rider and horse fell hard in the sandy soil. The lone Indian on the ridge had found his mark. He stood with his arms in the air, shouting and gesturing like he had won a great battle. He seemed unencumbered by the knowledge that his companions had fallen. Asa, loading his rifle to return fire, wondered for a moment how a person could be so callous toward the loss of his companions.

Before he could shoot, the figure on the ledge vanished. The fifth Comanche had not appeared. Asa kept ready, looking quickly in all directions. Gustav dismounted and rushed to Juarez, whose leg was pinned under the dying horse.

The stomach-shot Comanche crawled through the sand toward the creek. He plopped in the water and drifted face up in the slow current. Asa raised his rifle. The bullet pierced the Comanche's neck, and the body sank, bobbed up, plowed into a rock, and drifted lifeless downstream. Stew ran from the buckboard, his rifle ready.

Ben untied his horse from the wagon, mounted and raced across the stream after the scattered horses.

"Wait!" Asa called after him. "We don't know where the other Comanche is!"

His shouts were in vain. Ben sped away.

"Stubborn mule!" Asa called.

Gustav, with considerable effort, pulled Juarez from under the horse.

Juarez rose, rubbing his elbow. He brushed off his shirt and pulled his sombrero back onto his head. "Aye, mi caballo esta muerto. He was a good horse, now dead." The stallion lay in a pool of blood, little indentions in the sand where its last breaths had blown, and its legs were already stretched straight from its last death throes.

Juarez kicked the sand. Gustav patted him on the shoulder consolingly.

Asa wasted no time. "Mount up, gents. We've got horses to round up. Juarez, you stay here and guard the wagon. If more Comanches come back, don't take any chances. Just get the hell out. Stew, you and Gustav take out up the middle and gather as many as you can. See if you can find where Paul took the major part of the herd, or if he even got them to stop. I'm going after my bullheaded little brother."

The wranglers mounted quickly and charged across the stream. Juarez stood, disconsolate, looking at his dead horse. With a considerable struggle, he removed the saddle, blanket and reins. He walked over to the buckboard, gathered the team from their harnesses and tied them under a short blackjack oak. He put his saddle and reins on one of the horses in case he had to escape more Indians, then sat in the shade. Looking about, he thought that, were it not for the dead Indians and horse, this might be a very peaceful spot. "Un sitio tranquilo," he said.

Something caught his eye, moving in some bushes a little way up the creek bank.

THIRTEEN

SLAVERY IS A WEED THAT GROWS ON EVERY SOIL

SAME DAY, AUGUST 20, 1861
NORTHEAST OF DALLAS

In late afternoon, the wranglers returned with the horses to the creekside. Juarez stood by a new fire, chuckling, his bushy mustache dancing up and down. He had a surprise for them.

Paul was grimacing, gingerly holding his right leg. Stew and Gustav were laughing at a ribald joke. Neither Asa, nor Ben looked in any way pleased. Asa's lips were pulled tight, and he sat on his big stallion straight as an arrow. Ben moped, barely raising his head.

The five men steered the tired herd into the ankle-deep section of the creek. All the horses drank. Stew and Gustav broke off to watch the herd.

Paul dismounted and limped to sit and lean against a boulder. His lower leg had been shattered in a fall when breaking a horse years previously and had never healed completely. Tough riding always made the ache almost unbearable for him. He let his dapple-gray wander about the creek, the reins dangling down.

Ben dismounted and said to Juarez, "Don't ever try to figure out what Asa wants. If you do it one way, he wants it done the other. Nothin's ever good enough." He laced the reins of his horse into a short bush.

"Well, mi amigo," Juarez chimed. "I think I have something to cheer you up." He stepped across the lifeless horse.

"And what might that be?" Asa retorted, glowering and still seated on his horse. He was such a strong man, intimidating to almost anyone, that Juarez shrank a little, thinking maybe his surprise was not so good after all.

"Well," Asa growled, "are you gonna tell us the surprise or not?'

Juarez stumbled backward over the dead horse, barely escaping a fall. "Alright, Señor Asa, I have a surprise. Ahora, es possible que no you think it is a good surprise, I...."

"Just tell us."

Juarez did not respond, but nodded his head in the direction of a boulder, behind which a man was tied to a sapling. He was a black man in tattered cream-colored shirt and pants. His head hung on his chest.

Asa dismounted and walked over to the Negro who sat with his bare, scarred feet sticking out from under the tree's insufficient shade. Ben and Juarez followed, and Paul rose to join them.

"He's a slave," Ben announced.

"Well, do tell," said Asa, "as if the obvious is not obvious enough."

"He's an escaped slave," Ben continued. "He probably has a reward on his head."

"I found heem crawling around the bushes" Juarez said. "I thought he was a Comanche, so I surrounded heem and he cry like un nino. He awful big for a baby."

"I was lookin' for a way to cross this here creek," the escaped slave blubbered, "and I'm scared of water. Then you all come in a fightin' and I didn't know what to do, but hide. I be on my way if you set me free. I won't trouble you."

"How long you been gone from the plantation?" Asa asked.

The man dropped his eyes and mumbled, "A long while."

"I told you," Ben said. "I bet he's from a plantation around here. We turn him in, we'll get a bounty."

Asa squatted next to the man. "What are you really doing out here, friend?"

The man looked up, his face showing perplexity. He swallowed hard. "I be goin' north to find my wife and my children. I think she up north. I just want to visit, then I go right back to the plantation."

"Hmmph!" Ben smirked, "Do you really think we would believe that, Nigger?"

Asa barked, "That'll be enough, Ben!"

Ben's face burned.

"This here colored man ain't done you any harm," Asa continued. "Now you best get over whatever's eatin' you."

"And what do you propose we do, Asa?" Ben was not to be restrained. "Let him go on his merry way?"

Asa did not look at Ben, but returned his gaze to the sweating runaway. He said, "Juarez, untie him, and get him out of the sun before he dies of thirst."

Juarez untied the slave, helped him to his feet, and led him to the creek to drink. "What is your name, amigo?"

"My name is John Coincoin." He was about forty with a balding scalp, strong muscled arms and legs, and deep black skin. He cupped his hands in the stream and slurped the water.

Paul turned to Asa. "So, what *are* we going to do with him? We can't just let him go. That would mean we're guilty of aiding a slave. Last time I heard, that was breaking the law. He belongs to somebody, and I bet they'd like their property back."

Asa brushed past his brother and began gathering tinder for a fire.

Paul shook his head wearily. Stew rode in, so Paul mounted his horse and joined Juarez and Gustav moving the herd up to the meadow beyond the creek. Stew took the branches from Asa and started a supper fire.

Ben grabbed John Coincoin by the collar and pushed him from the creek and made him sit near where Stew was cooking. "Don't you look at me!" he yelled. "You keep your eyes down. Don't think we're gonna give you any pity. If I have my way, you're goin' back to your master."

Asa came up behind Ben and grasped him on the shoulder. "That's enough. Go put some grease on the buckboard axles. I'm sure they took a punishing today."

Ben shoved Asa's hand off him and stormed away.

In a short while, Stew had pork sizzling in a pan and coffee perking. The setting sun burned the long streaks of clouds to orange and gold, and a gusty wind fanned the cottonwoods lining the creek. John stared into a vast nothing. Asa whittled a stick. Ben sat by the creek, fuming.

Stew was pulling biscuits from a cast iron pot buried in the embers when he looked up for a moment and noticed that John was gazing piercingly right past him. "What you lookin' at?"

John pointed beyond Stew at boulders atop the mesa cliff, partially hidden by the tall cottonwood trees. "I'm lookin' at those two Indians up there on those rocks. You might want to hide yourself."

Stew swirled around just as an arrow flashed across his brow and stuck in a nearby tree. He dove behind the wagon. Asa leaped up and ran for his rifle that leaned against a rock. A bullet pierced the sand at his feet. Ben scrambled from his spot by the creek to gain cover behind a bush. He drew his pistol, scanning the rocks to see where the shots had come from, but the trees blocked his view.

John swept past Stew in a run and grabbed the short man's rifle propped against a tree. In rapid motion, he cocked the hammer, aimed, and fired toward the boulders. One of the Comanches tumbled to the sharp rocks below, dead. The other Comanche raced away into the brush, escaping over the top of the hill.

Asa fired after him. Ben jumped up with his pistol to pursue, but Asa grabbed him by the arm. "I think they're done, little brother. Comanches never work alone. He's going back to get the string of horses they started with, and to count his blessings, that is, if Comanches even believe in a God."

The brothers rushed to the prone Comanche to ensure he was dead. He had a bullet in his skull. They turned to see John had returned the rifle to its original spot and again sat.

Stew busied himself trying to keep the pork from burning. His pallor was blanched, and his hands shook. When Asa and Ben walked up, he said, "I was almost in my grave. That nigger saved my life."

Asa walked over to John. "Get up," he commanded.

John rose slowly, proudly. Asa extended his hand. John took it.

"Thank you very much, John Coincoin," Asa said. "Next time, would you mind killing the other Indian, too?"

They both laughed.

Ben squinted an eye. "Where'd you learn to shoot like that?"

"My master — he grew very sick. I was the only slave left. The plantation go down, so he gives everyone they freedom papers. Me, too. But I didn't wanna have no freedom. I had no place to go, so I stayed and ran his house, and one day, he shows me how to shoot a gun. I do the hunting for my master. He had many guns. Shotguns. Rifles. After a long time, I am shooting deer. With the shotgun — pheasant and duck on the fly." John held up his arms as if holding a real shotgun and mimicked following a flying bird for a shot. "The Indian... I guess I be lucky."

Daylight dwindled, and twilight settled around the mesas. Stew called, "Supper's ready." Still shaken by his brush with death, he could not bring himself to his usual smile.

The wranglers, including John, gathered around the fire. Gustav was keeping watch on the herd. When Juarez finished eating, he loaded a tin plate with the grub and mounted a horse that danced and jigged with the new rider.

Asa called after him, "That little roan with the bit-off ear is the best broke horse. Ride that one! Not that bay horse."

Juarez turned and nodded. "Sí, Señor. Thees horse is muy facil."

"Yeah, you say it's easy," Ben said. "Just hope that partial broke horse don't throw you."

"Sí, I be careful." He trotted the twisting, prancing horse out to the herd.

The fire began to subside. Stew gathered a tarp and curled up in the rear of the wagon. Ben pulled a blanket from his saddlebag and settled on it, leaning his head against his saddle.

Paul, when he figured Ben was asleep, leaned toward Asa. "What do you plan to do with the nigger slave?"

"He stays with us as far as Fort Smith."

Paul waited for Asa to say more. When he did not, Paul said, "And then what?"

"Let 'im go."

"You can't do that, Asa. It's wrong. The nigger is someone's property. We have a duty to return him to his owner. It's the right thing to do."

"Do you honestly believe that, Paul?"

"Yes, I do. The darkies are not much brighter than a good horse. And certainly not worth as much. No matter what you think about him saving Stew's life, he can't make it on his own. I heard tell that all the slaves that escape to the north end up stealing or begging or starving to death. Most end up dying in the streets or living in flop houses. If you let him go, you're dooming him to a life of misery."

"Wherever do you get your reasoning, Paul? Sometimes I wonder if you're not adopted, and Ma and Pa just didn't tell us."

Paul removed his spectacles and wiped them with his kerchief. He was sure of his reasoning, feeling good inside that *he* was the truly compassionate one. He felt sorry for his older brother, and he wished he could knock some sense into him, but, like he always had done in the past, he kept his thoughts to himself.

He stood to join Juarez and Stew to keep second watch on the herd and be on lookout for more Comanches. He knew his older brother probably would sleep very little, keeping watch at the camp. He looked at John, curled up by a log not far from Juarez's dead horse, snoring loudly. He figured that by morning the slave would have sneaked away, and then he would not be their problem anymore.

FOURTEEN

∞

MARINERS OF
THE PLAINS

AUGUST 21, 1861, EARLY MORNING
NORTHEAST OF DALLAS, TEXAS

John Coincoin had not crept away from his wrangler captors during the night, but was up before dawn. When Ben awoke, he saw him adding dead branches to a fresh cook-fire he had stoked from the previous night's embers. "So, you still here, slave? Are you hopin' for a free breakfast before you skedaddle to your family up north?" Ben sneered.

"Well, suh, last night's meal was the first real food I had in several days. I am obliged, but I don't intend to take nothin' I don't earn. I is willing to work. Whatever you want me to do."

Ben was surprised. "Well, if you don't beat all. I always thought you niggers were a lazy, sneaky lot. Directly we'll give you plenty of work."

"That's right, we'll put you to work." Asa strode up beside the pair. "Johnny boy, can you ride a horse?"

John smiled cheerfully. "A little bit. Yes, suh. I can."

"Then after you help Stew get breakfast going, we'll see if you can ride."

"And your backside will be plenty sore, you black mule," Ben enjoined. He wanted to insult the man, but John paid no heed to his words, instead grinning broadly. He joined Stew who was stirring up a batch of biscuits.

Stew's face showed he was mulling something over. Finally, he said, "John, thanks for saving my life." Stew craned his neck to look up at the muscular Negro.

"Yes, suh. You woulda done the same for me."

"Maybe I would have. Anyway, thanks again. Now grab a spoonful of that lard and grease these pans."

John dutifully followed that direction and every other order given him, and when the wranglers came in for breakfast, he served each one their pans of food and went around with the coffee pail, pouring fresh cups.

Before heading out, the wranglers dragged the Comanches' corpses on top of the dead horse, tossed branches over them, poured kerosene from their lanterns over the pile, then set it ablaze. Black smoke billowed up in a dense brume. "Better that we burn them," Asa said. "If it comes a rain later, their carcasses would foul the water. If I was farmer downstream, I wouldn't take too kindly to that."

When the fire had completed itself, the wranglers drove the horses across the north Texas plain toward the Red River for Colton's Crossing. Asa wanted to put as much distance as possible between the herd and any new Comanches seeking revenge. John rode bareback on a pinto horse and struggled to stay seated. The sun blazed. The tall prairie grass, wilted yellow and brown, trembled in the wind. Here and there, small creeks trickled where the wranglers always stopped long enough to let the horses drink.

They encountered yet another herd of bison clustered around a watering hole. The wranglers moved the horses around the edge of the mass of black beasts.

When at last, the bison were out of view, Paul and John rode up beside Asa who had stopped on a low hill and was peering across the prairie. Paul said, "What's the hold up?"

Asa pointed. "Do you see those houses yonder?"

Paul nodded.

"Yes, suh. I sure do," John exclaimed.

"Do they appear to be sailing across the land to you?"

The three watched the houses in the distance, their whitewashed walls glowing in the sun like clipper ship sails, flowing across the tall, tremulous grasses that undulated in a brisk breeze. The houses looked to be floating on a grass sea.

"They sure do," Paul exclaimed. "The one in front just slid past that tree. Is there a river there? Could that be a house loaded on a boat?" He paused. "Yes, it's moving. It's sailing!"

"Paul, go back and tell the others to move the herd more to the right. John, come with me. Let's go take a look."

Paul headed back to the others, and Asa and John trotted their horses toward the phenomenon of land-bound ships.

Asa recalled a visit as a boy to Mobile Bay where he had been enamored with the tall frigates sailing gracefully in and out of the harbor.

When they drew closer to the houses, they saw a couple dozen men and women and a half-dozen children standing around the front house. Nearer them, Asa noted two mules were harnessed to a wagon filled with tools, tack and household ware.

Four men carried a twenty-foot-long log to the front of the lead dwelling. Asa and John halted to watch the event transpiring. Three men in black jackets and hats, likely a father and sons, strode forward from the wagon with rifles aimed at them. John held his hands up. Asa leaned forward over the withers of his horse.

"Thee best stay back, if thee desires to live!" the older man called. He bore a long, curly, black beard. Above his pronounced nose, his dark eyes sunk in the caverns of his sunburned face.

Those with him looked to be like peas in a pod, only clean-shaven. To Asa, they appeared angry and ready to fight.

Asa tipped his hat.

"Like I said, thee best turn around unless thee want a belly full of lead," the old one said.

"We mean no harm," Asa announced and held up his hands. He looked past the armed men and watched as the four men lay the log in front of the porch, and walked around and behind the house. Then all the men and women pushed the house across a traverse of several logs laid in sequence underneath it. The house rolled forward about ten yards, and those pushing stopped. Again, four different men picked up a log from the rear of the house and carried it to the front and set it down.

The armed men shifted from foot to foot. Asa and John said nothing, but merely watched. Shortly, the group of house movers went back to the second house and did the same procedure for it.

"Did you know?" Asa began.

The oldest man cocked his rifle.

"Did you know that your houses look like they're sailing across the land?"

"I know as much," the old one said. "Thee best state thy business, for I'll not wait much longer."

"Fair enough. I'm Asa McGavin. My brothers, my friends, and I are driving a herd of horses to Fort Smith, Arkansas." He pointed behind him to the rim of a far hill where the herd could just be seen. "We'll be on our ways. We just couldn't figure how the houses were moving. Kinda floating across the prairie grass."

"I am Solomon Jarrell, and these are my boys." The old one pointed his rifle down. His sons lowered their rifles. "Why does your Negro companion not have a saddle?"

"Oh." Asa hesitated, considering a response. "He lost his saddle in a fight with Comanches some ways back."

"I see. We are Quakers and have had enough of Comanches."

"Quakers? I thought Quakers were peace-loving people, not inclined to shoot a man."

"That is true. When we learned what John Brown had done in Virginia, we foresaw the clanging of the swords of war. By God's command, many of us moved our families west to avoid the coming conflagration. My brothers and our families came to Texas. What we did not expect was the Comanches and the lawlessness here. By God's providence we are yet alive. But God has told us we should arm ourselves against the savages and outlaws, and that much we have done."

"I understand. I see you have a saddle in your wagon there and you don't seem to have any horses, just mules. If you'd not mind parting with it, I'd like to purchase it for this colored man to use."

The old man glanced back at the wagon and the sailing houses. He turned his eyes to heaven and whispered a prayer. Looking again at Asa, he asked, "How much are thee willing to pay?"

"Ten dollars gold," Asa said, pulling a coin from his pocket and holding it out."

"Fair enough," the old Quaker took the coin and bit it. "Elias, get thee to the wagon and fetch the saddle and blanket."

The wooly-headed young man nearest Solomon walked back to the wagon and retrieved the saddle.

In a few minutes, John, with Asa's help, had saddled his horse and mounted. He grinned.

"Well, then, Mr. McGavin, if thee has no more business with us, we must be on our way."

"I just have one question," Asa said. "Why are you rolling your houses across the land? Wouldn't it just be easier to rebuild somewhere else?"

"That's two questions, Mr. McGavin. Have thee seen the paucity of trees around here? Just thorny mesquite trees, which are a bane from the devil. There are no trees with which to build a house. However, there's a town name o' Sherman just a couple of miles over that direction." He nodded his head toward the West.

"We've had too many Comanche attacks where we first settled. I lost three of my sons — killed by the murderers. My brother, Abel, lost a daughter. The savages kidnapped her. We're moving closer to the town for safety. We've got some land to farm adjacent to it already purchased. Now if thee don't mind, we've a hard days' work ahead of us."

"My condolences for the loss of your loved ones. We've had enough trouble with Comanches ourselves. Godspeed."

Asa and John turned their horses.

"We will pray for thee both," the Quaker called after them. "And especially for the safe passage of the runaway slave."

"I wonder how he knew you were a runaway," Asa asked John.

"I hear a lot down on the plantation from people passin' through. All us black folks know about the Quakers. We know that if we run, the Quakers help us be free. 'Specially in a place called Ohio. I figure it is a high place in the mountains that the bounty hunters can't get to."

Asa chuckled to himself at John's rendition of the meaning of Ohio. "So, there's Quakers in Ohio?"

"Yes, suh, Massa Asa, a whole passel of 'em, I hear."

"Well, don't be getting any ideas of trying to join up with those Quakers. This ain't Ohio, and you ain't out of danger yet. Besides, they have enough to worry about without hiding no runaway slave. You go get with Gustav and have him train you some more. We'll make a wrangler out of you yet."

When John trotted away, proud of his new saddle, Asa looked long and hard at a coal-black mass of thunderheads gathering to the north. Across the whole prairie for as far as he could see, there was no cover. The herd and the wranglers were in the direct path of the storm.

FIFTEEN

❧

To Ride upon a Storm

August 21, 1861
Fifteen Miles South of the Red River Northeast of Dallas

In the late afternoon, the thunderstorm that had been stoking itself up broke with a vehemence unlike any the wranglers had ever seen. Driven by a tortuous wind, the rain blew sideways, striking like a whip, first from one direction, then another. Despite wearing their waxed coats, the men were drenched. John slipped twice from his new saddle, landing in ankle-deep mud.

Asa called a halt under a copse of oaks. The wranglers huddled there.

"I can barely see the herd," Gustav said. "The rain's like a curtain."

"If some of the herd runs off," Asa announced, "we'll just go get 'em."

"There's a funnel cloud dropping over there." Paul pointed.

The wranglers looked where he had directed at a blackish tube cloud stretching down, then hitting the earth about a mile away, its snake form sashaying across the grassland. It moved parallel to them, clouded in the storm, but markedly visible like a dastard whore dancing behind a veil. If it turned toward them, there would be hell to pay.

"What is that?" John asked. "I ain't never seen anything like it."

"That," Asa replied, "is a twister. It'll gobble you up and spit you out in pieces." Asa worried about the tone of his voice. Did he sound calm enough? He had answers and strategies for most anything, but felt vulnerable in the face of nature.

The tornado drew closer. At one great turn of the spiraling column, the herd fled in all directions. Ben pulled his hat tight, and buttoned his top coat button, leaning forward in his saddle. "I can catch 'em."

Asa took hold of Ben's arm. "Wait. We'll get them later. I need you alive."

The tornado, aslant into the torrid black cloud, swept ever closer, wearing out the land for several more minutes. Then, without any recognizable cause, it raced back into the clouds, whipping its tail in a snap, before vanishing.

After the rainstorm abated, the miserable group spent the better part of the evening and the next day rounding up the horses that had run off.

Once the herd was gathered, they traveled along a mucky trail, the Texas Stage Road. They camped on a rock outcropping.

The next day, Ben looked at the evidence of a prodigious quantity of hoof prints of shod horses on both sides of the road. "I'll bet those hoof prints are from a Confederate cavalry regiment," Ben said to Gustav. "I'm joining up when I get to Fort Smith."

Gustav twirled his mustache. "Mon cheri lost her father in Napoleon's war. Be careful, my young friend. War can mean death, not just glory."

"I ain't joinin' to fight for no glory. I plan to keep the Yanks from takin' our land from us. That's what they aim to do. Take our land. Take our slaves. Our women. Hell, there's no accountin' for what they'd take if we let 'em." Ben pounded his gloved fist into his palm.

Gustav made no comment. He cantered away and joined John who was struggling to hold his own horse on keel.

In late afternoon of the next day, they arrived at the bluffs above the Red River crossing that Asa had sought. Gustav rode slowly down a path cut in the bluff to a sandy beach dotted with scrabbly bushes. The stretch of sandy, boggy river bottom below the cliff ran out for a mile in both directions from where he sat on his horse. Beyond the sand was the wide river.

The recent deluge caused the river to run chocolate brown and roiling, and it was impossible to tell the water's depth.

Gustav pulled the neckerchief from his neck, removed his top hat, and wiped his brow. He waved at Asa on the cliff. Asa motioned to the others who got the horses moving. The horses proceeded slowly, following the black boss mare. The bay leader stallion brought up the rear. Thirty head of horses, some of them fully broke, others partially broke, were accustomed to the moving and stopping, and then moving again. Asa was grateful for the adaptable creatures.

Single file, they followed the boss mare, treading just behind Asa down the sloping path, each horse patiently taking its turn in the descent. Paul rode after the first four horses. Juarez and Ben encouraged the horses down, carefully and deliberately. John walked down last, leading his horse. Stew drove the buckboard rattling along a ragged road along the top of the cliffs; the long way around. He would cross at a toll ferry five miles downriver and meet up with them on the other side.

Finally, the herd was gathered on the sandy riverside. Asa dismounted and went up to the edge to peruse the depth. His boots sank deep into the watery sand. The river was far muddier and moving faster than he had hoped. Broken trees long ago dislodged from the riverbank lay tangled in the river weeds, many stretching their dark branches into the rapidly flowing river.

"How deep is it?" Ben asked.

Asa pulled out a map. "I don't know. This should be the crossing, but I'm not sure. It's powerful muddy."

Paul dismounted and limped to the river edge. He grabbed a stick and tossed it in the current. The stick swept away quickly, and then dived into a whirlpool. "What're we going to do, Asa?"

Asa stroked his thick mustache, deep in thought. He walked several paces along the bank first in one direction, and then the other, his boots sinking in the sucking sand. At last, he said, "I don't like all the mud. The herd could get stuck in it if the bottom is too shallow. There may be impediments under the water that we can't see — bushes, tree stumps."

John walked up, leading his horse. In a soft voice, he said, "I sure hope these horses can swim, 'cause I can't. Is this where we supposed to cross?"

Asa put his hand on John's shoulder. "Don't you worry. There's a ferry crossing downstream from here. That's where Stew is taking the wagon. I'll let you ride with him on the raft."

Paul, wiping his spectacles with a kerchief, said, "So are we going to cross here or not?"

"I don't know. I thought this would save some time instead of going all the way down to Colton's Crossing. Maybe it wasn't such a good idea." Asa mounted his horse and turned it toward downstream. "Stay here. I'm going to go see if there is a better crossing point further down. John, you take your horse back up the path and catch up with Stew. He shouldn't be too far along that road to the ferry. You cross with him. The rest of you sit tight. I'll be back soon."

Paul, Ben and Juarez sat down in the shade of a mesquite tree. John led his horse back up the cliff. Once there, he found a tree stump and used it to mount. He rode at a trot to catch up with the wagon.

Gustav stayed in his saddle, monitoring the herd. He noticed how deep the horses' legs sank into the sandy bottom along the river's edge, water pooling in each hole. He looked in the direction that Asa had ridden. "Wonder how far Asa is going. I can't see him."

"He'll be back soon enough. He knows what he's doing," Paul said, but a strange anxiety came over him. He strained to watch down the river. He could not see Asa.

Asa galloped his horse along the sandy bottom land, dotted with bushes, grasses, and fallen trees and broken limbs left by many floods.

SIXTEEN

∞

THE METTLE THAT FEW ATTAIN

August 23, 1861, Mid-Afternoon
Red River, Texas

Under a sweltering sun, sweat poured from Asa's brow. He guided his horse through tough, scratchy sagebrush, broken branches, fallen trees, and boulders that lay in the wide river bottom. With the storm of the previous night, the river was up, flowing with waves and eddies. White froth gathered along the shoreline. The sandy soil yielded puddles of water at every footfall of Asa's sturdy stallion.

The big horse struggled at negotiating the tangled brush and soggy land, often sinking past its fetlocks.

Then Asa saw what looked like a decent crossing, a small sandy stretch leading to a slower flowing portion of the river where it had narrowed to perhaps forty yards across. The water ran generally clear over a flat, rocky bottom.

"Yes, this'll do nicely." He galloped his horse toward the river's edge.

The stallion leaped a deformed mesquite, its trunk running one foot above and parallel to the ground. The horse stumbled downward, its legs diving deep into a sandy, watery pit. Asa almost pitched head first from the saddle, the reins tangling around his arms. He punched his horse hard with his spurs, and the horse lurched forward, and then turned on its side, thrusting Asa halfway into the sucking sand. The horse, its eyes wide in terror, was struggling to keep its head up. Its struggles pushed Asa farther into the muck.

"If you'll just stay still!" he yelled.

The horse continued to churn its legs, forcing Asa down.

Then the big stallion twisted again, and its two legs shot loose from the slop and into the air, its full weight pressing on Asa's body, driving him deeper.

Wet sand poured over him. He turned his head, barely above the sand, left and right, fully realizing his plight. He strained with everything in him, struggling to free his leg and lower body from under the horse to no avail. He searched to see if he could grab any tree root, but all around him was wet, bubbling sand.

As the horse's head went under, it raised it enough to shriek in panic and thrashed about, dragging horse and rider farther and farther down.

Asa reached for his gun to fire a signal. At that moment, his horse rolled to its left, its legs went up and its head sunk, leaning its full weight on Asa. His body pinned, his head slipped under the ooze.

Straining, he just got his head above the muck and gasped for air, but his body was sinking fast. He tried to grab the saddle horn, but his movement pulled him deeper. He raised his gun, but when he squeezed the trigger again and again, it failed to fire. He could barely see, the sand pouring over his face, and he twisted to keep his head above the surface.

Then the bog issued a slow, deep, guttural sound, and he sank under the surface. Only his booted foot still in a stirrup extended above the sand. His body struggled for over a minute, and then went still.

The quicksand coursed all around his body, bubbles rising to the surface here and there. The horse, its head now buried, ceased to move. Its belly and two legs showed above the still roiling sand pit.

John was riding along the top of the embankment close to the edge. He heard the horse's scream below him at the river, and he looked down and saw Asa in his death struggle. He called, "Mister Asa! Hold on!"

Stopping too quickly, he tumbled from his horse and rolled to the edge of the clay cliff. "Oh, no. Oh, no," he said repeatedly, gaining his footing and watching Asa's head go under. He scrambled down the side of the embankment, accidentally clubbing a knee against a large rock and collapsing at the bottom.

Holding his knee, he limped forward, only to have his feet step into the edge of the quicksand where the bog wavered and flopped, his feet sinking several inches. He fell backward and dragged himself onto firmer soil.

He stood and hobbled as fast as he could to where he knew the wranglers were waiting, a half a mile upstream.

When he saw the wranglers, he immediately began screaming, "Come quick! Come quick! Mister Asa done gone down in a marsh or... a bog... or I don't know what!"

Gustav, already in the saddle, galloped his horse to John, now sweating and out of breath.

Leaving the herd untended, Ben, Paul, and Juarez quickly mounted and followed with all speed. They arrived as John was fumbling for words. "He down there. Down in the sand. Oh, Lord, I ain't never seen anything like it. The ground done swallowed him up."

Juarez pulled John onto his horse behind him. The wranglers raced their mounts, leaping over downed trees and rocks. They drew up a few yards from where Asa and his stallion lay sunk in the quicksand. Ben leaped from his horse and raced toward his fallen brother. He hit the quagmire at top speed, only to sink to his ankles. Two more firm steps and it was up to his knees.

Paul grabbed his lariat from his saddle strappings and tossed the loop end to Ben, his face in abject panic. Ben grabbed the rope with both hands, remembering to stay still. Paul stopped for a moment to stick the spectacles in his vest pocket. He then wrapped the other end of the rope tight around his pinto's saddle horn and bade the animal to back up. The horse backed steadily, dragging Ben out. He scrambled up, tossing the rope aside. "What're we gonna do? We gotta help him."

Paul pushed his brother out of the way. Gustav, Juarez, and John had dismounted and were looking at the scene in dismay. They led their horses in an arc that ultimately brought them closer to Asa's body, yet standing clear of the pit. John stood in the back.

Juarez threw his lariat, the loop landing directly beside Asa's right hand that still floated at the top of the quicksand. Juarez flipped the end, so the rope jumped slightly on the bog, but then began to sink. He withdrew his rope. Gustav, Ben, and Paul paced up and down the edge of the pit, each seeing how far forward they could venture before they began to sink into the pit.

"Best I can tell," said Paul, "it's a good twenty yards through this mess to get to him. I don't...."

"We gotta get him out!" Ben screamed, and repeated himself at a higher pitch. Stepping back and with a running start, he raced forward leaping five yards into the pit and was just able to grab hold of the half-buried mesquite tree and pull himself up. He stood teetering on the charcoal black bark of the bent trunk that swept along for a dozen feet just inches above the bog, before dipping into it. The outer gray branches rose out of the sloppy soil, tiny green leaves glistening. Its roots were firmly planted in heavy boulders.

Wet sand covered the lower half of Ben's body. Beckoning to the others, he shouted, "Throw me a rope! Maybe I can loop him from here."

Paul hung his head, conceding the futility of their efforts, knowing his older brother was dead. He put his hands on his hips. "What're you going to do, Ben? Loop the rope around his neck and strangle him?"

Ben stood, balancing precariously on the bumpy trunk. He looked back at where Asa lay mostly buried, his arm still floating, and his foot caught in the twisted stirrup being the only parts of his body showing. For a long while, the men stood silent, shuffling their feet and looking down.

Finally, Ben called again. "We can't just leave his body there." He bit his lip, and turned his back on Paul and proclaimed loudly, "It ain't Christian. He needs, at least, a decent burial."

"I don't know what to do, Ben," Paul replied, "We could walk out really slow, but trying to pull Asa out won't work. His body's under the horse. Trying to get him loose will just drive us deeper. Besides..."

"I'll go get him," John said.

The wranglers kept their backs on the runaway, but Gustav looked over his shoulder. "And how would you accomplish this, my black companion?"

"I think I can do it. Back in Louisiana where I first lived before I was sold, they be a whole lot of bogs and marshes. And one time, a white chil' got herself out on a log in this marsh, and we don't know how she did, but we can't go get her, lessen we take a rope what keep us from sinkin'."

Paul, Ben, and Juarez turned to stare incredulously at John.

Seeing them all staring at him, he hesitated.

"And what?" Paul commanded.

"All right, all right," John's voice quavered. "Well, we run the rope over a tall tree limb that hung over the bog, and the master done tied the rope around me so I could go out in the bog while they done hol' onto the other end, like when you liftin' a cotton bale up into a loft. So, I done swim out to her...."

"We get your gist." Paul turned to the others. "This is a better idea than all of us trying to pull him out, and getting stuck ourselves. Juarez, toss your rope over the big limb of that oak." He pointed to a massive oak. The trunk of it stuck out of the embankment well away from the river, and the limbs snaked toward the river; one extending several feet over the quicksand pit.

Juarez threw the rope over the limb; the loop end dangled a yard above the edge of the pit.

For a long time, the wranglers looked at John. Finally, he took a big breath, stretched out to grab the loop, and secured it about his chest under his arms. Gustav, Juarez, and Paul took hold of the other end.

Paul said, "John, if you have the mettle, you head straight out to where Ben is on that Mesquite trunk."

He turned to his brother. "Ben! When he gets out there, help him up beside you. Flip Juarez's rope out as far on the limb as you can. You should be able to get it just over Asa's body..." His voice trailed, sorry that he had said the word 'body.'" He looked hard at Ben. "Then when John goes in for Asa, help hold the rope. Get it right, Ben."

Ben nodded.

John took several deep breaths, attempting to bolster his courage. "Remember now. I don't know how to swim, so you keep me up."

"You don't have to swim," Paul replied. "Just don't stay too long in one spot and no sudden movements."

Stepping tenuously forward, John felt the three wranglers tightening the slack of the rope against his chest. He stepped slowly into the pit, sinking only a little, but each step went deeper than the one before.

The wranglers pulled on the rope raising his body up from the mire. "Keep going, John. We got ya!" Paul called.

John trudged forward, sinking with each step, and made it to the half-sunk mesquite trunk. Ben grabbed John at the elbow and helped him up. John held on to the large, upward pointing limb. His entire body shook as if the sand were a monster bent on devouring him.

Ben patted him on the back. "Good job, so far."

John nodded. He held onto the sturdy mesquite while Ben flipped the rope farther out on the narrowing oak limb. Ben turned to John, his face disconsolate. "I sure hope you can do this."

John gave no answer, but looked out across the distance he needed to traverse.

Taking more deep breaths, he slid off the trunk and into the frothy, undulating sand. He sank past his knees but kept moving forward, stretching his arms out in a balancing motion.

He felt sudden tension on the rope and was lifted higher. The rope was not quite far enough out on the limb. He could move no closer to Asa's body.

Ben called, "We have to release the slack or he'll never make it to Asa!"

"Are you sure?" Paul yelled back.

"Yes, I'm sure. He's just hanging there."

John stood still, slowly sinking. He felt the weight of the sand gripping his legs.

With Gustav and Juarez gripping the rope, Paul released his hold and walked a short distance downstream to better view the situation. He paced a few moments. "All right. Here's what we're going to do, John! When I yell 'Now,' we're going to release the slack. You get quick to the horse and push it off Asa best you can. Get his leg out of the stirrup. Then dive your hands under him, lock your hands and pull hard. Right when you signal, we're gonna pull like there ain't no tomorrow. So, don't dare let loose of him. You got that?"

"Yes, suh!" John called back.

"Ben, you ready?" Paul barked.

"Yeah. Let's get it done."

Paul took the tail end of the rope that extended on the ground behind the wranglers and tied it to his horse's saddle horn, and then returned to grab his section of the rope. Then he called, "Ready! Now!"

The three wranglers let the rope go slack. John immediately took rapid steps. The quicksand rose to his thighs. His right hand found purchase on the saddle. Bringing his other arm around, he pushed against the saddle, raising himself upward in the effort.

Slowly he shifted the heavy stallion about six inches. He could do no more.

No longer thinking clearly, John tugged at the boot in the stirrup. It would not give. Asa's hand that had been visible before slipped below the surface.

Yanking with all his strength, John felt the foot slip out of the stirrup.

He dove his left hand like a pile driver into the pit and grabbed Asa's collar, pulling the body up. He then slid his left arm around the torso and reached his right hand over to take hold of his left.

"Pull!" John felt such a jerk on his body that he almost lost his grip of Asa's body. Asa's head and upper torso came up from the bog.

John gathered a stronger hold on the deceased man. The others, aided by Paul's backing horse, pulled mightily until John, the body wrapped tight in his arms, skidded across the top of the watery slop and slammed against the crooked Mesquite trunk.

Straining, he and Ben raised the dead body onto the tree. Ben then helped John climb up. John's body was covered in mud up to his chest.

Juarez tossed a looped lariat perfectly to Ben, who, with John's help, placed the rope around Asa's body across the chest and under his arms. The wranglers on dry land pulled Asa the rest of the distance out of the pit. John took Juarez's next tossed rope and was pulled to safety. Ben came last. The five men collapsed beside the dead body. After a moment, Paul went to his horse, retrieved a cloth from his saddlebags, and began carefully wiping the sand from Asa's face and hair.

He turned to John. "Thank you very much, John Coincoin."

"That was exceptionally brave. I salute you," Gustav said.

"Ees very good job. Muy bueno," Juarez said. "Tu tienes un largo corazon."

Gustav translated for John. "He said you have a big heart."

Ben began pounding his fist on the ground over and over. "It ain't right that Asa should die."

Paul put his arm around his little brother. When Ben stopped his tirade, Paul palmed Ben's shoulder. Tears formed in his eyes.

John was so exhausted, he lay on his back with his arms stretched out to the side. Tears clung to his closed eyelids. *Now that Asa is dead, what is to happen to me?*

SEVENTEEN

◯

REPRIEVE

S ara trotted Esther along the Cross Hollows Road under a blue sky peppered with mounds of cumulus clouds and an early moon. A Confederate sentry stepped out from behind a tall elm, stopped her and made her dismount.

"Turn around," he demanded.

She did. Then he pointed his rusty musket at her. "How will I know you're not a spy?"

"Because I'm not. Spies are sneaky, and act charming to fool a stupid soldier, and I know you're not stupid, so I couldn't fool you. And I'd just as soon knock your head off for making me get off my horse. I'm here to join my fiancé."

The young private looked as if he were facing a bear. He lowered his rifle. "Fair 'nuff. But don't be tryin' nothin' sneaky. I'll know it."

"Fair enough." Sara mounted her horse and continued.

She passed more Confederate sentries, some on horseback, some on tree limbs. Everyone waved a friendly hand. Several swept their slouch hats from their heads and made bowing gestures. Grinning, she passed one sentry who had taken to pole fishing in a shallow stream. He was too busy watching the cork bob.

Another came out of the bushes, pulling up his trousers, and almost fell backward when he saw her.

Sara followed Father Antonio's directions, and the journey to the Confederate camp took less than two hours from the burned-out farm. The baby girl she had saved was in good hands with the Cherokees, and the old squaw had chanted a blessing onto Sara just before she left, tapping her on the head with a gourd rattle.

The handsome and humble Father Antonio led the Cherokees east while Sara had headed west.

The noise Sara had heard echoing for some time through the dense forest was now becoming a din, a clanging of metal, hammering and sawing, mules braying, wagons creaking, and men shouting.

At a break in the foliage, the cause of the clanking, inharmonious symphony became evident. Sara beheld a capacious valley between tree-crowded, rocky hills. Up and down the valley lay an array of half-built cabins and shacks beside tents of various sorts. Soldiers strove with alacrity everywhere, as did many slaves. She identified the brash officers by their jackets worn in the sweltering heat, strutting around, shouting and pointing and directing all manner of endeavors.

The soldiers and slaves were generally clustered on the periphery of an expansive parade ground, erecting cabins of tongue and groove boards. Most were stripped of their shirts and were swarthy with sweat and grime. Some men slung stacks of boards onto their shoulders from overladen carts. Other men gathered whittled pegs from buckets and drove them into augered holes in the boards and beams to pin them together to form the walls. On the roofs of other cabins, the laborers pounded iron nails into board shingles.

Sara had never seen so large a town as was being constructed, bigger than Springfield. One building was a commissary, another had a cupola perched atop it with a filigreed cross — a church. Blacksmith shops were scattered here and there where the big-armed smithies hammered away, making horseshoes and wagon parts. A bakery with two huge rock chimneys exuded a tantalizing smell of fresh-baked bread.

Sara rode slowly up a sloped road through the cantonment. Men were hoeing and weeding gardens with homemade tools, many with wooden blades, not iron. At one garden, stout soldiers shoveled manure from a muck cart onto the upturned soil, fertilizing it. To her left, a gardener hollered, "Look what I found!" He held up a six-inch long, flint spearhead. Though his comrades were not as pleased as he, the man pocketed his find and smiled. Some gardens were already growing turnips, cabbages, onions, and pumpkins.

In one arbor of trees, laundresses bent over their large tubs, churning the soapy clothes in steaming water with thick, hickory staves. Sheets and clothing hung on long lines. If she could find Joseph and gain his commitment to marry, she would find work doing such chores as those women.

She was so captivated by all the hubbub, she almost plowed Esther into a Napoleon cannon. She halted the mare just in time. Before her lay an assortment of forty or so cannons, caissons and accoutrements. Pyramids of cannonballs and shell boxes rested in the center of the array.

All about her, soldiers and civilians hustled to one urgent task or another. Water bearers carried buckets on yokes and ladled water to the workers.

She looked up past the cannons and saw atop a rise an immense, two-story-tall sawmill, butted up against the White River. The owner's name was posted in large gray letters across the length of it. "Peter Van Winkle." Such whirring and clanking from the building she had never heard, and the sound almost overwhelmed all the other noises of the valley. The smell of fresh-cut lumber flowed out as a fragrant bouquet. "I love that smell," Sara said.

After weaving a route through the cannons, she chose to dismount at a row of completed cabins. Each edifice, like a hotel, had a title handsomely inscribed on a board above the door. One sign said "Wildcat Den," another read "Alligator Retreat," and a third stated boldly "Manassas." The cabins had two doors. A wall and a rock chimney fireplace ran between the doors, separating them into two barracks.

Sara tied Esther to a post and strode confidently inside the open door of "Pelican Rifles Retreat." Tidy, wooden bunks, three high, stood against all sides, save the chimney wall. Some soldiers were sleeping, others lay on their bunks, reading. Three men sat teetering on narrow tree stumps at a crude table, playing cards.

Sara cleared her throat.

Every man, save the sleeping ones, looked astonishingly at her.

"You fine men best close your mouths before you catch a fly," she commented bravely. "I'm sure you have all seen a woman before."

A sergeant, wide of girth and wrinkled in face, rose from the table and limped awkwardly toward her, fairly dragging his left foot. His nose bore crisscrossing red veins, indicating his fondness of liquor. He doffed his battered kepi, revealing a mop of gray hair, and spoke in an odd accent that Sara had never heard. "Ma chil', you do us here d' honor magnifique and chu can fin' we am sportin' 'appy to 'blige you of your wishes."

Sara took a moment to make sure she understood the man's words. "So, you're sayin' you will help me?"

"Sho' 'nuff."

"I'm sorry, I didn't understand that."

The sergeant took her hand in his rough fingers as gently as he could and said, "Oh, bon boo, don't you be make a bahbin or hont, I's just a grand beede in dis here army." He stopped when he saw her confused expression.

"I'm sorry," Sara said, withdrawing her hand from his. "Is there someone here who speaks English?

"By my Defan Papa and me Pouvre Maman, I have offended you." The man showed remorse across his face.

"Let me see if Ah can help by some measure." A lanky fellow arose from a bunk. He wore a long mustache stretched an inch outside of his cheeks, curled and waxed at the ends, and bushy eyebrows sat over his eyes. He approached, his bearing dignified. His drawl indicated he was from the deepest South. "Ah am Corporal Jaquez Toutant, Third Louisiana, company K. It took most of us several weeks before we could begin to understand what Sergeant, Monsieur Rabaneaux, was orderin' us to do. But we have his tidings and chansons well in hand now."

He turned to the sergeant. "If Ah may, sir?"

"Oo, ye, yi. May, oui. Of course, Toutant." The sergeant retreated a few paces, twisting his kepi in his hands.

"Mademoiselle," Jaquez said, facing Sara. He made a slight bow. "We, the men of company K, are here to assist you." He made a wide gesture to the rest of them. The men got up from their bunks and stools and gathered behind Jaquez in a semi-circle. A few whistled, at which point Jaquez glared at them. "Please excuse, Sergeant Rabaneaux. Calls himself a Cajun. Part French, part alligator. He was sayin' that you ahw a sweet young lady, and he is distressed that you would be embarrassed or troubled because of him. As you all can see, he is mortified, having invoked the names and the prayers of his deceased parents. What do you desire, Mademoiselle, uh, yo name, please?"

"My name is Sara Reeder, and I'm looking for ... my fiancé, Joseph Favor. He's in the Third Texas Cavalry. Would you know where that regiment is camped?"

The soldiers began murmuring with each other, shaking their heads, but the little crowd of men inched nearer to Sara.

Jaquez, who had never taken his eyes off her, said, "Mademoiselle Reeder, none of mah comrades here know where the Third Texas might be. We are mostly infantry encamped in this valley. Let me show you." He directed her eyes to the floor. With his brogan, he rubbed a foot-long skid mark on the floorboards. "We are here in this valley. Cross Hollows."

Sara watched his shoe trace across the floor.

"Fayetteville, Arkansas, is here." He pointed the bulky shoe at a knothole in a floorboard. "Below and south of the town is grazing land for horses." He pointed his shoe some distance past the knothole. "That is where most of the cavalry are positioned. Beyond that, Ah know no more."

Sergeant Rabaneaux, said, "You ask de officers in de front, o'er der." He pointed. "Dey miy know."

"Yes, they might know. Good idea." Sara nodded understanding.

"Tonigh', you are here wid us." The sergeant limped forward. "We fix up big batch o' boudain and crawfish gumbo." He grinned from ear to ear.

All the men hooted and clapped. "Here, here," or "Please, ma'am, stay."

Corporal Toutant took her hand and kissed it. "You can stay in our cabin tonight. We will all sleep outside." He turned to the admiring soldiers. "Isn't that right, gentlemen?"

The soldiers bobbed their heads yes.

"Very well," Sara answered. She was becoming more and more comfortable with these strangers from the deep South. *This is a big wide world I am learning*, she thought. *Filled with friends as well as foes.* She had not slept in an actual bed in many days. The idea sounded delightful.

"Excellent," Jaquez said. He clapped his hands. "Quickly, men, who's going for fish? Who's the cook tonight?"

Sergeant Rabaneaux selected five men to prepare the meal. The men gathered their belongings and hurried outside.

Sara had numerous comforts provided her. One soldier brought in a feather mattress. He put his finger to his lips to indicate not to tell that he filched it. Another brought her bright colored pillows. He said, "Shhhh." A third, all the while watching over his shoulder, hauled in a rocking chair. She wondered laughingly if she had fallen in with a den of thieves.

Sara unloaded her belongings from Esther, and a soldier took the mare over by other horses where there were heaps of hay and water buckets.

In the cabin alone, Sara used a bedpan to relieve herself. With several wooden buckets of water available in the cabin, she washed her arms and face in a tin basin, using a chunk of her own lilac-scented soap. She chose not to use the simple yard-long, metal tub to bathe, for though the shuttered windows were additionally covered with golden, almost opaque, waxed parchment, she desired no man to see her naked.

She sat for a while in the rocker, leaning against one of the pillows, reading Don Quixote and finding it pleasing. *If only I had a Sancho Panza to join me on my quest.* That thought led to her affections for Joseph and the hard loneliness that carved at her heart. She thought about disrobing just to glide her hands over her own skin and imagine Joseph naked beside her, together on the feather mattress.

A rap at the door drew her dreaming to a close. She rose, released the rawhide latch and opened the door that hung on leather strap hinges.

EIGHTEEN

❧

TAKE THE EARTH BY ITS EDGES AND SHAKE THE WICKED OUT

— BOOK OF JOB

AUGUST 24, 1861, EARLY EVENING
THE RED RIVER, NORTH TEXAS

While Juarez and Gustav returned upstream to bring the herd up onto the higher ground, Paul, Ben, and John used ropes to raise Asa's corpse to the top of the cliff. Then they carried it some yards to a spot under an expansive oak.

"How'r we gonna bury him?" Ben asked. "We don't have any shovels." He kicked at the hard clay.

"One of us will ride to a town and purchase some," Paul replied.

No sooner had he said this than a mule drawn wagon topped a rise, approaching from the west.

Juarez and Gustav herding the horses down the road circled around the slow-moving, lone wagon. They settled the herd in a grassy, tree-shaded spot, fifty yards from where Asa's body lay. When they joined Paul and the others, the heavily-laden wagon drew nearer.

When it was close enough, John recognized the Quaker elder and a son sitting on the wagon seat. "They's them Quakers."

Paul raised his eyebrows. "Do tell."

Solomon Jarrell pulled the wagon to a halt beside the men. He looked past the group before him at the prone body of Asa. He took off his hat and looked upward, his lips moving silently. He stopped and said, "I was going to offer blessings for God's glorious day, but I see one of thine has passed. I am sorry."

"I'm sorry for thy loss," the Quaker son said, and lowered his head.

"I don't believe we've had the pleasure, Reverend," Paul said.

"I am no reverend. We are all brothers in Christ."

"Well, my name is Paul McGavin. This is Ben McGavin. These men work for us. Juarez and Gustav... and the colored fellow, John." Paul pointed at each man.

"My name is Solomon Jarrell. This is my son, Elias." He stepped down from the wagon and walked over to the dead body then turned to face the wranglers. "I recognize him. He's the one who spoke to us earlier today. He was with the Negro."

"Yes, suh," John said. "I remember you, Mister Solomon."

"Your arrival here is fortunate," Paul said. "We need shovels to dig in this hard clay. If you have some, may we borrow them to give him a proper burial?"

"Of course, thou mayest." He reached in the wagon and pulled out two shovels. "Use these. My son, Elias, will assist. He owes you that."

Paul did not ask why the Quaker thought his son owed them the work, but was glad to let the young man help. The men took turns spading the almost unyielding soil until they had reached a four-foot depth. After removing Asa's gun belt, pocket watch, knife, wallet and the few coins from his pockets. Paul stowed those items in a saddlebag. He removed some grimy papers and telegrams from the interior pocket of Asa's jacket. One was a torn telegram from a Captain Sheridan of the Union army. He brushed the sand and grit from the papers, folded them, and placed them in his vest pocket. The Sheridan telegram he placed in his shirt pocket. *This may be important.*

The men laid Asa's body in the grave and shoveled the soil over it.

When the mound had been tamped down and a small cross erected at the head of it, Paul asked Solomon. "Could you say some words over our brother? I don't think any of us could muster a decent prayer."

"If thou wishes." He pulled a worn Bible from under the wagon seat and read several scripture passages, primarily dealing with hope.

While Solomon was reading, Ben wept. At the end of the quotes and prayers, Gustav and Juarez made the sign of the cross. Gustav pronounced, "In the name of the Father, the Son and the Holy Ghost. Dear Lord, please receive Asa into heaven. He was a good man. He feared no evil. He actually feared little at all. Amen."

Paul turned to the Quakers. "We appreciate your help, Solomon. I have to wonder why you drove your wagon all the way here though."

"I've come on God's errand. My son has put thy Negro in jeopardy."

"How's that?" Paul asked.

"Shortly after we spoke with thy brother and John, three men of the most wicked sort rode hard upon us. We kept our guns on them, but they showed no regard for our weapons. The leader, an old man with one arm, asked if we had seen any Negroes. Of course, he called them *niggers*. Before I could stop my son, Elias said that we had just seen one today. He did not mean any harm, but I had already recognized them as bounty hunters, looking for runaway slaves. After years of hiding runaways from the likes of them, one comes to know their ilk."

"So, you help runaway slaves?" Ben's voice spiked.

Paul slung his arm sideways and slapped Ben in the chest. Ben doubled over coughing. Paul said to Solomon, "Go on."

"Fortunately, I maintained the wherewithal to point them away from thy path in the opposite direction. But it will not take them long before they figure out my ruse. We came to *warn* thee. They are vile men who stop at nothing to take back a slave, I fear even if it means killing anyone in their way. Thou must make haste before they find thee. My son insisted he come along. He has something to say."

"I beg thy forgiveness," Elias said. He looked sadly at John.

John nodded. Paul noticed the dread on John's face.

"We must be getting back," Solomon said, mounting the wagon. "My family and I will be praying for thee, and the Lord will shake the wicked out." After Elias climbed into the seat, Solomon turned the wagon and headed in the direction from which they had come.

"Thank you again!" Paul called after them. He lowered his voice, "If I can think of a prayer, I'll say one for you, too."

Ben stepped in front of him, almost to his face. "What're we gonna do with the nigger? I say leave him here for the bounty hunters. He was runnin' when we found him. Let him run now."

"We'll do no such thing. Now that Asa's gone, we need all the help we can get. John stays with us. Let's get this herd moving." Paul looked once more at the grave of his older brother, raised his eyes to hold back tears and placed his hat on his head. "We'll head to the ferry. It'll cost, but we're not going to try to cross anywhere else. Agreed?"

Each of the men nodded.

"On the other side of the river," Paul continued, "it's the Choctaw Nation. They're friendly and won't hinder us. We'll stay on the Texas Road, then onto the Butterfield Stage Road. Should be easier the rest of the way to Fort Smith. You men have worked hard and deserve your pay. Asa would've had it no other way. I'm honored to know you."

"When we've sold the horses, I'm done," Ben said, hurling his words. "I ain't never drivin' horses no more. I'm joinin' McCulloch's army soon as I can. And don't try to stop me, Paul."

"Well, Ben, I'm thinking I might join up, too. Without Asa, I think it may be the best thing we could do." He placed his spectacles on his nose and mounted his horse.

NINETEEN

∞

SOME ARE DELIVERED, SOME ARE DETAINED

OCTOBER 10, 1861, DUSK
SOUTH OF IRONTON, MISSOURI

Lucas and Workman stood with the slave, Elisheba, under the slanted porch roof of the dismal cabin, the gray storm pouring all around them. The jovial, round slave had knocked several times on the shoved tight door. She had even pushed on it. Lucas worried that the rain falling so violently would leak into his trunk on the wagon before they could secure it in a drier place. In his clandestine plan, he needed his old uniform, laid inside the trunk.

Finally, Elisheba pounded so hard on the door, Lucas thought she might splinter the wood.

"Who der?" came a meek voice from inside.

"It's Elisheba, now let me in."

"You got any money?" the voice asked.

"No, you ol' skinflint, where you think I get any money?"

"You let me have you naked tonight?"

"You listen hea. Balthazar, I have two very kind white gents wid me who is most weary and wet from dey travels, and if you don't open dis door I'll break it down, and you knows I can."

The door creaked open wide. With the dark storm outside, and no light inside, Lucas could not make out anything except a flash of white teeth and the whites of a Negro man's eyes. The three shuffled inside, rainwater from their clothes slopping the floor.

"Ain't you got no light in hea?" Elisheba said. Her voice echoed.

"When I heard the wagon comin' up de road, I doused the lantern. So's no one knows I'm here."

When Balthazar lit two lanterns, Elisheba said, "That's a piece better."

The dwelling's interior was drab and had only a few pieces of furniture, the most pronounced was a large four-poster bed shoved in the back corner. The rest of the furniture was hand-turned, and every chair and the lone table wobbled, for one leg of each was shorter than the other three.

The four sat and stared bleakly at each other while the storm lashed and boomed outside. The man, a thin Negro that Lucas guessed to be about his age, was missing one arm, cut off ragged at the elbow. His face had few wrinkles, and he seemed overtly fidgety. In his one hand, without looking, he held a deck of cards that he deftly shuffled, turning and inserting the cards over and over.

Workman arose and pushed his hat down on his head. "I'm takin' the horses and the wagon under cover in what's left of that barn."

"You be careful in that old barn," Balthazar said. "That old roof might tumble any time. And dey's rats so I'd get out of der mighty quick. Don't go lookin' in no corners."

Balthazar leaned over and whispered into Elisheba's ear.

"Of course, dey ain't bounty hunters!" She pushed his arm so hard he fell from his chair. "What bounty hunters do you know of ride in an old wagon filled with their belongings and travelin' nice and slow, like these gents?"

Lucas heard her well enough. "We're not slave hunters. Except I'm looking for... a freeman that might have come through here. An older fellow. Gray hair and beard, riding a fine horse." Lucas monitored Balthazar's reaction who gave no indication of knowledge of Abram.

Balthazar hunched his shoulders. "Ain't seen sech a man."

For several minutes, the three sat quietly, save for Elisheba's humming of unknown songs.

"How'd you lose your arm?" Lucas asked Balthazar.

Balthazar held up the nub that was scarred and purple at the extremity and looked like an edge of bone stuck out farther than the rest of the flesh. "Got it stuck in a cotton gin. Swole up and got ugly, so I just cleaved it off with an ax. Yes, suh."

"Hmmm mmm. I was der." Elisheba added.

"You cut off your own arm?" Lucas was incredulous.

"Hmm, mmm. Ax is over der in de corner. Want to play some cards?" Balthazar flicked the cards in his hand faster. "I got some nickels if you got some."

"I'll pass." Lucas scooted his chair back a measure, not sure how to evaluate the man.

Workman returned, slapped his soggy clothes with his hat, slinging the rainwater about. "Done. The horses are under cover, so's the wagon." He sat. "And..." he said loudly, and then paused.

The other three looked at him, and then Balthazar jumped up and stormed to a back corner. "I knew it. I knew it!" he exclaimed.

"Yeah, I saw the runaway slaves," Workman said, sitting down cross-legged in his chair, folding his arms, "and they were as sceered as church mice cornered by a bobcat. I just waved at 'em and told them no never mind. I've got enough on my mind than to worry about some runaways."

Balthazar rejoined the group. "You mean you ain't gonna turn us in?"

Both Lucas and Workman nodded that they would not.

"What is this place, Balthazar?" Lucas asked.

"This be a half-way house for runaways," Elisheba broke in. "We on the underground railway. All the slaves 'round here knows it, but not the white folk, not yet anyway."

"I've read about the underground railway. Never thought I'd find a place where they actually hid." Lucas rubbed his trousers, sliding off the rainwater.

"I don't get what the deal is with slaves runnin' away," Workman announced. "I've seen plantations. They got a house to live in, raise 'em a family, get their own garden and some chickens. Yeah, they have to work, but don't we all?"

"You get whupped across your back wid a lash, you know right 'way it's not that pleasant bein' a slave," Elisheba said. "Ain't never happened to me, but I seen it 'nuff times. Hmmm mmm."

Workman rolled his eyes. He did not wish to get into an argument with a big black slave woman, whether she *gonna be free* or not.

"Can we sleep here?" Lucas said. "That bed sure looks inviting."

"Full o' bedbugs. You wouldn't wanna." Balthazar said.

Lucas could tell the man did not wish to relinquish his one treasured belonging.

"Very well, we'll sleep in the barn."

"I decided to sleep here tonight," Elisheba said, looking out the one window at the blowing storm.

"Suit yourself," Workman said.

Lucas and Workman headed to the barn. At the rear of the barn, barely under the burned roof, a family of seven Negroes had cloaked themselves under piles of hay, and the mama intermittently shushed a fussy baby.

Lucas and Workman found hay to sleep on at the other end of the barn from where the runaways had bedded down, and they pulled blankets from Lucas's chest on the wagon. Lucas lifted out his old cavalry uniform, feeling the tight-weave wool. He sighed, now even more determined about his plan to stop the war. He fell asleep circumscribing details of his perilous scheme.

TWENTY

∞

A DEBT PAID

SAME DAY, OCTOBER 10, 1861, 10 AM
FORT SMITH, ARKANSAS

The wranglers had little trouble herding the horses through a late morning mist that floated atop the shallow eddies of the Poteau River. Dogwood petals floated like a pink carpet in the sloshing water. The horses trotted up the gentle rise to the imposing, sun-bleached, white, stone walls of Fort Smith. A dozen Confederate cavalry pickets escorted the wranglers. They had met the wranglers a mile back on the peninsula that jutted out to the convergence of the Poteau and Arkansas rivers.

On the parapets, guards waved their hats and whooped vigorously. Paul rode in front, up the steep, slate rock embankment and stopped just outside the open gate. The jubilation from the men in the fort ratified the wranglers' long drive.

I'd say they're glad to see these horses, he thought, smiling through gritted teeth, for the month-long drive had tormented his bent leg. He took off his glasses and wiped the lenses.

The herd trotted through the gate. Ben rode up beside Paul and noticed him wincing. "You could take some laudanum, you know. I bet they got some in the fort."

"Don't want any. I don't like the way it makes me feel when it wears off."

Stew drove the wagon up beside the brothers and doffed his hat. "We done it, gents. My compliments to you both."

"Yes," Paul said, "and you've earned a good rest."

"I'll vote for that," the little man cheered and headed the wagon into the fort.

Juarez rode up. "Mucho suerte. We had good luck in the last of thees journey, sí, señors. No more Comanches, no more death. I want a siesta, but I want una cerveza, too."

"You've earned a few drinks," Paul said. "I'll bet some soldiers have some corn liquor hidden somewhere." Paul thought that he, too, would enjoy some liquor to perhaps forget, for at least a while, the death of his brother in the quicksand. *Why there? Why did he die at a river he's crossed a dozen times?* He pinched his lips to stave his remorse. *Later, I will mourn.*

Juarez whistled at the last horses, herding them through the gate and into a holding pen. Gustav came next, a broad smile stretching his thin mustache.

John rode up the incline last, his face more somber than it had been in days. His bald scalp glistened with sweat, and his threadbare pants were tattered almost to shreds. In the two months from the Red River, Paul knew that John had developed into an accomplished horseman. John forced a smile at Ben and Paul.

After he passed, Ben said, "He doesn't look too happy. Guess he knows this is the end of the line for him."

"We'll see. Asa wanted to take him as far as Fort Smith, and then let him go free."

"But..."

"No buts to it, Ben," Paul was adamant. "Asa said he planned to let him go, and even though I'm not sure I agree with his wishes, I'm going to honor them."

"Paul, do you seriously think these soldiers are going to allow that to happen?"

"We'll tell them he's a freeman already."

"But he ain't free. We should've sold him to that old Choctaw Indian. He offered us good money."

"That old chief had enough colored slaves, plus slaves from other tribes. He didn't need one more, but we did need John's help. With Asa gone, he was the extra hand we had to have. Besides, when he came to us, he *was* free. His master was dead with no heirs. No one owned him. As far as I'm concerned, he's free now. And furthermore, he risked his life to get Asa's body out of the quicksand. Doesn't that mean anything to you?"

"Yes... no, he's a nigger. They're supposed to work for us white men. They do what we tell 'em. They ain't got enough sense to... to..."

"To what, Ben?" Paul wagged his head in disgust. "To learn how to herd horses with no previous experience, and not complain about anything we told him to do, to save Stew's life, and risk his own damn life for a dead man when nobody asked him. You best shut your mouth for once." He loped his horse through the gate and up to some soldiers who immediately directed him to the officer's quarters.

Ben fumed. "It ain't right. Next thing, we'll be settin' the table for them. He surely pulled Asa outta that bog, and I'm grateful to him for that, but he's still a no account nigger."

Ben and Paul sat at a table in the officer's dining hall eating beef steaks, potatoes, cornbread, and collard greens. Ben scowled, despite the tasty fare. The door flung open, and Gustav and John entered. When Gustav saw them, he strode forward a few steps. John hesitated.

"What's that nigger doing in here?" piped a rotund lieutenant.

John froze, and then backed out the door. Gustav came to Paul and whispered in his ear, "We saw the bounty hunters just come into the fort. Had to be them. Three of them, one gray-haired and missing an arm."

Paul rose and limped out onto the porch.

"I came to tell you, Suh," John said, "I don't want to go back to no plantation. I want to see my family."

"Don't worry, John." Paul leaned toward his ear. "I'm going to see if I can get a horse with a saddle, and let you ride out of here a free man." Paul watched John's eyes light up, and his lips spread to a large grin.

"Lay low," Paul said, "I hope to finish up the sale of the horses soon with Major Clarke. In the meantime, you join some of the other darkies. Just pitch in. Blend in. Don't give anything away." He gave a wan smile. "Gustav, keep a close eye on him. If those bounty hunters get close, try to head them off."

"I will do my best, mon Capitan," Gustav said. His eyes showed worry. He left to tell the other wranglers.

John joined some slaves who were sharpening bayonet blades on a grinding stone behind the quartermaster's building.

Paul left his meal unfinished. Leaving Ben inside jawing with the officers, he stepped out onto the parade grounds. Some officers' wives in pretty, flowered skirts and bonnets tended simple gardens in front of the two-story affair. Paul took a moment to take in the fort's immense rock walls. At nine feet in height, they were much more than was needed to ward off an Indian attack. A few guards patrolled on high platforms. Hundreds of Confederates sat about in shady areas eating their noon meals. Seeing the quantity of soldiers garrisoned in the fort, he anticipated no vicissitude in selling the herd at a good price.

The aroma of baking bread from the bakery ovens hung on the air, but it was mixed with a preponderant stench of horse and cattle muck.

Three horse pens were within the fort. The pens for the cattle were outside the wall, and when the wind shifted, the reek of manure inundated the air.

Despite it being a sweltering day, a half-dozen blacksmiths stood before a large shed foundry, pounding hot iron on anvils for horseshoes and wheel parts. Paul hobbled over to one of them, a swarthy fellow with deep wrinkles like ruts in his face, black hair covering his bulky, sweating arms and chest. He wore no shirt, but a leather apron hung from his neck down to his pants cuffs. He was pumping the bellows of a blazing furnace.

"Hello, smithy, how you do?"

The blacksmith glanced up and continued to press the bellow arms. "Hot. Tired."

"I see there's a passel of you working now. Don't you get a lunch?"

"No time. I've got some bread and beef over there on that salver. I munch on it of an occasion." He tonged a heated-to-orange, iron rod from the fire and set in on the anvil, then commenced to beat the piece into a horseshoe with his heavy hammer. "Maybe you're just making polite conversation, or maybe you don't know there's a war. The horses need shoes, or the cavalry can't ride."

"I just was curious about the urgency."

"Word's come that General McCulloch is arrivin' soon. He wants the horses right away and shoes for them. Trouble is, a third of these horses ain't broke. And in this entire army," he pointed his hammer in a wide arc at the fort grounds, "there ain't a single man out of the seven hundred or more what can break a horse."

"Well, I can break..." Paul felt a surge of pain in his leg as if it were telling him *no*.

"You can do what?" the smithy stopped pounding.

"I was just saying I have a brother who can break horses. That's what we do."

"Do what?" Ben, munching on an apple, sidled up. "What can your brother do?"

"We both can break horses," Paul said. "That's our way."

"Yeah, so what," Ben retorted. "And don't be volunteering me for no duty. I'm fixin' to join up at the recruitin' table over yonder." He pointed to a sergeant seated beneath a cottonwood, behind a rough table where a short line of new recruits had formed. Two wore Sunday best, two others wore homespun and were barefoot.

"Ever since the word came down about us winnin' the Oak Hill battle," the smithy announced sardonically, "anybody that can walk is trying to join up. They don't wanna miss out on the fightin' before it's all over." He set to pounding again on the horseshoe, and then stopped to wipe his forehead. "And if you're lookin' to get a job breakin' horses, you best talk to Major Clarke when he gets back from his ride." The smithy smirked like he knew a secret.

"His ride?" Ben asked.

Paul bid goodbye to the blacksmith and pulled Ben aside. "The major's not too popular here. One of the officers at the dining table said he's gone off to reconnoiter, but another officer whispered to me he's gone to visit an Indian woman off in the hills."

"Is that true?"

"Probably just a rumor. Don't spread it. That's worse than whoring. When Major Clarke returns, we'll dicker with him about the payment for the horses. When he pays, we'll pay the wranglers their wages, and then, and only then, do we join up. And that's after we put our money in a bank in the town."

Ben nodded, gave the apple core to a horse stretching its neck over a corral fence, and followed his brother.

They walked across the broad expanse of the compound, filled with wagons and carts, piles of hay, mounds of cloth sacks of lentils and cornmeal under sheds, barrels of molasses, salt and dried pork. Beyond that, a city of tents of all shapes and sizes spread, many formed up like teepees. Under one sprawling lean-to affair, forty or so women sat at rough-hewn tables upon which bolts of tan and ash colored cloth lay. White women, slave women, and Choctaw squaws were serried together, cutting fabric and sewing uniforms.

Dozens of boys of the three races jibed and capered about, laughing, playing chase, shooting marbles, or kicking rawhide balls. The girls of the three races sat in circles with rag dolls around little tea sets and makeshift dollhouses.

"Afternoon, ladies," Ben announced to a quartette of younger women. He swept his hat from his head, his blond locks falling across his eyes, and made a deep bow. All the women giggled, but a stern stare from a beady-eyed crone prompted them to turn their eyes down and return to their work.

"When I get me a nice uniform," Ben said, "I fancy a number of pretty ladies will line up to meet me."

Paul chuckled. "I'll bet." Walking, instead of riding, was lending a measure of relief to his leg.

Beyond the tents, the grass was beaten away by months of the passage of thousands of treading feet. Cannon balls were stacked in several neat pyramids. Squads of men pitched dirt onto ramps for the cannons to roll up and then fire over the walls.

The brothers climbed the steps to a guard platform. Standing beside the private stationed there, they looked out at the cozy town of Fort Smith. Wagons and people moved with fervency about the streets. Closer to the river, a circle of teepees marked the more subdued small village of the Creek Tribe, with visiting chiefs considering joining the Confederate cause.

"We're none too sure about them Indians," the private offered, pointing at the village. He was a mousy fellow with a droopy black mustache, fairly swallowed by his pasty gray uniform.

"Why's that?" Ben asked. He held his hand to his nose, for the cattle pens opposite the wall were redolent with stench.

"They done voted for neutrality. Seems to most of us that that's the same as sidin' with the enemy."

"I hadn't thought much about the Indians choosing sides in this war," Ben said.

"Cherokees gonna fight with us. Choctaw, too," the little private said. "General McCulloch's got General Pike out in the territories, negotiating with the Indians to get 'em to fight. Lots of stories flyin' about. Not just about the Indians but about all kinds of folks. If you'd care to hear, I can tell you some good 'uns."

"Not really," Paul said, turning to go. Ben followed after him.

"I can't stand a gossip," Paul remarked. "Gossip stinks worse than those beeves."

At that moment, a bugle sounded. Soldiers on the parapets again hollered and waved their hats. Paul and Ben watched General McCulloch in his black velvet jacket and broad-brimmed black hat ride in with an accompanying squad of officers and soldiers. They galloped up to the expansive, red-brick, two-story officers' quarters.

"Looks like," Paul said, "we're going to sell the horses to the general himself."

TWENTY-ONE

∞

SATIETY AND WANT

SAME DAY, OCTOBER 10, 1861, 2 PM
FORT SMITH, ARKANSAS

B en and Paul slouched on the steps of the fort's headquarters
watching the camp's goings-on — companies of soldiers
marching in drill, a cavalry squad rehearsing maneuvers,
and a long line of mule and oxen-drawn wagons arriving, laden
with supplies. Teams of men rushed to unload the goods, change
out the animals, and send the wagons out again.

The door to the headquarters opened. The brothers rose and
were met by two tall Indian chiefs exiting. One was bedecked
with a profligate myriad of beads and animal teeth necklaces
over a buckskin shirt and trousers. The other wore a business
suit, a white shirt and tie and a stovepipe hat. They walked in an
arrogant fashion, both with their large hawk-like noses in the air.
Ben marveled at their pomposity. "Looks like they're enjoyin' the
smell of the place." He chuckled.

A sergeant beckoned the brothers inside. Their spurs jingling
on the pine floors, they walked toward a large desk near the back
wall. Major Clarke stood there, his jacket off and the sleeves of
his heavily starched shirt rolled up. The collar was buttoned tight
around his thick neck. He indicated chairs to them. They sat. The
major looked down, reading through some papers spread on his desk.

To Ben and Paul's left, General McCulloch leaned against one of the large support posts, looking out one of the six windows toward the fort compound and the storm brewing. He puffed on a pipe filled with an aromatic tobacco. He still wore the dusty, black jacket. His dark eyes seemed expressionless to Paul.

A lieutenant sat at their right in front of a large stone fireplace. He occasionally swatted at flies that chanced to land on his desk.

Paul looked around the wide room. Heavy timber rafters ran under the vaulted roof. On either side of the door, large, paned windows let in considerable light. Several heavy, dark wood chairs lined the back wall.

After a few minutes, Paul cleared his throat, attempting to gain a comment from someone in the room. Ben picked at a torn fingernail. He leaned toward Paul. "Aren't they even going to introduce themselves?"

Paul shrugged his shoulders.

"I would like to presage...." General McCulloch finally said. He tapped out his pipe on his boot and kicked the burnt dribble into a crack in the floorboard. He turned to the wranglers, took off his jacket, and set it on the back of a chair. He turned the chair backward and sat straddling it, facing the wranglers. "That you would like to sell your herd for top dollar and you would like payment in silver. I am General McCulloch."

Paul turned his chair toward the general. "General McCulloch, pleased to meet you." The three shook hands. "My brother, Asa McGavin, told me quite a bit about you. You've met on several occasions."

"That is correct," the general said. "This officer to my left is Major Clarke. He's the quartermaster for this Army of the West."

Major Clarke looked up just long enough to nod.

"He's not one to dicker, so I'll do the negotiating of the price per head. And you'll forgive him if we let him do his job. He has the arduous task of feeding, clothing, and arming this multitudinous flock, this rabble, this, may I say, congregation of believers who scrabbled together to fight a war. We take them all, be they banker, beggar, or thief."

"Yes sir," Paul said.

"And your names are Paul and Ben McGavin. The lieutenant informed me. And where might your brother be?"

Paul cleared his throat. "He died, sir, on the drive here. At the Red River...." Asa's death weighed heavily on his heart.

"I understand. My condolences for your loss. He was a good man."

"Damned right, he was," Ben said. "And he died so this army could have them horses. So, we better get a good price." His face had turned red.

Paul turned to Ben with a stern look.

General McCulloch nodded. "And you shall have as good a price as the army can afford. I have little time to quibble. A quarter of my army a few miles northeast is quarantined with measles. At least a dozen have died from the disease. The army needs horses almost as much as men. Tell me what you have."

"We have," Paul said, "thirty head, ten stallions, twenty mares."

"Mares are good," General McCulloch leaned back in his chair. "I find mares are more tractable, not as sturdy, but generally calm in battle."

"That's right," Paul said. "And one of the mares foaled, so we have one filly. She's doing fine."

"That's good. How much you want for them?" When General McCulloch asked the price, the major looked up and his eyes pierced the wranglers.

Paul rubbed his chin. "Fifteen dollars a head. I've got..."

"I'll give you ten," General McCulloch said.

"Thirteen." Paul leaned back and crossed his arms. "I've got wranglers to pay."

"Would you take twelve?" the general asked, his face impervious.

Paul looked at Ben who nodded agreement.

"Very well," Paul said, "on three conditions. First, we're paid in silver. That was the agreement Asa worked out with you."

"Agreed," the general said.

"Second, when Paul and I sign up for the cavalry, we get to keep our own mounts."

General McCulloch leaned forward. "That's agreeable. Write that down in the bill of sale, Lieutenant."

"Yes sir." The lieutenant dipped his quill in the ink and wrote on a ledger page.

"And what's number three?" General McCulloch's eyes betrayed no emotion.

Paul hesitated, formulating his thoughts. "The Negro in my company gets to pick one of the horses for his own. That's his pay. You pay us for the horse, but he gets it."

General McCulloch sat poker-faced. The major huffed and straightened his papers noisily.

"He's a freeman," Paul continued. "He worked hard helping us bring in the herd. We... couldn't have done it without him. That's his pay." Paul did not look at Ben, not wanting to meet his eyes.

"Freeman, huh?" General McCulloch said, leaning back and stroking his beard. "Well, Paul McGavin, I know they do things a little different here and there, and maybe especially from where you're from. But we're in Arkansas now. What does your freeman plan to do?"

"He's going back... north to be with his family."

"I see."

The air in the room seemed to grow heavy to Paul. He glanced out the window where charcoal clouds had gathered over the camp and hung like billowing sailcloth.

"And you're aware of the Fugitive Slave act. He may not be considered a freeman if he has no papers to prove otherwise."

"He has papers." Paul was lying, but kept his eyes square on the general.

"Then I have no problem with the Negro joining his family up north as long as he is a man of character. *Is he a man of character*, Mr. McGavin?"

"I can vouch for him," Paul answered. He was beginning to regret his decision. But he shook it off. "Yes, sir, he's a good, ethical man."

"Very well," General McCulloch said. "Write that in the agreement, Lieutenant."

"Thank you," Paul said.

"Yeah, thanks," Ben said sarcastically. He stood and strode rapidly across the room.

Paul watched General McCulloch's dark eyes follow Ben to the window nearest the lieutenant.

"And you young men are ready to join and fight for Southern freedom?" General McCulloch pointedly remarked. "You're old enough." His eyes were still on Ben.

"I'm twenty-six, sir, and Ben is twenty. He just looks young," Paul said.

"And I'm sure you have your reasons for joining the army."

"Yes, sir," Paul replied.

"Yes, I do. I got plenty of 'em!" Ben said, spitting the words on top of Paul's answer. He advanced toward the general, his finger pointed accusingly at his brother. He halted when he beheld the general looking at him like he was watching a prancing pony. He dropped his arm and halted his tirade.

General McCulloch rose and patted Ben on the shoulder. "Yes, most everyone's got a reason. The Yankee shopkeeper has a reason, the barrel cooper, the plantation owner, even the *Texas horse wrangler*. Southerners are fighting because they don't want anyone telling them what to do. Yankees want to control the economy, make more money. Colonel Greer, your regimental commander after you enlist, wants to make sure the South keeps the slaves.

"I hear some Yanks are fighting to save the Union. If that ain't a pitiful thing. What difference does it make if there's two countries or one?" General McCulloch shook his head. "The Southern plantation owner wants to keep his *king cotton*, and thinks having slaves is the only way to turn a profit. I can tell you now that cotton is smothering us in the south."

"What do you mean? Cotton is the best crop." Ben felt bewildered.

"Is it? Yes, we have plenty of it, but no mills to twist it into threads, no manufacturing plants to turn the thread into uniforms or even blankets. Cotton has been shoved down our throats and we're choking on it!" General McCulloch's voice had become strident, the complaint of a man in desperation. "We have no ability here in the west to manufacture even one gun. We're subsisting on the guns we've confiscated from Union armories and on fighting gear we've cobbled together from wagons and farm tools. And the politicians, they just like to hear themselves thumping their chests like baboons. 'War!' they shout. 'War!' as if it were a church picnic."

In the interim of his diatribe, Ben said meekly, "General McCulloch, I'm just here to fight the Yanks."

"Yes," said the general, "because your disdain for the Northerners is so intense, and you don't want to miss out on the fight. You and half the others in this army. Some of 'em saw what war is like at the battles of Wilson Creek and Carthage, with the carnage and sorrow, and they ran away either to hide or join the marauders. But the ones that stayed want revenge."

He threw on his jacket and stormed out the door. He stopped on the porch and called over his shoulder, "Lieutenant, finish the bill of sale. Twelve dollars a head. The Negro gets one horse. Major Clarke, issue these men three hundred sixty dollars… silver." He stepped off the porch, and thunder slapped the air. Heavy raindrops began pelting the compound. In a moment, the deluge burst, and the soldiers, seamstresses, and slaves raced for cover.

TWENTY-TWO

∞

LET LOOSE THE FURY

SAME DAY, OCTOBER 10, 1861, EVENING
CROSS HOLLOW, ARKANSAS

When Sara opened the door of the cabin loaned to her by the Company K, Louisiana Confederates, Sergeant Rabaneaux was standing on the steps, rocking on his heels. He immediately looked down and held out to her a dress and pressed undergarments on a wire hanger. Speaking to the ground, he said, "Mademoiselle Reeder. Dees are for you." He held the clothes out toward her, his eyes still averted.

Sara surveyed the dress. "What is this?"

"Dis pretty ting and de new ladies' delicates, you'll pardon me saying, mon bee. De Captain, he gi' his fondest regards, but he be about mourning his wife. You see." Rabaneaux held up his hand toward the sky. He appeared to be fumbling for words.

Corporal Toutant stepped forward, twisting the ends of his mustache. "Mademoiselle Reeder, you are the picture of loveliness this evening. May I say you look as sweet and delicate as a rose. Before you think I am flirting with you, I will explain. Our good Captain Tunnard. His wife, a sweet young thing of about your stature, arrived here two weeks ago on a convivial visit. She immediately contracted the dysentery and despite the most prudent work of our surgeons applying every known remedy, she could not be made healthy. She couldn't maintain her water and wasted away. Now she is with the Lord."

Sara gasped. Immediate memories of the Confederate officer's wife at Wilson Creek whom she had attempted to console after her loss of her husband in the battle flooded Sara's mind. Now, this officer had lost his wife.

"The captain is in mourning," Jacquez continued. "He heard about your less than fetching attire, and feels it would be a kindness to give you one of his wife's dresses. One he had purchased for her but was never worn."

"Thank you, Corporal and Sergeant." Sara took the dress and latched the door behind her.

Inside, she lifted the hem of her own bedraggled dress, replete with rips and coral-colored stains. Her dress had changed from a calico blue to a soot-gray, and even her pantaloons were torn. *It is beyond repair. After all, I assisted in burying five bodies.* She shuddered thinking of that endeavor, one she had accomplished almost with no sentiment, a blindness at the time, but now the effort seemed most loathsome.

A mirror in a sturdy frame, one removed from a vanity, hung on a wall.

She held up the new dress. The dress was elegant with silk embroidered sleeves and waist. She fingered the lace pantaloons and the stiff corset with whalebone stays.

She went to the corner farthest the door and disrobed. Pouring a bucket of water into the two-foot-wide metal tub and using the last sliver of her soap, she washed her hair and entire body, the water streaming off her skin to puddle on the floorboards. She took her old pantaloons and dried herself with the cleanest part of them. With the door firmly latched, she sat naked on a pillow in the rocker in the corner awaiting her hair to dry.

She could not help reveling in the luxury of being free from days of filth. She stroked her face, arms and legs and, ultimately, her most intimate area between her thighs in slow, back and forth fashion, soft at first, and then with more force. She watched herself in the mirror, admiring the light glistening on the roundness of her breasts and erect nipples. In her simple understanding of human anatomy, she considered herself something of a beauty, but only ever having seen a few neighbor women bathing in Wilson Creek, she was not certain. She had not had the luxury of a mother to explain the elements of womanhood, and neighbor women refused to answer her questions on the basis of their predisposition to Victorian propriety.

She gazed in a sort of innocent astonishment at the lantern light glimmering on the tiny, soft blond hairs on her strong thighs and calves. Then, thinking of Joseph naked, she ran her fingers across her breasts, and down to her knees, tracing with delicate touch slowly up to the hirsute notch between her legs, lingering there. Her yearning was so aroused, she began panting.

At that moment, she caught sight of an eye of an unknown soldier peering through a knothole, not leering, but with a sort of amateur fascination. She flung the old pantaloons at the knothole, then fled to the opposite corner and quickly dressed. She tied her still wet hair up with a ribbon.

"Supper'll be ready soon," Jacquez called from outside. "We'd be honored if you joined us."

Sara looked once more in the mirror, then smirked a little that a soldier found her of acute interest, enough to risk having his eye poked out.

Outside, the evening was falling into a gray haze under a source-less sun. Cook fires blossomed everywhere, the smell of spicy food almost tormenting. Roasting meat odors, baking cornbread, and herb-flavored stews rose in a serendipitous, tangy effluvium. Sara walked to a table with a checkered cloth spread on it. Sergeant Rabaneaux pulled out the single chair for her.

Hung on a stout pole over the cook fires, two large pots steamed and hissed under clattering lids.

The soldiers perched on a circle of logs just beyond where Sara sat. They poked at each other like schoolboys, and a few of them chortled at ribald jokes. When the men finally noticed Sara, they became subdued and carried on quiet conversation, but Sara noted that most of them stole glances at her. Corporal Toutant came from around the cabin carrying chairs and followed by a boy of about thirteen with a chair of his own. In short order, the three had seated themselves beside Sara.

"This young man," Jaquez announced, "is our drummah boy. He is also the colonel's son. The colonel is away on duty or he would have joined us here, but, in his stead, we are fortunate to have Wayne with us."

The callow boy sat quietly. He had dark hair, golden brown eyes and a dimple in his chin. He wore a smart gray uniform with a white strap across one shoulder. His kepi was too large and tended to slip down over his brow. His nose whistled when he breathed, evidence of a cold.

"You know," Jaquez said, "they say a dimple in the chin means the devil within." He grinned at Wayne who gave a winsome smile in return.

"I doubt this boy has ever had a devilish thought in his life," Sara said.

"Oh, I wouldn't be too sure," Jaquez said. "The other day, I saw him tossing rocks at an old crow in a tree just to pester it."

"Not so," shot the teen. "Crows eat corn, and the army needs corn." He lowered his eyes.

"Very well, young drummah boy," Jaquez said. "I stand corrected."

All of a sudden, three soldiers stood by the table with tin plates steaming with boudain, bowls of crawfish gumbo, and huge chunks of honeyed cornbread. Sara was inclined to believe she had never experienced such delightful smells.

She bowed her head to say grace. Her table company joined her. "Dear Lord," she prayed, "please bless this food and the hands that prepared it, and bless the Confederate army to victory, most especially company K of Louisiana."

"Amen," they said.

Before Sara could dip her spoon in the soup, Sergeant Rabaneaux arose, pulled a small bottle from his shirt pocket containing ground, green-gray tea leaves. He pulled the cork from the bottle. "You must have *filé* for de gumbo." He hesitated until Sara nodded, and then he sprinkled the leaves over her gumbo. "Der," he said, "you dine sufficient now. Bon appetit."

Sara relished the dinner, sopping up the roux with her cornbread. She shared in the lively conversation, though she did not always understand the sergeant's frequent pronouncements.

The night patrolled the cantonment and then penetrated it, laying its long black cloth throughout. Soldiers hung lanterns on poles and tree limbs. Slaves added logs to the fires, and the camp became as illuminated as a plantation house parlor at Christmas.

Musicians of every sort appeared up and down the valley. One fellow blew on a cornopeon, a horn fashioned somewhat like a short trumpet. Several strummed guitars and banjo-like instruments. The tin whistles and wooden flutes piped throughout the cantonment, and the assortment of musical renditions from the diverse companies often conflicted, but sometimes blended together.

By the Company K campfire, a thin soldier banged on a three-string guitar and Wayne brought out his drum and beat an unsteady rhythm. But when Jaquez bowed his fiddle and Sergeant Rabaneaux squeezed his concertina, the mellifluous ballads and ditties truly commenced. The vibrant tremolos and allegros were new to Sara and the songs possessed a tempestuous rhythm. The remaining soldiers danced jigs and reels, dosey-doeing with each other and bowing as if to a sweetheart or wife. Sara could barely contain her joy, tapping her foot and clapping.

A few laundresses, accompanied by their husbands from neighboring companies, joined the musicale. Sara noted the laundresses' forearms were red raw from their labors.

At the end of one song, Jaquez told Sara, "You know, Reverend Felder, who comes here of an occasion, says the fiddle is the devil's instrument, but I..."

"You know Reverend Felder? From Springfield?"

"Yes, he does a circuit through heah of an occasion and offers a sermon. All the men gather round and listen, even us Catholics. He's a mighty speaker. The Lord is in his corner."

"He's a good man." Sara beamed, knowing that her own minister served the army here.

Jacquez and Rabaneaux struck up a plaintive melody that slowed after a few measures to a sort of dirge, recalling the sadness of loss. At the end of the melancholy piece, Jacquez maintained a long pull on his bow, lasting for several seconds at a point when there was no other sound in the valley, and the note to Sara sounded akin to the song of a dying swan that she had read about. Jacquez lowered the bow and took a deep breath. The entire regiment was silent. A few dried tears.

Then the two musicians began a jolly waltz. Once more, the soldiers flung themselves around the circle with untamed wildness. Several soldiers offered to escort Sara to the impromptu ball dance area, but she declined.

"I'm engaged to be married," she lied. Once again, her heart pined for the touch of Joseph, remembering their dances at the party that General McCulloch bestowed on them at her home on the hill above Wilson Creek, Missouri.

She held up her right hand that had clasped Joseph's in the final waltz of that evening, her fingers tingling.

Spreading her fingers, Sara looked past her hand and saw beyond the tall blaze of the campfire that cracked the night sky a sight she had hoped she would never see again. She gasped.

Beyond the circle of men, in partial dark and flickering firelight, standing by a couple of horses and speaking to some officers, the man's scarred profile was entirely evident. Richards, the man who had tried to rape her.

Sara shrank down in her chair, put her hand over her brow to hide her face.

"Psst," she called, "Corporal Toutant." She called his name again. He ended the piece he was playing incomplete and looked back at her. She motioned for him to join her. He got up from his seat and sat on his haunches beside her.

"What is that man doing here?" She pointed quickly.

"Who?"

"That man there." She pointed again. "Talking with those officers." Jaquez took a long look. "You mean the man in the deerskin jacket?"

"Yes. Do you know who he is?" Sara's voice trembled.

"I don't know his name, but he delivers the mail from the cantonment to the tavern at Elkhorn and out to Fort Smith. See those large saddle bags on his horse."

"That man tried to rape me."

"What?" Jaquez rose, his eyes fierce. He set his fiddle on the table. "When? Where?"

"He burned down my house. He's not a Confederate at all. His name is Richards. He came at me to..." Sara gulped, too frightened to speak.

At that moment, B. Franks Richards, as he had called himself, jumped into his saddle, and the horse bolted away into the night.

"Stop that man!" Jaquez called. "Stop him!" He raced after Richards, leaping logs, and weaving between soldiers around their campfires. The rider disappeared into the abyss of black.

When Jaquez returned, he asked, "Did he see you?"

"I don't know." She trembled. "I must get away from here."

By this time, the remaining members of Company K had gathered around the table. Jaquez explained to them what Sara had told him.

"Don't worry," one said, "we'll take care of ye."

"We'll guard you," another said.

Sara looked up into their well-meaning faces, feeling numb. The memory was too gut-wrenching and too clear. Sergeant Rabaneaux took her arm and helped her to her feet. He guided her to the cabin door. "We will post a guard at dat der door. Mon Cherie. You be mighty fine here, ya hear." His words offered little consolation. Sara treaded slowly through the door, closed it, set the latch, and leaned against it, her heart skittering in a race.

She could not fathom how the very man whom she wished to never see again had invaded such a joyous evening to destroy it by his very presence. She had for some days marginally put him out of her mind, though his crass bearing and vicious voice had echoed often in her thoughts.

On her father's simple farm in Missouri, she had never felt afraid. Then the war came with its suffering, great loss, and death, followed by the arrival of the heinous Richards. She had learned fear.

She reflected that in her unrestricted wanderings around her farm, she had often marveled about the workings of the world, the absolute order of things. Small trees could never grow under large ones, so the large trees put out seeds, and birds ate the seeds, then their droppings landed in new soil where the new trees could grow. The seeds even had an initial pile of manure. Foul matter would encourage growth. So, the ongoing flow of life continued.

Early on, she knew that she could not grow into the woman she wanted to be while always living under her father's roof. She recognized this even before meeting Joseph. Was the burning of their house part of God's plan? *Drive me from my home so I may either thrive or die?*

Was the never-ending quivering of life about every shrub and flower part of a greater plan? Bugs crawled and chewed on the plants, and lizards ate the bugs, and birds devoured the lizards, and the plants grew on and on and spread. Some of them were edible, some poisonous. Sara knew the poisonous ones. She briefly thought of Workman, such a skilled nurse, who had taught her much about which herbs and plants helped cure.

She could barely countenance the bitter memory of the night Richards had come so close to raping her. She dared not be near when the man returned to the cantonment. Her fear left her bereft of careful analysis, fidgeting, wanting wholeheartedly to dart away into the night as fast as she could to anywhere but there, though she might well be rushing directly into his clutches. She sank down to sitting on the floor.

After a long time, and her thoughts calmed, she resolved she would ask for a pistol. She had a few silver coins sewn into her bodice. She would offer to buy a revolver, for if she ever encountered the beast again, a one-shot rifle would not do.

A light knock at the door. "Miss Reeder. This is Corporal Toutant. May Ah come in?"

"Yes." She stood and opened the door.

Jaquez entered, his hat in his hand. "Miss Reeder, Ah don't know what to say, but all of us want to help. Can you give me some details, so when that post agent, Richards you called him, returns, we can capture and try him?"

"Try him? And what would that do? Would he have a lawyer?"

"He's not a soldier. Perhaps we could get him one out of Fayetteville. Ah suppose...."

"And I would have to give a testimony in front of some men, perhaps friends of his. And perhaps his slick lawyer would get him free. What would I do then?" Tears were runneling down her cheeks.

Jaquez mumbled something to his shoes.

"What did you say?"

He raised his head. He took a delicate kerchief from his pocket and handed it to her. She wiped her face and blew her nose, though her body still quavered with sobs.

"Ah see that you are right," said Jaquez. "But without evidence, we can't do anything to him, other than run him off. And you say, he's not aligned to our Southern cause."

"When he attacked our farm, he knew we supported the South. He, or one of his men, killed a soldier who was helping guard our home. He called me a 'sesech.'"

"Well enough, mah dear young lady. Allow me to find out what Ah can, and we will have a comeuppance for him. That much, Ah assure you." He strode forward, lightly lifted the kerchief from her hand, tenderly wiped her moist face, and gave her back the kerchief. He took her hand and kissed it. "You will be safe tonight. We can plan tomorrow."

"No," Sara said, "I will be leaving early tomorrow. My plan is to find my fiancé. I *will* find him."

"Mais oui, Mademoiselle." Jaquez exited and softly shut the door.

Sara heaved a deep breath, and clinched her fists. "And tomorrow I will barter for a revolver, and watch for him myself, and I will unleash my fury on him."

TWENTY-THREE

✿

THE UPRAISED ARM
OF THE WICKED

SAME DAY, OCTOBER 10, 1861, LATE AFTERNOON
FORT SMITH, ARKANSAS

B en and Paul stood under the roof of the long porch of Fort
Smith headquarters, staring at the clouds that bled steely rain.
Though the negotiation for the price of the horses with
General McCulloch had gone well, Paul waded through ambivalent
thoughts. Had he done the right thing — covering for the Negro?
Ben and he could earn the bounty with one quick remark. But that
was not what Asa wanted. Paul, after considerable rumination,
determined he would follow his deceased brother's wishes. He
looked out at the smoking remnants of the doused cook fires in
the parade ground that turned the air a dun color.

He often glanced toward a lean-to filled with firewood, thirty
yards across the way, where stood his immediate concern. Under its
shabby pine slab roof were three men, who, by Paul's estimation,
had to be the bounty hunters. Paul nudged Ben to look at the three
scowling men. Ben nodded, but looked uninterested.

A hound-faced man with a bald pate and one arm cut off at the
elbow stared bleakly out at the rain. He clinched a cigar in his teeth.
In his one hand, he held a brown dollop of a hat that he used to

swat flies. Under his gray jacket hanging open, two revolvers stuck out prominently from his belt. Beside him, two callous-looking fellows, both in waxed long-coats, ambled back and forth, kicking at the dirt and straw. One of them was huge by human standards, taller than most, with a chest as broad as a horse's. His face was hidden beneath a thick, black beard that covered all but his nose and eyes. He carried a shotgun. A Bowie knife was slung in a scabbard at his belt. The third man was wiry with a neck like a stalk of celery, a shrew face, and a bent nose. A revolver protruded from his belt and he had a lariat over one shoulder.

Behind them, in the shadows against the back wall of the lean-to, an emaciated Negro cowered. The one-armed man turned and pointed at him. The massive bearded man grabbed the Negro by the collar and tossed him, tumbling, into the rain. The three laughed uproariously. The Negro scrambled up from the sloshing mire and attempted to flee, but the wiry man tossed his lariat that looped around the Negro's shoulders and dragged him to the ground. The three of them pulled the runaway into the shed. They continued their bawdy guffaws. The Negro crawled to the back of the shed. The shrew-faced bounty hunter pulled a knife from a sheath and carved from a plug of tobacco. He shoved the chaw in his mouth and spat into a puddle. Paul felt immediate disgust at their gaucherie. Ben merely watched, deadpan.

Single drops of rain often plopped from cracks in the roof to land on their hats and shoulders. A chilled wind set Ben's arms to goose bumps. He turned his sleeves down.

Paul had seen enough of the bounty hunters.

"Come on, Ben. Let's go," he said and ran out into wall of rain.

"I ain't goin' out in this storm!" Ben hollered after him. "Suit yourself!"

Paul raced to a lookout platform under which Juarez, Stew, and John huddled. Beneath the meager cover of the platform floor, Paul pulled John aside, out of earshot of the other two. They sat on some hay bales. "I saw the bounty hunters... just over there."

John nodded. His jaw was set. "I ain't goin' back. I'll fight 'em."

"Don't worry. I've got a plan to get you free." Paul leaned over and whispered, "You know, John, I don't know much about you. Do you really have family up north?"

"Yes, suh, not sure where, but I believe they be up in Ohio. If I get there, I'll keep lookin' until I find 'em."

"Kids?"

"Four of 'em. You see, my wife's pa is a free man. He got enough money and paid a white man to come down and fetch his daughter and grandkids, but they wasn't enough money for me. So, I had to stay."

"So, the white man took them away up north?"

"Yes, suh. He mentioned somethin' about Ohio. Must be a place near the Ohio river."

"Yes, John. It is. How long ago was that?"

"Three years. The white man said he'd be back in a year but he never came. And I hated to leave my master, Mr. Jameson, with him dyin' and all, so I stayed. Kept the little place runnin'. He sold off most of the plantation. When he died, I stayed around a day or two, buried him proper. He was a good man. A lot nicer than that colored woman, Mistress Coincoin. That's where I got my name. She owned my pa and ma and me. Afore she died, she set her children free and sold my pa and ma and me to Mr. Jameson. She used to whip a slave once in a while and...."

"Wait a minute," Paul interrupted. "You say your ma and pa and you were owned by a colored woman? A Negro?"

"Yes, suh. I was just a li'l boy down in Louisiana. She owned the plantation and a passel of slaves. My parents and me were some of 'em. I was about seven years old when she sold us. I saw the paper where she writ the sale to Mr. Jameson."

Paul stared incredulously at John. After a long moment, he said, "I'm sorry, John, but that's hard to believe." He shook his head.

"Believe what you want. But it's the honest truth."

"Well," Paul still shook his head. "Any man that's been a slave of the white man and of the black woman, I guess has a right to be free. Do you know where Gustav is?"

"Yes, suh, he be outside the walls settin' up our tent he bought in the town for us to sleep tonight. He say he would set it by his self."

Thunder banged like an explosion and shook the platform. The men jerked in surprise.

"Dang," Stew said. "God flung a thunderbolt right at us."

"We best go help Gustav with the tent," Paul said. "He can't put it up by himself in this downpour."

"Sí," Juarez said. "I should have help heem. I bring my lariats and tie the tent muy fuerte. Strong."

The men plodded out from their cover into the deluge and past the southern gate walking abreast toward the field where soldiers had constructed a village of tents and lean-tos, almost invisible in the grayness of the rain's curtain. Twilight had arrived, lending opacity to the entire area.

Some forty yards beyond the gate on the downward trail, the one-armed bounty hunter stepped out from behind a tree square in their route. He pointed a revolver at them.

Paul, Stew, Juarez, and John stopped quickly, Juarez almost falling in the slippery, mire-like mud that was cascading across the path.

"I'll have your weapons now," the man barked. "Drop them."

Paul placed his hand on Stew's arm who was about to grab his revolver from his belt. "And what if we don't?" Paul said, his voice placid. "You look to be one against four."

Juarez allowed his hand to drop close to his revolvers. Stew straightened. Paul caught John's arm and drew the Negro behind him. "Get ready to run," he whispered.

The bounty hunter smirked. "Ain't four against one. They's three of us." The large, bearded accomplice stepped out from another tree a dozen feet to Paul's right. His shotgun was raised to his shoulder. The shrew-faced bounty hunter came forth from the left some fifteen yards down the steep path, a revolver pointed at the wranglers. He held a rope in his other hand, at the end of which he wrestled the wrist-tied Negro, five feet behind him. The Negro's face was brimmed with despair. He wore only shabby, patched pants, no shirt.

"Just drop your weapons, fools," the gray-haired man said. "We have no problem killing you, and there ain't a soul in this southern army that'll cry a single tear if a few filchin' slave thieves die. Soon as we have your weapons, we'll take the runaway. Funny how niggers will talk. We just asked a few questions, and they pointed him out."

Lightning and thunder cracked the sky, and the rain poured like a waterfall, all the men drenched. Paul regretted for a moment his decision to have even tried to let John go free, then a surge of pride swept over him. He was glad he was a southerner, but that did not mean he had to abide with slavery. *Well, Asa, what would you do now?* he thought.

"Now! You hog filth! Lose your weapons," the one-armed man shouted.

"Now!" The massive bounty hunter growled like a bear. He stepped within three feet of Paul.

"All right, men," Paul said, "put your guns on the ground."

Stew and Juarez carefully lifted their revolvers from their belts and laid them in the muddy runoff. When Paul reached for his revolver, it was not there. *Did I lose it somewhere?*

He realized that John had reached around and taken the gun from its holster. John, standing inches behind him, held his revolver out of sight. He figured the bounty hunters had not seen him take it.

Paul held his hands in the air. With night coming fast and the rain falling so hard, he could barely see through his glasses, but that meant that the assailants surely had difficulty seeing as well. The lead bounty hunter stuck his gun in his belt, walked forward, and leaned down to pick up Juarez's pistols with his one hand.

"Now, John!" Paul yelled, ducking. John swung around and fired the revolver into the big man, the bullet piercing his neck and spinning out the back of his head. The man collapsed, the shotgun roaring into the clouds. The shrew man ran forward firing his gun, but his grip on the slave's rope threw him off balance. He slipped and fell in the slop, his shots scattering. One bullet grazed Juarez in the arm, but not before the stout Mexican planted a boot square under the chin of the older bounty hunter.

The man tumbled backward, sliding in slimy grass, grabbing for his revolver in his belt, but Stew reached his own gun from the ground first. He fired, plugging the man's chest. The bounty hunter went limp. Stew swirled to take aim at the shrew man, but saw that he was already lying motionless in a mud-filled wagon rut, a bloody hole between his shoulder blades.

Gustav walked up out of the rainy gloom, his revolver in his hand. He kicked the skinny bounty hunter's body. The man made no movement, his eyes staring fixed. Their runaway Negro escaped into the gloom.

In seconds, guards were shouting from the fort walls and lookout platforms. Before Paul could turn around he heard thirty or so men racing toward him and his wranglers. Other soldiers stormed up the road from the encampment, all with rifles in their hands. The wranglers were soon encircled. In the downpour, Paul could not tell whom to address, so many men were shouting. A few lanterns covered with wide rain shields and held high on staves finally revealed a captain who strode to the center of the circle. He held up his hand and all became quiet. "How many are dead? I see one here."

"They's three dead bodies!" a voice called.

"Who can tell me what's happened?" the captain asked. He turned toward Paul.

Paul hesitated, looking at his wranglers who had dropped their guns and raised empty hands. Dozens of rifles pointed at them. Paul drug his boot in the mud. The rain was like a cataract, and his heart would not calm down. Then he heard Ben. "What's goin' on, Paul? Paul. Paul!"

Paul looked about the many stern faces staring at him, but could not find his brother hidden behind the crowd.

"I said," the officer reiterated, "who can tell me what's happened here? Tell me now or I'll pack the whole bunch of ya to the stockade."

An idea formulated in Paul's mind. "Yes," he said. He knew he could not tell anything close to the truth, so this new idea would have to work. He remembered what was in his inside shirt pocket. "Yes," he repeated. "These dead men are Yankee spies. They knew we were going to report them so they tried to kill us. But we got the best of them."

"Yankee spies? Prove it." The captain raised an eyebrow.

"Sure. We saw them the other day when we were bringing in our herd. They were talking with some bluecoats about fifteen miles back. One of the bluecoats handed the one-armed man a paper, a message. When they saw us, they all rode away. Vanished."

"And?"

"I don't think they expected to see us at the fort. They came in pretending' to be bounty hunters, but their nigger was creeping' around by the windows listenin' to what was being said inside headquarters. Our nigger here ran him off." He pointed at John.

"Sounds like a story. I'm not believin' ya." He directed some nearby soldiers. "You, take these men and shackle them to the floor in the storeroom. We'll have a hearing tomorrow and get to the truth."

"No, wait. I can prove it." Paul knew he had to pull off this part of his ruse perfectly. As the circle of men parted, he slowly made his way to the prone body of the one-armed bounty hunter. He bent down close to the mud-defiled corpse so as to hide his actions. He pretended looking through the pockets of the dead man, then carefully slid the paper from his own pocket that he had gathered from Asa's jacket at the burial. He held it up. "Here. Here's the proof."

He handed the torn page, half of a telegram, to the captain who covered it from the rain with his hat. He pulled a soldier holding a lantern closer, the light glancing off the telegram. He read it aloud, "Need more details. Signed. Captain Philip Sheridan, Quartermaster US Army of the Southwest."

"You see. They were Yankee spies. Whoever that Sheridan is, he wanted more details about the army here." Paul and the other wranglers held their breaths.

"Very well then," the captain stated. "You men did a service to our army. Thank you." He shook each of the wranglers' hands, except for John's. "Sergeant, select a burial detail. I'd just as soon burn these rats, but they're too wet." He raised his voice. "Let this be a lesson to all of ya that the enemy isn't just up there in St. Louis, but they're creeping around looking for ways to outfox us. Be on your guard. Be careful who you talk to. Now, all you men disperse." He turned to Paul again. "Can you write?"

"Yes sir, I can."

"Tomorrow morning, I want a written report I can give to General McCulloch." He turned on his heel and slogged his way behind the soldiers returning to the fort.

Ben joined Paul and his friends. "Paul, what's this all about?"

"I'll explain later."

"The tent is up and is cozy as a harlot's boudoir," Gustav offered.

"Yes," Paul said, "let's get out of this rain." He was not sure that his story would hold together. Morning would reveal.

TWENTY-FOUR

☙

THE PARTING

A fter their battle with the sanguinary bounty hunters, Paul had difficulty calming himself. He knew that the morning would tell the tale.

The wranglers sat on relatively dry cots inside a large tent. John sat on an empty nail keg. They had swaddled themselves in dry blankets pulled from a covered barrel. They shivered, though at least they were out of the rain. Paul sat in a corner, still re-living the episode in which he and his friends could have died. He agonized over how he should word the document the officer requested.

Ben carved at a hangnail with a knife.

Juarez struggled with the bloodied torn fabric of his shirt where the bullet had grazed the meat of his arm. Occasionally, he daubed the wound with a wet kerchief.

Gustav had spread juniper thresh thick over the muddy ground to make a suitable rug. Two lanterns glowed on stools in opposite corners. The men chewed on strips of dried beef, pickles, and wheat bread, and sipped ale from the town tavern.

Paul looked up to see each of the men were deep in their thoughts, having come so close to being killed and then almost being imprisoned. Paul, himself, felt undone, and his body shook not from the cold, but from realizing how close he had come to dying.

Only Ben had not faced imminent death. Paul shook his head, for Ben seemed oblivious as he took to whistling a tune, "The Water is Wide."

"I bought the tent for a pittance from the dry goods store in Fort Smith Town," Gustav announced, "and hired four privates to set it up for a nickel a piece. I purchased the barrel of blankets and the cots from a peddler living in a wagon on the street. He was drunk, so any price I offered was agreeable to him. He offered me his whore, too, but I turned him down. Her face could stop a clock. I do have my standards." He twisted his mustache.

Juarez and Stew sniggered.

"You did well purchasing this tent, Gustav," Paul said. "All of you have your pay now." He glanced around at his friends. "Our labors, my international band of misfits, are done. It's been a pleasure working with you. A Frenchman, a Mexican, and, Stew, correct me if I'm wrong, but don't you have some German in you?"

Stew nodded. "And Polish and Dutch and ..."

"And half burro, mi amigo," Juarez chimed in. "Muchas gracias for shooting those bad men. Muy malo hombres. You are a good shot, sí?"

"Well, I was aimin' to shoot the skinny one in his derriere, but Gustav beat me to it."

The men's initial snickers turned into laughter, Stew the most. Paul appreciated Juarez lightening the mood. Their day had been harrowing and he was grateful for the reprieve. He looked out the tent flap at a clearing of the rain clouds. Only drizzle fell.

He stood. "Tomorrow, us two Scotsmen, Ben and me, are putting our money in the bank in town. I encourage you to do the same. I've selected a good horse for John. Once he's safely on his way, Ben and I are enlisting. The rest of you are welcome to join, too. If we don't commit now, the war's likely to be over, and at any time in the future, if someone asks, we'll be able to say we did our part."

Stew, Juarez, and Gustav gave grunts of approval.

"Why you wanna do that?" John said, his voice tired and sorrowful. "Ain't nothin' gonna happen in the war but a whole lot of men dyin'."

The wranglers' eyes widened.

"Ain't no men gonna be dyin' except a whole bunch of Yankees," Ben responded.

John shook his head. "I know about war. They was a war in our county between two families what took to feudin'. No one won. They all died. Except one, and what did he have to live for? His kin folk's dead. His enemy family dead. He got on his horse one day and rode away. Ain't no one heard of him since."

Only Ben wagged his head. "Well, that ain't gonna be the way with this here war. One Confederate can whip a dozen Yankees."

Deep silence. To Paul, each of the wranglers appeared to retreat into his own world, one apart from their current situation. He looked at the dark-skinned man sitting across from him. He observed the man's smooth features, his balding scalp, and the skin tone showing through the threadbare clothes. John was as wet as any of them, he had worked as hard, and, at that moment, seemed a great deal wiser. Paul reflected on how John had saved Stew's life, pulled Asa's body out of the quicksand, and, by his quick thinking and skillful shooting, saved the lives of the lot of them. He wondered, *Did John draw the gun as a do or die fight against being thrown back into slavery or for a heartfelt desire to save them all?* He would never know the answer, but he still admired John Coincoin immensely.

"You know, John," Paul finally said, "you make a lot of sense, but sometimes... a man's got to stand for something, not just for staying alive, but be able to look his friends in the eye and say 'yeah, I did my part. I didn't hide because I wanted to live... I hope you understand that."

John made no answer, but looked piercingly into Paul's eyes.

"Makes no never mind what a darkie thinks," Ben said, full of his own piss and vinegar. "He'd make a pitiful soldier anyway."

"For me," Juarez said, "I go home to Mexico. I miss my señora. She miss me, too, I bet." He looked pensively out the open flap of the tent. The rain had abated and a few stars twinkled in the clearing sky. He wrapped a dry bandage around his arm wound and tied it off.

"I'll pass on joining the army," Gustav said. "I think I'll go to Canada. I have family there. I am not much interested in war. I am grateful for this drive I've shared with all of you." He grinned.

"Well," Stew smiled, "ain't no army gonna take a man my size anyway, so I'll go see if I can find a ranch or farm to work on. Who knows?"

Paul went to the lanterns and blew out the flames. "Good night, gentlemen." He spread his body out on his cot and put his hat over his head. Each of the others followed his lead and fell quickly to slumber, except for Ben who kept mumbling curses and threats enough to cover all Yankees in general.

In the morning, the wranglers sat naked with blankets about their bodies in the tent while their clothes dried on a line under a hot sun. When the captain who had accosted them the previous night came to their tent accompanied by General McCulloch, Paul secured the blanket around his waist and stepped out to explain to the general the aspects of their fight with the bounty hunters outside the fort.

"So, you had the wherewithal to kill some Yankee spies," General McCulloch said, "and saved us the trouble of a trial. I like your spine, McGavin. In fact, I've noticed your limp. You'd be of no use in a hard fight either to the infantry or much to the cavalry, and I need an additional adjutant. If you want it, I'll make you a lieutenant. Help me run my affairs. Can you write middlin fair?"

"Yes, sir. I can write clean and readable." Paul rubbed his scrabbly beard. "What do I do?"

"When your clothes are dry enough to wear, find this captain and he'll take care of getting you signed up and getting you a uniform. I need you in headquarters by this afternoon. Don't worry. You'll be busier than any other man in this army."

Paul grinned.

Dressed in dry clothes, Paul deposited Ben's and his silver in the Fort Smith town bank. He went to the horse corral and chose a sorrel gelding for John. He saddled the horse and led it by the reins to the tent.

John sat on a stump, trying on a pair of brogans Gustav had purchased for him. He wore a new pair of pants. When he saw Paul leading the prancing, snorting horse, he sprang up and raced to meet him. "You done mean it. You gi' me a horse and lettin' me go."

"Yes, Mr. Coincoin," Paul said, "slave of the white man, slave of a colored woman, expert shot, life saver, good… not just good, but really, damn good man. Yes, the horse is yours. I bought some parchment from one of the sutlers and wrote out this order that says you're a freeman. I think it looks official. So, you pretend it is if anyone asks." He handed John a folded paper.

John opened it and looked at the pen strokes. He merely nodded. "That be good for me."

"Do you know where you're headed, John?"

"To Ohio to begin with, then I don't know."

"Stay away from towns if you can. Go around. Move like you've got a purpose when you pass people by. Don't look afraid. And I'd ride fast as I could until you get to Illinois. In fact, there's a whole passel of Southern sympathizers in the south part of Illinois, so keep headin' north and east. That's when you'll find Ohio." He handed John a new rifle and a cartridge box with twenty rounds.

Gustav passed John a haversack, a rolled blanket, and a sack of cornmeal. Stew stuck a cook pan, hardtack wafers and a tin of lard in a saddle bag.

Juarez came up last. "Thees is my best rope. I want you own it, mi amigo." He hung the lariat on the saddle horn.

John shook all their hands. "Where is Ben?" he asked.

"Oh, I sent him on an errand," Paul replied. "I'll tell him you said goodbye. Now get on your way before I change my mind and make you join the Confederate army with Ben and me."

The wranglers chuckled. The idea so tickled Gustav that he bent over laughing. John mounted his steed looking proud. "So, I's really a free man."

"As free as you'll ever be," Paul said.

"I's gonna follow the drinkin' gourd. North." John turned the gelding and cantered it out to the Butterfield Stage Road.

"And thanks for everything you did for us," Paul said, though he knew John could not hear him. Under his breath, he said, "And thanks for making me a better man."

He hoped for good things for John, but considered that he may not get far before another band of bounty hunters trapped him. Now, he had to worry that his ruse about the dead bounty hunters was not found out. His spectacles had fogged, so he took them off and wiped them clean.

TWENTY-FIVE

FEW AND EVEN SCARCE VIRTUES

THE NEXT DAY, OCTOBER 11, 1861, 5 AM
CROSS HOLLOWS CONFEDERATE ENCAMPMENT

Sara awakened the next morning at the muffled jabbering of soldiers moving about the camp and the sound of firewood being stacked. Lying in abject darkness, a stab of fear racketed through her, remembering Richards' earlier proximity in the camp.

Then she remembered where she was, safe in the Louisiana Company K cabin, and that she had slept on a feather mattress. She wallowed in its softness. Warm under the blanket, the crisp morning air tickled her face. The room was dark as crow's feathers. Easing herself out of bed, she felt her way to the single window, peeled back the waxed paper, pushed open the shutter a measure, and peeked out at the dark mass of trees beyond the valley under a sky the color of lampblack. Night birds of some sort swooped and veered across the face of the moon.

Before her in the valley, men were already banking the coals under fresh kindling for breakfast fires.

To her far left a bugle signaled, and then another one closer to her, then three more, followed by an entire concerto of tootles and blaps throughout the camp. Upon her closing the window, a jumbled noise arose, the beating of shoe leather on hard ground and horses trotting back and forth. Men were jawing and hollering. The camp was quickly full awake.

Sara felt her way in the opaque room to her bed, drew out a stub of a candle and a match from her haversack and lit it. She soon had a smoky lantern glowing as well.

She got dressed, drawing the new corset around her and tying it in the back as best she could, and she wondered whether the undergarment would allow her to cache a small pistol.

After breakfast and the soldiers' morning rollcall and drill, Corporal Toutant located a spare Colt revolver for her as well as a small pocket pistol. He gave her a pouch with twenty rounds. Sara tucked the revolver in a saddlebag. The pocket pistol, an over-under, two-barrel device, and of miniature dimensions, she stuck in the top of her high-top shoe, snug. For that gun, she had but four rounds.

She practiced reaching for the revolver while sitting in the saddle should Richards or any of his sort show up again.

Sergeant Rabaneaux sauntered by while she was practicing and held out to her a sack of money. "De monsieurs, dey pitched in for you, Mademoiselle."

The various coins and Confederate paper added up to about forty dollars. Sara smiled and hugged the sergeant. "Tell every one of them thank you. And I have something for you." Sara brought forth the worn music box, wound it, and handed it to Rabaneaux. When he opened the lid, the tinkling melody sprinkled the air. He smiled and held the gift to his heart.

About mid-morning, she bade the men of Company K of Fourth Louisiana goodbye, Sergeant Rabaneaux bawling as if he were losing a daughter.

Sara headed out of the valley and toward the cavalry regiments, south of Fayetteville, camped on the Arkansas River.

The ride took longer than she figured, and she was bound up with worry. *What if Richards saw me? And is following me even now?* She could not shake her anxiety. She had fought off Bushwhackers at the barn and found courage to shoot one, plain and simple, but this disquietude was different, like wrestling with a demon in a dream.

She reached Fayetteville in a brisk afternoon and was astonished to see the clean, sturdy-looking town bustling with commerce. She stopped at Dindle's Bed and Café and purchased a sandwich and milk and then went to the dry-goods store and bought food for a week to store in her saddlebags. *Surely, I'll find Joseph within a week.*

Ferreting her way through the roadways south of town, overgrown with wildflowers and Joe Pie weeds, she at last topped a rise and beheld hundreds of horses grazing in a jumble of simple corrals. Evening was casting a taupe dullness to the tents and cabins, similar to those she had seen in Cross Hollows.

Soldiers carrying rifles were posted at each enclosure. In one corral, a dogged rider was subduing a bucking bronco. She came even with him at the fence about the time the horse settled into a mild trot, circling inside the rails. The rider doffed his bowler, and Sara wondered how he had not lost it in the ride. Other soldiers lined the fence.

She drew Esther to a halt, expectant to learn the whereabouts of her beloved. She dismounted and walked up behind a row of men hanging on the corral fence. "Ahem. I would like to inquire about a soldier. Might you be so kind and..."

"Well, lookie what we got here," a pock-cheeked private with ratty hair hanging about his face interrupted her. He jumped down and advanced, stopping a foot from her, sniffing. "Smells good, don't she? Much better than the whores in Van Buren." He looked back at his two companions who were stepping down from the fence. One of his buddies was as dark as saddle leather and had pale whitish-blue eyes, the other was stub-nosed with snot hanging off his mustache. Before Sara could react, the three were walking toward her, she backstepping.

Stubnose wiped the snot with his sleeve and advanced directly up within a foot of her and began snorting at her neck like a hog. Sara kept backing away but found herself pinned against a wall of a simple shed, the three surrounding her.

The pock-cheeked fellow lifted a handful of her hair. "What is it you're wantin' to ask us, sweet thing?"

"Excuse me," Sara choked out. "I was looking for someone, but you men obviously don't know him."

"How do you know we don't know him?" Pock-cheeked asked her.

By this time, the three had come within inches of her, leather-skin lifting her skirt with the tip of his boot.

"What's this?" a voice called from behind the three accosters. "You men step away. Now!"

The men retreated, bowed their heads, and gave half-hearted salutes to a captain in full dress uniform.

"You men, get back to your duties. Clean those stalls. That's an order."

The men slunk away like club-beat dogs, each taking a leering glance back at Sara.

"I am Captain Griggs of the Sixth Texas Cavalry. I apologize for the behavior of those two-legged reptiles. Not all are of so low a caliber, I assure you. We've had to curtail soldiers' visits to Van Buren or Fayetteville because of some of their tawdry behavior."

Sara, trembling, nodded. Gaining her breath, she said, "I'm looking for a cavalry soldier. He's a corporal. His name is Joseph Favor."

"What is your business with him?"

"He's my fiancé."

"Is he expecting you?"

"I think so. He invited me to come so we could make plans for the wedding." Sara felt her lie getting deeper.

"Well, he's not in our regiment. If I were you, I would head up to each regimental headquarters and inquire of him."

"I believe he's in the Third Texas."

"The Third! By thunder, young woman. The Third Texas is not here. They're all the way up in Missouri. I believe near Carthage or Springfield or some such. General McCulloch ordered them to guard against any Yankee advance. You have been misguided coming here."

Sara's heart sank. Curious soldiers were gathering in a loose circle around her and the captain. "Very well, Captain. Thank you for your valuable information. I shall make my way back to Fayetteville."

"It's getting late, Miss."

Sara turned to look where the final glow of the sunset had turned the high stratus to marmalade orange and pink.

"I have no place to stay other than there."

"Safe journey then, miss." Captain Griggs put a finger to his hat and directed the small crowd to leave.

Sara mounted Esther and headed at a trot into the tree-lined road toward Fayetteville.

In an hour, the moonless sky built a castle of dark around her, and every third tree looked like a frozen knight or goblin of a dark realm. She had slowed her mare to a gradual walk, and peered into the black cloak night.

Of a sudden, a hand grabbed Esther's halter, pulling the horse to a halt, then another hand held up a lantern, flipped the panel open and threw blinding light at Sara. "My, oh, my, it's a woman, Frederick," a male voice said.

Sara did the best she could to determine the threat of the man holding Esther. She immediately beheld a gentle, smooth-shaven face under a floppy-browed hat. He was smiling with benevolence.

A second figure stepped up to the other side of her and patted Esther's neck. "Easy girl," said an almost girlish voice. Looking at this new person in the glimmering lantern light and her eyes adjusting, she saw that he was perhaps a boy of eleven or twelve. He and the older fellow wore Confederate gray jackets and had rifles slung on their backs. Neither looked malicious.

"I say, lady," said the older one, "we didn't mean to alarm you, but if we hadn't a stopped you, you might've, in this dark, sailed right off a cliff on this useless excuse for a road. Are you all right?"

Sara was speechless at first. "Yes, I'm trying to get back to Fayetteville. And I...."

"Not tonight you're not. Trust us, we mean you no harm, but you need to stop here and take your rest. We've a fine cabin about a rod over yonder. Name's Junior." He extended his hand.

Slowly, Sara extended her hand and shook his.

"This is my brother, Frederick. We're new recruits in the Cause for Southern Rights."

"Pleased to meet you," Sara said.

"Pleased to meet you." Junior was already pulling Esther by the halter along a bush-heavy path.

Sara held her breath, unsure of these two rovers who had crossed her path. The younger boy walked behind the horse, whistling *The Arkansas Traveler*. Were these two a welcome reprieve? Sara was unsure, and she slid her hand into her open saddlebag and felt the Colt's hard steel, her finger found the trigger.

In a moment, Junior held up the lantern to reveal a sorry, unpainted shack, the roof partially collapsed. No porch, no corn crib, just a shabby dwelling.

"This is it," Junior announced. "This is where you can stay."

"I'm not sure I want to stay in there. It looks like it will fold in on itself at any moment."

'It's safe enough, and there's a bed." Seeing Sara's face, he said, "And don't worry, Frederick and me gonna sleep out under the stars, it bein' such a pleasant evenin'."

He extended his hand. Sara took it and dismounted. She immediately unlaced the saddlebag that held her revolver.

"Frederick," Junior said, "take this lady's horse by the hayrick yonder."

Sara saw no hayrick. "Wait, I need my things. And don't take my mare far." Her thoughts were conflicted, not sure whether to accept these pleasantries.

"Certainly," Junior said. "Frederick'll tie the horse yonder at that elm."

Sara slung the saddlebags over her shoulder and carried her haversack and rifle. She watched Frederick tie Esther and remove the saddle and blanket. He lay them at the foot of the tree. She followed Junior into the one room dwelling. *At least it has wooden floors.* The lantern light glanced off the wall, and when the young man turned around, he appeared no more than fourteen. He gave a glowing smile.

"This is your home tonight. The bed's there. Wash stand by it."

Sara saw a board frame with a corn husk mattress stretched across crisscrossed ropes with two pillows. Under a shutter-less square gap in the walls that may have been meant for a window, her eyes alighted on sacks of corn with holes nibbled in the bottom where varmints had gained entrance. Beside the corn sacks were two large wood tubs and some copper coils leading into a metal caldron sitting on a stove.

"So, you make moonshine for the soldiers," Sara said. She knew the small pistol that had bothered her foot all day was shoved in her laced shoe. She could reach it if needed.

"No, ma'am. Us and Pap make our livin' helpin' the poor soldiers with their aches and pains with our elixir of health. We call it juice. Isn't that right, Frederick?"

"Mmm mmm," Frederick said, just entering.

"Where is your pap?" Sara could not hide her trepidation.

"Oh, he's off some a where's a dealin' the juice." Junior stood taller at that remark. "Won't be back 'til tomorrah night. He told us to be hospitable to whoever come up, soldier or commoner. And you're a commoner I'll wager, so we're bein' hospitable."

Sara relaxed her guard a little.

"Here," Junior said, pushing Frederick out of his way, "I'll let you sample some of our juice." He grabbed a bottle from a collection on the floor and pulled the cork. "Here you are. You must be thirsty and worn from your travels."

Sara hesitated.

"It's just juice, honest. Like apple cider." He poured himself a dram in a tin cup and quaffed it off.

Thunder rumbled, and the initial drops of a rainstorm plopped on the roof. Not wanting to appear ungrateful for the hospitality, pitiful as it was, and not relishing spending a dark night drenched to the skin, she took the bottle and drank a swig. It was very smooth, a musky apple spice concoction. Unlike any liquor or wine she had ever tasted.

"It's tasty," she said.

"Sure, it is," Junior said.

"Sure, it is," Frederick echoed.

"Have all you want." Junior lifted her hand with the bottle to her lips. "We have plenty."

Sara took another drink, smooth and soothing to her dry throat.

"Well, you make yourself to home now. There's a candle on the bureau by the bed. We're gonna leave you now. 'Til the mornin', and we'll see you on your way."

Then the youths were gone, and all was dark. Their footsteps bled slowly away. Sara felt her way to the side of the bed and found the candle and matches on a crude drawer structure that Junior had called a bureau. The rain increased to a steady shower. Lightning flashed regularly.

Sara took out some jerky from a saddlebag and gnawed on it. Having nothing else to drink, other than walking outside and holding her tongue to the rain, she sipped on the mellow brew. She leaned her rifle against the wall in easy reach and slid her saddlebags under the bed. Rising, she began to feel dizzy and overly sleepy. She tried to unlace her shoes but fell back onto the pillows. The candle dwindled down until it guttered and put itself out, and she slept hard.

When Sara awoke, the sun shone bright through the torn gap in the wall, rainwater still dripping from the eaves. She blinked, rubbed her eyes, and sat up. She noticed that the sacks of corn, the tubs and copper tubing, cauldron and bottles were no longer in the room, though a rat scurried around feeding on the dribble. Her exhaustion overtook her, and she lay back on the bed. *Where are the pillows?*

She stood quickly, swooning considerably, then knelt to look under the bed. Her saddlebags, haversack, and rifle were gone. She wobbled like a top to the wall breach. Rain had blown in through the opening and slopped the floor. Looking out, she saw that Esther was gone. She traversed the floor in a zigzag fashion to the yard and called for her mare.

After searching the vicinity for a considerable time and treading through mud over the tops of her shoes, she stormed back inside, slamming the door.

She was dithered like a small bird with a claw caught in a cobweb as to any strategy to pursue.

Then she noticed the paper underneath the bottle. Some of the liquid sloshed inside when she lifted it. She wondered what else besides liquor was in the juice. The note read: *Sorry Lady. Pap came home early. His figuring is your horse and your things would be just enough to pay rent for the room. The pistol is mighty comely. Junior*

Sara clenched her fists. She stepped out on the porch and stopped long enough to take a long draft from rainwater dribbling from the roof, then tore off in the direction she hoped the thieves had taken Esther. Though hoof prints were going in both directions in the muddy road. She guessed they would not go toward the encampment because soldiers would recognize the horse was hers. She surmised they went toward Fayetteville, there to sell and make a handy profit.

Despite the sludge of the road, Sara ran at a steady pace.

TWENTY-SIX

☯

SCOURGE AND MERCY

OCTOBER 12, 1861, NOON
SOUTH OF FAYETTEVILLE, ARKANSAS

S ara had run for miles trying to chase down the thieves who stole Esther and her means of living. She was winded, and the mud-slogged road made her pursuit laborious. She had seen nothing to indicate that she was even on the right track. She felt drained of purpose and will.

All her belongings were gone — her food, her books, her rifle and revolver, and her dear horse, Esther. *Why would men be so crass to do that to a woman? What manner of creature are they?* Her mouth felt like it was filled with cornmeal, her legs and lungs burned. Covered with mud that had spattered even up to her face, she deemed herself a slattern, a woe-body.

Then she spied the spring. Just off the road in a little rock outcropping, the water bubbled up amidst emerald moss and some late-blooming purple daylilies and yarrow. She went to it and drank several handfuls of water. At length, feeling some relief, she sat on a mossy rock and looked at the once beautiful dress, now splotched brown from mud.

All of a sudden, she heard a horse galloping. *Perhaps that's Esther, escaped!*

She sprang to her feet and raced to see the horse, but becoming aware that the rider may not be a friendly one, she hid behind a tree. The galloping was at a reckless pace. Sara peeked around to see. The saddled horse was rider-less. It sped down the road, breathing its steady pant, disappearing out of sight.

Sara stepped out onto the road and gazed in the direction the horse had run.

Turning, her face came up against a deerskin jacket, hung over a half-open shirt, revealing a hairy chest, heaving. Raising her eyes, she beheld the scarred scowl of B. Franks Richards. With stringy black hair hanging over his grizzled face, his red, peeled lips spread into a vile sneer. "I've been following you since you left the camp, Sesech. Thought I'd lost you. I circled back the next morning after I saw you with them Louisianans, and trailed after you when you left, but my horse threw a shoe. Hell of a thing. But now, here you are on foot." He took hold of strands of her honey-golden hair. "Now, we meet again, Sesech. Just old acquaintances."

Sara's every fiber yelled *run*, but she knew she could not escape him.

Richards whistled, and his horse trotted up to stop a few feet from them. He smirked. "I learned that little diversion of a horse without a rider from some Dakota Indians. Well, now. You're looking mighty dirty here. You need a bath. Let me take you over here and we'll get this filthy dress off you."

Sara was juddering now, but a fresh thought blew the bellows into the fire of her courage and anger. She glared at her captor. She was *not* going to be despoiled. "Oh, please, don't hurt me." Making her voice full of lament and bending down, her hand went to her shoe.

"I don't have any desire to hurt you," he bellowed an insolent chortle. "At least, not yet." He grabbed her hair, pulling hard, and slapped her cheek.

Cringing from the pain, Sara saw him bending his head back in a belly laugh.

She rose.

When Richards looked down, he instantly saw Sara's pocket pistol, cocked, flush against his bare chest. "Well, isn't that a pretty toy. Why don't you put that little thing away and we'll...?"

"This toy will kill you at this range just as sure as a cannon shot." Sara's words were piercing.

He raised his hands. "Very well, you win, sweet one."

"You call me that one more time, and I'll dispatch you right now. Drop your revolver. Fingertips only."

Richards gently lifted his revolver from its holster and tossed it a few feet away. Sweat beaded on his brow, the color spent from his cheeks. "I tell you what. I'll just get on my horse and never bother you again. How about that?"

"Go!" Sara followed him, the pocket gun thrust in his back. When she passed his revolver, she picked it up and aimed it at Richards while he slowly gathered himself into the saddle. He looked back at her and saw his own gun pointed at him. "Don't let that thing go off. You wouldn't want to kill a man."

"Try me." Sara cocked the hammer.

Richards lowered his arms and laid a hand on the butt of his Springfield rifle.

"You touch that gun and I'll blow you apart," Sara said. "Ride south."

Richards took hold of the reins, then shook them. The horse trotted away at a good clip.

When he was out of sight, Sara plunged into the woods and ran as far from the road as she imagined was safe. She dared not approach the road. All she could think of was why she had shown him any mercy. *Why didn't I kill the rat? I have no answer. I have no answer. Now I must run and hide. God forgive me, I wish him dead.* Her mind toiled for hours about her mistake in not shooting Richards dead.

TWENTY-SEVEN

DOES THE EAGLE FLY AT YOUR COMMAND?

SAME DAY, OCTOBER 12, 1861, LATE AFTERNOON
SOUTH OF FAYETTEVILLE, ARKANSAS

S ara fought her way through undergrowth so thick with vines she reckoned it would have made a respectable spider web. Branches reached out and grabbed at her clothing. Other branches threaded out like the arms of an octopus, entwining in her hair and tearing at it. She knew she had left numerous strands in the tangles. Copious vines wrapped about her legs and spilt her in a tumble several times. Burrs collected about her dress.

She dared not try to attain the road, for surely Richards would be searching for her.

Why didn't I bust Richards wide open? Why'd I not kill the sorry dastard?

Evening was closing, and she had not eaten since the morning before. The last water she had drunk was at the little spring just before Richards accosted her. Her dress was rent in the front and back, her face, arms and legs scratched and bleeding. The small pistol she had shoved back in her shoe was lost when she scrambled under a thorn-spiked bush. She held Richard's revolver in a slap-dash fashion.

Often, she had to climb over, or crawl under, bushes crammed together and threaded tight by vines. Her efforts were thwarted again and again by undergrowth so dense she had to veer for yards and yards around just to find some path forward.

She was becoming fully aware that everything she owned, save the wretched clothes she wore, were now gone, probably forever.

She collapsed onto a murky stream and could not bring herself to rise. She lay listening to the conversation of the creek, trebling over round stones and crushed leaves, little words of "give up, sleep now." She tried to lap up the water, but it tasted foul, and she spit it out.

Having been possessed of unbridled hope when she first began the search for her horse and the thieves, she believed she would indeed catch them, then throttle them one by one. Her persistence would prevail. Now though, every hope was dashed, every sense of a decent future crushed. Her life had become a husk of its former self.

Pursuing a zig-zagged course in what she hoped was the direction toward Fayetteville, she continued more out of obsession than for any logical reason.

Passing through a small break in the underbrush and tree canopy, she caught sight of the road about forty yards to her right. Watching the road, she crashed against a compact, trimmed hedgerow of juniper bushes, finely shaped, reaching taller than her head. She could see nothing on the other side, but heard, beyond the hedge, the unmistakable sound of bubbling water.

Not anticipating anything, but hoping to quench her thirst, she surged through the hedgerow and sprawled face-first on a lush grass lawn.

"Who goes there?" yelled a shrill, harpy-like voice. "I'll have you tell me who you are. I shall call my man and he will shoot you down."

Sara looked up wearily, though she did not know the source of the voice. Too exhausted to stand, she croaked, "It's just me. May I have some water?"

"What is your name, child?" Shoe leather clicked on a rock walkway.

Sara also heard the knock of a cane. She raised her head but a little and looked at polished, high top shoes and a long midnight blue dress. The woman began poking Sara in the side with her cane.

"Get up!" the woman demanded. "Who are you?"

"Water," Sara murmured.

A sharp-heeled shoe stepped on her hand holding the revolver. The shoe kicked the revolver away. "Billie Sue," yelled the voice. "Where are you, child?"

"I's right here Missus Fairchild." A voice with the pleasant tone of silk stroked over burlap, soft but scratchy, was racing closer.

Sara saw dusty brown feet and ankles and the ragged hem of a simple dress.

"I's here, Missus Fairchild."

"See who this creature is. I can tell she's a girl, but not much else," Mrs. Fairchild said.

"Yes, ma'am." A kind, brown, freckled face showed next to Sara's bleary eyes. "Missus Fairchild, this poor woman is terrible injured. She all cut up and bruised, and her dress be torn to shreds. Oh, my!"

A second face, bending from above, came within inches of Sara's. The face was of an older, but not unattractive woman, her eyes coated white. "Do you think she's dangerous, Billie Sue?"

"No, ma'am. She terrible hurt. Poor chil'."

"Well, bring her inside. Posthaste. And where's that Theophilus? He better not be hidin' again."

"He here. I round him up."

Sara closed her eyes. When she opened them again, she was being carried by a muscular Negro, his sweaty odor ripe, but his arms strong, and his hold gentle. In her field of vision, she beheld a manicured lawn, a bubbling fountain with crusted, green, moss-covered statues, and a two-story brick edifice and a huge oak door. She drifted to a fatigued stupor.

When she awoke, she was aware that hands were lifting her head and pouring water into her mouth. Nothing had ever tasted so good to her, and she attempted to guzzle it. The hands steadied her head back onto a soft pillow. She sank into the comfort. Her eyes still closed, she became aware of calloused, but gentle hands softly touching the scratches and gashes on her body, applying an agreeable, mint-scented ointment. Her clothing had been removed, and she was lying uncovered.

Suddenly aware of her nakedness, she opened her eyes with a start. The young Negro woman was the only person in the room and was tending to Sara's wounds. She smiled. "Oh, there you are. I's so glad to see you awake. You been sleepin' a while now. I's Billie Sue. What's yor name?"

Sara smiled and closed her eyes, but could offer no reply. Billie Sue pulled the sheet over Sara's lower body. She ran her hands gently up to the side of Sara's right breast, just under the arm, and Sara became aware that the woman was pulling a thorn from deep in her skin. It came free, stinging. Sara had so many injuries, she had not even noticed the thorn. Billie Sue cleaned the wound with a damp, soapy rag, applied the mint salve, and pulled the sheet to Sara's shoulders.

"My name is Sara Reeder," Sara said. "Thank you so much, Billie Sue."

"Oh, she's awake!" Mrs. Fairchild called from the hall and hastened into the room, then knocked into the bedside. She leaned into Sara's face. "Your voice sounds young, child. How old are you?'

"Seventeen, ma'am."

"I heard your name is Sara Reeder." The woman smelled of heavy perfume and liniment. Sara searched the gray-haired woman's smooth face, bereft of wrinkles save a few crows' feet, indicating she had seldom smiled or frowned in her life. Her high-collared dress was of a burgundy silk with many refinements.

Sara stole a glance around the lamp-lighted room. Four large lamps sat on corner tables. A polished and brocaded wardrobe sat across from her. Fine furniture rested about the room. Elegant paintings of bucolic countrysides adorned the walls. Lace curtains hung at the windows.

"Well, is your name Sara Reeder?" Mrs. Fairchild demanded.

"Yes." Sara's mouth was still dry.

"How do you spell it?"

"S-A..."

"Your last name, dolt! Why would I wish the spelling of your first name?" Mrs. Fairchild hmphed.

"R-E-E-D-E-R."

"That's incorrect. It should have an 'a' after the first 'e'."

"But that's how my family spells it. I'm so tired and sore. May I have some more water?"

"In a moment. Why were you in my yard? Are you a common bandit, bent on robbing me at the point of gun?"

Billie Sue handed Sara a glass of water. Sara held the sheet to her neck and sat up to gulp the water. "No, ma'am. I was the one robbed. They took my horse, my food, my money...."

"Can you read, child?"

"Yes, ma'am, I can."

"Leave us, Billie Sue. Attend to your chores." Mrs. Fairchild drew up a chair and sat on it, erect and proper, her hands on her knees.

Billie Sue exited, closing the door.

"You smell of mud and muck, as putrid as anyone I've smelled, dear one." Mrs. Fairchild's tone softened, though still ringing. "My name is Edwina Fairchild. You may stay here and get better on one condition. As you can see, these cataracts on my eyes, these plates of white film, have made it so I cannot read. Nor can I see all the pretty things I own. I can barely see you. Oh, the surgeons applied all manner of salves and drops, but they only made it worse."

"Yes, ma'am." Sara was near to swooning, but she did her best to pay attention to the woman.

"My husband and I never had children. I used to read all the time, for what else was there to do in this big house? It gave me such pleasure. Then, when I could read no more beginning two years ago, my late husband read to me. That is, until he died riding one of his stallions from his stable. He was so impetuous. He thought the eagle flew at his command. It threw him and broke his neck. He's buried in the backyard by the fountain. I was there visiting his grave when you startled me almost to my death, crashing onto my lawn." Mrs. Fairchild halted her monologue. Sara could tell she was endeavoring to assuage a desire to cry.

"I'm sorry, ma'am."

"Yes, well, here's the condition for your remaining here. You must read to me whatever I want you to and whenever I want."

"That would suit me dearly. I was going to say the criminals who made off with my horse, food, and rifle also stole my books. I would love to read to you."

"Excellent. You begin work in the morning. You can tell me the dire details of your travail later, though I cannot say I will pay much attention, but I will give you that deference." Mrs. Fairchild stood, her demeanor once again sharp. "Billie Sue! Why have you not fed this woman? Where is that soup?" She careened from the room, bumping furniture and the doorway, but walking as fast as a sighted person.

Sara slumped back onto her pillow. The bruises and torn skin were making her nauseous. She could only count her losses—her horse, all her belongings, her beloved books, her Bible. She had the devastating realization she would probably never see Joseph. *I tried so hard.* She turned her head into the pillow and bawled.

In the morning, Sara found even the slightest movements difficult, for every muscle seemed to ache, and the bruise on her cheek where Richards had smacked her made her whole head hurt. She weaved downstairs to the kitchen where Billy Sue and the other household slaves made a fuss over her. She was fed a sumptuous breakfast, after which she felt a bit strengthened.

Billie Sue took to massaging Sara's shoulders and back. Sara's breaths came easier.

Mrs. Fairchild stormed into the kitchen. "Sara, you have one hour to prepare yourself to read. If you are to dwell here, you are to work. Wounded or not." The woman turned on her heel, hands outstretched in front of her, and tottered into the front foyer and stood before a window.

"She ain't lookin' at nothin'," Billie Sue whispered. "She just rememberin'."

One hour later, Sara sat in the mansion's parlor and read to Mrs. Fairchild until her voice gave out. The entire time, the woman leaned back in her chair, her cold ice eyes staring up into nothing. Finding her demeanor at first disconcerting, Sara grew used to it and enjoyed reading a new fiction as well as a treatise on spirituality.

TWENTY-EIGHT

IT'S NOT ENOUGH FOR A MAN TO KNOW HOW TO RIDE, HE MUST KNOW HOW TO FALL

OCTOBER 15, 1861
FORT SMITH, ARKANSAS

On a crisp autumn morning two weeks into October, Private Ben McGavin, now serving in McCulloch's army, stood ready to mount a mean-spirited, un-broke stallion in a Fort Smith corral. The horse snorted, jerked, and kicked over and over.

Another private held the rope that tethered the horse tight to a post in the middle of the corral, its nose almost touching the post. A third soldier held a cloth over the horse's eyes and tried to keep his feet from being tromped on by the angry horse. Ben walked confidently toward the horse and put his left hand through the reins and onto the saddle horn, the right on the saddle pommel, left foot in a stirrup. The horse jigged a little, sensing Ben's presence.

Hesitating only a moment, Ben swung lithely into the saddle, and the soldier holding the rope released the hasp on the halter. His partner removed the cloth, and both men ran for the fence.

The horse, with Ben clinging to the saddle horn and mane, bucked, pranced, and leaped, and then raced the circle of the fence before stopping and bucking again, all four legs air-born. Ben stayed in the saddle, his movement fluid, as if he were skimming rapids in a canoe. A hundred Confederates hanging on the fence and perched on roof tops cheered.

General McCulloch sat in the shade of a porch watching the young recruit calm the horse. Beside him, Paul McGavin, now adjutant to the general, leaned against a nearby post.

"Lieutenant McGavin, your brother is a remarkable rider," General McCulloch called over the raucous shouting.

"Yes, sir, he is," Paul called back.

"Clearly, he commands the respect of these men after only a few days here."

"If he doesn't get his head broke getting thrown off. Sometimes, he doesn't know when to quit."

"With the horse before this one, he got thrown off five times. And every time, he got back on." General McCulloch chuckled. "I'd wager he *never* quits."

"Yes, sir." Paul was often amazed by his brother's horse skills. He had quickly adjusted to and even enjoyed the new army life. His wranglers had gone their separate ways, and though he missed their camaraderie, he had gained new confidence in his own worth. General McCulloch looked to him for attending to many paperwork issues, freeing up the lead adjutant, Colonel Armstrong, for other duties. He was respected and saluted by privates and corporals. He liked that.

The bronco finally relented of its bucking, and Ben galloped it around the circumference of the corral, reined it, and trotted it the opposite direction. The cheers exploded, subsiding only when Ben finally dismounted and handed the reins to a private. He took off his gloves and chaps, and said, "I'm done for today. Five horses are enough." He paced his bowlegged walk across the corral, jumped on the fence, and sat atop it. He saw Paul and the general and smiled a toothy grin.

"What ya quitting for, Ben?" Paul yelled.

"I ain't quittin'. I'm just hungry." He jumped from the fence. He sauntered up to Paul and the general and saluted.

"Your brother tells me, Private McGavin," General McCulloch said, "that you boys grew up in northwest Arkansas before moving to Texas. Is that so?"

"Yes, sir," Ben said. "We grew up there, rode all over kingdom come. Hunted. Tracked and killed bears and even tracked some Indians. Not to kill 'em, just to say we did it."

"So, you'd say you know the terrain pretty well."

"Yes, sir, all up and down the Boston Mountains from here around the fort to Sugar Creek and on up as far as St. Louis, Missouri."

"I'd have to agree there's not a trail or broken path we haven't traveled," Paul added.

General McCulloch stroked his beard, reflecting. "Very well, then. I'm promoting you, Ben McGavin, to corporal. You and your brother will ride with me as my scouts. I need someone who really knows these parts. But you must show me your mettle. If you can scout and report as good as you bust broncs, then the army may fare better against the Yanks when they come our way."

"Yes, sir. Thank you, sir," Ben said. "But beggin' the general's pardon, I'm really hungry."

"Eat hearty, my *cowboy* scout. We leave this evening. It's jerky and hardtack for quite a while. Lieutenant McGavin, you and your brother make ready to ride. Pick your finest horse. Have Major Clarke issue the new stripes and new pistols, a Springfield, and a saber apiece."

"What about Ben breaking the rest of the horses?" Paul asked.

"Someone will step up. This is the army. If they crack a few bones, then so be it. The sooner we get going, the sooner we may end this war."

TWENTY-NINE

∞

MUFFLE THE DRUM

OCTOBER 20, 1861, 8 AM
SOUTHWEST OF FREDERICKTOWN, MISSOURI

When Lucas and Workman arose in the barn the next day, the runaway slaves had moved on in their escape. Workman discovered Elisheba and Balthazar had gone as well.

The storm had turned the road into an impassable mire. They could not leave.

Workman spied a lone chicken strutting about the barn. He chased it down, his long arms flapping around like a scarecrow in the wind. He grabbed hold of the chicken's neck, gave it a rapid, spinning yank, and the body popped loose from the head. The bloodied torso flopped about for a few minutes and ultimately stopped. Workman boiled a pot of water, dunked the carcass in the pot. The feathers came loose easily with a few tugs. After splitting the chicken with a large knife and removing the giblets, he dredged the pieces in rye flour and salt and dropped the pieces in a pan of bubbling hot grease.

Lucas baked some pone with the last of their cornmeal in the hot coals.

They dined on their first cooked meal in a week. "Directly," Workman said, patting his full stomach, "I'll pursue us some game. We're delayed here anyway. Might as well make use of the day."

When Workman returned from his successful hunt with a tiny shoat in a tow sack, the two men worked together to dress the pig, roast the pork, and boil out the lard for soap.

When evening approached, they sat in the window of the barn loft, their legs dangling, and enjoyed a fair view of a vermillion-streaked sunset. Their vantage point afforded them a view of some distance out to the road and beyond.

About midday of the next day, the road was still too muddy to risk traveling it. They climbed the loft again and were telling stories of their war experiences. Workman heard the distant rattle of a drum and held up his hand, then pointed out the hayloft window.

They witnessed a column of Federal infantry toiling its way up the road that had become a half-mile wide bog of rainwater and mud. The troop was forced to slow and march either into the marshy fields or, with great care, through the sloppy road. The soldiers fanned out.

Workman climbed down and strolled out to watch more closely. He stood on a rock outcropping and called to a lieutenant inching his horse through the mush, "What outfit you with?"

"Eleventh Missouri," came the pinched reply, for the man's horse was struggling in the sludge.

"The rain last night was like the Bible's mighty deluge," Workman pronounced.

"And this swamp they call a road is like the Red Sea flood."

"I'd liken it to that. Where you headed?"

"What I know," the sergeant replied, "is that the rebel General Jeff Thompson and some Missouri guards, is up the road a piece toward Ironton and Fredericktown. We're aspirin' to send 'em a runnin'." He jerked hard on his horse's reins to keep it from stepping in a deep hole.

"Who's your commanding officer?"

"You answer me first why you ain't in this army helpin' us fight the Rebs?"

"The consumption," Workman faked a cough. "Army won't take me." By this time, Workman was hollering at the soldier going away.

The lieutenant nodded as though he figured as much. "To answer your question, General Grant is the man leads the army from Cairo, Illinois. He sent us out to squash the insurrectionists. He has no benevolence toward them. The regiment's colonel is Panabaker."

He said something else that Workman could not hear for more horses and foot soldiers slogged through the sucking mud, causing a calamitous noise.

When Lucas and Workman resumed their journey the next day, the sound of battle coming from the direction of Fredericktown was evident miles away. They pulled off the road and waited. Late in the afternoon, a dozen Missouri Guard Confederates, unburdened by their weapons, came rushing past them, obviously fleeing. A tiny drummer boy did his best to keep up with the men and to muffle his drum. When Workman called to them, they did not respond but continued their trot down the road.

"Looks like the war has followed us here," Lucas said.

THIRTY

༄

COURAGE BY NECESSITY

TEN DAYS LATER, OCTOBER 30, 1861, DUSK
SPRINGFIELD, MISSOURI

T wo companies of Colonel Greer's regiment clustered on a hill just outside the sleepy town, watching the movement of Union soldiers on the streets.

In the waning daylight, the Confederates stooped low, hidden in a copse of trees and underbrush. Their horses were tied half a mile back.

Joseph, his vigor returned after his bout with the measles, crouched with an advance force of ten cavalrymen ahead of the rest of the troop. He knew that Springfield had been again occupied by Federal troops, this time under the command of General Freemont, the Pathfinder. He wondered what their mission was.

Not far from Joseph, Captain Henche Mabry and Captain Alf Johnson both sat on their haunches, hidden behind scrabbly bushes, observing the town made quiet by the army's curfew.

Joseph knelt behind a fallen tree watching Federal soldiers tread about the streets. With the night closing around them, jack-o-lanterns, their candles flickering in the grotesque grins, sat on a few porches.

Not a hundred strides away, a Union sentry coughed and adjusted his rifle noisily. Captain Mabry, his chubby face smiling, whispered to the small group, "I know a prosperous woman in that house yonder who could probably tell us a great deal about the Yanks' comin's and goin's. She's been to our camp before with valuable information she'd garnered. If we can get down there, I'd like to see her again."

"I'm sure you would," Captain Alf Johnson, short and strong-muscled, whispered back. Tobacco juice dribbled down his chin. He wiped it with his sleeve. "She's a durn site prettier than any females I've seen lately."

"Why you lookin' at the married laundresses in camp?" Mabry shoved Johnson in the shoulder.

"I ain't lookin' at them. I'm watchin' the officer's mistresses that come callin'."

Joseph wondered if the Union picket could hear their chatter. He glanced at the blue-clad soldier who was yawning. Directly, the soldier slumped to the ground and leaned against a tree, pulling his cap over his eyes.

"See that," Mabry stroked his short chin beard. "The Yanks ain't expectin' nothin'. Now's our chance to get down to Miss Lowry. We'll be able to give a good report to Colonel Greer from what she tells us."

Johnson nodded. "All right. But wait, we don't need all these men comin' with us."

Captain Mabry eyed the eight other men. "All we need is a lookout."

He pointed at Joseph. "You, Corporal Favor."

"Yes, sir."

"You be our lookout whilst Captain Johnson and I converse with our spy." He turned to the remaining soldiers. "You, there." He pointed at a private. "Make your way back to the rest of the men up yonder. Tell 'em to stay put. We may be an hour or more. The rest of you men keep a sharp watch, too. If you see some Federals approaching that house yonder, you give a whistle to this corporal. Understood?"

The men nodded. The private slunk away to the rest of the cavalry.

"Very well," Captain Mabry whispered. "Come on, Johnson. You, too, Favor."

The captains crept out of the bushes and past the sleeping Yankee guard. Joseph followed close. With pebbles clattering down the hill with each step they took, the three descended to the end of the street to the backside of a leaning shanty, its paint peeling, a trickle of smoke coming from its chimney. Their backs to the house wall, they pulled their revolvers. Captain Mabry peered around the corner. A Union infantry company was marching farther into town and turned the corner out of sight. After they had disappeared, the captain motioned for Joseph and Johnson to follow him.

Alert to any movement, their spurs jangling, they crossed the street to a well-lit house, neither grand nor mundane, but with filigreed lattice along the roof's edge. The light of the home spilled from the shade-less windows into lighted rectangles stretching into the dusty street. From inside, a piano was playing.

On the porch, Captain Mabry rapped lightly on the door. "Annabelle Lowry. It's Henche Mabry. Let us in."

The sun had drifted below the hills, early stars sparkling. Joseph peered out into the dark street, watching for any blue-coats, and listened hard for any approaching steps. His heart had lumped into his throat, his breaths were short.

When no one answered the door, the three men took turns, peering through a front window at a gentlewoman in the parlor, playing a soft waltz. Captain Mabry stepped off the porch and looked in a side window. When he came back, he accidentally kicked a jack-o-lantern and sent it tumbling into the street a good twenty paces. "Damn it all," he said aloud.

A nearby dog launched into a barking tirade, followed by a chorus of yips and howls from other dogs up and down the long street.

A pretty woman's face appeared in the window. She gave an expression of recognition of Captain Mabry, and she swiftly opened the door. The house had a warm, inviting interior, filled with lamps topped by pretty, brocaded lampshades, thick-cushioned armchairs, and the piano.

Beyond was a dining table under a chandelier. The table was laden with mounds of food — a dinner party. A Negro maid entered the dining room from the kitchen and placed a platter of ham on the table.

The woman of about thirty years with curly blond hair leaned out the door and fairly sang her greeting. "Captain Mabry. Henche, how good to see you."

Suddenly, a half-dozen guests dressed in their finery entered from the kitchen, laughing and chattering. The woman tugged the captain's sleeve, then stopped him short, placing her delicate hand on his face. "These are all *our* people. You needn't worry."

She removed her hand and stepped back from the door. Captains Mabry and Johnson swept into the house and removed their hats with a flourish. Several huzzahs and welcoming comments came from the dinner party group.

Captain Mabry turned to Joseph. "Favor, if some filthy Yanks come near, three knocks." He banged his knuckles on Joseph's chest. "Got it?"

"Yes sir." Joseph saluted. The captain returned the salute and shut the door. Joseph stood on the porch, a new north breeze blowing. The door had been open long enough that he could smell ham, roast duck, pumpkin, nutmeg, and cloves. His mouth watered.

He took a position, crouching behind a large potted geranium bush on the porch.

The twilight rolled into moonless night, and the first blasts of a cold front signaled, sending the houses' weathervanes twirling. Joseph became aware of thuds and clangs and yells throughout the town and recognized the sounds of the Union army camp outside the town.

He looked up the hill where the Confederate cavalry was somewhere waiting. He saw nothing on the hill, only cavernous black. *Where are the rest of our troops?*

Most of the homes down the long street had doused their lights by eight. Only the two-story brick building in the distance where the narrow street met the main street remained well-lit. The edifice's windows glowed. Joseph could just make out shadowy silhouettes pacing back and forth in each window. A hundred or so more men clustered below. He could not determine the purpose of the building nor the doings of the men, save that he sometimes heard raucous laughter emanating from the place.

Twice, a lone sentry paced halfway down the street in the direction where Joseph patiently waited. Then the sentry marched back.

The night toiled on. From inside the spy's house, Joseph heard silverware clacking on plates and light conversation. Later, the house clamor grew as drink took hold of the partiers. Someone played the piano, and those inside warbled the jaunty tune, "The Bonnie Blue Flag," and other favorites of Southern society melodies. Joseph stole a glance inside and saw Captains Mabry and Johnson, both with drinks in their hands, their mouths wide open on a chorus. Each man appeared to be trying to outdo the other.

He turned back toward the street. Out on the hill where the two companies were waiting, the dark trees began heaving back and forth in the burgeoning norther. He hunched his shoulders against the cold. He could see at least a dozen tiny orange glows twinkling on the hill. The bored soldiers were smoking cigars or pipes.

He lowered his stare into the street. After watching the party in the bright house through the window, his eyes took a while to adjust to the dark. Then he saw the man. Directly in front of him in the street, his feet astride the earlier kicked jack-o-lantern with its candle guttering, the Yankee sentry looked up at the hill, his rifle still shouldered. Joseph knew the Yankee picket saw the glowing pipes and cigars, too.

The soldier suddenly turned and gawped. He said nothing as he brought down his rifle, aiming at Joseph.

Before Joseph could react, instead of firing, the sentry raced up the street toward the building surrounded by Yankee soldiers. He yelled, "Rebs! Rebs!"

Joseph knocked hard on the house door three times, his breath bated. The music and singing had swelled. The revelers were harmonizing on "The Bonnie Blue Flag." No one came to the door. He banged harder, bruising his knuckles. No response.

Joseph looked quickly around to gauge his options. He saw an almost opaque stack of firewood. Across the street, the old dark shanty was surrounded by tall barren trees. He wished he had a boulder to hide behind.

Down the street, soldiers were reacting to the sentry racing closer to them.

Joseph grabbed the knob and forced the door open. "Yanks are coming!"

The singers were at their loudest. Some did not hear him at all. Finally, the pianist calmed her hands. The last of the partiers quit their reverie and turned toward Joseph.

"The Yanks are coming!"

Mabry and Johnson began stumbling around searching for their pistol belts and sword scabbards, bumping guests. The Lowry woman kept attempting to hug Captain Mabry.

A few dozen Yankees were speeding from the brick building, first visible in the vanishing window light, and then opaque when they reached the lightless portion of the street. They appeared as phantoms sweeping toward Joseph. The rapid tramp of feet and clanking gun metal sounded a demon's symphony in Joseph's ears.

Joseph could not wait. He raced from the porch to the rear of the shanty across the street.

He fired his revolver, aiming high, hoping to slow the rushing Yankees. They did slow, then stopped.

Immediately, bullets battered the shanty wall just as Joseph saw the flashes of the rifles.

"Spread out, men!" an officer's voice called.

More feet rushed down an alley behind the houses, moving toward the rear of the spy's abode. Shadowy forms took up positions in the street fifty paces from Joseph and just outside the house's window light.

For a moment, all was silent.

Then the house lights went dark. Two almost opaque forms dashed from the door, spurs jingling like little bells, sabers clacking against legs. Suddenly, every being was in motion.

Joseph shot repeatedly at the dark line of Yankees running and kneeling in the street.

Bright flames from the Yankee rifles ripped the night. More Yankees stormed from the rear of the house onto the porch and into the open doorway. Women' screams emitted from the darkened home. In the abject darkness, soldiers were stumbling and falling, in collisions.

Mabry and Johnson fired on the run — Mabry with his shotgun, Johnson his revolver. A big Yankee leaped up from the shadows and caught Johnson by the collar. Johnson swung around and drove a Bowie knife into the man's ribs. The big form seemed to fall in slow motion.

Blazes from the rifles flared into the dark like shooting stars. Women in the house continued to shriek and call for mercy. Bullets pelted the shanty where Joseph stood, one shot chipping wood an inch from his head. He dived and rolled to the edge of the street and lay prone.

Johnson went down, hit in the hip, tumbling in a heap. Mabry turned back and was trying to drag his companion when a bullet crashed into his left arm. Joseph, but a few feet away, saw the blood spew from the wound.

A jarring roar swept all around them. Scorching rifle fire spewed from every quarter. Then the volleys ceased.

Yankee officers ordered, "Reload."

While the Yankees were reloading, Joseph knew he had one chance, only a few seconds, but a chance. He raced to Mabry's side, and the two of them helped Johnson to his feet. Joseph supported the failing Johnson, almost dragging him. Mabry was trying to tie a tourniquet on his arm on the run. Just then, another soldier sprang on Captain Mabry, but the captain produced a large hunting knife and plunged it into the man's chest. The man collapsed.

Joseph struggled with Captain Johnson, grabbed him by the belt with one hand, the other pulling on his shirt. They reached the rear of the shanty when a new volley splintered the brittle wall to shreds.

Joseph peered around. The Yankee company was reforming. Men with lanterns were rushing up to join those already lined up in the street.

Then the rifle fire from atop the hills burst like a string of loud fireworks. The cavalry companies were providing covering fire at the Federals below.

With the shielding fire, Joseph and Mabry grappled their way up the hill, each on either side of the weakened Johnson. Behind them, an entire regiment of Union soldiers began filling the street.

When the three Confederates reached the dismounted cavalry, Captain Johnson was taken in hand by several privates. A corporal retied Mabry's tourniquet. Some soldiers knelt, firing their carbines into the dark town, aiming at flashes. Other Confederates mounted their horses, preparing to retreat. Bullets whizzed high in the trees, showering leaves and branches on top of their heads.

Exhausted, Joseph leaned against a tree, breathing hard. It dawned at him that he had fought in his first battle with the Third Texas, small as it was. He watched a hefty sergeant lift Captain Johnson into his saddle. Captain Mabry mounted his steed. A bullet fired from the street hit Joseph in his left shoulder. It stung something fierce. He went to his knees, grimacing, clutching the wound. *Here I go back to the hospital.*

A private rushed to him and stuck his finger in the bullet hole. Joseph yelped.

"Bullet went all the way through!" the private shouted, withdrawing his finger. "You're gonna be fine." He wrapped a towel around the wound. "Get on your horse, and hold that tight."

Joseph wearily rose to his feet and mounted his mare. He heard a lieutenant ask the wounded Captain Mabry if they got any valuable information about the Yankees.

"Nary a thing," Mabry called, wincing. "Ran outta time."

In a few more seconds, the companies were on their way back to camp, bullets from the town below pinging off the trees.

THIRTY-ONE

To Give a Fair Share

S ara was recovering handily from the bruise caused by the blow from Richards. The bruise had softened from purple to yellow and the scratches and tears of her skin were also healing.

Mrs. Fairchild threw away Sara's fetid dress and gave her three of her own elegant dresses, and though they fit well enough, save the longer hem, Sara felt out of place in such refined attire. After a week in the large home, she discovered a bolt of gingham cloth in a closet, and with scissors, needle, and thread, and some help from Billie Sue, fashioned a dress more to her liking.

Mrs. Fairchild had Sara read to her three times a day, once at breakfast and twice more later in the day. By the fifth day, Sara's voice had gone hoarse and Mrs. Fairchild gave her a day's reprieve. "I want that girl to have tea with lemon every hour. Do you hear me, Billie Sue?"

"Yes'm," Billie Sue answered.

"Well, stop dawdling. Get to it. Then get that ironing done."

Sara sat in the kitchen sipping the tea while Billie Sue ironed sheets and underwear and dresses. The iron rattled while the young slave maid shoved it across the fabric.

"Why does your iron rattle so, Billie Sue?"

"Well, Miss Sara, since Mrs. Fairchild can't really watch to see if I'm workin', she purchased this here rattlin' iron so's it makes this sound while I does the ironin'. If she can't hear me rattlin', she figures I ain't workin', then she set to me terrible."

"Is that why you wear the jingling bells on your apron? So she can hear you?"

"Yes'm. She don't take kindly to any of us slaves takin' 'vantage of her. She used to slap me all the time. Usually on the hiney, but two times on the face 'cause she thought I wasn't tellin' the truth. But I was."

"I'm sorry for you, Billie Sue. I would never treat a slave that way."

"Oh, it all right, I reckon." She pushed the hot iron across the last creases of a nightgown, and folded it, setting it in a basket. She lifted the heavy basket and walked toward the door, but stopped to add, "Mrs. Fairchild don't know this, but three of her slaves done run off to the Union army. I don't have the heart to tell her. 'Specially after she saved my life." She trotted down the hall and up the stairs.

Sara's voice was too hoarse to even ask how the matron had saved the sweet slave's life.

The next day, Sara continued reading aloud books on subjects from medical leeches to astronomy and then the fiction, *The Hunchback of Notre Dame*. Sara was enthused to read this book, one of her favorites. Each day bled into the next for weeks. Often, Mrs. Fairchild insisted Sara slow down her reading, or speed up, or speak more clearly, or with more inflection, and Sara did the best she could to comply. Whenever Mrs. Fairchild said, "Enough!" and trounced from the room, Sara set the book mark and went to help the slaves with the chores around the house.

When she was not reading, or helping the house slaves, Sara wandered the extensive house, gazing at the numerous paintings, smelling the redolent roses, lilacs and other flowers that were always fresh in numerous vases throughout the house. She wondered how so many flowers were available in the fall.

She spoke candidly with the half-dozen household slaves who went methodically about their chores. They were always pleasant, but markedly reluctant to engage in conversation. Billie Sue was the only one not reluctant to converse.

Once, she entered Billie Sue's room. Bare accommodations of a small bed, a dresser, and a ladder-back chair. Beside a tin washbasin atop the dresser, Sara found a two-inch-square silver jewelry case. Hardly more than a token, though it bore fine etchings. Inside was red velvet. A tiny silver cross and chain was the only treasure. She closed the lid when she heard Billie Sue singing a hymn full out on her way down the hall.

In the middle of the first week of November, Sara attempted to go out the back to view the yard and fountain. The big hound-faced slave of about forty years, Theophilus, sat whittling in front of the kitchen exit and informed her she could not go outside. He folded his arms and leaned his chair against the door.

"Fine," Sara said, not to be dissuaded. "I'll go out the front." Arriving at the front door, she found it locked. All the windows were nailed shut. She considered breaking a window, but thought better of it. She was a prisoner in the home. *This is not to my liking at all.*

Sara stormed to Mrs. Fairchild's room, but found her sleeping, stretched crosswise across the bedspread. She was ready to wake her with the demand to be released, but she stopped. In one hand, Mrs. Fairchild loosely held a handmade card with little drawn roses and romantic verse in fine penmanship signed by her late husband. In her other hand, she held a lock of gray hair. Sara could see that the woman's face had been awash with tears, the face lucent with the dried moisture.

Billie Sue's jingling alerted Sara that the maid was drawing near. She turned to see Billie Sue enter quietly. She went to the old woman's bed, lightly lifted her head onto a pillow, took the card and lock of hair, and placed them on the vanity. Then she spread an afghan across Mrs. Fairchild's legs. Billie Sue took Sara's elbow and drew her out the door.

In the hall, Billie Sue whispered, "You be a prisoner here, and that bothers you, doesn't it?"

"How did you...? Never mind. Yes, it does bother me. Why can't I leave?"

"Sara, you must realize that this earth is *not* our home. We're all prisoners of it in some form or fashion, no matter if you be a rich banker or slave like me."

"But I should not be her prisoner."

"No, nor should anyone be a prisoner of another, not when der's been no crime done."

"So..."

"Think for a moment, Sara. You tol' me you self you ain't got no family or friends what can care for you. If you left, where would you go? You could starve. Mrs. Fairchild is keepin' you here for your own good."

"But I'm not her slave."

"Oh, but think again. Do you read to her when she demands it?"

"Yes." Sara's face flushed.

"Always?"

"Yes."

"Do you by any force of your own will think you can resist her? The fire in her voice is like a storm arrivin'. I'll answer the question for you. The woman is most blind. She ain't got no one to read to her. To give her de will to live. Without her books, she will waste away and die. She almost died of heartbreak when her husband passed. She became a shell of who she was. Us slaves couldn't help with the readin'. We don't know what one letter sounds like, nor the next. By the grace o' God, she fought her way back from de brink of death. Now, you have given her hope."

Sara was flustered. But she knew that Billie Sue was right.

"What do I do? I can't stay here my whole life. I must find my fiancé."

"It is not for you to decide. When you fell onto the lawn at the feet of Mrs. Fairchild, dat was God's will. Amen. And it will be God who lets you know when you are to be free from here. I know that, someday, He will let me know when I is free. In my mind, I already is free."

Sara stared incredulously at the petite, pretty slave. She wished she had the depth of understanding of the order of the world that this young woman seemed to have.

"How will I know when it's time for me to be free from her?"

"You will know. God will let you know." Billie Sue walked away, holding the tiny bells of her apron in her hand so they made no sound.

Sara returned to the library and selected a new book, one on human anatomy. The drawings, simple as they were, excited her. She spent considerable time perusing the drawings, especially of the male figures. Page after page, she carefully viewed the colored drawings, complete in detail. She thought again of the tender kiss Joseph had given her, how he looked, splashing the clothes in the water of Wilson Creek, and how strong his chest and arms looked. She closed the book, flushed.

In the most surreptitious fashion, she held the tome to her side, hidden by her dress, and secreted it upstairs to her room. Once there, she closed the book and disrobed. She stood naked before a tall mirror and examined the curve of her body and rolled her hands around her soft round breasts and then lightly pinched her nipples. In her naïveté, she whispered, "So this is what men find so attractive." She hesitated there, closed her eyes and imagined Joseph beside her, flesh to flesh.

"Sara!" came the sharp tone of Mrs. Fairchild, "Where are you child? Get down here this moment!"

"Comin'!" Sara called. She dressed quickly. When she reached the bottom of the stairs, Mrs. Fairchild was holding to a bannister post, tapping an impatient foot.

"What took you, child?"

"Oh, I was going on a brisk walk on the upstairs hallway. I do that because I'm so used to walking about the farm, and..."

"Don't bother me with your trivialities. I did not hear you walking?"

"Well..."

"I have decided that with the darker hours coming upon us this season that we won't read in the parlor. We will use my husband's conservatory. It is much airier and allows the sun in through its many windows. I think it shall be a welcome change. Come. You'll read this book today." She handed Sara a Shakespeare play, *The Merry Wives of Windsor*.

Sara followed her to a low-slung door beneath the stairwell. It was dusty and seldom used. Sara had figured it was merely a storage closet. When Mrs. Fairchild fumbled with her keys, they both heard noises from inside the room, a sort of soft moaning and a shushing. Two voices.

At last, Mrs. Fairchild keyed the lock and opened the door, revealing a room filled with wall to wall windows and potted plants of all sorts, some tropical. Toward the back of the room on a table, Sara witnessed the hound-faced Theophilus, his trousers off. He was lying on top of one of the younger maids, her shapely body completely naked, sleek with sweat. Sara gasped. When the man rose, a surprised look on his face, she saw briefly his manhood, not unlike the drawings in the anatomy book. She was amazed at its tumescence, twitching in the air, as it was.

"Who's there?" Mrs. Fairchild demanded.

The man pulled on his trousers, tied the rope belt about his waist, cleared his throat, and in the most convivial tone, said, "Why, it's only me, Theophilus. I's in here waterin' the plants like you tol' me, trying to be quiet as it were."

The young maid slid from the table. She stood for a moment, her broad, round nipples perked, her coffee-toned body thin and curvy. She bent down and gathered her dress and held it in front of her.

"Who else is here? Tell me straight, Theo. I won't have you lyin' to me."

The teen stepped behind Theophilus.

"Why, tis only little Tilly. She wanted to see how I waters the plants and cleans the place. And, you never know, I might come down wid de rheumatis' and be laid up. She could back me up. So, she learnin'."

Mrs. Fairchild stood a long time tapping her foot, twice wiping her eyes, as if doing so could allow her to see. "Very well, Theo. I will take you at your word, but next time, ask my permission."

"Yes'm. And the plants, they all watered. Let me just get my diggin' tools and waterin' can." He gathered his shoes and socks. Theophilus and Tilly slipped cautiously by Mrs. Fairchild, between her and Sara. When the two fairly raced down the hall, Sara beheld the soft rounded buttocks of the young woman and her strong legs, her long black hair flowing down her light brown back.

Mrs. Fairchild closed the door.

Sara took in the conservatory. She could not help herself stepping up to several plants, touching them and smelling the tangy, vibrant odors. Despite Mrs. Fairchild's admonitions, she strode around for a couple of minutes, examining palms, pineapple plants, lime and lemon trees, plus myriad purple, gold and emerald flowers. "I must look at these beautiful plants."

"That is quite enough. If I can't see them, then neither may you. Be content with the smells and feel the warmth of the sunlight in this room. Sit and read, Sara. Now!"

Sara took a seat in a deep heavy armchair with velvet upholstery across from Mrs. Fairchild.

"Wait." Mrs. Fairchild held up her hand. "I smell something familiar, a sort of fresh smell, a sweet, earthy odor and … something else."

Sara glanced at the work table, still moist with human sweat. "Oh, that's just me from my exercise."

"Oh. Then read, child. Stop wasting time." Mrs. Fairchild sat back.

Sara did the best she could to read the Shakespeare play. She had never read a play before, let alone aloud. Mrs. Fairchild constantly interrupted her with the correct pronunciations, insisting that she use different voices for the different characters, and otherwise complaining of Sara's efforts.

At the end of the fifth scene, frustrated to the point of tears, Sara paused and looked out the tall east window. Beyond the yard, there was a red stable, some eighty yards afar. Five stalls, the half doors open and two horses with their heads out. A sturdy Negro stable hand was walking along, forking hay from a hay-wagon through the open doors. Sara dropped the book. Her thoughts raced. *There is my means of freedom. I have worked for this woman. She owes me a horse. I will find Joseph.*

"What are you doing, child?"

"I'm sorry. Let me get the book and continue. Such a great story."

"It's a play, not a story."

Well this is one actor in this play who will soon be exiting, stage north.

When evening plaited the sky with rusty colors and purplish clouds aglow, Sara pried open a window of her room, took foothold on a trellis and climbed to the ground. She stole across the yard, slipped through a small arbor gate and made her way to the barn. She brought a sack of additional undergarments, soap, and a second sack of dried pork and biscuits. She had long ago found Richard's revolver, hidden by Mrs. Fairchild, and she now tucked it in her coat pocket. Though she had only the bullets in the gun's chamber, she would not be without it. Further, she brought a lantern and matches.

Reaching the barn, she opened the unlocked door and slipped in. After lighting the lantern, she saw five horses. They nickered and stamped, unfamiliar with a night visit. Sara strode quickly past each horse in stalls, eyeing their comportment.

When she came to the last stall, she almost lost her breath. Esther immediately recognized her mistress, came forward and nuzzled against Sara's chin. Sara stroked the mare's white blaze. *Thank you, God. Praise to you. You have showed me my freedom and given me this gift.*

She grabbed tack and saddle. When she had finished preparing Esther to ride, the barn doors sprang open. Two shadowy figures stood.

"This is my horse, the one the thieves stole from me."

"I figured as much," came the voice of Billie Sue. "Just before you arrived, a man with two boys come through here and offered to sell the horse, sayin' it was too wild to ride. One of 'em complained of his backside whence he'd been thrown by the horse. Mrs. Fairchild was apparently feeling generous, offering a bed to share with the man, but he declined. She paid him ten dollars for your horse."

"How did you know this is my horse?"

"When you told your story, I done figured it out. I didn't want you to leave 'cause o' your many hurts."

Theophilus, his bulky form casting a large shadow in the flickering lantern light, sauntered up beside Sara who had set one foot in the stirrup. "I have somethin to say."

"Yes," Sara said.

Theophilus cleared his throat. "You could a tol' Miz Fairchild about me and Tilly, but you didn't. You see, Tilly is the love of my life, but Miz Fairchild won't let no preacher come here to hear us take our vows. So, we has no choice but to hide and such. Anyways, I wants to say I's mighty grateful." He patted the horse's neck. "You done earned this here horse. She won't even know it's gone."

Sara mounted Esther. "Thank you, both."

"You welcome." Billie Sue extended her hand and shook Sara's. "Now you as free as I am." When Sara withdrew her hand, Billie Sue had placed in it the silver jewelry box. "I knows you like that little box. I've not a use for it. I have a whole houseful of pretty things to look at."

"Thank you, Billie Sue." Sara placed the tiny gift in a coat pocket. She sighed. "Give my best to the others. And tell Mrs. Fairchild, I will pray for her, and... never mind."

"Good luck findin' your beau." Billie Sue smiled.

"I will find him and build a good life." Sara shook the reins and galloped Esther out into the crisp, starry night.

THIRTY-TWO

In Much Wisdom, There Is Much Grief

November 9, 1861, 11 am
South of St. Louis

Lucas, driving the wagon on a dusty road, gazed at a familiar scene, one remembered from years back. He recognized a limestone quarry and a lonely barn, gray and austere alongside a swift running stream. Atop the barn was a weathervane of a leaping frog, rather than a cock. Workman and he were near the Dent plantation.

Moreover, he recognized the sloping land on both sides of a running creek where Mr. Dent, Julia's father, raised cotton. The fields were fallow, preparing for winter. He passed a shabby piecemeal, two-room house, new since he visited last, many years ago.

He looked forward to seeing Julia Dent Grant, his deceased wife's old and dear friend. His long search for Abram proving fruitless, he hoped that his old friend had come to his senses and found his way to live here under Julia's watchful and caring eye. He smiled, for Julia and his wife had been good friends, even attending preparatory school together. He remembered their schoolgirl-like laughter at the slightest event.

Workman, sitting next to Lucas on the wagon, was fidgeting. He had injured a thumb and his lower back endeavoring to put new shoes on one of their horses. He succeeded in shoeing the horse, but his pain was now abundant. He kept shifting to various positions. "Makes no difference how I sit, my back is stove up like a crane what swallowed too big a fish. I am pried open with hurt." He grimaced.

"We'll be there shortly," Lucas said.

Just when he said the words, they topped a rise and the Dent Plantation house, barns, and slave cabins spread below them, the full creek flowing sleepily amidst walnut trees and hickories. In one field, a dozen slaves were picking the dregs of a cotton crop, stowing the fibers in long cloth sacks. Following them, three slaves with plows pulled by sleek black mules were turning up the soil. Across the creek, a red barn was situated. Behind it, the two-story plantation home, named White Haven, with its long front porch, stood hidden in the shadows of imposing cottonwoods. It was painted a solemn gray.

Beyond the big house about fifty yards, slave cabins, each with small autumn gardens of orange pumpkins and green cabbages, resembled a patchwork quilt. Farther on, cattle grazed.

Nearing the house, they crossed a narrow bridge over the creek. A bewhiskered Negro waved his ragged straw hat at them and beckoned them to proceed up the pebbled drive. For a moment, Lucas thought the old smiling character might be Abram, but his hope was dashed when they drew closer.

When Lucas pulled the wagon to a stop before the house, Julia Dent Grant rode up on a stallion, the horse full of piss and vinegar, jigging left and right, almost leaping while she reined it confidently.

"I recognize an older face of a dear friend," Julia called, "and widower of one of my dearest friends. Hello, Lucas." Her hair was pinned in a bun under a forest green hat. She rode side-saddle, her dress of elegant emerald silk and hand-fashioned lace cuffs, her boots high-glossed.

"Good afternoon, Julia. You're as pretty as ever." He remembered she was slightly cross-eyed, giving her a look during a conversation as if always inquiring of something deeper. "This is my good friend, Dred Workman."

Workman barely gave a wave. He slid uncomfortably to the ground and leaned his lanky body against the wheel, blowing hard through his bushy mustache.

"Pleased to meet you, Mr. Workman. You seem in a measure of discomfort."

"I am, dear lady. I would be obliged if I could make use of a soft chair." Pain rifled through him and he buckled.

"I most certainly have a chair." She dismounted, and the old slave was immediately there to take the reins, hook a bridle to the harness, and waltz the steed back to the barn. He spoke soothing words, and the animal calmed.

Lucas hurried to help Workman up the porch steps. Workman inhaled jerking breaths. He went to his knees at the door.

A tall man with a white goatee and handlebar mustache opened the door. He wore a broad straw hat, pristine gray jacket and pants and was pinning a carnation to his lapel. He unaccountably tugged on his white, pasty goatee beard and finally looked down at Workman. "I say, I've had niggers bow to me before, but never a white man. I may get used to that."

"Papa, your jest is ill-spoken," Julia reprimanded her father. "This man is in agony as anyone can plainly see. Kindly step out of the way.'

A petite Negro maid swept past Mr. Dent. "Scuse me, sir. This man done gone down wid the cramps and the cricks. Let me help."

Mr. Dent retreated from the doorway a few steps, allowing Lucas, Julia, and the maid to half-carry Workman to an elegant mauve-toned sofa in the parlor.

"Not that one, his clothes are soiled. He'll ruin the fabric," Mr. Dent complained.

"Papa, do hush."

They laid Workman down easily on the sofa, and the maid placed a pillow under his head.

"Thank you, Lotty," Julia said. "Now return to your chores. But see if Miss Mary has some of her special tea."

"Yes'm," Lotty said. The teen slave was thin as a sapling, but spry and pleasant in appearance. Her homespun clothes were clean and starched. Despite having to dodge around Mr. Dent, who seemed to Lucas to be intentionally getting in her way, she had a twinkle in her eye, and an undaunted air.

Lucas was listening with his ear trumpet. He extended his hand to the Southern gentleman. "Mr. Dent. We've met, but you may not remember. I'm Lucas Reeder. My companion is Dred Workman."

"I am Frederick Dent." He looked up at the ceiling, stroked his mustache, and then waved off a handshake. "I don't remember the pleasure of making your acquaintance, but as you are a friend of my daughter, we will speak later. Please excuse me. I must attend to the affairs of my plantation."

Once he had departed, Julia said, "That means he must watch that the Negros don't abscond. He's not whipped one yet, but threatens to do so almost daily, and I believe he would go through with his promise of whipping a man's wife and selling his children if the man ran away. Already, though, he has had to sell some of our people to pay debts, and... oh, I do go on too much."

"Julia, surely your father remembers me or at least knows I'm a family friend. Why would he not shake my hand?"

"He's odd that way. Until he knows whether you champion the Southern cause or favor whom he calls the Yankee invaders, he will have nothing to do with you. If you support the North, he would demand you leave. If, on the other hand, you had come in and given a revered homage to the Confederate flag there on the wall, he would have met you heartily. I apologize for his rude behavior. But these are rude times."

"I see. Actually, I endorse neither cause, and would see the war delivered on a platter of olive branches this very day were it up to me."

"His dis-communion with visitors has worsened because of my husband, Ulysses. He's off to war, and I miss him and am sore grieved."

"So, Ulysses is your husband's name? I'm sorry I was not earlier appraised. I would have sent a wedding gift. I'm sure you are proud of him being in the army."

"You needn't apologize. I'm sorry I was not there for Emily. Word of her death devastated me for a month. I have such welcome memories of her."

Lucas nodded.

"Yes. I am proud of Ulysses and deeply worried. Our children miss him, too. It's as bad for me as it was when he was stationed in California. It might as well have been the other end of the world. I think that tour of duty did him mischief. He took to drink and wrote often about his depression."

Julia stopped suddenly and fixed her gaze out the window. Her voice airy and removed, she said, "He proposed to me out there on the porch. I turned him down, but he would not relent. I'm glad he pressed for my hand, and I'm glad I gave it him, though our engagement lasted years. Whenever we were together, we would ride all day across this lovely countryside, then talk for hours here in these very chairs."

Lotty returned to the room, curtsied to Lucas and to Julia, and set to fluffing the pillow for Workman. "Are you comfy, sir?"

"Powerful lot better, thank you." Workman took his hand from his back and patted the young woman's hand. "You are kind."

"Well, she better be," Julia remarked, smugly. "I would have her no other way. Else she'd be out working with the field hands."

Lucas noticed the maid's slightest cringe, followed by a broad smile.

A gray-haired, stout Negress, wearing a starched gray dress and white apron, tottered into the room bearing a large mug of a beverage, heavy with a spicy aroma. "Here 'tis, Lotty."

"Thank you, Miss Mary." Lotty took the steaming cup, handed it to Workman, and slid her arm behind his pillowed head and raised his upper body. "Drink that all down, y'hear. Best rem'dy for the spells."

Mary stood rocking on her heels, moving her head up and down as if encouraging each of Workman's swallows. He slugged back the brew and handed the cup empty to Mary. Lotty eased his head back down. Lucas and the others watched expectantly.

"I do say," Workman announced after a short while, "the room appears to be swimmin' round like a fish in a bowl."

"Miss Mary," Julia said. "Your remedy is a Godsend."

The old woman smiled, curtsied, and returned to the kitchen. Lotty followed her.

Workman began to snore. Julia and Lucas tiptoed into the opposite room with an elegant dining table, candelabras, ornate vases, and bronze table statues. They sat. Julia removed her feathered hat and placed her laced cuff hand on Lucas's for a moment. "Dear Lucas, it is so good to see you again. What brings you here in the middle of this horrid conflict in our land?"

"I had to leave. My home was destroyed by Jayhawkers."

Julia gasped, putting her hands to her cheeks. "Oh, my! How dreadful."

"Now I journey with Workman to find a desk job in Richmond. I believe I could serve the army well. My original plan was to leave my manservant, Abram, with you, knowing that he would be well taken care of."

"Yes." Julia gave a smug look. "Why is he not with you?"

"He begged his freedom, and, with lack of foresight, I gave it to him. Now I wish I hadn't. I don't know how he has fared. I'm devastated at the loss of his... service."

"I understand. Oh, and I forgot. I have a gift for you. It was supposed to be for you and Emily since your birthdays are so close in date." She rose and hastened up the stairs. She returned with a gold-plated compass with a leather cord and handed it to Lucas. "I've had this for so long. I know you enjoyed looking at the stars. I hope this compass can support your hobby."

Lucas looked at it for a minute, fingering the etchings on the back. "I am grateful for this. Unfortunately, when marauders destroyed our home, they smashed my telescope. Not to worry. Perhaps I will purchase a new one." He forced a smile, and placed the piece in his pocket. "Well, tell me about your husband. Did they give him an officer's rank when he reenlisted? Does he lead a regiment?"

"I am quite amazed at his gumption. When he resigned from the army years back, he tried his hand at a host of occupations. He chopped and hauled wood in a cart, then worked as a rent collector, but he was too kind to the renters and was let go." Julia hung her head for a moment and sighed.

"He worked for a while helping run my father's plantation, even built us a farm house a short distance from here. Called it 'Hardscrabble.' Of late, before the war, he'd been working for his father's tannery in Galena, Illinois. That is our home now. I'm only visiting my family for these few weeks. I needed the air. He's stationed now near Cairo."

"You say he helped run this plantation, but fights for the North? Would he not be in favor of the South?"

"Not at all. He hates slavery, as do his abolitionist parents. My goodness, they were followers of that wretched John Brown. My papa and Ulysses engaged in regular arguments about the merits of slavery. I found myself at times at sixes and sevens. Papa has threatened to sever ties with us, though he has not followed through yet. I know my place as a woman and take neither side. Ulysses was given a slave as a gift at our wedding. He released William back in fifty-nine."

Lucas sat, his mouth slightly agape.

"Come now, Lucas. You know as well as I do that there are large numbers in the North who want the South to win, and just as many Southerners who hold for the North."

"You are right. But what of your husband?"

"By good fortune, he was promoted to General and is in charge of Eastern Missouri and Illinois soldiers."

"I wish him well. I have seen enough to know this war will go on a very long time."

"Surely, you jest, Lucas. The war will be over in fewer than six months."

The old Negro entered from a rear door, hat in his hand.

"Zacchaeus," Julia said. "Why are you bothering me? You can see we have company. At least you remembered what door you're supposed to use."

"Yes, ma'am." Zacchaeus nodded. "I put Firestorm in his stall, groomed him, and...."

"And what?" Julia interrupted.

"I went to town earlier and picked up the St. Louis Dispatch, like you asked." He handed her a newspaper.

"Oh, I'd forgotten. You are a dear." Julia rose and embraced the slave, giving him a kiss on the cheek. "Thank you, Zacchaeus. You may go now."

"Yes'm." The slave started for the front, but caught himself and left out the rear door.

Julia unfolded the paper on the table. "Must keep up with the news. No telling...." She stopped abruptly.

Lucas looked at the headline: *General Grant Leads Attack at Belmont, Missouri, Federal Army Repulsed.*

Julia began quivering like a fall leaf clinging to a branch in a gale, her eyes brimming. "What of my Ulysses? Is he dead?"

The banner story gave no reckoning of General Grant's condition.

"Surely," Lucas offered, "if a general was wounded or killed, the news would be stated here."

Julia ran from the room, sobbing.

∽

THIRTY-THREE

HOPE AND PLANS

TWO DAYS LATER, NOVEMBER 11, 1861, LATE EVENING
DENT PLANTATION HOME

With all the house lamps turned up, Julia Dent sat reading a just-received letter from her husband, Ulysses Grant. She was crying again, but this time, tears of joy slid down her cheeks. He was alive. The letter explained how his surprise attack on rebel forces at Belmont had been successful, but the Confederates had counterattacked, forcing the Union army to fight their way out.

Her personal slave, Jule, stood behind her, leaning in to read the post as well.

"Look at this, Jule," Julia called over her shoulder, "he says it was good practice to both win a scrap, then escape from a much larger army."

"Yes'm." Jule had ginger-toned skin and freckles. She was thin and muscled. Julia often said that with those powerful legs, Jule could push a locomotive. Julia had long ago taught her personal slave, a gift to her at birth, to read.

Julia turned to face her handmaid. "Jule, I wish father were here, instead of in town on his 'business,' so I could share this happy news with him."

"He may not be able to listen if he comes in roarin' drunk from his bidnis like he's likely to do."

"Don't say that. Father does drink a little too much, but...oh, what am I saying? You're right. I hope he's sober enough to listen when he arrives home."

"Yes'm."

"If only mother were alive." She dropped her head and sighed, and then dabbed her tears. "And Ulysses says further," she pointed at the letter, "that the children and I are to join him in Corinth at his headquarters as quickly as possible."

"That be fine news indeed. Do you wish me to come, too?"

"Well, of course, Jule. You and I are a team. Besides, I will need help keeping watch on all four of the children in an army camp. Now, you go up to my room, prepare my clothes trunk, take out my mauve riding dress and the pretty pink hat for me. Of course, gather your own belongings. It will be a long trip."

"Yes'm." Jule departed upstairs.

Zacchaeus tiptoed in through the rear slave entrance. He stood quietly in the dining room while Julia began reading the letter again to herself. He cleared his throat. She looked up.

"Why, Zacchaeus, why are you here at this hour of the night, and sneaking up like that enough to scare the spirit out of me? And look at your dirty clothes and your cottonfield filthy shoes, leaving a mess all over my rug. Shame on you."

Zacchaeus shifted his weight and hung his head. "Yes'm," he said several times, always looking at the floor.

"All right, all right, what is so urgent that you should trouble me at this hour?"

Jule trounced down the stairs with a hat in each hand. "Miss Julia, which of these two hats do you want for tomorrow?"

Julia turned to Jule. "The one in your right hand."

"Why is Zacchaeus here at this hour?"

"I am trying to find out." Julia rose and walked to the slave. He was trembling. She put her hand on his shoulder. "It's all right, Zacchaeus. Take a deep breath and tell me what it is."

The old slave raised his head. "Miss Julia, I's sorry to bodder you at dis hour, but dey's a man out back, says he knows you and wishes to speak wid you."

"A man? Did you not call the overseer to train a gun on him?"

"No, ma'am. He be most insistent that you know him. He's a colored man like me. He say he a freeman and showed me a paper. I couldn't tell nothin' of it in the dark and all. He say to tell you the name Lucas Reeder, and that…"

"Lucas Reeder? Why! He's not here. He just left yesterday with his companion. Did this colored man give you a name?"

"Yes'm, he say his name be Abram."

"Jule, bring a lantern and come with me." Julia barged past the still trembling old man and made her way out the back slave entrance.

Jule set down the hats and gathered a lantern and was attempting to light it when they both arrived on the stoop. In the dark, Julia could just make out an opaque form of a man. "Jule, where is that light?"

"Right here, Miss Julia." Jule lit the lantern and held it high. In the soft, comfortable glow, Abram Reeder stood, twisting his battered hat in his knobby-fingered hands. His white beard was longer, his cataract-coated, white eyes reflected the light eerily, like a phantom's.

"How do, Miss Julia."

"Well, hello, Abram, my dear friend's servant. But you just missed Lucas. He was looking for you. Were you looking for him?"

Abram took a step forward, placed his hat firmly on his head, and stood more erect. "I ain't a slave no more, Miss Julia. I's free. Lucas Reeder was my friend and he gi' me my freedom. It say so right here." He drew a paper from a shirt pocket. "And I can read it, so I know it's official."

"So why are you here? Do you wish me to send a courier to catch up with Lucas?"

"No, ma'am. I don't want nothin' to do with no Lucas Reeder. Our friendship is through." Abram stamped his foot and spit on the ground.

Julia harrumphed and put her hands on her hips. The lantern's glow flashed all about the yard. In the outer reaches of the light, several of the plantation slaves had gathered, watching.

"Two reasons," Abram continued. "One, I's tired of bein' a slave. I didn't come here to be a slave. That's what Lucas wanted. To come here an' be yor slave. I come here 'cause I know you and know you would treat me right, 'cause you such a good friend of my mistress, Emily Reeder, befo' she died. So, I come here in the hopes of bein' a hired hand. That or nothin' at all."

Julia softened her glance. She stepped down and hugged Abram. He felt embarrassed and attempted to squirm loose, but she hugged all the tighter. At last, she stood back from him, her hands still on his shoulder. "And what would the second thing be, freeman Abram?"

Abram weakly held up two fingers of an arthritic hand. "Two, I's also tired of bein' a freeman if it means starvin' to death. I's scarce had much to eat for a month. I's powerful hungry. So, if you have anything to eat, I'd be mighty grateful. An' I has a horse tied up and hid, and I can skedaddle out of her quicker than mercury." He crossed his arms.

Julia smiled and turned to Jule, who by now had shifted the heavy lantern to her other hand. "Jule, please prepare a plate for my dear friend's freeman."

"Yes'm. I'll go down to the slave cabins and fetch up…"

"You'll do no such thing. Abram will dine on the house meal tonight. Warm up what's leftover of the pork roast that Mary and Lotty prepared for me tonight, and he will dine at the house table. He's not a slave. He's free."

Jule's mouth flew open. Abram raised his head, a proud look on his face.

"And, Abram, you will now be in my employ. Jule and I are traveling to Galena, Illinois to gather up my children at my cousin's house, then we are heading to Corinth to join my husband, Ulysses. Can you drive a carriage and handle a rifle?"

Abram twisted his face in disbelief, then in wonder, then smiled broadly. "Yes, ma'am."

Jule took hold of Abram's arm and led him inside, chattering at him and asking him how he got there all the way from south Missouri. "All right, Mr. Abram, Freeman. Can you really drive a carriage?" she asked.

"If I can ride a horse, I sure can drive a carriage. I'm a hard worker, too."

"We'll see about that. Now you watch your step around all de fine furniture and vases and statuary in de house."

They stopped in the bright dining room, Abram blinking and eyeing the statues and vases and embroidered furniture.

Julia sent Zacchaeus on his way, shooed the curious slaves back to their cabins, and then returned inside. "Jule, after you've fed him, find him some fresh clothes, then hide him in the spare room upstairs. I don't want father knowing we have a Negro freeman here. He will have the fits. We'll leave early in the morning for Galena before Father awakens from his drunken snooze. You, me, and my old friend, Abram." She hugged him again. "And Abram, you will be a reminder to me of my boon friend, Emily. So, you must tell me all about her and her children. Do you hear?"

"Yes'm" Abram looked up. *Thank you, Lord. Glory be.*

"And," Jule added, "we'll see how well you can take care of little kids, old man. Especially when those two strappin' boys take out and pretend dey soldiers."

That night, Abram knelt before a four-posted bed, the first of its kind he had ever slept in, and said prayers until his old knees wore out. "I am finally free," he whispered.

THIRTY-FOUR

∞

THINGS LOST,
THINGS REGAINED

WINTER, FEBRUARY 16, 1862, 10 AM
CROSS HOLLOWS, ARKANSAS CANTONMENT

Joseph's left arm was healed from the wound in the October fray in the streets of Springfield. He vowed he would never assist in spy work again.

He was daydreaming of riding his new horse. In drills, he could dash at a fast gallop, bring the horse to a quick halt, and still draw his saber and slash it about as if he were taking on the entire Union army.

Deep into February, though, he could only fashion imaginings of battles on horseback, for he sat on a stool in a wooden plank cabin with snow piled on the roof and mud daubed in the chinks between the boards. Poor ventilation and a bent metal pipe chimney on the stove allowed smoke to drift into the room. That smoke and eight men puffing on their pipes day in and day out left a hazy cloud across the upper half of the cabin.

All the men coughed regularly, and Joseph was no exception. Two of the men had sweated out a bout with pneumonia and were barely recovering. A month previous, a member of their mates had died of dysentery. He and his bunkmates shared one of dozens of sturdy, but drafty, part tent, part log cabins in the cantonment of McCulloch's infantry regiments in Cross Hollows.

Joseph was playing chess with a man from England, recently joined, who spoke with a decided accent. Ebie Dollander had arrived in Galveston two months before the war, and on a lark when riding through Jefferson, Texas, enlisted in the Third Texas Cavalry.

In this chess game, Joseph had maneuvered his pieces, leaving the chap with a challenging puzzle. Ebie, a gangly cross between a stiff-legged crane and a pudgy pig, was taking an inordinate amount of time reconnoitering the board.

Joseph's mind drifted to the visage of the beautiful woman with green eyes of his dreams he knew had to be important in his life, but the few stray memories of her that had risen in his mind served only to frustrate him. Elements of his past life had trickled back into his cognizance, and he thoroughly remembered his mother and father, both dead, for he recalled their funerals, and that he had lived in Tennessee in his youth along the Mississippi River.

He remembered the muddy river's vastness. He even remembered playing on the bluffs above the river with childhood friends, and he knew their names. All else of his more recent past remained lost, and straining to remember never brought any satisfying results, only consternation.

He wished for something to read. Their camp, so far removed from towns, meant that newspapers were a rare commodity. The men had shared each other's books from home, but Joseph had read them all, some twice. The handful of newspapers that came did help fill in some of the holes of his lost memory. He knew now that Lincoln was the United States president; Davis led the Confederate States. A general named McClellan was leading the Union forces around Washington. General Joseph Johnston commanded the Confederate troops in Virginia.

He had read several editorials about the North's atrocious and bewildering behavior. "Loathsome Yankee Invaders," the papers called them. One diatribe fomenting rage against freeing the Negro slaves ate at his conscience. He felt a great opposition to slavery though he could not ferret out the origin of his beliefs. It just felt wrong. It was in his nature that he found any oppression of another human as rancorous. He had concluded, based on discussions with his cabin mates and from reading the southern newspapers, that the Northern, commercial money-grubbers were bent on oppressing the South, to turn the Southern states into serfdoms. Thus, he felt comfortable fighting for the cause of Southern freedom.

Tired of waiting on his chess competitor, Joseph rose and stepped out into the frosty morning. The weather had warmed under a pleasant sun and icicles dripped from the roof. Above the door, a cabin mate had fashioned a sign that read "Cross Hollows Hotel." Most of Colonel Greer's regiment was cantoned fifty miles south near the Arkansas River, but Joseph's company was established as a sort of vanguard cavalry north of Fayetteville where the weather was cooler and the foraging more time-consuming. Two times this winter, the company had driven ox carts south to bring up loads of hay for their mounts.

Joseph needed no coat this morning. The cold did not bother him. He stepped around ice patches to a latrine some thirty paces from the dwelling and relieved himself. Next, he traversed along a set of wobbly boards stretched across a muddy patch to the corral where several of the company's horses, with blankets spread over their backs, crowded under a lean-to and munched on oats. He whistled a set of tweets, and his black mare trotted over to him. "Hello, old Card Trick." The horse nickered. Stroking the blaze on the horse's head, he drew a sugar lump from his pocket and palmed it to the horse.

He trekked back to the modicum of a porch and looked out at the expanse of cabins of McCulloch's Army of the West. Each cabin had a chimney from which lazy smoke drifted. Across from his lodging was a larger tongue-and-groove planked affair that served as the headquarters of Colonel Hebert, third in charge after General McCulloch and Brigadier General McIntosh. The youthful Hebert sat on a log bench, almost motionless, smoking a pipe. Joseph nodded hello at the colonel who nodded back.

Refreshed in the brisk morning, Joseph's thoughts flew as they often did to Sara. He had seen other women in the last months, and had spent an evening observing the female gender in the party before the scrape in Springfield.

He had seen farmer women, then town women in Carthage and later, in Fayetteville after his recovery from the bout with measles, but none compared in beauty, nor appeal, to Sara. He possessed such a pining for her that was akin to being on fire, and he thought often of asking for a leave to return to the Reeder home to sweep her up in his arms. The letters he had written her were never answered.

His will to find and embrace her fell short because of certain elements of his memory that intruded. He felt often like he was a thin sheet of muslin stretched too far and at the point of tearing. "Sometimes," he said to himself, "I don't believe I have any sense at all."

He was stepping inside when an assemblage of Confederates galloped hard into the cantonment and directly up to Hebert's cabin. In the lead was a robust, hefty officer with clean-shaven face, silver hair, and an impeccably clean, silver-shaded uniform. A supporting entourage of Confederate Missouri Guard in motley garb followed. Their faces were intent.

Colonel Hebert stood to greet them. "What ho! General Price," he said. "You seem in a hurry." He saluted.

"Indeed, we are, the Yankees are pressing us," General Price shouted." They have driven us from Springfield with vast numbers, and despite our efforts at halting their advance, they are too many." General Sterling Price of the Missouri Guards rolled his almost three-hundred-pound girth from the saddle. "Come, Hebert, let us inside, for the matter is urgent! We must meet the enemy and hurl them back!"

Hebert, Price and the lesser officers rushed into the headquarters. Their discussion was so loud, Joseph could hear aspects of the heated palaver. He leaned in his cabin doorway and announced to his companions, "I think we have some Yankees comin' our way. We may have a fight soon enough."

The men scrambled outside. Crowded around him, Joseph explained what he had heard. Then, unabashedly, the lot of them crept across the barren yard and onto the porch of Hebert's cabin and held their ears at the headquarters door and thin walls.

"Odd bodkins," Ebie said. "We appear to be headed for a bit of a row."

THIRTY-FIVE

∽

THE CHANCE LOST

FOUR DAYS LATER, FEBRUARY 20, 1862, NOON
FAYETTEVILLE, ARKANSAS

Sara, wearing a pristine white apron over her hooped dress, brought plates of food to a group of salesmen. They barely acknowledged her, but watched out the cafe window at the groups of nervous Confederates accumulating on the boardwalks. Sara watched as well through the café's frosted windows. Thirty or so gray-clad soldiers took up positions in and around the blacksmith's barn across the street that had been turned into a Confederate storehouse.

In a moment, a troop of cavalry splashed through the muddy street, the wind whipping their flags. Piles of melting snow lay against the boardwalks like little dunes, crusted and dirty brown. Every low spot in the street held puddles of water covered with thin sheets of ice. The cavalry officer signaled a halt.

Sara carefully examined each man when they dismounted, hoping to see Joseph. She had almost given up hope of ever finding him. She gazed out the window in a sort of languid daze.

Her employer called from the kitchen.

"Coming," Sara replied.

She had worked at this Fayetteville boarding house and café shortly after fleeing from the termagant Mrs. Fairchild. When she applied at the Dindle Boarding House and Café, she happened to mention that her father was a major and had fought in the War with Mexico. She did not say he was no longer serving in any army, but that was enough for Miss Dorothea Dindle, a spinster of fifty with a face like a cherub and a torso like a gourd, thin in the bosom and heavy along the bottom tract. She hired Sara and gave her room, board and modicum salary.

Every day, Sara wrote letters to Joseph in the hope of receiving a return post. No letter ever came.

In early November, she gained permission from Miss Dindle to twice travel to the camps of the Missouri Guard and McCulloch's army that had joined together at Pineville to thwart a threat from Union General Freemont's massed troops who had once again wrested Springfield from the Confederates. She was not the only woman amongst the troops, so she traveled freely in the camps and once joined with the troops for a meal. The constant shifting of the regiments to new positions left her frustrated. No soldier knew of Joseph's whereabouts.

Confederate squads and regiments often moved in and out of Fayetteville, but never the Third Texas.

She refused to believe he might have been killed. It did not occur to her that he might have been wounded and was elsewhere recovering.

By late November, she had worried herself into not eating and had grown as thin and unsubstantial as a sapling, and her skin had taken on a ghostly pallor. Finally, Miss Dindle gave her a good scolding and made her eat.

When December filled the Boston mountains and valleys with snow, she made no more forays into the camps splayed out from the Missouri border to Fort Smith.

A healthier Sara changed sheets, emptied bedpans, fed the chickens, tended the garden, washed clothes, helped cook, and waited on soldiers and civilians alike in the small café.

On this bright, frosty day, Sara came to the kitchen where the dowdy Miss Dindle stood at the stove stirring an olio. "Have you fed the peacocks, dear?" Miss Dindle asked.

"Not yet. I'll do it now."

"Thank you, dear. It's very important we keep the peacocks happy. They're better than watchdogs. If some critter comes sneaking around the smokehouse, they scream, don't you know. There's many a time they sang out, and I took my buckshot to some nasty varmints."

"Yes, ma'am, and the bears."

"Yes, the bears."

Sara and she chuckled. *Bear* was their code word for the occasional soldier who crept to their storage shed in search of a ham or a steak. Sara admired the self-made woman who, during the winter, kept meats fresh because she paid men to cut chunks of ice from creeks, and then set the ice atop straw on shelves in her little cedar smokehouse. The meat lay under cheesecloths.

"I pay our neighbor hunters good money for that meat," Miss Dindle said, "and that's why folks keep comin' back, because they like my steaks and chops."

"Yes, ma'am." Sara stepped out the back door into the agreeable sunshine. She retied the blue ribbon around her flowing blond hair. She went to a barrel, scooped out scratch, and tossed it about the yard in front of the smokehouse. The peacocks and chickens fluttered from the trees.

Then Sara went to the corner of the house, and, hoping in an oblique mist of memory and desire, she surveyed the soldiers. Many Confederates were posted before the smithy's barn and the two ammunition warehouses. Joseph was not among them.

When she entered the boarding house, one of the salesmen hollered from the café, "Say, look at this. It looks like the whole army's marching. Glory be."

Miss Dindle and Sara hurried to the front windows. They beheld the spectacle of thousands of Confederates, eight and ten abreast hurrying haphazardly through the streets in a bare semblance of order.

The men clad in gray or mustard brown and some in palest blue uniforms drew up abruptly. Sara looked to see why they had halted. Then she saw the staunch, bearded man she knew well, General McCulloch, in the middle of the street astride a tall, grayish white stallion. Beside him, a young colonel sat on a bay horse, his palm upraised.

"Soldiers! Gentlemen!" McCulloch's voice rang like a church bell. "We vacate Cross Hollows to increase our strength with the Missouri Guard. Soon we will halt the Federals' advance and send them crying back to their mamas. We are *not* retreating. There is no cause for alarm..." He waited a moment. "Nor panic. We are Southerners. Proud, fearless. Fighters, not trembling sheep."

Two thousand men, packed in the wide avenue, stood quietly, barely a shuffle of feet sounded. McCulloch eyed his men. "As we re-establish our position, we cannot afford to let the enemy gain our supplies here in Fayetteville. Therefore, on my order, take whatever you can carry from these warehouses. Bring it with us south to our new camp. Leave nothing for the Yankees. They shall have no prize in Arkansas. Go now, then follow me south." He galloped away with the colonel close by.

The soldiers broke first at a fast walk, then into a run to the warehouses. They mobbed the buildings, struggling, pushing, shouting, and grabbing boxes and sacks, crates of bullets, anything they could carry. It was not long until the throng of men spread out beyond the warehouses, forcing their ways into the stores, even into homes. "Nothing for the Yankees!" Sara heard over and over in the swirling hurricane of men.

Sara watched in horror the men toting not only sacks of flour and cornmeal but ornamental vases, suitcases, umbrellas, books, candles, chairs, and every sundry item they could lay their hands on. The handful of wagons were soon stacked high with such loads as to be unmovable. She observed one cavalryman with a rolled rug across his saddle and a birdcage in one hand. Two privates held bayoneted hams on their rifles.

Miss Dindle's café doors burst open. A dozen soldiers bumped and slid in, a tangle of arms and legs. Some, already burdened, stole tablecloths and silverware and pulled down the curtains. Two men raced upstairs. Others gamboled into the kitchen. Miss Dindle held her hands out to the men, pleading. "No, no, please!"

Sara pulled her back from the onrush. In a few minutes, the men emerged from upstairs carrying a mattress. They left and tossed the mattress on top of a tall stack of loot on a buckboard. Just then, the smithy's shop burst into flame, black smoke pouring out the doors. The startled horses hitched to the wagon jerked and reared, pulling it slowly down the street. Citizens of the town rushed to the streets. Many of them called the soldiers any number of cursed names. Several took to fisticuffs, belting the soldiers.

The soldiers from Miss Dindle's kitchen appeared, heading to the door. "No, please, not my steaks," Miss Dindle called. Their arms were filled with cheesecloth-covered slabs of meats.

The last man exited holding two dead peahens in his thick fingers. "Thank ye, ladies," he chuckled. "Nothing for the enemy."

Sara and Miss Dindle looked again to see the hurly burly of soldiers slowly sliding out of the town like quicksilver across a table. Smoke billowed into the street from the blacksmith's barn while the citizens formed a bucket brigade to keep the fire from spreading. Numerous straggler soldiers, some on foot, others on horseback, meandered down the street, their arms full.

A loud bang like a hundred tiny cymbals crashed. Across the street, two men who, in attempting to carry away a pump organ, had dropped it on the boardwalk, destroying it, sending keys and pipes spinning into the dirt. The men sped after their comrades, but not before picking up articles dropped in the street.

At that moment, through the smoke, a young soldier rode by the café. Sara immediately knew the rider was none other than

Joseph. He wore a smart gray uniform and a saber. Though the puffing smoke clouded the street, she knew it was he. With a rifle in one hand, hung on his saddle horn was a sack of cornmeal. Sara flew out the door, hurtling down the street, weaving through the crowds, calling, "Joseph! Joseph!" The disharmony of the men and women yelling drowned out her calls.

Then a new devastating sound erupted. A second fire had been set in the ammunition storehouse. Pops, bangs and booms exploded within the brick walls. Sara was running full out past the blazing storehouse calling after Joseph, now out of sight.

Then the building blew like a dam bursting. Sara was thrown amidst bricks and debris across the street, her body slamming against a store wall.

Sara opened her eyes slowly to a darkened room. The people and objects in the room looked bleary. She attempted to raise her head and felt a knife-like pain in her neck. She closed her eyes. Soon a rough, wet cloth was being wiped gently across her face. She raised her hands to her eyes when opening them again to clear her vision. Even her arms ached. Wiping her eyes, she immediately noticed that her right leg was splinted at the calf and raised on pillows. Now that she was awake, pain flowed through her like a raging river. She saw two women standing by the bed smiling. They appeared to be whispering, the younger one mouthing words to her. A loud whooshing wind swept about in her ears. Is there a storm?

She could not guess the reason for the noise. The second woman, a matron with a pinched expression on her face, opened the drapes allowing in the light of a blue sky. There was no storm.

Sara noticed Miss Dindle sitting on a chair in the corner. Her employer rose and was flapping her lips like she was speaking. The other ladies seemed to be mocking the ability to speak as well. Then Sara realized she could not hear them. She raised her aching arms, stuck her fingers in her ears and twisted the digits about.

Removing her fingers, she heard nothing but crashing waves. She batted her ears. The sweeping sounded abated to no sound at all.

"I can't hear. I can't hear!" But Sara could not hear her own words, only a faint pressure like someone whispering in a vacant cathedral. The three women's faces showed great distress. Miss Dindle plopped to the chair and buried her head in her arms, sobbing.

She attempted to rise, but the pain in her leg and the back of her head knocked her down. The younger woman gently opened Sara's mouth and poured in a spoonful of liquid. Tears poured down Sara's cheeks. Her leg was broken, so she could not pursue Joseph. And now, like her father, she was deaf. *Even if I do ever find Joseph again, he could never love a deaf woman.*

THIRTY-SIX

⌒

OUR CRAVINGS OWN US

THE NEXT DAY, FEBRUARY 21, 1862, 10 AM
BUFFALO, NEW YORK

"It says here that the president's son, Willie, died yesterday." Leah Fox read from the Buffalo, New York newspaper. "That is a pity. I can't imagine losing a child."

"How'd he die?" Maggie asked.

"The story doesn't say, just that he'd been ill. And that the President's family is in mourning. There is much ado about the White House, and the president has postponed all cabinet meetings."

"Why'd they wait so long to announce that he was ill?"

"It says here that Mrs. Lincoln forbade anyone saying anything about his illness. It goes on that she hoped even for days while his health was sinking that he would recover to a full life."

"She sounds like a good prospect for our séances. I'll bet President Lincoln would pay a healthy fee for our services. Or, at least, Mrs. Lincoln would."

"You know, dear sister Maggie, since you swore off drink you've been ever so much more agreeable and...."

"Conscious. You can say it. I hope to never drink again. My sister and I have our job to do." Maggie's cheeks were rosy now because of more robust health. Her hair was kept in a well-coiffured cut. Though sixteen years younger than Leah, she looked as wise as a matron.

Leah smiled sardonically at her much younger sister. "We have a job to do tonight at Bascomb Hall. With the Presbyterian and Unified Bible churches supporting it, it's bound to bring in quite a crowd."

"It's almost becoming boring now to do these performances. I'm tempted to try something more daring."

"Don't even think of it." Leah's face was livid. "No chance. Do the act, make money."

"But you know, with the last show in Baltimore, all those people protesting out front, even in the sorry weather; if we did something more outrageous, we could silence the critics."

Leah thought for a moment. "No, it's too risky. We'll be heading out west to Ohio in two weeks. If there's any risk taking, we'll do it there, as long as there's a fast train to get away."

THREE DAYS LATER, FEBRUARY 24, 1862, 1:45 PM
THE WHITE HOUSE

The storm over Washington wailed and beat against the walls of homes and businesses and thousands of tents in the camps surrounding the city. The rain flooded the latrines, the garbage piles, and gutters, and washed the disease-infested water throughout the city in rivers of sludge that rose over curbs to slip under the doors at the thresholds and into the stables and barns, pouring ultimately into the streams that fed into the Potomac. The businessmen of the town crowded into the bars; mothers, huddled in their homes with their children, cradled their frightened babies and sent their older children to set towels at the window sills and pails under the roof leaks. The less fortunate reprobates and rascals residing in the nation's capital gathered under bridges or in covered wagons to plan and conjecture about their next filch or con. The prostitutes lounged in their sorry edifices, bored and anxious.

The hundreds of runaway slaves who had begun slipping away from their owners at the beginning of the war never stopped coming. Those who had not yet been processed by the army found corner eaves of buildings to crouch under and to wish momentarily for the fleshpots of their wretched slave hovels. They wondered why they had run away in the first place. The Union's capital was not the paradise for which they had hoped.

President Lincoln, sitting in his office, thought wearily on these subjects — the increase in crime in the city by virtue of the numerous land-dwelling privateers who had invaded like rats, hoping to weasel soldiers and civilians alike from their earnings. He knew that, despite the best labors of generous civilians and valiant efforts of the army's officers, the steady influx of runaways had almost brought the city to its knees. All these vexing thoughts rattled around in his brain, but he could not think on them now. No solutions for those problems today. On this day, at this hour, he was distraught beyond explanation.

He sat in his uncomfortable chair, staring out the window draped with funeral crepes at the rain falling like a Biblical deluge. Lightning divided the clouds over and over, throwing barbs of hot light into the sky, then the curtain clouds closed again. Thunder rumbled a tale of trouble and ruin at the president, and he tilted his head back a little to hold back tears.

He picked absent-mindedly at a loose thread of the hastily-made jacket he was wearing for his son's funeral. Willie had died of Typhus, the same disease depleting the great northern army. No bullets were necessary to thin the ranks. Typhus was sufficient.

He thought for a moment about the jacket with its dull gloss and paper thinness. It appeared shoddily made. He concerned himself with it because he had received reports that the cloth of many of the armies' uniforms manufactured by the lowest bidders seemed to ball up like lint at the first washing, and the threads peeled away like scabs from a wound.

Is it not enough that I have to worry about winning a war that I did not want, he thought, *and deal with the death of my son?*

He stared at the vacant flag pole in the yard, no flag flying in this downpour.

He was lost in the malaise of his soul, mesmerized by the gray wall of water plummeting out the window.

With violent force, a bolt of lightning struck the flagpole, sending sparks and fire flying. Thunder like a cannon blast created a vast shuddering of windows and walls, and he nearly fell from his chair.

He heard calls of alarm from the maids and from funeral attendees in the house that went on for a few moments, then the somber silence ensued for another half hour.

His secretary, John Nicolay, entered quietly behind him.

President Lincoln heard his cautious steps. "Is it time, Nicolay?"

"Yes, Mr. President. Everyone has assembled in the East Room. As you requested, Dr. Phineas Gurley, the Presbyterian pastor, will deliver the eulogy. He has prepared some sterling remarks. I've seen them. And sir, General McCulloch is here, and a considerable number from the Congress as well."

"And is Mrs. Lincoln ready?"

Nicolay cleared his throat. "She bids me tell you that she will not attend the funeral service nor the interment."

The president made no reply, merely nodded his head. The two men proceeded to the East Room where little Willie's body lay in repose in a metal coffin, stained to look like wood.

THIRTY-SEVEN

JUDGE NOT BY THE PEAK ATTAINED, BUT BY THE JOURNEY TRAVELED

FEBRUARY 25, 1862, LATE AFTERNOON
TELEGRAPH ROAD, SOUTHWEST OF SPRINGFIELD

"I can barely believe we have traveled this road for a whole day and have not encountered a single cavalry troop, guard or picket," Cyntha said. Dreary shadows dwelled under her tired, green eyes. She had hardly slept the night of hers and Constance's escape from Springfield, and her mind was crowded with thoughts of either her husband, Joseph, and his soul in torment, or of her brother, charged with theft from the bank where he had worked.

To her right, Reynolds lightly shook the reins, the horse tugging the carriage along the Telegraph Road. Cyntha knew marauders ranged in the area and wished Reynolds kept the pistol in his belt instead of hidden in Constance's bag.

On the other side of Reynolds, Constance Carver stretched her bony arms after waking from a snooze.

She blinked and looked out at the wooded environs with traces of snow in the shady spots under the crowded trees and shrubs. The road stretched downhill into a valley. "We did pass them supply wagons, but they didn't give us a never mind. I imagine them Yanks think, since they closed up Springfield so tight, that no one that shouldn't be would ever be on the road in the first place."

"But what if soldiers with questions do come upon us?" Cyntha said.

"You just stick to our story. I told you I met the general's wife visiting him at the boarding house awhile back, and you look enough like her you could be her sister. You just claim to be Mrs. Belinda Curtis, and tell them we're fetching this here doctor's medicine bag to a sick officer." She pointed to the bag between her feet. "For all they know, that trunk of yor'n is filled with medicine and bandages. T'aint nothin' to worry about."

"All right, all right." Cyntha bit her lip. She looked at Constance, dark-skinned and angle- boned but well-proportioned in her bosom and waist, and with shiny black hair tucked under an unbecoming slouch hat. Her face had a sharp nose, high cheek bones, and smooth complexion. She wondered where Constance had gained such confidence. Was it from her Cherokee mother?

"Pretty soon, Miss Cyntha," Reynolds remarked. "We're goin' to have to stop and make camp. This old mare needs a rest, too. She done pulled us all day."

"Why, of course," Cyntha replied. "Watch for a good spot to camp off the road."

The moment the sentence left her lips a dozen blue-clad cavalrymen broke out from the foliage and surrounded their carriage. A cavalryman grabbed the horse's harness and brought the gig to a stop.

Cyntha's stomach churned. Her face blanched.

A sharply-dressed captain in his mid-twenties stepped down from his horse and strode with marked steps up to the carriage. "Hello, ma'am." He touched a finger to his forage cap. "Hello, ma'am," he said to Constance. He ignored Reynolds, but stretched out a hand and plucked the reins from him, turning to Cyntha. "Ma'am, I have to ask you what in heaven's name you are doing on this road. Didn't you know it's closed to travelers?" His tone, though cordial, was somewhat condescending.

Cyntha drew herself up and tried to look like she was put out by the officer. "Of course, I know the road is closed. We're heading south to bring medical supplies to General Curtis's army. He has an officer wounded who needs immediate attention."

In the dimming light, Cyntha could still see the suspicion in the captain's eyes.

"Ma'am, why don't you tell me your name, and...."

"Why don't you tell me yours first? Can't you see we're on an urgent errand of mercy?"

The captain glanced back at some of his soldiers who were snickering. "Very well, ma'am. I'm Captain Davis of the Fourth Missouri Union Cavalry. The Hussars."

Cyntha leaned forward, "Davis? Isn't that the name of that traitorous Confederate president? Is he your cousin?"

The snickering of the cavalrymen turned to outright chuckles. The captain held up his gloved hand, white in the early moon glow. The laughter subsided. "Now, why don't you tell me your name, ma'am," he said to Cyntha.

"I am Mrs. Samuel Curtis, wife of your general. This is my traveling companion and nurse, Mrs. Juniper Watson." She thumbed at Constance who gave her a surprised look. "Can you not see the doctor's bag at her feet? Our mission is urgent, and you are thwarting our progress." Cyntha sat back in the seat and tried to show as much disdain on her face as she could. "Now why don't you tell me where this fourth cavalry is camped? That is where we were told by Quartermaster Sheridan we were supposed to rest for the evening."

"Excuse me, Mrs. Curtis. I had no idea. But why are you riding out here all alone? Isn't the general afraid for your well-being?"

"Well, of course he is. We had a fine escort of a half-dozen soldiers, but they were called back on pressing business just a few miles back. The captain said we would come upon the Fourth Missouri cavalry in a few strides and, apparently, we just did."

"Yes, ma'am."

"I only wished we'd found them to be gentlemen, not suspicious scallywags." She harrumphed and crossed her arms.

The befuddled Captain Davis shifted his weight, stuck his thumbs in his pants pockets, and looked around at his men. A few of them shrugged their shoulders. He handed the reins back to Reynolds and mounted his horse. "Follow me," he shouted. He pointed his arm down the road, and the cavalry troop trotted after him.

Reynolds flipped the reins, and the carriage kept pace with the riders. Cyntha leaned over and threaded her arm through Reynolds'. "Dear Josiah, I'm sorry I didn't introduce you. You are a cherished friend, but...."

"No need to explain, Miss Cyntha. If you hadn't done what you did, I'd be on a work detail in Springfield." He gave her a knowing nod.

Cyntha's heart pounded like a blacksmith's hammer, and it took her entire will to catch her breath. She looked over at Constance who had broken her usual stolid expression and was smiling ear to ear at her. "You done good, Miss Cyntha. Proud of ye'. But my name ain't Juniper." She shook her head but still smiled.

Reynolds began sniggering as the little troop sped along. "We done tricked 'em."

Cyntha remained deeply worried. They were not out of the woods yet.

THIRTY-EIGHT

To Loosen the Bonds of Orion

Same Evening, February 25, 1862, 7 pm
Union Cavalry Camp, Telegraph Road

Reynolds drew up the carriage. Cyntha, Constance, and he were immediately aware of an extensive camp aglow with fires, hundreds of horses, and several tents. Captain Davis dismounted and helped both women step from the carriage. Cyntha kept the doctor's bag in hand. A private, at the captain's orders, took the reins from Reynolds and bade him step down. Reynolds complied. The private drove the carriage out of sight, though Reynolds strained his neck to watch where it had been taken.

"Don't go far," Reynolds hollered. "Miz Favor, er, Curtis will be needin' some things from that chest."

The carriage disappeared into a shadowed grove.

Captain Davis escorted the women to a tent with guards on either side of the opening. He told the women to wait. Cyntha, shivering from cold and more from fear, squeezed Constance's hand. "Lord, help us," she whispered.

In a moment, Captain Davis reappeared and held the tent flap open. "Colonel Meszaros will see you now." When Cyntha saw the man sitting behind the desk, his head down writing by lantern light, she thought perhaps that Captain Davis had been jesting with them. The colonel appeared no more than a youth. She glanced furtively at Constance who seemed as astounded as she.

The young man at last looked up. He had an angelic boy's face and could not have been more than in his early twenties. "Hello, Mrs. Curtis. I'm Colonel Meszaros."

"Hello, Colonel Meszaros. Let me introduce my traveling companion and a fine nurse, Mrs. Juniper Watson."

Constance again gave Cyntha a sly look.

Colonel Meszaros stood, swaggered around the small desk, and came directly in front of the women. Without looking at Constance, he spoke inches from Cyntha's face. "Pleased to meet you, Mrs. Curtis." He glanced at Constance. "And you, Miss, or is it Mrs. Wilkens?" He smirked.

"The last name is Watson, Colonel, and it's Mrs." Constance twanged.

"I see." The colonel turned on his heels, walked to his desk, and opened a tin decanter from which he pulled a long cigar. He bit off the end, lit the cigar, and puffed away, not saying a word. "I didn't see a wedding ring."

"Lost it carin' for the wounded."

Cyntha's unease was growing. Her armpits were wet, despite the overall chill of the tent. Her breaths came in short gulps. Constance was rocking on her toes and heels.

"I would offer you both a chair, but I only have the one." Colonel Meszaros blew an elongated smoke ring and settled himself on the desktop, one leg on the ground, the other dangling. His stare penetrating the women. "General Curtis is known for despising slavery. I'm surprised you have a slave with you."

Constance began to realize the man's ploy, attempting to catch them in the lie he suspected. "He ain't no slave. He's a freeman. His name is Josiah Reynolds. You can go ask him yourself. He is a man of integrity and is employed by Mrs. Curtis."

"Oh, my apologies, Mrs. Curtis." Colonel Meszaros tapped ashes from his cigar. He looked up at the tent ceiling. The smoke hung in a haze between him and the women. "Mrs. Curtis. There's nothing like a good cigar. I hear your husband prefers Panama cigars. They're rare now with the war on." He again looked straight at Cyntha's eyes.

Before Cyntha could formulate an answer, he coughed several times, his face down, spit flying from his mouth. In that moment, Constance tapped Cyntha's foot with her own. When Cyntha glanced at her, Constance made a slight shake of her head.

When the colonel quit his coughing spell, Cyntha said, "My husband does not smoke. Nor does his son, Major Henry Curtis."

"Oh, yes, of course. I forgot." Colonel Meszaros rose and paced around the desk, "I was thinking of sending him a gift for his birthday, which is...?"

"October fifth." Cyntha declared, having no idea what the correct answer was.

The colonel's dark eyes darted back and forth several times. "Yes, of course." He sat again at his desk. He called, "Captain Davis."

The captain entered the tent.

"See to it that Mrs. Curtis and Mrs. Watson are well taken care of." The colonel smiled broadly and stuck the cigar in his teeth. "Tell the officers of company E and F to give up their tent for one night. Please see to these ladies' accommodations." He turned to the women. "I hope you'll forgive my questions. One can't be too careful. We must be diligent against these rebel rats, the dross of humanity. So, welcome, Mrs. Curtis and Mrs. Watson."

Cyntha and Constance spent the evening in the officers' tent amid the Fourth Regiment of Missouri Union cavalry. Two privates brought Cyntha's trunk to the tent. She had no idea where Reynolds had bedded down, but chose not to look for him. They went without supper, and asked for none. Cyntha figured the less contact with any soldiers, the better. They decided they would sleep in the dresses they wore, aware of their situation and abashed of any sense of impropriety, being, as they were, surrounded by men.

Constance curled up on a cot with several blankets and her buffalo coat over her and fell quickly to sleep. With the clattering and campcraft din, horses whickering, and the incessant tread of feet past the tent, Cyntha lay awake staring into the dark.

When the hours had passed well into the blackest elements of morning, the noises died away. She arose and turned up the lantern a measure, barely enough to see. She looked at her companion buried to her shoulders in blankets. Her cocoa-colored skin shone in the lantern's glow, a few tendrils of her dark hair hanging lightly over her lips and fluttering faintly with each breath. Cyntha wondered what it must have been like to be raised by a Cherokee woman, one that seldom spoke or smiled.

Cyntha had learned quite a bit about Constance's rough edges during their covert meetings while planning their escape. She wondered how Constance must feel, being abandoned by her husband, having no children and no means to survive except by her own obstinacy. She looked at the smooth face that held a wild beauty to it, a wolf-like furtiveness.

Cyntha had undone her hair bun and let her shoulder length tresses hang loose, and she lifted some of her own black strands where she could examine them, not too unlike Constance's, though not as long, nor as dark. She peered at the strands a moment. She could not fathom the quality of beauty of other women, whether one was truly more striking than another. She could not bring herself to call herself attractive, and she considered it to be a horrid lack of humility to think so. She was only grateful that Joseph had thought her beautiful. Not just he, but many other beaus who had sought her company.

In evaluating a man, she had no problem identifying the traits she felt were most handsome, most appealing, indeed which ones excited her rawest passions.

Constance gave a gentle moan, probably the most childlike, innocent sound that Cyntha had ever heard her utter. Cyntha turned down the lantern and made her way to the front of the tent and untied the laces of the flap. She leaned her head out into the starry night.

A warm breeze threaded across her face. She pursed her lips, and her breath did not plume vaporous as it had for so many cold days previous.

She gazed up through the wavering tree boughs, caught in the ebb and flow of the southerly wind. She spotted the Big Dipper. Ursa Major. The Large Bear. And wondered why it was called so. *What did the Greek astrologers see in those ancient skies?* She plumbed her thoughts. She had never seen any shape in the stars resembling a bear. *The Greeks brought the world democracy. Was it really such a good idea? The Union is a democracy, but Southerners felt disenfranchised. So, they left the Union and made their own democracy. Their slaves certainly have no say in what they call their democracy, and Freemen barely can vote in the North. And yet, we all say we live in a democracy.* "Two democracies, filled with passion and with hatred," she whispered into the stars, "fighting each other as if their foe was a vile tyrant leading an army of Philistines." She shook her head at her own realization.

She stepped out of the tent and breathed in the crisp sweetness of the piney air as she gazed up at the ephemeral cloud of the Milky Way. *Why so many stars?* she wondered. Unable to divine any larger meaning for night's glittering spangles, or for democracy, or for war, she felt that *ignorance* was a gift God had given her. She was not supposed to know why men fought and why democracy was so imperfect. She could only hope for some good to come in the future. She slipped inside the tent, lay on her cot, and slept, dreaming of sweet encounters with her husband, Joseph.

In the morning, Reynolds was calling lightly at their tent, "Mrs. Curtis. Y'all up? Wake up. It's time to get ready to go."

Cyntha, in her wrinkled dress, arose and greeted Reynolds at the tent opening. She was so overjoyed to see his gray-bearded face she reached out, pulled his head down and gave him a kiss on the cheek. "Thank you, Reynolds. The sooner we're out of here, the better."

While Cyntha combed and secured her hair in a bun, Constance brought out deer jerky from her doctor's kit. The three sat on camp stools outside, chewing on the stringy beef. A young private came shuffling up, bearing three tin cups of coffee. He pulled hot biscuits bulging from his pockets. Along with the biscuits, he gave Cyntha a small jar of peach jam and a spoon. "Compliments of the colonel," he called over his shoulder, departing quickly, his long sabre clacking against his legs.

The coffee could hardly pass for the name, but it was hot, and the warm biscuits with jam brought smiles to all three. When Cyntha and Joseph four years previously had moved to Iowa, she grew used to the flour breads, different from the cornbread of Tennessee where she had been raised. With Reynolds' help, they grew wheat on their farm.

Cyntha reveled in the sunlight glancing through the trees. The weather had warmed considerably.

"I done found where they stowed the carriage," Reynolds commented, licking his lips of the jam, "and I found our mares. They fed them oats, hung a grain maul over their ears. They was a munchin' away. I got the fresh one hitched up and ready to go."

Colonel Miszaros came strolling up to their tent and inquired of how they had fared during the night and of their destination. Cyntha told him that Elkhorn Tavern was to be set up as a field hospital. In short order, he afforded them an escort of a half-dozen cavalrymen all the way to the tavern.

When they arrived at Elkhorn in early evening of the second day from Springfield, Cyntha's cousin, Polly Cox, stepped off the porch with a delighted countenance. Cyntha rushed to hug her cousin. Polly was a woman of meager height, broad of waist and hip, and with intense, tightly woven freckles across her face. Like Cyntha, she wore her hair tied in a bun. Her dress was embroidered, indigo homespun with a single hoop.

"Cyntha, whatever are you doing here?" Polly asked, smiling broadly.

Cyntha waved the escort troop away. They galloped north up the Telegraph Road. "I'll explain in a bit," Cyntha said. "First, I want you to meet my two friends. This is Constance Carver and Josiah Reynolds." Constance extended her hand, but Polly merely nodded at them.

"Well, for goodness sakes, come in," Polly said. "Get out of the cold. It is so good to see you."

"And to see you as well. Is your husband, Jesse, to home?"

"He's off selling cattle to the Union army. He's been gone for weeks up north." Polly stopped on the front porch of the stout stone and wood plank, two-story tavern. She pointed out to the low peaks of the Boston Mountains. Cyntha, Constance, and Reynolds turned to look. "I love this," she said, almost in a whisper, "in the evening when the moon shines over the mountains. Our little piece of heaven here atop the Pea Ridge plateau."

The group stood admiring the first glimmering stars and the sliver of a moon above sleepy, dark purple mountains. In a moment, they heard children laughing, trampling feet, and jockeying against furniture. "That would be my younger boys, Elias and Franklin," Polly said, shaking her head. "I don't know why Joe doesn't have more control of those rag-tags."

"Your son, Joe, is here, too?"

"Yes, with his wife, Lucinda. They're helping me run the place with Jesse being absent for so many weeks. With all these armies passing through, I don't know how I would have handled it. First, the Rebels come crashing down the road from Springfield like a bear was after them. They looked a mess. They slept in the orchard and the yard." She pointed at the barren trees. "Then took every piece of fruit and vegetable from our root cellar. They unloaded a few sick ones here and just left them in our care."

Polly pointed in a wide arc of the front yard and frowned. "Then the Federal armies came through. Some kept going, but some stopped and camped over the entire grounds. You couldn't walk in a straight line without bumping into a dog tent. Then other Federals marched back from the other way. One regiment sweeps in here and takes over the tavern like they own it. Then they leave again. Wagons pass through here regular. It's very troubling. So, I come out here and look at the mountains. It gives me peace."

"Indeed, such a tranquil piece of land, away from war." Cyntha said. "And it is so good to see you. I only wish I could see Jesse."

"Yes. Jesse's been away for a while, but we've managed. Elkhorn Tavern has not been the same quiet rest for travelers for weeks. Since the Yanks came chasing the Missouri Guard down the road, we haven't had a single regular customer, nor a single Butterfield stage since December."

"It must be a strain."

"Well, Joe and Lucinda do most of the hard work. And, of course, with your brother, Anthony, and his wife here, they've been such a big help." She stopped abruptly when she saw the astonished look on Cyntha's and Reynolds' face.

"My brother? He's here?"

"Why, yes. I was surprised when I saw you step down from your carriage, but then I figured you knew he was here, and that was the reason why you journeyed all the way from Iowa to visit. And to meet his new wife and step-daughter. Though you picked a harsh time to come."

"Well, I did *not* know he had come here. And you say he's married? That *is* news! But I do so wish to see him. I heard he's been in some trouble."

"Trouble? How's that? He never said anything."

"Never mind. That would be just like Anthony not to mention it to you. Let us go inside and catch up."

When Cyntha and the others entered the tavern, Anthony and his new bride, Jeanette, were just making their way down the stairs. His wooden leg clacked on the stairs. His face showed deep amazement.

THIRTY-NINE

ONE WHO HEEDS THE WIND WILL NOT SOW

THE NEXT DAY, FEBRUARY 27, 1862
ELKHORN TAVERN, ARKANSAS

In mid-morning of the day after their arrival, Cyntha sat in the parlor across a table from Anthony. A soft fire glowed in the fireplace. Greased paper filled the pane of the window which had been broken recently by rowdy soldiers and allowed in a milky light. Anthony tapped his fingers lightly on the table. A mantel clock ticked what seemed to him inordinately loud.

"So, you're not going to tell me why you are accused of stealing from the bank?" Cyntha glared at her older brother.

"What would you like me to tell you, Cyntha?" Anthony tried to remain calm, but the argument had gone on for a half hour. "Would you like me to tell you something that you would then feel compelled to tell my new wife and dash our hopes of a life together?"

"What sort of life will that be? A life built on deceit? On theft?"

"Did I say I stole anything?"

"The telegram said you did?"

"So, the telegram is proof?"

"Can you not go back to St. Paul and prove yourself innocent?"

"That sounds easy. Just skedaddle on up there through all this war, pay my way back up the Mississippi where river traffic is reserved entirely for the army. Put my wife and child in harm's way to prove what?"

"That you are innocent. You still have not told me why they accused you of theft. Why?"

"Do you know why?"

"Stop asking me questions and answer mine."

"I will not." He folded his arms across his chest.

Cyntha opened her mouth to speak, but stopped, seeing the futileness of the effort. She stood abruptly and stormed upstairs. *Can he not see my distress?* She thought, *I have lost my husband, my only love, and have no means of maintaining our farm or even paying Reynolds his wages? Can he not know that I needed my brother to support me in this dreaded hour?*

She tightened her jaw, slamming the bedroom door behind her. *I will not cry another tear. I have borne too much already.* Her life seemed bare of flesh, all bone.

Anthony sat alone in the parlor, a sharp wind flinging ice at the walls. He wanted to tell her the truth. He had wanted to tell as much to General McCulloch, but could not bring himself to do so. His thoughts tumbled back to the tumultuous week at the beginning of the war. The week that Tennessee seceded, he had wired his father's good friend, General McCulloch, and offered to secure gold for the Southern cause. Then his conscience had taken over, and he almost recanted his overly enthusiastic proposal. He felt he was in error even as he was developing the heist. But he considered himself a man of honor, and he had promised to help the Confederate states break from the shackles of the northern commercial hypocrites. He had seen first-hand how the bankers he worked with decried the southern morality, all the while making a fortune off southern goods, especially cotton.

He had stolen no money from the bank. His accomplice, a teller named Brown, had absconded with all the coins after Anthony had given him plans and a private key. They had agreed with a handshake to share it, but when the evening came for them to meet, the teller never appeared. The gold was missing, but not by the means Anthony had proffered. The teller had somehow stolen the coins by a completely different method.

Panicked, Anthony resigned the employ of the Minnesota State Bank. Before leaving, he shuffled into his valise a pile of old paper stocks, made nearly valueless in the 1857 financial crash. When he lost the valise in the sinking of the Aurelia, he had not forfeited anything of real value. He kept that bit of truth from General McCulloch, thinking that if the South prevailed in the war, he would have recourse to the general in finding him a position, perhaps in the Confederate government or banking industry. The only gold coins he had from Minnesota were his life savings stored in the chamber of his wooden leg. He gave most of those to the southern cause, keeping a few coins for his marriage, buying new clothes for himself, his new family, and for Owen, and then enough to secure a horse and carriage for travel to Elkhorn Tavern.

"Indeed, dear sister," he whispered to no one, "how could I tell you that story? What would you make of me? I now have a wife who wedded me despite my obvious disability, and she has made some salient points about saving the Union and working things out among the states. I cannot take the chance of losing Jeanette by being imprisoned for a plan I only formulated but never implemented. Someday, Cyntha, I will explain everything."

Jeanette came into the parlor. "Anthony, I saw your sister in the hall. She looked quite distressed. Is everything all right?" She took his hand in hers, her bright eyes shining.

"Yes," Anthony said, standing. "She's lost her husband and was counting on my help with her finances. She needs assurance... and...." He could not bring himself to say any more.

Jeanette pulled him close and kissed his cheek. "Come. Our daughter is drawing a picture in the dining room. We'll talk later."

Anthony felt dread that he would blurt out the truth to his wife. He was torn from his former self, cleaved by conscience and need.

Suddenly, a clattering of hooves sounded outside the tavern. They looked out the window to see two hundred Union cavalry arriving in the yard. Officers dismounted, rushed up the stairs, and knocked.

When Polly Cox answered the door, a captain announced, "We are in need of rest. In the name of the United States government, this property and this dwelling is now for the use of this army."

FORTY

∽

PERHAPS A PLAN
FOR VICTORY

Paul and Ben McGavin crept forward through dense brush, accompanied by General McCulloch. They halted behind a rock outcropping on a ridge. Paul pointed toward a niche in the forest across a boulder-filled gully. "There's some pickets. See them smokin' their pipes."

General McCulloch lifted his spyglass and held it to his eye. "Yes, I see them. I see two more that've laid aside their guns and are playing a game of checkers."

"I don't believe their soldiers're too worried about what our army might do. Over there," Paul pointed again, "the Yanks've been clearing trees and building their redoubts and barricades. Further up the hill you can see some stronger fortifications with cannons."

"So, General Curtis has taken a defensive position," General McCulloch said, scanning the Union lines thoroughly. "Lieutenant McGavin, I see two regimental flags. Have you an idea of the number of Yanks positioned here around Cross Hollows?"

Paul removed his glasses and wiped them with a kerchief. "Well, sir, their general picked a strong defensible position. If we come up here looking for a fight, it may not matter how many men they have, because they could hold a long time. Also, Ben moseyed around the entire affair the other day and night. Tell him what you found out, Ben."

"Best I can tell," Ben said, running a hand through his blond locks, "the army tuckered out, so their General Curtis has the army spread out far and wide tryin' to fetch up some provender. I talked to some Yanks who were chasin' wild turkeys. I don't know who was smarter — them or the turkeys. They didn't seem to have much sense. They believed me when I told them I was a Yankee supporter lookin' to join up. I could've sold 'em snake oil. They told me Curtis is worried about holdin' this spot. His supplies is comin' all the way from Rolla."

Ben pointed to the north. "Their line's strung out, but they could easily move together rapid as quicksilver. They've cut through the woods connecting their interior lines. I'm estimatin', based on their tents and regimental flags, between four and six thousand just here. Hundreds more stretched out coverin' their supply line all the way to Springfield. Not many cavalry, though, that I've seen. I'm still unsure of that. I think he's sent them off raidin'."

"Makes no difference," General McCulloch said. "The Yankees pushed General Price's men out of Missouri. President Davis himself told me not two weeks ago the only help we'd be receiving is a new general to put Price in line. General Earl Van Dorn is arriving soon to take charge of my troops *and* the Missouri Guard. If he can handle that dullard, Price, I'm all for it. I hear Van Dorn's the kind of man that can get it done."

"Do you think he'll try a frontal assault on Curtis's position?" Paul asked.

"Not if I can talk him out of it. We need a way around this position. Get between him and his supply line."

"Ben and I think we know a way to get behind them. We plan to reconnoiter this evening." Paul looked long at Ben. "In three days, we'll know for sure. If I remember correctly, we might be able to sidestep the Yank army here, then hit 'em from the rear."

"Very good, Lieutenant McGavin. Inform me as soon as you can. I can't see Van Dorn launching an attack in the winter, but the Yankees *have crossed* into Arkansas, and that sticks in a lot of people's craw, including mine. I need to get a good look at Curtis's deployment. Think I'll move closer."

"Sir!" Paul almost yelled, before dropping his voice to a whisper. "I wouldn't advise that. You take too many chances as it is. Let us do that."

The general thought a moment. "Very well. I'll have Brigadier General McIntosh take some cavalry around and bust up the Yankee supply line. Shake 'em up some." He slid his spyglass into a deep coat pocket, and the three crept away.

FORTY-ONE

⌒

To Suffer the Grievous Loss

FEBRUARY 28, 1862, LATE MORNING
ELKHORN TAVERN, ARKANSAS

"It's time I went home, Cyntha," Constance said. She hoisted a haversack over her shoulder and pushed her floppy hat down on her head.

"But you are welcome here at Elkhorn Tavern. My cousin Polly has said as much several times. She so appreciates you helping tend to these soldiers who pass through. And...."

"I do feel welcome, Cyntha, but the truth is I'm no closer to my husband and farther still from my farm. I'm going home, and maybe if this infernal war ends soon, I'll see my no account..." she sighed remorsefully, "husband come strollin' 'cross the yard, and we'll get back to doin' what we should be doin'. Farmin' and makin' babies, not warrin'."

"I wish you'd reconsider. I owe you a great deal. You helped us escape Springfield. I'll miss you."

"You'll be all right. You got family here. Your cousins, and your brother, Anthony, and his wife, Jeanette. And that little gem of their daughter."

The two stood in the tavern parlor looking past the white-lace curtains through a frosted window toward the Boston Mountains. "But how will you get around the guards and troops moving up and down Telegraph Road? You've seen how many troops pass here. And a lot of them don't speak English. If they catch you, what then?"

"I don't plan to stay on the road much." Constance turned toward Cyntha. "I'll go over land. I need to get home, make sure my place ain't fallen to ruin."

Anthony limped in from the kitchen. "I hear you're leaving us," he said. "Can you not wait until Spring? That's what my wife and I are doing. Waiting until Spring, then heading to Texas."

Constance, biting her lip, shook her head. "Naw. I'm done here. My home is calling." She pulled on her buffalo coat and stuck her big floppy hat down tight on her head. She wore pants and a shirt now, ones given her by Polly's son, Joe. She gathered up two haversacks of provisions and two canteens and trudged toward the door. Opening it, she stood for a long moment with the wind whistling a wild chant through the doorway. She nodded at Cyntha and Anthony. "Give my thanks to the Cox family. I ain't much on goodbyes." With that, she was on the porch, then down the steps, the door latching behind her. She climbed on her horse that was already laden with her sacks of food and canteens. In a moment, she was down the road a few dozen yards before angling her mount toward a break in the trees and vanishing.

THE SAME DAY, FEBRUARY 28, 1862, 11 PM
BENTONVILLE ROAD, JUST NORTH OF ELKHORN TAVERN

Ben McGavin, astride his mount, craned his neck and stretched, trying to stay awake. He looked up at the starry sky with long streaks of leaden clouds gathering. The moon was a silvery bark drifting among smoky colored waves. With less than two hours of sleep in over two days, he was losing his lucidity.

Paul and he rode along the Bentonville cutoff road, circling the Pea Ridge big mountain in far northwest Arkansas. Ben listened to the clip clop of their horses' hooves and the occasional squeak of the saddle leather, and found the sounds somewhat melodic. He hummed "The Yellow Rose of Texas" lightly and fought against his drowsiness.

Paul, equally exhausted, listened for the possible sounds of approaching horses. The two had ridden deep into Union army territory, scouting for General McCulloch to find a way to slip unnoticed around the Federals. The seldom-used road they traversed now, though narrow and with deep wheel ruts, was passable. Valuable information to share with the general.

Ben slumped forward in his saddle. The tightly packed trees along the road pervaded his line of sight, and the sagging snow-laden pine branches looked to him like a regiment of a vanquished army laying down its weapons. He was dwelling on this perception when he drifted to sleep, nodding like a cork bobbing in a pond.

Paul leaned over and swatted Ben on the back. He waked, startled. Paul held up his hand, and they drew to an instant halt. "Listen," he whispered. After a moment, he said, "Thought I heard horses."

"I don't hear nothin'," Ben yawned and stretched.

"Neither do I. But ever since we passed McKissick Creek and Siegel's division, I've had a hunch that someone saw us and has been trailin' us." The brothers had been on constant alert, moving sometimes within yards of enemy outposts, creeping on foot, their horses tied far back, oftentimes crouching in shadows for hours until Union sentries moved away.

"Why would anyone be following us? We're just two men, not a cavalry company."

"I guess I'm worrying over nothing. Still, there's bound to be Yankee patrols about, even at night."

"Stop worryin'. If some Yanks show up, we ride hard and get away."

"What if they start shooting?"

"Well, we shoot back."

"Ben, neither one of us has ever shot a man, or even shot at one."

"Well." Ben paused a long while. "The army gave us these nice Colt pistols. I reckon I could shoot a Yank if he was shootin' at me."

"I prefer not to shoot at anyone."

A mean, biting wind careened through the valley. Clouds covered the moon. The brothers continued slowly in the coalmine of night. Nearby, wolves howled a mournful serenade. Paul focused more and more on the prospect of someone shooting at him. He wondered, too, if he had the wherewithal to shoot a man. He suddenly felt dizzy and a little nauseous, and the alarming new cold caused him to tremble. He glanced at Ben who appeared merely drowsy.

Ben rose in his saddle and stretched. He noticed Paul's shaking. "You cold?"

"Naw. Well, yeah. A little."

"Dang it, put on your coat, big brother. I'm middlin' cold myself."

Paul reached in a saddle pouch and drew out his riding coat and flung it over his shoulders.

"How far do you think we've come?" Ben asked. He tugged his own heavy coat about his thin, strong body.

"I'm estimating we've come directly behind Sigel's army by several miles. We're about ten miles northeast of Bentonville."

Just then, the brothers noticed lights flickering in windows through the trees in the distance. "That must be Elkhorn Tavern," Paul said. "This is where we turn around."

"Let's go see."

"Not a chance. Probably full of Yanks."

Ben ignored his brother and cantered his horse forward. A light sleet began drifting down.

Paul sighed heavily and followed after his brother, calling in a whisper, "Ben! Ben! Don't! You're not thinking straight."

He caught up with Ben at a rail fence about thirty yards from the tavern. Every window glowed, golden and inviting. He grabbed Ben's horse's reins. "Stop, Ben!"

The first shot pinged off a fence post five feet from Ben, then grazed his horse in the flank. The horse reared and screamed. More shots came at them from all angles. Paul wrenched his dapple gray around and sped back down the road, but Ben bailed from his saddle, still holding the horse's rein, while it danced and leaped. He pulled off his riding gloves with his teeth and drew one of his revolvers. He fired at gun flashes in the cavernous dark. Almost simultaneously, several bullets hit his horse, and the animal slammed to the earth like a hewn tree. Ben jumped to the ditch by the road, firing into pitch blackness in the trees around the tavern. Union soldiers carrying rifles poured onto the lamp-lit porch of the tavern. Voices called for Ben to surrender.

He looked down the road. Union cavalry spilled like locusts from the trees and rode hard pursuing his brother. "Paul!" he shouted. He thought maybe he heard Paul returning his call, but the noise of gunfire was too overwhelming. Bullets thudded into the dirt and fence rails all about him.

He scrambled up and dove for the cover of the woods. A bullet tore into his ankle, snapping bones and sending a torrent of pain up his leg. He forced himself to struggle deeper into the forest, the pain washing over him in waves.

Sleet was pouring from the sky.

He limped hurriedly along the ice-caked ground, careening into trees and bushes. The dense undergrowth grabbed at his clothes and scratched his hands. His leg began to feel as heavy as an ingot of pig iron. When he could no longer hold his revolver, it dropped from his hand. His mind went black, and he collapsed.

Paul drove his stallion onward. The cavalry pursuers were relentless in their chase down the Bentonville detour. His eyes flashed left and right watching for a break in the trees in which he could hide. The winter storm wind threw sleet into his face, burning cold. Though he drove his mount hard, the Yankees seemed to be gaining on him.

For miles, he galloped in the dark, barely missing brush entanglements and leaping fallen trees in the road. Finally, he pulled up and looked behind him into the lightless void. He heard horses galloping, but the sound was receding from him. The Yankees had given up the pursuit. Panting, he dismounted and walked his tired horse off the road into the cover of trees. "My fool brother," he said aloud. "He either got himself captured." He swallowed hard. "Or killed."

He loosened the neck cord of his hat, and the hat fell to his back. He bit his lip and paced, listing his options in his mind. At length, he mounted his horse and moved stealthily once more back toward Elkhorn Tavern. The ice storm abated. The air grew colder.

The morning sun sat in a cleft between mountains, and the sky was sooty when Elkhorn Tavern, where he had left Ben, came into his view once more. He guided his horse off the road, deep into the junipers and blackjacks, and tied it there. He had lost his coat in his escape, and a bitterly freezing morning sliced his frame like a saber. Revolver in hand, he crept alongside the road, darting from tree to tree, keeping alert to any picket. Nearer the tavern, he caught sight of Ben's dead horse, crystalline ice atop the rigid body.

He shrunk back behind a skinny oak and covered his face with his hands. He succumbed to tears.

He peered once more around the tree at the fallen horse. At that moment, two blue-clad soldiers in heavy overcoats cavorted down the tavern steps, lighting their pipes and talking loudly. Two more soldiers, pickets, ambled from the trees behind the house toward the two smokers, rifles on their shoulders. Not twenty feet from him, a third guard called to the others and traipsed out of the trees onto the road and made his way to the group. Paul held his breath.

"Kinda noisy last night," the picket yelled, rubbing his eyes and yawning, "shooting at them Rebs." The others chided him for his comment and offered him tobacco for his pipe. The soldiers stood jawing and smoking.

"One of 'em got away," Paul heard a guard say.

Paul turned, tears streaming down his face, knowing he would have to mourn his brother later. The army of thousands of men needed the information he had. He made his way back to his horse and rode south, keeping to the trees as much as he could.

FORTY-TWO

∞

THE MERCY OF
AN ENEMY

FEBRUARY 28, 1862, 11:30 PM
ELKHORN TAVERN

In a troubled sleep, Cyntha was awakened by the rattle of gunfire outside the tavern. Wrapping herself in her robe, she hurried downstairs where Anthony, who was strapping on his wooden leg, met her. They were soon joined by Polly, Joe and Lucinda, the younger Cox boys, and Anthony's family. Anthony, his wooden leg banging noisily, herded them into the kitchen.

Unions soldiers who had been sleeping in the downstairs parlor and kitchen were up, slinging on coats, tying brogans, and grabbing rifles and ammunition. Soon they were rushing out the door, some with lanterns in hand.

"Where's Reynolds?" Cyntha, crouching by the pie safe, asked Anthony.

"I saw him go outside a while ago," Anthony replied, shielding the children with his body. "He said he wanted to smoke his pipe."

"Oh, dear." Cyntha moaned. A bullet thudded the wall, and she ducked behind a chair.

Outside, when the shooting started, Reynolds was standing with his back to the fireplace wall, his pipe tight in his lips, his hands tucked in his armpits. He ducked to the ground and witnessed what the Union soldiers were firing at — a figure on the ground, and then his horse falling violently to the earth. Enough light came from the new-thrown lantern light to allow Reynolds to see the youthful man dart to the trees, take a hit, and stumble into the forest.

Some minutes after the shooting stopped, a lieutenant led a dozen men with lanterns into the forest. Reynolds waited in the shadows unnoticed.

Ben lay unconscious in a deep pile of brown moldy leaves and almost completely under a broad, dense juniper bush. He awoke suddenly. His leg felt like it was on fire. He knew he was losing blood. With great effort, he yanked off his belt and secured a tourniquet below his knee. He realized the shooting had stopped. Pulling the tourniquet tighter, he slipped again from consciousness.

When he regained presence of mind, the pain seemed to defile his entire body. He bit his wrist to keep from screaming. Silence surrounded him, save a falling leaf or twig. To his left, a raccoon gamboled along, crackling the foliage. Looking up, Ben saw the sleet clouds had slid quickly away. He watched glittering stars through the trees. The tall pines bent and riffled at their tops in a stiff breeze, hiding the stars, then revealing them again. "What a nice place to die," he said in a whisper. The deep mound of leaves warmed him like a blanket. He smelled the musty aroma of the leaves, but he also caught a whiff of salty iron—his own blood.

Then he heard the manifold footsteps of soldiers and calls of a Union officer. The Yankees were searching for him. Lanterns glowed through the maze of the trees and brush. He counted eight lanterns. The soldiers kept calling. "Come on out, Reb. Ain't no use in hidin'. Give it up."

The officer continually shouted orders for his men to move left or right or search in a different direction. "Scour the woods, men. Scour it. Dig out that Rebel rat."

Ben's heart pounded. He knew he could not run. He knew, too, that spies, if they counted him as one, faced firing squads. He inched himself deeper under the heavy, dark bush and brushed as many dead leaves as he could up over his legs and torso. His head lay against the stump of the bush, the low branches scratching his face.

The footfalls came closer, paused, and then closer still. Different feet walked within a few inches of him, the lanterns shining out in flashes and glimmers. Once, a light like a flare appeared to shine right at him, but nothing happened.

After what seemed like hours, the officer ordered his troops back. "If he got away, he'll bleed to death or freeze. That's all for tonight."

Ben fell into restless sleep. When he awoke in the icy morning, the leaves no longer provided warmth. Frost clung to his clothes, hands and even his face. The chill reached inside him, trying to take his breath away. His mouth was dry, and his teeth chattered like a clattering train. His lungs ached from sucking in frozen air. Puffs of moist breath plumed from his mouth.

Shivering uncontrollably, he managed to pull his second revolver from his jacket pocket and lay it across his chest and attempted to rise, but fell back, heavy, exhausted. He had never felt such cold and such weakness. He drifted into unconsciousness. When he waked again, he knew he had to summon his strength and attempt escape. His purpled fingers were numb, and despite his willing it, he could not grasp the revolver. It slid to the ground. With great effort, and pushing away the bush's branches, he gained a kneeling position.

"Oh, there you are," he heard a honeyed male voice say. "I been lookin' all night and half the mornin' for you. You is a good hider. Yes, suh. You is a good hider."

Ben turned to see a Negro of fifty years with a salt and pepper beard striding toward him. The man bent down next to him and put his hand on Ben's back. "Why, you is as cold as ice, young fella. We need to get you in the house."

With shivering lips, Ben mumbled, "No. Don't take me inside, the Yanks'll shoot me. D-d-d-... don't, please."

"Well, I don't know what Yankees will shoot you. They all done rode off. Ain't nobody here but the nice folks what runs the tavern."

Ben, feeling like the insides of his muscles were lined with boards, not bones, allowed the man to lift him and carry him into the tavern. He again succumbed to sleep. When he awoke that evening in a soft bed covered with a sheet and blankets, a fair skinned woman in an emerald dress, with her black hair tied in a bun, was placing a damp cloth on his head. Her voice seemed so pleasant to him. "You have a fever, sir. My cousin, Mrs. Cox, wanted to bleed you, but I think you've lost enough blood already."

"Who are you?" Ben managed to mumble.

"My name is Cyntha Favor. That's Mrs. Favor to you. You're very lucky, Ben McGavin. Yes, you told us your name, though I doubt you remember. Mr. Reynolds there," she pointed at Reynolds sitting to the side, "cleaned your wound and stitched it closed. The bullet went through your leg. It split your ankle bone, but Reynolds pulled out the bone chips and re-set the bone, or what's left of it."

Ben looked over at Reynolds. "The nigger there reset my broken bone?"

"Yes, and you can thank him later for searching that forest for hours, finding you and saving your life."

Ben's lips bent into a bewildered smile, and he waved a weak hand at Reynolds.

"If we can get your temperature down," Cyntha said, "you may be all right. Here, take this calomel. It will calm your fever." She gave him a spoonful of the quinine medicine then walked to the fireplace to add two logs onto the fire.

Ben's thoughts flowed like errant breezes. He said, "Thank you, ma'am. Say, why are you so pretty? Uh, I meant to say." He fell asleep before he could complete his thought and just as he saw her cheeks blossom to red.

∞

FORTY-THREE

MEMORY IS THE MOTHER OF ALL WISDOM
— SAMUEL JOHNSON

MARCH 3, 1862, 8 AM
CONFEDERATE ENCAMPMENT SOUTH OF FAYETTEVILLE, ARKANSAS

General McCulloch drummed his fingers on the camp table and puffed on a cigar like a chugging train. At last, he said, "Your brother's dead. I'm indeed sorry." He waited for Paul to speak.

Paul said nothing, but looked down at his mud-crusted boots. His leg was sore beyond reckoning, and he rubbed it hard with his fist. He looked at Colonel Armstrong, standing outside the flap of the tent. He raised his reddened eyes to his general.

"And your brother," General McCulloch said, "paid the ultimate price for the information you have. I am beyond grateful. If you had your mother alive, I would write her and extend to her my pride in her sons."

"Yes, sir, it's just me now. Parents are dead. Both brothers dead. Just me." Paul sucked a long breath of the crisp air. "The road past Bentonville is basically unguarded." He pointed to the map he had drawn where a faint line indicated a road and traced the road with is finger.

"You know, I had scouts riding all over northwest Arkansas. Not a one of 'em knew about this road. And you and your brother found it."

"Your other scouts hadn't lived here like us. It's not well known. If you go quickly up to Bentonville at McKissick Creek, you'll slice the Union army in half. Siegel doesn't have pickets out. I think he believes that if we do anything, we'll assault Curtis at Sugar Creek. And this Bentonville detour road runs around the Pea Ridge and gets precisely behind them. It's there. Move fast. You can corral and whip Siegel, then turn, and you'll be directly behind Curtis, cutting his supplies."

"He'll have no choice but to attack on the ground we choose." McCulloch stubbed out his cigar on his boot. "I'm going to inform General Van Dorn. He's the one to make the call, but he won't say no. It's too good an opportunity. Price will go along with this, too." He rose and extended his hand. Paul shook the general's hand, but did not rise, continuing to rub his leg. McCulloch left the tent.

Paul sat alone. "Just me," he said. In his weariness and sorrow, he slumped in the chair into a fitful sleep. In his dream, he was racing away from wolves, knowing all along that the wolves were devouring his brother.

THE SAME DAY, MARCH 3, 1862, 1 PM
OUTSIDE FREDERICKTOWN, OHIO

Leah Fox felt the train jolt like it had hit a boulder. Deafening banging filled the air. The train was shuddering to a rapid halt, the passengers thrust forward, several falling to the floor or hitting their heads on the seatback in front of them. Leah managed to lift the window and looked out. Black smoke poured from the engine boiler, and fire flew out in spurts under the wheel carriage. She immediately looked for her sisters, Maggie and Kate, who were seated farther back in the train car. Both were wearing their matching, highly fashioned, purple hats, and their eyes were wide with terror.

Leah remained calm, despite the turmoil of the falling and screaming passengers and the incessant banging from the engine. She closed the window and rose. Stepping stealthily over some women still flailing on the floor, their hooped skirts a-kilter, she grabbed each seatback and waded to her distraught sisters. She put on her most tranquil face.

The screeching of the wheels against the rails slowed.

"Don't you love an adventure?" she said, tilting a little backward when the train finally came to a halt.

"More like a calamity, if you ask me," Maggie said, chastising.

"Tsk, tsk, my poor little sisters who are unafraid to speak to the dead, but worried over a mere malfunction of a machine. It's like listening to a circus calliope."

Both spiritualist sisters frowned.

"Why are we even going on this journey?" Maggie complained.

"Yes, what's wrong with staying back east, at least no farther than Pennsylvania?" Kate said.

"There is a growing community of believers in spirituality in Ohio, thousands by one newspaper's estimate. And because we are renowned, and the crowd is less accustomed to how the eastern papers often dismiss our little charade, the pickings are good. We may make a fortune."

"I wish I had a drink," Kate announced.

"There, there now," Leah said. "There will be plenty of time for celebration when we make what should be a fresh fortune. We have left early enough that this little delay will not disturb our plans."

Maggie and Kate both rolled their eyes.

A conductor entered the front of the car and told all passengers to take their luggage and prepare to walk to the next town, Fredericktown, two miles away. The Fox sisters donned their elegant capes and muffs. Leah paid a Negro and his teenage son, who had come out to the stranded train to offer help, a dime each to carry their luggage, which they handled with some difficulty, strapping suit bags on their backs and each taking a handle of the clothes trunk.

Leah paid no heed to her complaining sisters, plodding across an icy field, and then to a muddy road into the quaint village of Fredericktown. When the group arrived at the train station, Leah turned to her luggage porters. "Put the bags here, the trunk there. Here is an extra dime for your efforts."

The older Negro took the coin. "Thank you, ma'am. Is there anything else you be needin'? My name is John. This is my son, James."

"Hmm." Leah put her finger to her chin. Her younger sisters plopped onto a bench, huddling and grumbling.

"I will give you each a quarter," Leah told the man, "to take this flier to the newspaper office over there. Have the proprietor print fifty copies. He'll have to set the type to match these words, and tell him to send me the bill for his labor." She handed John a page with large printing. "After you get the fliers, hand them out to everyone, stick them on windows and fences, until they're all gone. Do you understand?"

"Yes'm," John said. "Where will we find you when we be done?"

"At the boarding house. I will tell the owner to allow you to our room. Do you have a last name?"

"Most certainly do, ma'am, it's Coincoin. My wife is cook at the boarding house, and I does the odd jobs. James here helps, too."

"Good, Mr. Coincoin. You must make haste, for the day is almost done. Do not disappoint. I hope to have a large crowd in attendance to our séance tonight."

"Séance?"

"Yes, my sisters have the capacity to speak to the dead."

Both John and his son's eyes widened.

"Be off now. If the job is not done, no pay."

John and James hurried on their appointment.

By nightfall, almost the entire town's occupants had gathered in the foyer of the single boarding house to hear the Fox sisters commune with the dead. Once Leah had culled the naysayers from the room, the intimate show went off without a hitch.

John watched the event, peeking from behind the kitchen door. "I wonder if they could speak to Asa McGavin," he whispered to his wife.

He did not have the gumption to ask the Foxes that night. After the crowd left, he watched Leah's face beam when she counted their take. He scratched his head. "I wonder."

FORTY-FOUR

∽

The Measuring
Line of Earth

The Same Day, March 3, 1862, 2 pm
a Few Miles Southwest of Springfield

Constance Carver stood with fists tightened before the blackened remains of her home and barn. Brown, curled, brittle vines clung to the few charred posts and boards still standing. The ground around the two buildings was primarily black with patches of despoiled grasses and weeds. The house's front door had fallen forward and escaped much of the flame. The hinges had rusted, and shards of window glass lay spilled across the yard. Constance kicked at the door.

She wandered to the barn and dug out the rusty iron plow, its handles burned away. She tossed it aside. A piece of a wedge-shaped frow and pitchfork lay in the black rubble. Bones of chickens and a pig lay about the charcoal like chips of chinaware. Nothing of value remained.

"I wonder when it burned." A crisp wind whipped her long black hair. Her mind was dazed and her heart pitifully saddened. She went back to the remnants of the house and dug around where the kitchen floor had been. She found some blackened hard potatoes, more like rocks than vegetables. She found the metal box she had searched for, but it was popped open and the contents mere flakes of ashes. "Now I don't even have the deed to the place. Can't even prove it's mine or my husband's."

The wind picked up and snow clouds were gathering. She took time to search the surrounding forest looking for game. She heard the gobble of a wild turkey and, in short order, spied it and shot it. She tied the carcass to her saddle horn, rose onto the horse, and made her way to the only place she felt she had friends—the Reeders' home.

When their burned-out home came into view, she shook her head, astonished. "Well, damnation, them Jayhawkers done got us both." She surveyed the grounds, first the destroyed barn. Then she discovered that a swayback horse was tied to a tree near the still erect southern wall of the house. Smoke was wafting from the chimney. "Well, maybe someone is to home."

She dismounted and treaded up the rickety steps to the back door and knocked.

"Come in," a tortured voice said from inside.

She entered and found, in the garish light, Reverend Edward Felder sitting on a tree stump for a chair, a Bible on his lap. No other furniture was in the room, though a stack of theological books lay on the floor. Constance removed her hat. "How you be, Reverend?"

The man of the cloth stared vacantly at her for a moment, then recoiled as if he had seen a ghost. Shaking, he gathered himself together and lay his Bible on the floor. Finally, "Hello, I'm fine. How are you on this blessed day the Lord has given us? I don't believe I know you. Are you from around here?" He sported a large red welt on his cheekbone and had a plaster of sorts applied to his neck. His stark black hair hung stringy about his head.

"I could be doin' a lot better if my farm tweren't razed to the ground. And I don't see how you can say this is a blessed day. Yer sittin' in a burned-out house with nothin' much even to sit on. Yer horse looks to be as old as time. There's a storm brewin', and it don't look like you got much kindlin' there for your fire." She pointed beside the fireplace.

Reverend Felder turned and evaluated his lack of firewood. "Yes, you are right. I shall have to find my ax." He looked down, disconsolate. "Who am I kidding? My fate is...." He buried his face in his hands.

"I saw yer ax leanin' against the wall outside." Constance stepped forward, then stopped. "How'd you get yer face so beat up, Reverend?"

Absentmindedly, Reverend Felder touched the wound on his cheek and cringed. "Oh, that. I was attempting to shore up the west wall, and a bunch of boards fell on me. I thought I was going to die. It bled a lot."

"Yeah, head wounds bleed a mite harder than the real hurt."

They were silent for a while, Constance shuffling her foot on a dusty but solid floor. The reverend kept his hands over his face. Then, he began to whimper. Constance saw a drip of wetness fall to the floor at his feet.

"If you're a grown man carryin' on a like a little baby, then I don't have any use for ya." She turned to leave.

"No, wait. Please stay. Your farm is burned. My church is burned. The Yankees did it, or, at least, someone who had a bone to pick with me did it. I've been turned out of Springfield now that General Curtis and his heinous invaders have stolen it. That Captain Sheridan. He's the one. He said I was causing unrest. He called me a 'secesh traitor.' No freedom for me to spread the Gospel. No freedom to speak the truth. He told me that if I didn't leave, he'd have me hanged."

Constance was unsure how to react. She had problems of her own, but no one had threatened to hang her. She fumbled for words. "I see," was all she could muster.

The gaunt reverend rose and paced the floor. "I have no place to stay. I've been here freezing half the time since the twentieth of February. Two weeks in a frigid hell. The Sharps are not God-fearing and would not have a man of God near them. The Rays and the Edwards have sided with the north. They said they knew my type. They said I twisted the word of God. I don't understand. The Rays have slaves but they won't support the southern cause. This burned remnant," he passed his hand across the southern wall, "was the only place I could find." He pointed into the front bedroom. "As you can see, there's a bed and a dresser and a wash bowl, and...." He pointed to the fireplace. "And I can cook and stay warm. I don't know where the Reeders went, but I'm sure they wouldn't mind me staying."

"Well, that's all good for you, but I've got to find a place to stay myself." She looked out the door to the North where the sky had turned the color of melted pewter. "That storm is building, and the temperature is droppin' quick like."

"I have an idea. Stay here. Two can always make a better way than one alone. We can help each other. That is, until we can find better conditions." He stopped when he saw Constance's doubtful expression. "As it is, I'm not accustomed to faring for myself. I fear I may not make it through the winter. I have no food even now."

"Very well." she nodded. "I'll stay for a day or two until it warms up, then I'm findin' another place. But where we gonna sleep. Just one bed."

"We'll work things out. Please."

Constance trudged out the door, unsaddled her horse, and tied it beside the reverend's horse. With the reverend's ax, she broke up a charred but sound portion of the west wall that had fallen in the yard. With Reverend Felder's help, she erected a sort of stall to block the wind from the horses. "Ain't no use in lettin' the snow kill them horses," she said. Next, she chopped off the turkey's head and claws, stripped its feathers, stuck the carcass on the spit in the fireplace, and the two sat, making small comments, watching the bird turn a rosy brown. They ate supper before a roaring fire. The reverend ate like the starving man that he was. Licking his fingers after the repast, he patted his full stomach.

Constance tore the rest of the meat off the bones and placed the carcass in a pot of water on the coals, boiling it. "We'll have some broth if we can find some potatoes or turnips worth throwing in it." She wrapped the remaining meat in waxed paper from her haversack and stowed it on the mantle.

That evening, a snow storm heaved against the worn house, piling drifts against the north and east walls. Though they had gathered firewood, the house, missing its west wall, half the south wall, and much of its roof, was empirically cold. Constance shivered in restless slumber in the creaking bed. Reverend Felder slept in the kitchen next to the fireplace on two saddle pads with a saddle for a pillow and covered with his coat and Constance's buffalo coat.

Constance awoke with her teeth chattering. She wrapped herself in the single blanket and walked to the fireplace. She nudged the reverend with her foot. Bleary-eyed, he looked up at her.

"You're single, ain't ya?" she said.

"Yes."

"Well I don't intend to die by freezin' to death. If you was a married man I wouldn't ask, but you get your cold hide up and help me move the bed next to this here fire. Then we'll share the bed. Nothin' else mind you. Just for keepin' warm."

Reverend Felder nodded.

"What's your first name?"

"Edward. What's yours?"

"Well, Eddie, my name is... Juniper."

Reverend Felder was too weary and too cold to figure a better strategy. With a bit of a struggle they maneuvered the bed frame, and then the mattress, into the kitchen by the fireplace. Constance added logs to the fire. Avoiding any comments, they fell asleep backside to backside.

FORTY-FIVE

SORROW KNIT TIGHT

THE SAME DAY, MARCH 3, 1862, 3 PM
ELKHORN TAVERN, ARKANSAS

"The president's son is dead!" Cyntha stood at the top of the stairs of Elkhorn Tavern and wailed. "Oh, lamentable day! Willie, the little one, is dead." Crumpling the St. Louis paper in her hand, she bawled. "Oh, the poor dear. Our dear President and his wife. What a tragedy. And dead almost two weeks. What terrible woe." Having taken the paper from the morning breakfast table she had come to check upon her Confederate convalescent in an upstairs bedroom. With the newspaper dotted by her copious tears, Cyntha came in and perched on the edge of Ben's bed.

Ben sat up, looked bleakly at her. With an effort, he mumbled, "What's the matter, missus?" His fever had subsided, but he was still weak. The laudanum made him groggy.

Cyntha turned to him, caught her breath, and dried her eyes with her sleeve. "Our president has lost a son from an illness. It is such a tragedy. He is a good man who deserves our prayers."

"Who?"

"President Lincoln, of course."

"Lincoln," Ben spoke somewhat incoherently. "I'd spit on his grave."

"What? You cannot mean that. Oh, yes, of course you would. You are a heartless rebel."

"Heartless? Who're you callin'...." The laudanum plied against his will and he lost consciousness. His broken leg lay splinted on several pillows. His other foot stuck out of the blankets.

Cyntha rose and felt his forehead with her wrist. Seeing he was asleep, she leaned her cheek against his forehead.

Ben smelled her rose-water cologne and awakened, his eyes fluttering. "Sweet." He smiled.

Cyntha jerked back, embarrassed. She took a cloth from the basin of water, wrung it, and placed the cloth on his head. "You, Ben McGavin, are most likely an incorrigible rake. I do not trust you." Ben was again asleep, but she continued anyway. "Your type, you wretched slaver, you rebellious...." She searched for words. "Scamp!" was the only descriptor that came to mind. "Well, you are much worse than a scamp."

She so wanted to put him in his place — this Rebel, this curse upon the land. Yet she looked at his pleasant, tanned face and could not help but admire it. Asleep, he bore no malignancy in his expression. With a heavy sigh, she whispered, "Were that you were a man of the caliber of my late husband. I wish I knew what I wanted."

She looked again at the newspaper and flung it to the floor beside the bed. She stormed out, passing Reynolds, who was entering the room. He picked up the paper, sat, and began reading. After an hour, Ben waked, yawned, stretched, and eyed Reynolds.

"Watcha doin', old nigger? You pretendin' to read?"

"No, sir. I *am* reading. Shall I read it to you? Or do you want to read it yourself?" He handed the paper to Ben.

Straightening the paper, Ben tapped it with his knuckles and straightened it some more. "The St. Louis Sentinel, hmmm...." He glanced up and down the page. He pointed at a drawing on the page of a woman holding a placard and of a Union Zouave soldier in ballooned trousers. "Nice pictures," he said. "Nice. Nice. Say, the light's not good enough for me to see. You read it." He handed the paper back to Reynolds.

"I take it you can't read. Is that so, young man?"

Ben's brain was in too much of a haze to offer excuses. "No, I never learned. Should have. I had to work." He dropped his eyes. "Would you read it for me? I'd like to know what's goin' on in the world."

Reynolds read aloud for Ben who often groaned at the stories reporting Confederate defeats, especially hearing about the fall of forts Henry and Donelson. "Who's this Grant fella?" Ben asked.

"Appears to be a new general. Looks like the Rebels done took a beating there."

"Well, we'll win the next 'un."

Before Reynolds finished the paper, Ben had again fallen asleep. That evening, Ben's fever rose and he struggled with the pain in his leg, fiery red and swollen. Reynolds stayed with him the whole night, bringing in snow from outside in his bare hands and placing the snow on the wound. In moments of clarity from his delirium, Ben took notice of the care the Negro gave him. Reynolds smiled constantly. Ben marveled at his peaceful face. "You're a good man, old nigger," he barely whispered.

"Yes, and I'll bet you are, too."

THE SAME DAY, MARCH 3, 1862, 4:00 PM
MUDVILLE ENCAMPMENT BOSTON MOUNTAINS, ARKANSAS

Paul straddled a camp stool in the large officer's tent, seated beside five adjutants. General McCulloch leaned against a table, puffing on his pipe like a steam engine. He perused a page with scrawled lines, remotely resembling a map. To his left, General McIntosh stood. Colonel Hebert pawed through a box of rolled-up maps. Paul liked Colonel Hebert, the youthful face showed exuberance and a kind wisdom.

"Aah, here it is," Colonel Hebert remarked. He unrolled a printed map across the table. The three officers all spoke at once, pointing and extoling their points of view.

Paul looked over at the new general in charge, Earl Van Dorn, an austere-looking man in his mid-thirties with a high forehead, bushy mustache, and goatee. The general slumped on a cot, his jacket hung open and a blanket over his legs. His face was flushed. Sweat stood on his brow above reddened eyes. He blotted his watery eyes and seemed totally disinterested.

Suddenly, he blew his nose with a great honk, threw the handkerchief to the ground and stood, and then paced dramatically to the table. In a deep southern drawl, he said, "Tell me what you think, McCulloch. Ah have only just arrived, but ah dare not miss an opportunity to defeat the enemy. You say the men, despite being forced to forsake their cantonments, are in good spirits. Is that so?"

General McCulloch took the pipe from his mouth. "Yes, sir, General Van Dorn, our men are ready to fight. They're angry that the invaders have reached southern soil. They want recompense."

"I should think as much. Our many victories are unheralded in the Nawthen papers. Perhaps it is time we showed them the mettle of our boys and drive the Yankee invaders back to their serpent dens in the Nawth. Then to St. Louis. Huzzah!" General Van Dorn lifted a second handkerchief and snuffled in it. He wiped his damp brow with his sleeve.

Paul wondered how a man as ill as the general appeared to be would be interested at all in fighting. Paul fidgeted, unable to discern why he was even there.

"Ah have called this council of wahr," General Van Dorn said, "despite my tardy arrival, to ascertain the means of irradicatin' the sorry excuses for human beings, those blue bellies, from our southern soil. If it is not advisable, then we can wait, but not long. Ah have sent a courier to Brigadier General Pike to bring the Cherokee and Choctaw regiments from Indian Territory into our number. That is favorable. Now, it is March, and Spring is upon us. Ah feel the warmth."

Paul was sure the warmth the general felt was from his fever.

General McIntosh cleared his throat. "General Van Dorn, if I may. My cavalry has discovered that General Curtis is indeed relying almost solely on his supply line back to Rolla. His army is suffering. We've been harassing their lines, and...."

"Ah understand, General McIntosh, but ah wish to know if our ahhmy possesses the wherewithal to challenge the warmongering Yankee grub-worms and defeat them entirely."

"We can if we strike quickly," General McCulloch offered. "I have it on good account that the Union army is split. Here and here." He pointed on the map to Sugar Creek and to Bentonville. "General Sigel's German division is off here, unprotected and waiting to be destroyed. If we move quickly up the Butterfield Stage road here, then here," He drew his finger along a line on the map where no road was shown. "We'll slice them in half. My best scout, Lieutenant McGavin, certified it is passable and that the Union army lies unprotected."

He pointed at Paul, who stood at attention. After General Van Dorn gave a nod of acknowledgement, Paul sat.

"In addition," General McCulloch continued, "I have dispatched additional scouts at points up and down the road. They've reported the Yankees have little or no awareness of the precariousness of their position. If we strike quickly, we dispatch Sigel, then turn to be directly behind the main body of the Union army."

"And crush them like gnats." General Van Dorn coughed. "Ah like the plan. But what of General Price? Why is he not here?"

Paul could tell that General McCulloch was scouring around for words. "General Price felt he had to attend to some urgent matters with...."

"No need to make excuses for the man. Ah shall speak to General Price personally. How soon can your men be ready to march?"

General McCulloch looked at Colonel Hebert and General McIntosh, who both nodded.

"We can be ready by eight in the morning," General McCulloch said.

"Very well, have McIntosh's mounted infantry prepare to lead the column. We will have a strategy meetin' at five in the mownin'. Now, ah will personally inshuah that General Price is prepared."

Paul saw the fire in the General McCulloch's eyes and the other officers' eyes as well. Battle and glory were on their hearts. General Van Dorn buttoned his jacket, exited the tent, and, despite his fever, fairly sprinted to his stallion, mounted, and rode toward the Missouri Guard encampment and General Price. The rest of the officers and adjutants left quickly. Paul sat alone.

He rose and walked over to the maps. If the army struck the enemy at Bentonville, they would not be far from Elkhorn Tavern where he last saw his brother alive. The war was the cause of his older brother, Asa, pushing hard to deliver horses to the army and dying for it. The war was why his brother, Ben, had been killed. And his desiring that they would somehow still be alive did not make it so. His life now was solitary, a consuming oneness.

FORTY-SIX
❦
A Long Journey's End and Beginning

The Same Day, March 3, 1862, 7 pm
Elkhorn Tavern, Arkansas

B en looked to the end of his bed where the tall, gray-haired surgeon with muttonchops examined his leg. The Union medical officer prodded Ben's leg, tapped it vigorously along its dimension, and pushed on the still red, swollen muscle. Ben winced.

Behind the surgeon, Cyntha and Reynolds looked on with concern. Beyond them, a host of blue-coated soldiers filled the hall, jockeying for a glimpse. While the surgeon pried at the leg, Ben recalled the last fleeting moment he saw Paul. He was sure the Yankee cavalry had caught him down the road. *They were just too many,* he thought. *If he was still breathin' he'd a come back for me.* He believed unequivocally that, were Paul alive, he would have returned and rescued him, and that Paul's absence proved his demise. He felt overarching remorse and choked back tears.

Finally, the surgeon stood, looking bored, thrusting his medical instruments into his bag.

"Will it heal, sir?" Ben asked.

"It'll heal, young fella," the surgeon said brusquely, "but you'll have a devil of a time with it the rest of your life. They tell me you're a Rebel cavalryman."

"I fight for the southern cause, for our right to be left alone, sir. No offense."

"Well, cavalryman you are no more."

"What d'you mean?"

"I'm telling you that you'll have to ride in a wagon from now on. You put pressure on that bone in a stirrup on a hard ride, and you'll lose the leg. Just be grateful I don't have to saw it off. You can thank this colored man for saving your leg." The surgeon pointed at Reynolds.

"But... but."

"No buts to it, young man. Be glad you're alive." The surgeon bustled away.

Cyntha and Reynolds came in, closing the door in the faces of the gawking Yankees. "I don't think some of those boys have ever seen a single soul from the south," Cyntha said, "eyeballing you like you were a monkey in a zoo! I'm ashamed of them. Ben Favor, I'm so glad the surgeon will not have to remove your leg. Praise God."

"Well, not to let on I don't appreciate his help, ma'am, but that sawbones is not gonna keep me off a horse. No, ma'am."

Cyntha pulled the sheets up to Ben's neck. "You just rest and later on...."

"How can I rest? Later on, them Yanks are gonna take me out and put a bullet in me for bein' a spy."

"No, they ain't," Reynolds interjected.

Ben turned to Reynolds. "They ain't?"

"That's right. I went right up to the captain in charge and tol' him you came here under a flag of truce and your own gun discharged into your leg. He wasn't here, doesn't know what the other Union troop was doin'. Right now, you is a convalescent prisoner. That's all."

"Is that what he told them?"

"Yes, I believe it is," Cyntha said. "Without my knowledge, Reynolds has prevaricated on your behalf. I only agree to it now because I believe it would be un-Christian to allow you to be shot." She bit her lip. "Besides...." She said nothing, but looked at the face of a young man, near the age of her husband and perhaps not too different from him. She wished that somehow the word she had received about Joseph's death was incorrect and that he was somewhere alive and being cared for, even if cared for by a family aligned with the Confederacy.

"Ma'am, Miss Cyntha," Ben broke her thoughts. "I'm much obliged to y'all for carin' for me. You're good people. You and Reynolds."

"By the way," Reynolds showed Ben newly shined boots. "I took the liberty of fixin' that tear on yer boot where the bullet went through. Fixed 'em up proper."

"You did that for me?"

"Why not?"

"Well." Ben was at a loss for words. "If you don't beat all, nigger... er, Reynolds. Thank you."

Cyntha rose. "I must go help Cousin Polly in the kitchen. These troops demand so much. They have filled the parlor and kitchen, and both our families are confined to one bedroom, sleeping on mats and tatters of sheets."

Tears flowed down her cheeks when she exited the room. *My poor Joseph,* she thought. *Oh, that you were alive. My thoughts are all a jumble now. Why, dear God, did you give me this man now?*

She hurried down the stairs. The younger Cox boys, Elias and Franklin, despite being surrounded by soldiers, played by the kitchen table with cast iron, toy soldiers in a vainglorious battle. She saw Anthony sitting, drinking coffee, and talking to a lieutenant. She could not bring herself to even say hello to her brother. She felt ashamed of him. *Why is he lying?*

Arriving at the parlor window, she looked out at the new white snow, a few inches worth. Union soldiers stood about the grounds. *Who knows when I will ever go to New York to meet the Fox sisters to have them speak for me to Joseph's soul and set it to rest? I am as much a prisoner here as that confounded rebel upstairs, whom I cannot get out of my mind.*

She beat her fist lightly against her forehead. *I have no family. No brother. No husband. No hope. Because of this war, I am adrift.*

Upstairs, Ben was alone and uncomfortable in the bed. At that moment, it made no difference that he would be allowed to live. His leg was so damaged that he may not be able to ride again ever, and as far as he knew, Paul was killed by Yankee soldiers. "My brothers are dead," he said angrily, "Curse this war and all who abide in it."

MARCH 4, 1862, 5 AM
THE REMAINS OF THE BURNED-OUT REEDER HOME

Constance, who had chosen to name herself Juniper to Reverend Felder, felt a thumping against her buttocks. Snapping awake, she threw off the blanket and sat on the edge of the bed, listening.

Her loaded rifle needed only be cocked to fire. Beside her, the pale minister slept, now turned toward her, a gentle rush of air from his gaped mouth. The winter storm howled and slapped at the weakened house timbers and roof shakes. She looked out a frosted window to see their two horses huddled together with a layer of snow atop their backs. They appeared to be all right with the southern house wall and chimney blocking the icy blasts.

More awake now, she realized what had been beating against her backside. The reverend had a sleeping erection.

She grabbed some branches and a log and tossed them on the glowing embers in the hearth, banking up the fire. Still seated, she held out her hands, feeling the fire's heat. Soon, her entire body was infused with warmth. She reached over and pulled the blanket up to Reverend Felder's neck.

She thought about her husband, William, but not with cordiality. She had hidden her angst at his abandoning her at Fayetteville and marching off with the Guard. For all she knew, he made no attempt to save her from the Yankee encroachment, but ran like a rat from a sinking ship. *True,* she admitted to herself. *I was out cold drunk, but that was no reason to eject me like some useless, broken tool. Some marriage. Not even one child to show for it.* "William!" she ground out his name, then spit into the fire.

She sat there a long time, stoking the fire, feeling lost, almost as lost as the reverend beside her. The warming fire made her feel a yearning inside her and less obligated to her husband. She lifted the blanket from Reverend Felder and ascertained that his penis pressed hard against his trousers. She unbuttoned his trousers and carefully pulled back his long underwear just enough. The good reverend's man parts worked like most men's, erected and wooden, flicking in his sleep. She looked now at the reverend's wounded face. *Not a bad face at all,* she admitted. *And he's a real man, not like my sorry excuse for a husband.*

Then the desire rose in her, and before she had realized her own actions, she had taken off her pants and pantaloons, unbuttoned her shirt and removed the binding around her small, firm breasts. She was upon him, turning him on his back, pulling his trousers and flannels down to his ankles. He was momentarily only partially aware of what she was doing. His penis stood erect in the open air, quivering. He stared down at his nakedness, and then at the moderately pretty woman with bare breasts before him. Her dark hair gleamed in the fire's glow. She was smiling, and she was an animal of desire.

"I'm a man of God, and..." he choked, but said no more when she placed his hands on her breasts, and slid atop him and began grinding her thighs against his.

The hell with my husband, she excused herself. *He's probably dead anyway, and I'll not spend another night without a man.*

Soon, Reverend Felder was wanton in his desire for her, groaning and panting. He grabbed her thighs and thrust again and again, the two of them moaning, and then he felt the great relief he had forbade himself for so long. Constance collapsed upon the man's chest, her own breaths hard and measured.

"Thank you," Reverend Felder said. His entire body felt such a draining and a filling up. He could not recant his words. Such a grace as this was indeed a blessing.

After some time, Constance rolled off him. "Thank you, Eddie," she said. He put his arm around her, pulled the coverings over their bodies. She stroked his face gently, their legs intertwined. He smiled a rested, grateful smile. Wound up in each other, they dropped back to sleep until the night fell away.

In the burgeoning morning, Edward sat up and looked out the window. With the ground snow-laden, there seemed to be no boundary between the whitish gray earth and the same colored sky. *What has happened to my life,* he thought, *my calling? What has this war done to me?*

FORTY-SEVEN

All the Pieces Broken

March 4, 1862, 11 AM
Fayetteville, Arkansas

Lieutenant Paul McGavin cantered his dapple gray alongside five other Confederate scouts on the fire-blackened soil of Fayetteville's main street. The ground was a black sludge from ash mixed with melted snow, the walls of most buildings were begrimed from smoke, and many edifices were utter rubble. An entire city block lay in crusty, charcoal ruin. He knew now why there was such a line of citizens' wagons at the sawmill outside of town. People were trying to rebuild.

He slowed his horse and watched masons slapping up bricks for new walls of a large building that had been blown apart when the Confederates set it ablaze to keep ammunition from the Yankees.

Everywhere, the townspeople bustled about in the crisp, clear air, shoring up walls, nailing new boards, and sweeping away the remains of the town fire. He drew his horse up at an undamaged boarding house. "Dindle's Bed and Café," the sign read. He motioned for his comrades to keep going. Dismounting, he tied his horse to the hitching post. He was part of the vanguard of the Van Dorn's Confederate army on the move north and first to arrive in Fayetteville.

Paul had not had a decent meal in days, primarily because he had not felt much like eating after believing his brother, Ben, had died. He did not have to explain his stopping, for he had a carte blanche from McCulloch to do whatever he wanted. Now, he was hungry for a hot lunch. Standing on the boardwalk, he looked about the scarred town.

Colonel Greer's Third Texas Cavalry regiment approached at a rapid pace and trotted by him. He listened to the rolling rumble of four hundred horses' hooves echoing against the store walls. Colonel Greer rode near the front of the column. Paul saluted him and the colonel returned the salute. Paul observed a shaggy-haired young man of trim build, similar in appearance to his younger brother, riding near the colonel and perceived in the expression on the man's face a sense of such loneliness and confusion.

In a moment, the column had proceeded out of town.

Paul entered the café and accidentally kicked over a spittoon. A handful of customers in the café portion of the enterprise turned to look at him. He righted the spittoon to its original position. Looking up, he noticed that a young woman had not responded to the noise. She was trim and fair, and wore a faded, blue-flowered dress. She leaned on a crutch with her right leg in a splint. She was staring a piece of paper, a befuddled expression on her face.

He limped up beside her. She flinched in surprise at his sudden approach.

Paul was caught off guard as well, looking at her sweet face, blue eyes wide. Strands of blond hair fell in rivulets about her freckled face, and he immediately thought that he had never beheld more attractive features in a woman. He had seen so few women he would call pretty in the past several months. He was instantly charmed by her simple beauty. "Can I help?" he asked.

She shook her head no again and again.

"Really. I'm pretty good at deciphering poor pen marks. Let me see."

Without speaking, the young woman waved her hands by her ears and tapped the paper. She pointed at two men seated at a café table.

Paul still did not quite understand. "You can tell me how to help. With your broken leg...."

"I'm deaf!" the young woman shouted in frustration. "I have to make the customers write down their order, and I can't read this one."

Paul motioned with his hands in a pushing down gesture for her to speak softer and he nodded congenially. Gently taking the paper from her hand, he scanned it. "It says scrambled eggs and grits. Coffee." He looked at her face that showed no understanding. "Here." He reached up and deftly pulled the pencil from behind her ear, lifting some stray locks of her hair and sweeping them from her face. He re-wrote the order legibly and handed the paper to her.

She gave a sigh and a smile.

"My name is Paul."

Her face was blank.

Paul took the paper and wrote his name on the bottom of it.

She looked at his name and smiled again. "Pleased to meet you. I'm Sara," she said, placing her palm at her chest.

Paul smiled. "Let me help you." He indicated for her to go first and followed her into the kitchen where Miss Dindle kneaded bread at the stove.

"What's this, Sara? We have a rule of no customers in me kitchen." Her Irish brogue tickled the air.

Sara waved her hands back and forth in front of her. "I don't know what you're saying but he offered to help."

"What's this? Offered to help, did he. More likely, aspirin' to steal some of our few eggs. I've got no meat if that's what you come for, just some bacon to flavor the beans and collard greens. That's all...."

"Yes, ma'am," Paul said.

"That's Miss Dindle to you."

"Yes, Miss Dindle. Beggin' your pardon, but this young woman." He smiled at Sara. "She needs help. She's slow on the crutch, and apparently, she can't hear well. You'll lose customers."

"Not that I have that many," Miss Dindle retorted. "Since the Rebel army when they was retreating took almost everything and destroyed the town, there's been nary a bit of commerce, 'cept at the sawmill."

"Yes, ma'am. Let Sara help in the kitchen. I'll see to the customers and do the walkin' back and forth."

"Fine thing. And you a lieutenant, that's what ya be. I can tell by yer shoulder bars. Anyway, you look to have quite a limp of your own." She pointed at his leg.

Paul looked down and sighed.

Sara patted Paul's shoulder. "Thank you."

After the last lunch customers left, Paul carried the plates into the kitchen. "Now, may I order? Just anything hot. It's been a while since I've had a decent meal."

Sara nodded a thank you to him, and though she could not tell his words, she pulled out a pie from the pie safe and cut him a large slice. He took the pie in his hand and wolfed it down.

Miss Dindle put her hands on her hips. "Go sit down, Lieutenant Paul. Sara, you go with him. You can watch the army going by. I just hope they don't stop anywhere near here."

Sara did not hear Miss Dindle's remarks, but understood the older woman was shooing her from the kitchen. Sara had a reason to smile for the first time in a while. Here was an officer who was acting so kindly toward her. She saw his aggravated limp and felt sorry for him. Her own leg did not hurt, but it was splinted and throbbed if she stood on it too long. Beaming, she followed Paul into the café area.

Immediately, she saw the long columns of soldiers marching north through the street.

"What's happening? Has our army returned?" she blurted.

Paul attempted to answer, but seeing her confusion, grabbed paper and pencil from the front desk. He jotted: *The army is marching to cut the Yanks' army in half. If it works out, we'll drive them from Arkansas.*"

Sara read it and said, "Is it the whole army?"

"Just about." He nodded.

Sara read his lips enough to understand. "What about Colonel Greer's regiment?"

"As a matter of fact, I...." He wrote again on the paper, explaining that he was loosely attached to Greer's regiment, and that those troops had already traveled through the town hours before.

When Sara read his note, she rushed to the door, almost colliding with it in her struggle with her crutch. She flung open the door, the glass panes rattling. She wobbled out into the street almost right up to the column of soldiers. Some of them tipped their hats, others whistled. She whirled about and made her way back to the boardwalk where Paul stood. She flung herself on him and began beating his chest. "My Joseph! My Joseph! He's gone to battle, and I didn't get to see him. I never heard the soldiers marching. If I'd heard them I could've seen him go by." She sobbed.

Paul did his best to put his arms around her. The passing soldiers looked on in amazement. Paul knew some of them must be thinking of loved ones at home. Some of them, in a day or two, he knew would be dead. Sara's crying turned to a wail and, all of a sudden, the column stopped and turned toward her and Paul. Many soldiers removed their hats, watching this woman's anguish, and Paul imagined they felt that she was somehow foretelling their fates. Their faces were grim.

"March on!" Some officer somewhere called. "March on, I said." The soldiers turned again toward their unknown future and trudged forward, their feet heavier and slower than before. Paul knew the men's hearts and minds were on home and family.

He helped Sara inside and sat beside her on a worn, ragged sofa, patting her hand.

He saw in Sara's now quieter sobs an echo of his own remorse. How much loss had he already seen? His thoughts flooded to the faces of hundreds of soldiers who had already died, most of them from disease, remembering the agony or fear on their ghastly faces in the throes of death.

Paul had seen the change in the soldiers' attitudes from when they had first volunteered. The enticement of getting in on a splendid scrap had worn off. For months, they had drilled and practiced and waited and waited and, at night, dreamed fitful dreams. So many of them had died in the camps, not from bullet wounds but from wide-spread typhus, measles and dysentery.

Paul knew their concerns. He had spoken to many, and their plight was like his. Their desire for honor, their misguided sense of duty, and the fear of being chastised as a coward had torn them from their hearths and from their loved ones, believing they were defending vague and abstract concepts. Freedom for their state? Defeating the carnal invaders? Saving the South? Not letting the "niggers" take from them their jobs?

Other than Colonel Greer and a few officers, Paul had not met a soldier who owned a slave. *What a dreadful fix this nation is in,* Paul thought. *We're fightin' and we aren't even sure what for.*

Miss Dindle entered the parlor, empty except for Paul and Sara.

"How long has Sara been deaf?" Paul asked.

"For a few weeks," Miss Dindle replied. "She's lucky she's alive. I prayed to good St. Patrick. That's why you see her here gettin' around like she owns the place."

Sara ceased crying. Paul walked to the check-in desk and took paper and pencil. He wrote: *Why are you so upset? Who is on your mind?*

"I have lost my true love," she said. "He's in Colonel Greer's regiment. I've heard that he's alive, but I've been lookin' for him for months. Now he's gone to battle. If I wasn't deaf, I could've heard the soldiers marchin' and ran out and found him. Now it's too late."

Miss Dindle nodded her head. "That much I know to be true. She was lookin' for the man months ago when I hired her. As it stands now, I can't afford to keep her. I'm only lettin' her stay until…well…."

Paul saw Sara's bewildered look. He chose not to tell her what Miss Dindle said. He looked instead at the tender expression on Sara's tear-flushed face and wished that she might hold him in some regard. He felt his own sense of loss could be ameliorated were he to have a strong, sweet woman at his side. If not this woman, then some woman. At this juncture of his army career, he could easily ride away from the army and not look back.

Sara stood abruptly, gathered her crutch, and hobbled away in what seemed to Paul to be anger as well as remorse. He sensed the horrid storm in her emotions, and when Miss Dindle returned to the kitchen, his tears for his lost brothers finally burst forth. *I am like threadbare cloth*, he thought. *Ready to shred apart.*

He walked out onto the porch and was blasted by the first gust of wind and flurries of a snowstorm, fast approaching. He decided not to leave yet, but gathered a blanket from his horse's saddlebag, wrapped it around his shoulders and sat on a bench in front of the café. With the Confederate Army of the West plodding by, he watched awhile before nodding to sleep, and over the hours, with the cold came stinging ice and snow.

Sara had gone to her upstairs room, a small but tidy affair with a small dresser and rickety bed. She threw down her crutch and limped stolidly to the single window. Pulling aside the curtain, she marked the never-ending stream of men treading to war, their tattered, dusty gray and tan uniforms, their slouch hats, their rifles glinting on their shoulders. She realized fully that her concept of a glorious war was foolish. She had stayed long enough in Fayetteville to hear of death upon death in the camps from disease.

In addition, the terrors of her first encounter in battle at Wilson Creek never left her waking hours, and often shrieked into her dreams, as did her encounters with the scar-faced Richards.

She did not know that a few miles north, Joseph's wife felt alone and lost. Cyntha believed her husband dead and his soul lost in a tortuous limbo, and she was estranged from her brother.

Anthony, for his sake, felt his heart was disheveled. Jobless, a fleeing thief, and penniless. Even his new wife could offer him little solace. His wife, Jeanette, worried. The Union soldiers were constantly all around them, and both she and their daughter, Clara, suffered from ceaseless nightmares, driven by their memories of the encounter with the river pirates so few months ago.

Sara did not know that Abram had parted from her father. She did not know that her father had reached such a point of despair over the war that he was planning a most perilous effort that would surely bring about his own demise. She was unaware that the kind lieutenant who had comforted her believed he had lost his entire family. Nor was she aware that Paul's brother was despondent beyond consolation at losing his ability to ride a horse ever again, and that, he, too, believed his brother dead.

Nor did she know that the man who owned her heart was living in such a state of ambivalence and internal pain that he almost did not care if he lived or died.

Her father was gone now from her life, her entire family — mere ghosts. Abram, whom she loved almost as much as her father, was gone.

She felt trapped in a harsh eternity, working day in and day out not for her own home, but as a mere maid. *I should've never gone searching for Joseph*, she thought. *I am without family with no hope of finding Joseph. I'm deaf and lame.* She had plumbed the depth of her heart and found it shallow and dry. Her ears had begun ringing from her stress, but she paid them no heed.

Miss Dindle briefly watched Paul snoozing from her window, and then closed her café, lowering a cross bar across the door. She headed out back where she took the short supply of meat from the smokehouse and hid it in burlap sacks in drifts of snow already gathering under the trees behind her café. She came back inside, scribbled a note for Sara, and left it on the counter.

Putting on layers of coats, scarves, and a clumsy, battered hat, she slipped out the back and saddled a mule. In a few moments, she was cantering northward on seldom used paths.

The day wore into evening, and the weather worsened. Sara sat by her window watching, hoping that by some chance she might see Joseph among the troops marching through Fayetteville. Many of the troops upstretched their necks and looked at the upstairs windows. Sara withdrew her face from near the panes and pulled the curtains closed whenever she saw one do as much.

By early evening, the troops stopped and clustered in their companies for the evening. They built fires against the cold and gathered on the boardwalks, and several soldiers invaded the stores and homes to stay warm. Sara noticed they had no tents. The companies stretched in number far down the street and out of town. When it began to grow dark, Sara opened the window a crack. The aroma of coffee wound its way up to where she sat.

The ringing in her ears had subsided, and the vacuum quietness invaded once again.

All of a sudden, an idea sprung to her mind. One that involved the kind lieutenant she had just met. *I hope he hasn't gone.* She hobbled as quickly as she could downstairs.

FORTY-EIGHT

☙

UNRECONCILED STRIVINGS

MARCH 4, 1862, 5 PM
FAYETTEVILLE, ARKANSAS

S ara reached the bottom of the stairs, ignoring her leg's pain. The curtains were drawn, but shadows pervaded the café. She called, "Miss Dindle!" After shouting several times, she knew that the café's owner was gone. "Odd," she said.

She wrung her hands. "Why didn't I think of asking that kind lieutenant before now?"

She pulled a window curtain back. Snow whirled and dived and piled in drifts against the boardwalks. The soldiers huddled in groups in the street near hastily built fires, holding blankets around their shoulders. She saw two soldiers carrying a dresser and tossing it atop an already high fire. She almost closed the curtain when she spied Paul asleep on the porch bench. Wet snow had blown under the overhang and clung to his boots and pants legs.

He's still here. She removed the crossbar on the door, and using the key she kept pinned in her apron pocket, unlocked the door. On the porch, she exclaimed, "Hello, dear lieutenant!"

Paul stirred and wakened slowly. He pulled the blanket from his shoulders, lifted his hat, and shivered. He looked perplexed, blinking at the soldiers huddled around the fires in the street.

Sara limped up to him, knelt, and brushed snow from his boots.

"No call to do that," Paul lifted her hands away. He was immediately taken with the gentle feel of her palm and fingers and was wont to release them. He let go her hands and, after helping her to her feet, stomped the snow from his boots and stood. The snow dropped from his clothes. He removed his snow-speckled glasses and wiped them on his jacket. He placed them again on his nose. He smiled, for now he could see Sara's benign, lovely visage clearly.

When his stomach grumbled, he held his hand to it. "I haven't eaten all day, except that pie. Is the café still open?" Remembering she couldn't hear, he pointed to the café and made a motion like shoveling food in his mouth from a plate.

"It *is* for you." Sara opened the door. Paul's bad leg was stiff as a stick, and he chuckled at the thought that the two of them looked the part of a circus clown act. Sara lit lamps, but locked and bolted the door. "Come with me to the kitchen. I don't know where Miss Dindle has gone off to. Perhaps she's hiding her meats. The army took everything the last time. She may not be back for a while."

Lights from the fires in the streets glimmered through the partially open curtains and cast sprinkles of light across Sara's pleasant countenance. Paul, for a long moment, could not take his eyes off her. He wished to touch her face, to feel female warmth, so long unfelt.

Finally, he looked away and slapped his arms around his body to warm himself, stamped his feet again. "I can't believe I slept so long through all that noise outside. I should be on the road. General McCulloch will be needing me to...."

"Yes, of course." Sara did not know what he said, but felt she needed to be considerate. She reached behind the counter and brought out a fresh blanket. Before he could resist, she lightly placed the blanket about his shoulders and smiled. "C'mon with me to the kitchen. There's bound to be some eggs. Miss Dindle wouldn't hide those."

In the kitchen, Sara stoked the stove with kindling and ladled a spoon of lard from the tub into a pan. She pulled some already cooked sausage from the same tub and warmed it in the grease. She got a pot of water boiling and soon was pouring coffee for the man whom she hoped would help her accomplish her scheme. "Do you want cream for your coffee? I'm afraid sugar is short right now."

He waved no. "Black is fine."

Sara fried three eggs in the melted grease.

Paul sat at a sturdy table, watching her fluid movement, despite her broken leg. *She's like a graceful flower.* He felt a deep pang of desire for her. The touch of a feminine body, even only a hand, had been so long apart from his life. He had had a few belles, but knew he tended toward shyness around females, and he had never married.

When the eggs were done, Sara slid them with the sausage onto a plate and added a dollop of apple compote, then handed the plate with a fork and knife to Paul. Sara stood by the table, holding the coffee pot. After he took two sips, Sara leaned in to pour more.

Paul put his hand over the cup. "Set the pot down and join me." He indicated with his hand toward the chair opposite him.

Sara placed the pot on the stove and sat looking at her folded hands in her lap. She ultimately raised her eyes and watched Paul munch on his meal, savoring the taste of salty, hot food. When he finished, Sara rose and gathered sheets of paper and a pencil.

She wrote: *I need help. Will you help me?*

Paul studied the words. He hunched his shoulders.

She spoke, her tone pleading. "I need to find my future husband. He's in the Third Texas Cavalry."

Paul looked at the note. His hopes sank into disquietude. He turned in his chair so as not to look at her. Taking a deep breath, he wrote on the page: *We're going into battle. Third Texas in the lead. No way I can help.*

"Let me just follow you. I can find him if you just get me close."

Paul shook his head. He stood.

"Just let me come with you. Tell the officers I'm a nurse, or a spy, or...."

Paul adjusted his hat, buttoned his coat. "Thank you for the meal." He placed two nickels on the table.

Sara swept them to the floor and sank to her knees, her splinted leg sprawled to one side. "Please. I must see him before he dies. I'm deaf. What more do I have to live for? At least let me see him." She sobbed, her petite body heaving.

Paul's own sorrow buffeted him like a raging storm. He looked down at the poor, lovely soul, weeping and holding fast to his leg. He took her by the elbows and lifted her up, helping her to a chair, her tears still flowing.

He took a paper and scribbled: *I can take you as far as General McIntosh's brigade. That's all I can do. I must do my duty, and, right now, that is to scout for General McCulloch.*

He showed the note to her. Her smile gleamed.

"Very well," he said, "how will you come with me?"

She did not understand. He pointed to her splinted leg.

"I have a horse."

"So."

She understood his comment. "I have a carriage. When the Yankees took the town for that few days they were here, they took every horse they could find. I hid mine. Our neighbors, the Pates, had six horses. The Yanks took 'em all. The Pates just gathered what they could, put it on their backs, and walked away. I watched them go. They've not been back. But they left their carriage. My horse can pull it."

Paul blinked. He attempted to say something, grabbed a pencil to write, and gave up. "Very well, Miss Sara. Hitch up your horse." He shook her hand and smiled.

She hugged him. In twenty minutes, she had clothed herself in heavy sweaters and a hooded cape and brought Esther to the neighbor's open shed. The carriage, layered with snow, sat there. She began hitching her horse.

Paul mounted his own dappled gelding, rode around to the shed, and found Sara feverishly hooking chains and straps to her horse. He got down to help her. At one instance, on purpose, Paul brushed his hand on hers while fetching up the reins. From the touch of her soft skin, Paul wished to hold that hand, at least for a while. He brashly thought to ask to hold her palm to his cheek for a moment. But the opportunity passed. After slipping on her gloves she slid into the carriage seat and lifted the reins.

With arm motions, he indicated for her to follow.

When they entered the streets, weaving among the street fires, a bearded curmudgeon of a soldier sprang up and trotted alongside Sara's carriage. "Where ya goin', missus? Why don't ya join me, and we'll stay warm together?" He reeked of whiskey, and when he reached into the carriage and pinched Sara's arm, Paul rode his horse between the man and the carriage and booted him to the ground. The man rolled in the snow and mud, holding his belly.

Entering the forest beyond the town, Sara looked back to see the fires of Fayetteville dwindling. Into the pitch dark, with swirling snow, she did her best to keep pace with the lieutenant. They passed a handful of picket soldiers. They saluted Paul and gaped at Sara.

With the moon tucked in a hollow of caressing clouds, Sara was not only deaf, but might as well have been blind in the swollen night.

FORTY-NINE

⚭

A STORM FOR
A GARMENT

MARCH 4, 1862, 7 PM
THE TELEGRAPH ROAD, A MILE NORTH OF FAYETTEVILLE, ARKANSAS

General McCulloch rode along the icy road in pitch black night. Sleet and snow pelted him and the mounted infantry who marched beside him. The storm had renewed its vigor. He wiggled his gloved fingers, for they had gone numb.

Guiding his horse to the side of the road, he watched his Confederates bent over their horses' withers, all silent but for the tread of the hooves on the ice-crusted ground. The exhalations of man and beast in the frosty air shrouded them in a ghostly vapor halo. He stared down for a moment at the layer of sleet on his coat sleeves and on his horse's mane.

"Halt!" he ordered. "That's all for tonight, boys."

The column shuddered to a stop. General McCulloch looked at the men's faces, like rows of pale moons before him. He turned his gaze far ahead into the lightless void. Shadows of men, more like gray fence pickets wavering in a gale. He knew that many of his soldiers and Price's had halted in Fayetteville. More of the division were camped in and around the town and a short distance farther north. He hated the lack of regulation in the Missouri guard. He appreciated his Arkansas "Ransackers" and Texans. They followed orders and fought like wild men.

"That's all we can do tonight. The Yanks'll have to wait a little while longer to feel the steel of our bayonets. Take heart. Do the best you can to stay warm, keep fires controlled. Huddle together. Now, fall out!" The soldiers dismounted, trudged into clearings sprinkled among the trees, and began gathering spare tinder for fires.

Eyeing an officer nearby, General McCulloch ordered, "Captain, Tell General McIntosh up ahead to halt and spread the word to bivouac."

The young officer galloped north calling out the orders.

General McCulloch patted his horse's neck. He tried to light his pipe, but the matches were wet. He wished for whiskey or a steaming stack of buckwheat cakes smothered in blackstrap molasses. He had not eaten since the night before. *I wonder how General Van Dorn's doing in his comfy ambulance. Says he's still sick. We should've never attempted this march when we didn't know the weather.*

He dismounted and tied his horse to a tree. Colonel Hebert galloped up, dashing back and forth across the road, barely avoiding collisions with the soldiers retiring to the sides. "Are we bivouacking here?" he called to McCulloch.

"Yes, Colonel."

"What are your orders?"

"Check on the men. Set pickets north and east. Pick the ones with heaviest coats. Make sure the rest of the men are secure and warm. Find more blankets from the supply wagons if you can. Encourage the men. Check on them until you fall asleep in the saddle."

"Yes, sir," Colonel Hebert, the young officer with an angelic, serene face, saluted and trotted his horse back the way he came, vanishing into the dark.

McCulloch pulled a waxed tent cloth from a saddle bag and wrapped it around his shoulders. In a few steps, he found a vast oak with long, gray moss beards hanging from the limbs, the trunk's base hollowed out on one side like a cave. The bark had healed smooth around the opening and looked like the rear end of a horse. The hole was deep enough for him to sit comfortably on his haunches, barely bending his head. *At least it blocks the sleet.*

He sighed heavily. "Where is that confounded McGavin?" he whispered angrily. "This army needs him now. Damn!" He pulled his hat lower and backed as deep as he could into the tree scar.

Small fires lit up like rows of fairy lanterns along the trail. Somehow the men found enough dry brush and were using the fires to warm the ground so they could sleep on it once the fires were out. The low fires and the whispered grumblings of the soldiers eventually dwindled down. The general could distinguish only opaque blends of huddled forms and a few glints from the fast-dying fires. As the men grew quiet in exhausted slumber, he perceived somewhere nearby the faint babble of a rill, and ice melting off the tree limbs in a steady drip. An owl hooted a melancholy chant. In short order, he discerned the muffled, rhythmic snores of the men.

He sat, extending his legs out of the hollow, and then tossed his blanket over his legs. For a few moments, he thought of his artillery and supply wagons. He knew they would be having a rough time on the icy road, more so if the weather warmed, for the road would become slogged with mud. He considered perusing the maps in his coat pocket, but an intense weariness was overtaking him.

Smelling the sweet molasses and oats odor of his horse, and surrounded by almost perfect silence, he drifted to sleep.

He awoke suddenly at a gunshot. He glanced right and left, heard a hundred worried, demanding voices. Far to his left, a voice called, "Sorry, sorry! It was an accident!"

"Well, shut up and put your gun down!" a crass voice ordered. "You'll get plenty of chance to shoot it tomorrow. Now go to sleep."

Then all was quiet.

General McCulloch knew that at another time he would have put the man on report, but not tonight. He was too weary. Sleep would not take him again. His worries were too vast. He knew nothing of the Union movements or strength. He needed the report from his best scout, the Texan — McGavin.

A familiar voice called his name. "General McCulloch, I've got news." Colonel Armstrong, his tall, austere adjutant rode up and saluted. "We've found a house for you a short distance ahead."

FIFTY

To Chase
after Shadows

MARCH 4, 1862, 8 PM
NORTH OF FAYETTEVILLE, ARKANSAS

Sara traveled the dark road with snow blowing sideways under the top of her carriage and into her face. The road had more tight turns than she remembered. Ahead of her, she watched the gray, speckled rump of Paul's horse. He was not in a hurry, and well he should not have been. Twice, his horse skidded on an icy patch in the road. He held the gelding steady and proceeded even slower. He stopped once to ask directions from an officer.

Sara wished she could hear. The incessant buzzing had in the last two days diminished some, but now her ears felt like they were stuffed with cotton. Along the road, Paul and she passed Confederates huddled under lean-tos or down in a gully shivering under snow-covered blankets. Most men slept in pairs back to back to maintain warmth. Measly fires were mostly smoke.

Finally, after an hour of traveling straight into the frigid storm, the road turned sharply, and the trees provided a wind break. In a few strides, they came upon a well-lit farm house with soldiers bearing torches, the flames flickering in the stiff breeze. A Confederate flag hung limp, frozen to the pole. Lanterns danced in the wind on shepherd's hooks. Three tents sat beside the porch. A handful of soldiers, bundled in heavy garb, huddled on the porch against the tortuous storm.

Paul turned his horse and returned to the carriage. Sara reined Esther to a halt. He pointed at the house. He mouthed the word, 'general.'

"Oh, is this General McCulloch's headquarters?"

He nodded yes. Paul grabbed the carriage harness lead and guided the carriage directly beside the house, out of the wind. He dismounted and indicated for Sara to wait. A guard opened the door for Paul.

The window nearest Sara had curtains drawn aside, revealing a well-lit room. Sara watched Paul's form cross the room and shake hands with another man whose back was to her. The men sat and began conversing.

"Well, enough of this," she said aloud. She stepped down. *My pa is General McCulloch's friend. He'll understand.* She walked past the guard who had wandered over to comrades by the tents. Upon opening the door, the brightness and warmth of the home stung her face like a blast from an oven. She blinked, hesitating.

Paul and General McCulloch rose. Each were speaking to her, but she could not grasp their words. Finally, Paul led her by the elbow to sit at a third chair at the table. She began jabbering at her excitement of seeing the general again. General McCulloch merely smiled and nodded. Then she began telling the general about her deep desire to see Joseph.

Paul tapped her forearm and pointed at a paper on the table. He had scribbled a note. It read: *I told Gen. McCulloch your request. He said you can try to find Joseph. The Third Texas is in the van, advanced some miles ahead.*

Sara leaped from her stool, clapping her hands. Without thinking, she swept around the paper-strewn table and hugged General McCulloch. Gently lifting her arms, he smiled and pointed for her to return to her stool. He spoke to Paul who, in turn, wrote a new message that said: *He wants you to understand the peril you will be in. He cannot guarantee your safety.*

Sara read it and nodded.

Paul wrote again. This time, he bore hard on the pencil. If only he had a woman who loved him as much as this bold woman did her unseen betrothed. He had barely met her, but he felt like she may be her last chance for any tenderness in his life, for the coming battle could cut his life breath short. He considered further that he may well have escorted this beautiful creature to her doom. He dropped the pencil and stared into the vast longing of his desires and his confusion.

At last, he noticed the troubled look given him by General McCulloch.

He picked up the pencil and finished. The note read: *an escort will take you as far as General McIntosh's command. I must follow orders to reconnoiter the Union army to the East.*

After Sara read it, they rose. She shook hands with General McCulloch and hurried out into the driving wind. She started into the carriage and, suddenly, found Paul's strong hands about her waist, helping her ascend. She stepped back down, turned, and looked into his eyes that were almost pleading. He was saying words, but she could only guess at their meaning. Then, to her surprise, he took her gloved hand and held it to his cheek, his eyes closed.

Sara later thought that perhaps it was her mind numbed by the cold, but in the soft glow of light spilling from the window, the contour of Paul's face, even with glints of light glimmering in his glasses, appealed abundantly to her. She later figured that her gratefulness to him had conspired against her, and she felt her desires set aflame.

She withdrew her hand, removed her glove, and gently embraced his cheek. His eyes remained closed; a tear clung to his eyelid. He took her hand and kissed it, breathed a sigh, then limped toward to the house.

"Wait!" Sara called.

Paul returned. Sara took the little silver case Billie Sue had given her from her pocket and placed it in Paul's hand. "I have little need of it. Because of you, my treasure is forthcoming."

Paul looked a long while at the box shimmering in the window's light. At last, he said, "Thank you." He placed it in his shirt pocket. "Next to my heart." He patted his chest and gave a little smile. He turned and made his way back into the house.

Sara could only recall once when her heart had beat so fast.

She departed the small camp, north up the Telegraph Road, this time with an escort of riders bearing torches, so the pace was much quicker.

In a few minutes, the party arrived at a large two-story farmhouse, sparsely guarded by a handful of soldiers. One of the escorts unhitched and led Esther to a tall barn, and Sara was shepherded inside. The first thing she saw were two broadswords hung crossed on the wall, wide and long and reminiscent of an ancient time of war.

A half-dozen women, two being officers' wives, came down the stairs and greeted her. When they hurried her upstairs to a bedroom, Sara noticed several officers in what appeared to be a heated discourse in the parlor. She waved at her ears to the women to show she could not hear, but the women chattered away. Sara could grasp nothing of what they were saying.

When they reached the upstairs hall, one woman finally realized that Sara was deaf. She took an envelope and pencil from her apron pocket and wrote an extensive note: *We mustn't disturb Brigadier General McIntosh. Fortunately, the Yankee sympathizers who own this house departed in haste, leaving us the spoils of war.*

Sara nodded understanding, and the woman directed her to a bed to share with one of the ladies. She was tired, and the thought of finding Joseph in the morning gave her peace. Her hopes high, she slept easily.

When she awoke the next morning, the house was vacant. She found a note saying the army had marched north and that the women had departed south.

She dressed quickly, grabbed two blankets from the empty home, and discovered a lone private waiting on the porch who helped her hitch Esther to the carriage. Shortly after departing, she found herself blocked behind the army's wagon train. Despite her admonitions to let her pass, she spent the entire day trailing the freighters.

That evening, bundled with blankets from the abandoned house and sitting in her carriage, Sara removed the leg splint. She would ride bareback overland when the sun came up.

FIFTY-ONE

☙

So Quick the Candle
Could be Snuffed

MARCH 5, 1862, 6 AM
UNION HEADQUARTERS BESIDE PRATTS' STORE ON TELEGRAPH ROAD

G eneral Samuel Curtis sat in his tent, unaware that painful
death slithered near him.

Lantern light flickered off his tall forehead. He stroked
the graying beard about his jowls. During the campaign to drive
the Rebels from Missouri, he allowed his beard to grow.

Dressed in full uniform, his epaulets starched, Wellington boots
shined, he resembled a stodgy schoolmaster with goggled eyes. His
temperament equaled his appearance. Smiling and laughing was
only for children. That was part of his creed. The world was filled
with too many problems for joviality. His wide lips seldom cracked
into a grin at a joke or even at a victory of his own making. He sat
in his overlarge tent, ordered for him to his exact specifications.
He was a man of scrupulous attention to particulars and prided
himself so.

His precision with details was one of his attributes, plus an ample
amount of good luck that seemed to surround him. He looked up
from the letter he was writing and allowed himself a private smirk
at his good fortune. His Union Army of the Southwest had chased

General Price's Missouri Guard into Arkansas. His soldiers now occupied northwest Arkansas in an excellent defensible position atop the bluffs near Little Sugar Creek, and the Confederates had been driven back upon their heels, and, from all the reports he had heard, were in hiding.

His letter was to his wife, Belinda Buckingham Curtis. He continued thus:

As you know, Belinda, our army is too far extended into Arkansas in prudent retrospect. I have ordered continual strengthening of the supply line from Rolla, but the journey is arduous, not, mind you, for lack of an ample road, but from marauding bands of men who call themselves Confederates, but are no more than criminals conspiring to heist our provisions.

He paused, eyeing his broad table with its charts, maps, and notes, neatly ordered and ready for his avid attention. The light from the three lanterns hung at the tent ceiling flickered on the pages of details and numbers, and the pages beckoned to him.

He glanced down. Beside his booted foot, a three-foot-long diamondback rattlesnake wriggled listlessly, its tongue flicking in and out. He leaped from his chair, knocking it over.

He knew that wintertime was not when snakes moved about, but there it was, fangs swollen with venom.

The staff, milling about the headquarters camp around Mr. Pratt's general store, must have accidentally roused it from its cozy den, and it was looking for a new warm home. The Sibley stove parked in a corner of the tent provided just the warmth it wanted. The stove being behind Curtis, the snake slithered toward him, raising its head, the rattle clicking.

It swept past the general and behind the stove under some mail satchels, bridles, and a saddle.

General Curtis stumbled backward. "Captain Morse, come quickly!"

The rattler continued to slink deeper under the pile of leather accoutrements.

Captain Morse, a sturdy man with patent black hair and long sideburns past his jawline entered and saluted. "Yes, sir."

"There's a rattlesnake by the stove." Curtis pointed, breathing erratically.

Morse showed amazement, but quickly drew his revolver. Creeping toward the stack of satchels and horse tack, he carefully lifted a satchel. The snake coiled in two seconds and struck at him, missed, then shot out toward General Curtis.

With an immediate panicked reaction, and by sheer luck, the general raised his heavy booted foot and brought it down exactly on the rattlesnake's head, the sharp spur embedded behind the head. He ground the serpent into the soil, the snake's body flipping and twisting, even wrapping around Curtis's leg. But the general was relentless and did not give up the boot hold on its head.

Captain Morse drew his saber and sliced the snake in two. Still the snake writhed.

General Curtis was sweating, but he dared not remove his boot. The head could still strike; the fangs could still sink deep into skin.

After a minute, the snake lay mostly still.

When Curtis lifted his foot, the snake's head was clearly smashed flat. An eye popped out and blood pooled around the mouth.

"You killed it, sir," Morse said. "It's definitely dead. Fine foot work."

Curtis looked momentarily at his boot. "Yes, hmm. That's what our army is going to do to the Rebel traitors, not unlike this snake."

"Let me get that out of here for you." The captain used his saber to lift the heavy snake's body and half carry, half drag it from the tent.

Curtis sighed heavily, patted his chest for his heart still jostled, and settled himself again at his desk. He took up his stylus and continued his correspondence to his wife.

I have much to attend to, so this letter is brief. The Rebels have left little in the way of provisions, so our army is scouring for what fodder remains.

I apologize for my abruptness when you invited yourself to visit me at Springfield. Though I am grateful for the bouquet of gifts (particularly the whiskey) in celebration of our driving the Rebels from Missouri, your arrival brought me nothing but apprehension. I hurried from my duties and found that you had no ill news. For that I am grateful, but your timing of your surprise outing was poor. Must I remind you we are at war?

Furthermore, your arguing with that skinny, dark-skinned maid in the Schmidt boarding house, that Mrs. Carver, was an embarrassment to me. But what is done is done.

I hope that you are well on your way back to Iowa. Give my love to our children.

Yours, Samuel Curtis

He made no mention of his deadly encounter with the rattler, but blotted the ink with his blotter, blew on the page, and neatly folded it. He would post the letter the next day.

On this morning, he planned to review the numbers of new recruits versus those whose term of service had allowed them to depart the army. He also had to converse with his subordinates about what to do with the pesky Confederate cavalry and Bushwhackers raiding his wagon trains.

"General Curtis, begging your pardon," Captain Morse called from outside the tent.

"Yes, Captain."

The captain stepped inside the tent. "General Curtis, I have a woman outside, late arrived."

"Yes, what is that to me?"

"She says she sympathizes with the Union, and she has word that the Rebels are on the move, and she knows where they are headed."

"Send her in."

Captain Morse stepped out.

The stout, little woman, swaddled in coats and scarves and a tattered hat, entered. She swept the hat from her head, and made a curtsy like she was attending a palace court.

"General Curtis, I'm Miss Dorothea Dindle. I rode all night to get here. Van Dorn's Confederates are on the march. They are in Fayetteville now."

Captain Morse entered the tent once more. "A scout is just arrived as well. His report concurs with Miss Dindle's."

"Who is it?"

"Wild Bill, sir."

"Who?"

"Hickock."

"Send him in."

An audacious gentleman in a florid red shirt and buckskin jacket entered. His mustache was so long, he had it tied behind his head. "The Rebs are comin', General."

FIFTY-TWO

⌒

PREDATOR OR PREY

MARCH 6, 1862, 3 AM
TEN MILES SOUTH OF
BENTONVILLE, ARKANSAS ON THE TELEGRAPH ROAD

Joseph rose from his bivouac in the coal-black, icy pre-dawn. He had been dreaming that some creature was drawing near, snuffling and waiting to strike at his throat.

Though he knew not why, he dealt better with the frigid temperatures than most of his bivouacked comrades of the Third Texas Cavalry. He shook the crystalline snow from his meager blanket and wrapped the covering around his shoulders. His English comrade lay shivering, an inch-thick layer of snow and sleet atop his blanket, still snoring. They had lain on a bed of thresh, back to back to preserve their body heat.

Bleak evergreen trees, bent from heavy sleet, crowded the campsite like a cloister of ebony-cloaked friars bowing in prayer. Joseph heard the footsteps of pickets, stomping on crunching snow. Horses occasionally snorted and shook their hides. He could make out neither a figure of a man, nor horse, and could not see more than a few feet in front of him. Loosening his pants flap, he relieved himself. When he was finished, he pulled his wool coat collar up and flapped his arms to warm himself. He pulled the blanket tighter around his body.

Colonel Greer's tent was forty feet away. The slightest glow from a lantern emanated through the canvas walls, and Joseph's curiosity led him to stroll closer, perhaps to hear some whispered strategy.

Suddenly, a dark form was before him, the size of a large dog. He stopped, almost falling, and tried to determine what the creature was. His eyes slowly adjusting, he saw not only one, but several of the animals. Wolves! In the middle of camp.

They turned their burning, golden eyes toward him, not vicious stares, just curious ones. The moment seemed to last an eternity — him looking at the wolves and they examining him. Quiet as a baby's breath, the pack trotted away into the forest. Joseph realized he was shivering not from cold, but from the encounter.

At that moment, he had a flash of memory, clearer than any he had had in months, of standing in line in the dark alongside other soldiers. Where was that? Then he remembered Dred Workman had been standing to his left. The entire vision was as complete with detail as any he had yet remembered. He had become accustomed to experiencing so few memories during the last few months that he had basically given up hope of recalling much ever.

He tried to concentrate on the event, but Colonel Greer exited through the tent flap, followed by General Van Dorn. The light from the tent opening spilled out, lending an eerie glow. Joseph watched while the two officers exchanged pleasantries and shook gloved hands. Joseph could see General Van Dorn had dark circle under his eyes, and his face fairly raged red. He shivered under a heavy blanket. Finally, he strode off into the dark, mounted a horse, and galloped down the Telegraph Road south with his accompanying officers.

Greer's next in command, Lieutenant Colonel Lane, strode from the shadows and was immediately by his side. They whispered briefly to each other. Before Joseph could say a word to make his presence known, Colonel Greer spoke aloud to him, "Good morning, soldier. Up early, are you? Ready to fight? Ready to make the Yankees feel our cold steel?" He raised his gloved fist as in triumph.

Joseph saluted. "Yes, sir. Begging the colonel's pardon. I'm a light sleeper, and my mate snores a bit."

Colonel Greer chuckled. "Well, he won't be sleeping much longer." He turned to Colonel Lane, "Kind sir, get the bugler up. Wake the men assigned to feed the horses. Bring them all here. It is necessary we are mounted and moving well before the sun. We'll trap that German devil, Sigel, like a rat."

The colonel hurried away, and Joseph and Colonel Greer were left standing in awkward silence. Colonel Greer buttoned his coat and strapped on his saber.

"Did you know there were wolves just outside your tent, sir?" Joseph blurted.

The colonel gave a quizzical look and scanned the cobalt-toned trees. "Hmm. Strange. They weren't Yankee spies by any chance?"

"No, sir, real wolves. Just passing through, I guess."

"Very well. We are in wild country. This harsh, cold land. Arkansas. Not at all like Texas. Oh, Texas has wolves, mind you, and coyotes, too."

"Yes, sir." Joseph could not speak to his comment.

A wolf howled, followed by more wolves in a chorus of yips and yodels. Colonel Greer and Joseph peered in the direction of the howling. Colonel Greer grinned. "That, soldier, is the sound you'll be hearing from Sigel's Yankees at Bentonville when we cut them off from Curtis's main army and force their surrender."

"Yes, sir."

The aide returned with a host of burly men bearing sacks of oats. "Three handfuls of oats for each mount, twice that for the pack mules," the colonel whispered, and the hostlers hurried toward the horses. Two buglers arrived, yawning, pulling up their suspenders, and yanking on their overcoats. When they had finished buttoning their coats, Colonel Greer ordered, "Wake 'em up, my hearties."

When the buglers blapped their horns, Joseph returned to his friend. "Wake up, Ebie." He shook the Englishman, who groaned and pulled the blanket over his head. "Wake up, you slug."

Ebie Dollander rose on an elbow, bleary-eyed. "Why?"

"Why? Because we're in the army, and it's time to move out." Joseph tied a wool scarf around his neck, buttoned his heavy wool coat, and pushed his slouch hat down on his head, securing the chin cord.

When Ebie pulled his blanket above his head, Joseph kicked him in the rear. Ebie grunted and rolled into a standing position. He tucked in his shirt and slowly re-buttoned his coat.

The buglers ceased, and the commotion noise was of men rushing to sling saddles in place and tighten cinches. Joseph saddled his mount. The sleet ice clinging to the horse's mane and tail tinkled like fairy bells.

A few men stoked meager fires for a measly excuse for coffee, and the aroma drifted through the camp. Joseph joined the men at a cook fire and took a cup of the watery, chicory beverage. Each man munched on hardtack after dipping it in the coffee.

Designated soldiers dismantled the colonel's tent and stowed the canvas sections and poles in the regiment's one mule-drawn cart. The air filled up with grumbles and curses, clanks and clinks of sabers and guns. Joseph, too, tended his black mare, brushing the ice from its hair with a coarse comb. He checked his Springfield's load.

Ebie, more legs and arms than torso, eventually stumbled up to his mount and began fitting the reins' bit into his horse's mouth. "Damn it all! He chomped me." Ebie sucked his bleeding hand and struggled to saddle the ornery mount.

Joseph, leading his mare, jogged into a clearing for muster.

Ebie arrived just in time to answer when the sergeant called his name. Lieutenant Colonel Lane handed him the battle flag. "I think it's appropriate that a Limey carry the colors."

The men stood in a relaxed line, fingering their horses' reins and listening to Colonel Greer extol the virtues of their endeavor, but in Joseph's estimation, said little of importance. Joseph was in no mood to listen to a speech about maintaining a hale and hearty demeanor. The march had been as joyless and exhausting as any endeavor he could imagine.

"We don't know where the enemy exactly is," the colonel announced, "but we will find him and defeat him. And if he finds us first, we'll defeat him anyway." He chuckled, and the troops laughed.

At this pause in the colonel's discourse, a wolf emitted a lonely, haunting howl that echoed through the forest. The laughter stopped, and Joseph saw in the faces of his comrades that the lonely moan had an unnerving effect. The entire line fell solemn. It occurred to Joseph that he was not sure if the Confederates were the predator or the prey.

FIFTY-THREE

THE LONELY, SEARCHING HEART IS TIRELESS

MARCH 6, 1862, 6 AM
ELKHORN TAVERN, ARKANSAS

Cyntha drank coffee alone at the kitchen table of Elkhorn Tavern. So many sleepless nights had left dark circles under her eyes. The evening before, she had helped her cousin, Polly, parch and grind the fresh coffee beans given them by a generous Union soldier, one of many who daily passed through the little valley while escorting supply wagons. Every night, the muleskinner wagoneers and their guard detail camped in the yard and on the three roads that converged there.

She gazed out the frosted window at the glittering firmament that went on forever beyond the Boston Mountains. *I am so alone. I cannot even speak to my brother, Anthony. And the soul of my dear Joseph is in torment and I have no means to bring him rest.*

She sipped the coffee sweetened with honey, for sugar was nowhere for miles around.

The stairs creaked, and Cyntha heard the stuttering tread of Ben making his way down the stairs. She wondered if he would stumble over one of the many Union soldiers sleeping in the parlor.

When he came into the kitchen, he did not see her, for she sat in the dark. A single lamp glowed in the parlor behind him and flooded out to reveal Ben's visage. Cyntha examined the rebel while he stood there. *What a handsome face. I think I may have judged him too early. He has shown such a liking to Reynolds these last days and is always the gentleman to Polly and me.*

She set her cup in the saucer. Ben heard the clink and half hopped, half walked into the dark room. "Hello, my good lady." He tried to sound gallant, but the expression seemed awkward on his tongue. "May I join you? I sleep all day, then I'm up all night with this splint worrying my leg. I won't take the laudanum your cousin tries to give me. And the injured Yanks everywhere, all of 'em snore."

Cyntha could barely stifle a laugh. "At least your leg's healing. The infection has gone. And, yes, you may join me. Get a cup of coffee. It's hot."

Ben shuffled around the gloomy kitchen, gathered a cup from the cupboard, and did his best to pour the brew in the dark. He pulled a chair directly beside Cyntha and sat, his hip against hers. At first, she felt alarmed by his forward behavior, but then felt more at ease.

He laid his spare hand and inch from hers, holding the cup. Ben felt a yearning for her he had not known for any other woman. In his deepest heart, he knew it was inevitable. Somehow, she suited him. Directly opposite in character and beliefs to him in so many ways, yet he longed for her.

He lifted his cup and sipped the coffee, fighting his urging to pull her close and kiss her. "I have a feelin'," Ben whispered, "that this war that was originally meant to divide us will actually bring folks together."

Cyntha turned toward him, and a smile slipped across her lips.

"Think about it. I've met more different people in this war. Folks from all over. Arkansas, Louisiana, even from Germany.

Why, there's men what went all the way to fight in Virginia. I wonder what Virginia's like."

"I agree. It's an amazing outcome," Cyntha said. "You're the first Texan I've ever met."

"Is that a good thing or a bad thing?"

Cyntha smiled and ducked her head.

Ben gave a smirking laugh. "I ain't never met anyone from Iowa before. Are all the women in Iowa as pretty as you?" The question escaped him. He had not expected it to come out, but he sensed her breath coming quicker.

She looked at him with a piercing stare. She so wanted to hate this soldier of the loathsome enemy. He cared not for Negroes. But he cared for Reynolds. Her thoughts softened. Maybe he was changing. Maybe there was more good in him than she had first believed. She set down her cup.

There in the capacious dark, his face so close, she leaned over and held her cheek to his, and breathed deep sighs. Then she began to weep quietly. Ben did not pull back, but laid his hand gently on her back. She set a hand on his chest and felt his heart race.

After a minute, Cyntha pulled back and stood. She took the handkerchief from her dress sleeve and dried her eyes. "Thank you, Ben. I don't really know why I did that, but I appreciate you." She strode quickly from the room and up the stairs.

Ben did not drink the coffee. He limped to the window. He swept his un-kept blond locks from his eyes and stared out at the stars, and then at the first shimmering spears of silver and orange light slung from the sun over the mountains at the sooty sky. *A Yankee woman! And a fool abolitionist. Never under heaven.*

Somehow, he felt he had not convinced himself.

FIFTY-FOUR

THE BATTLE STRUCK, THE HEART REMEMBERS

MARCH 6, 1862, 8 AM
HALF A MILE SOUTH OF BENTONVILLE, ARKANSAS

Joseph Favor rode beside his companion, Ebie, several yards in the front of Colonel Greer's Third Texas cavalry, the vanguard of General James McIntosh's Mounted Infantry Brigade. Ebie held the furled banner of the Third Texas. Joseph knew the brigade was hard bent to trap General Sigel's Union troops, and he felt an element of lust for battle himself.

The two topped a rise and looked down at a wide valley, the town of Bentonville perched in the middle.

A hazy fog was rapidly sliding away in sections, like sheets let loose in a gale, revealing a placid white landscape of farmers' fields amid undulating hills. Stark, barren trees stubbed out on them like a dull-shanked haircut. The new sun gleamed on the crystalline snow, sparkling like a myriad of jewels. To the west, a dense snake of mist lay above the meandering, ice-choked McKissick Creek. Beyond that, blue and purple ridges, as yet untouched by the sun's glow, faded into the gray horizon.

East of the creek lay the village of Bentonville—a cluster of small shops and liveries and a two-story hotel. The town was blanketed with snow. In the main street, blue-clad Federals clustered like a treasure of sapphires spread on a lace tablecloth.

The Union soldiers stood mostly still and seemed unaware that the large Confederate army had approached.

"There they are!" Joseph pointed. "Sigel's army."

"Blimey. Looks like no more than a few hundred. Where's the rest of them?" Ebie's English accent rang in the chill air.

Additional riders of the Third Texas Cavalry arrived beside Joseph and Ebie. Lieutenant Colonel Walter Lane attained the hilltop first with about thirty cavalrymen. Colonel Lane was a hero of the Texas Revolution, a Texas Ranger, and often jested about the nine horses he had had shot out from under him. He was gaunt and gray-bearded and still spoke with an Irish brogue. To Joseph, the man's demeanor was one of fearlessness. Ebie and Joseph had played a few hands of Faro with the colonel in dull periods in camp.

A minute later, Colonel Greer came up beside Ebie, his horse snorting great plumes of pale vapor.

"We've got 'em," Colonel Lane said.

"At least some of them," Colonel Greer responded. He removed his gloves and took his spyglass from his coat pocket and studied the valley scene.

More of the double-file queue of cavalry moved in behind and astride the road, each soldier rising in his stirrups to garner a peek at the landscape below. The Union soldiers had still not noticed the gray column blended in amongst ash-colored bleak trees that crowded the hilltop.

Joseph squinted his eyes against the snowdrift's glare and listened to Colonels Greer and Lane discuss strategy, each of them pointing at features in the valley. More elements of McIntosh's Mounted Infantry Brigade of three thousand men were closing fast up the Telegraph Road. The Yankees in Bentonville would be overwhelmed.

The officers' conversation was interrupted by the approach of the clanking ambulance of General Van Dorn. The racket sent a roost of ravens careening, cawing. The cavalry troops moved their mounts out of the path of the oncoming enclosed wagon. When the wagon halted, General Van Dorn slowly emerged, bleary-eyed and looking as if he had awakened from the dead. He coughed roughly, spitting out sputum.

Wobbling, he came forward near Joseph and beside Colonel Greer, looking up at him and shading his eyes against the intense rising sun's gleam. Joseph smelled the overpowering cologne, mixed with menthol. *The man is rank.* He placed his hand to his nose.

Colonel Greer saluted. All the men nearby did the same.

"Do we have them, Greer?" General Van Dorn asked.

"We do, sir. We need to move quickly to cut off their retreat."

General Van Dorn's eyes lit like lightning strikes. "We have Sigel, then." He twirled the ends of his mustache. "Let me have a glass."

Colonel Greer handed him his spyglass. The general strode up between Joseph's and Ebie's horses, and looked through the spyglass, scanning slowly across the fields and town.

Joseph's horse skittered sideways. He stroked the mare's neck. "Easy, girl."

"Yes, I see," General Van Dorn said. "There's not very many of them. A few hundred by my count." Absentmindedly, he handed the spyglass to Joseph who took it and held his breath, for the man's smell was so appalling.

General Van Dorn walked back beside Colonel Greer. Joseph noted the man walked with his toes turned in. He had heard that men who rode horses a great deal sometimes developed that stride.

"Where's McIntosh?" General Van Dorn demanded. "Isn't this his brigade? Where's McCulloch?"

"General McCulloch is at the rear of the column," Colonel Greer said, "behind General Price's Missourians, with the infantry, trying to encourage our tired soldiers to keep going. And yes, sir, General McIntosh should be here shortly. In fact, here he comes."

Brigadier General McIntosh, followed by his staff sergeant, rode up at a gallop, scattering his own mounted troops to the sides of the road. Rounding the ambulance wagon, he drew up his snorting mount. The horse reared, and the general brought it under control. He saluted his superior. His brow was beaded with sweat. His thick, dark beard belied his youth.

General Van Dorn barely put a salute to his temple and turned from the bright-eyed, young general. "A map!" he demanded. His fevered illness seemed to flow away from him in his enthusiasm. His hands shook, waiting for General McIntosh to hand him a crumpled facsimile of the area, the map sketched by Paul McGavin. The general eyed the drawing up and down. "Yes."

"What are your orders, sir?" General McIntosh asked. Joseph heard the impatience in his voice.

"Well, look here." General Van Dorn stabbed at the map. His officers leaned from their saddles and peered at the penciled lines. "See here. There's this road that circles west around the town to the north, then turns and intersects on the eastbound road."

"Yes, sir, I see," Colonel Greer said, his eyes lighting up.

"I do as well," General McIntosh agreed.

"Yes, yes," General Van Dorn leaped slightly from the ground. "Colonel Greer, this is your Third Texas here in front, is it not?"

"Yes, sir."

"Who's behind them in column?"

"The Sixth, Ninth, and Eleventh Texas, and Arkansas and Texas battalions."

General Van Dorn fell silent and studied the map, turning it around at all angles, almost like a child not yet schooled, pretending at his letters.

General McIntosh, who had ridden up to Joseph's left, heaved a sigh, took a stub of pencil and a scrap of paper from his pocket and scribbled a note. He handed the order to his staff sergeant. "Take this to Colonel Elijah Gates of the First Missouri. Tell him to take his regiment east along this hilltop, then drop down and seal off that east road. Hold it at all hazards."

The sergeant saluted and raced his steed back toward the specified cavalry regiment. In a few moments, while General Van Dorn studied the map and paced back and forth, Joseph could hear the hastening horses of Gates' Missourians threading through the trees and brush eastward.

Joseph was curious about the Union soldiers milling around the town's main street and warming themselves at paltry fires. He raised the spyglass that General Van Dorn had handed him and focused it. Immediately, he witnessed two blue-clad soldiers scampering across the field below them toward the town, then two more from farther west began running. They were shouting and pointing back up the hill where the Confederates were gathered.

The clusters of soldiers in the town scattered like mice pounced on by a cat, some rushing forward to take positions behind houses and aiming their rifles up the hill. Others dashed behind the hotel and brought out horses in harness and began hitching them to a half dozen cannons and caissons.

Joseph was amazed at the scene unfolding. Turning his view but a little, Joseph saw one soldier vault up the steps of the hotel porch and meet a scowling, black-haired officer, holding a cup of coffee in one hand, a napkin in the other. "I think you better take a look," Joseph demanded. "They've seen us."

General Van Dorn rushed up to Joseph and tore the spyglass from his hand. He surveyed the town. "Ah, ha! It's old Sigel! It's him, Ah'm sure. On the hotel steps!"

The other Confederate officers trained their binoculars on the hotel. Colonel Greer lifted binoculars from a saddlebag and focused them. "Ah believe," Colonel Greer said in his rich southern drawl, "we have disturbed the man at breakfast. Is that a spot of egg yolk ah see on his uniform?" He smirked.

General Van Dorn spun around. "General McIntosh, take your brigade on this quick route around the West and North of the town." He slapped at the map. "We will inshuah that General Sigel's men won't escape. Quickly now! We must be in haste to spring our trap." He turned to Colonel Greer. "Colonel, you stay here with me and help with the reconnoiter. We must discern where the rest of Sigel's division is positioned. Send your subordinate to lead the column with McIntosh."

Colonel Greer gave quick orders to Colonel Lane. General McIntosh sent couriers down the line. In two minutes, Joseph found himself riding down the hill road beside Colonel Lane and his company captain, R.H. Cumby.

Ebie, who had unfurled the Confederate battle flag, rode just behind them. The flag snapped in the chill breeze.

They were in the lead of three thousand men riding in an arc around the town. By the time the brigade drew even with Bentonville's main streets, the Union troops had already left and were racing out of sight, eastward.

General McIntosh galloped up beside Joseph and Colonel Lane. He kept yelling back to the troops, "Faster, men, faster!" Joseph was pushing his mare hard, leaning forward over the horse's neck, the sharp wind slicing at this face, doing his best to keep up with Colonel Lane. General McIntosh halted his horse in a skidding stop. Glancing back, Joseph saw the general gather a riding crop from his saddle and begin striking at the cavalrymen's mounts as they rode by him. Joseph could hear him continuing to drive the men with shouts of encouragement as well as epithets. He could not remember witnessing such impatience.

The snow-laden road became a path and quickly narrowed in a thicket.

Turning a corner, Joseph, Colonel Lane, Captain Cumby, and Ebie accompanied by twenty of the Third Texas plunged headlong into a loose tangle of bushes grown across the road. Twigs and thorny branches cracked under the weight of the horses' passing while hundreds of branches on both sides of the trail thwacked and slapped each man from both sides. The meshed growth slowed their progress, but did not impede it completely. The companies slowed to a walk and resumed a double column. The seldom-used path seemed to be closing itself like a wound.

In a few minutes, General McIntosh forged his way to the front alongside Joseph. "Push through, men!" he spurred his steed. Joseph looked down and saw bloody scratches on his horse's neck and head. He felt a trickle of blood sliding down his own cheek and a stinging cut above his left eyebrow.

Soon, the brigade was forced to ride single file.

At one point in their mad rush, Joseph saw an open trail leading east, and said as much to Ebie. Still, the strung-out column followed the general who was striving with alacrity to hasten the brigade.

Rounding a corner in the vanishing trail, they came upon General McIntosh facing an impenetrable jumble of bushes and trees. The path had ended. "We've come too far. We've come too far!" the general shouted. "Turn around, turn around. We missed the turnoff. About face."

To Joseph, General McIntosh seemed to be speaking more to himself, but the general spun his horse and directed everyone to follow him. Struggling with the constricting brush, each soldier turned his mount and hastened back the way they had come. Joseph and Ebie rode now at the end of the column. Despite being surrounded by the crowded thicket, considerable gunfire could be heard to the east. Joseph guessed that the First Missouri was engaged with Sigel's Yankees.

In a while, the column turned onto the trail that became a road heading east, the one Joseph had pointed out earlier.

"I'll wager," said Ebie, "we rode three miles out of the way."

When the brigade reached the Sugar Creek Road, the one Sigel had used to flee Bentonville, General McIntosh called a halt and sent mounted pickets forward and back toward Bentonville. Colonel Lane led the entire Third Texas further east down the Sugar Creek Road and waited for orders from McIntosh. The various companies milled around, and Joseph and Ebie found themselves again near Colonel Lane at the head of the column.

The colonel pointed to the roadside where numerous haversacks, jackets, and even weapons from the Union had been discarded in their retreat. He took his revolver from his holster and examined the load, and then thrust it away. He drummed his fingers on the saddle pummel.

"Captain Baker!" he called.

The Company C captain rode quickly to the colonel's side.

"Baker," Colonel Lane said, "take your company up this road at all speed. Engage the enemy and try to slow them down. We're coming. Go now!"

Captain Baker saluted and gathered his company; they raced away.

In minutes, aggravated and concentrated gunfire and cannon blasts erupted to the east. Colonel Lane looked back at General McIntosh who was trying desperately to organize the melee of the remainder of the brigade. He did not hesitate. "Forward, men, at a trot." The column advanced down the road toward the retreating Yankees.

Joseph recognized an emotion he had felt before. His initial curiosity, then anticipation, then delirious excitement about battle had been replaced by a surfeit of dread. He knew this feeling. He was remembering the stark reality of his first battle, the sweltering heat among dark trees, a clearing night sky, and wading Wilson Creek.

He was trotting beside Colonel Lane once again. The colonel reached in his inner pocket of his coat and handed Joseph a folded parchment and his pocket watch. Without looking at Joseph, he said, "I've had nine horses shot out from under me. Nine! Never a dire bullet for me. But if this is the day the enemy aims a little higher, and if the good Lord takes me to His abode, be ye so kind as to gi' that to me beloved." Briefly, he squinted an eye at Joseph.

"Yes, sir." Joseph, unbuttoned his coat, and slid the letter and watch into his shirt pocket, and when he did, he remembered another time a very important letter was sequestered above his heart. The letter's words came flooding back to him. He almost fell from his horse.

FIFTY-FIVE

INTO THE GATES OF DEATH

MARCH 6, 1862, 9 AM
EAST OF BENTONVILLE, ARKANSAS ON THE SUGAR CREEK ROAD

Joseph was riding like a wild man. His remembrance of the words of the letter that had been in his pocket at the battle of Wilson Creek racked his mind. Such a realization while he was rushing toward battle. *The name*, he thought. *What was the name on the letter?*

The thunder of the hooves beat against his already throbbing head, paining him like he had been hit with the butt of an ax. He wished to leap from his horse, hide, and avoid the inevitable fight. Already, elements of the Company C cavalry were rushing away from the rifle and cannon fire.

"There must be a whole brigade up that road!" one cavalryman hollered while reining his horse to a halt beside Colonel Lane, who had stopped his own horse. Another couple of dozen cavalrymen galloped up to the column, their horses lathered even in the cold.

Joseph was near enough to watch Colonel Lane rise in his stirrups, attempting to see past the curve in the road where smoke was billowing like a factory's smokestack, creating wayward black clouds. Still more soldiers from Company C, along with Captain Baker, arrived and mingled among the rest of the Third Texas, filing in behind and to the sides. Joseph beheld a blend of worried faces, frustrated ones, and fearful ones. Each man held a different countenance.

Captain Baker saluted Colonel Lane. "Sir, they've been pouring it on us. They're dug in behind rocks and trees. I saw remnants of the First Missouri. They've backed off on one of them hills and were tryin' to maintain fire on the enemy when we arrived. One of their number came up to me and said they'd at first captured some Yanks from Illinois, but then the whole of the Yank army arrived and drove 'em off into the trees. Leavin' the prisoners behind."

"How many enemy can you estimate?"

"Hard to say with all the brush and rocks. They've spread out along the road, but they've got cannon just yonder on that steep incline to the left. If we'd take them cannon, it'd be a different fight."

"Good report, Baker."

The cannon and rifle fire abated. Colonel Lane drummed on his saddle pummel. "Captains Cumby and Mabry! A word, gentlemen."

The two captains rode up to the colonel.

"Cumby, Mabry, can you take your companies A and B and wrest those cannons so the rest of this army may proceed and whip Sigel?"

"We'll do it, sir," said Cumby.

Mabry nodded. "Yes, sir, in about two shakes of a lamb's tail."

"Very well," Colonel Lane ordered. "Arrange your soldiers for a charge up that hill and bring glory to our wives and sweethearts. For the South! Huzzah!"

Joseph found himself maneuvering his horse into an undulating line in and out of ravines about the road. Numerous trees separated the riders from making anything akin to a formal parade presentation. At best, it was a broken stripe.

Soldiers began checking loads in their revolvers and cocking their carbines.

Joseph chose to leave his rifle in the holster. He removed his saber, raising it so it glinted in the sun. *This is it.* His headache pounded. *Who am I fighting? Why am I fighting?* There was no time to discern a proper judgment. His mouth felt filled with cotton.

"Ready!" Colonel Lane, in the lead alongside Captains Cumby and Mabry, raised his sword. Eighty horses stutter-stepped. Eighty riders leaned forward, grasping mane and reins in one hand, weapon in the other, bending low to the horses' necks.

"Charge!" the call echoed up and down the line.

The companies galloped over the stingy terrain, dodging saplings, stumps, and full grown trees, their line broken into disjointed sections. Sooner than Joseph had imagined, the troop was pushing up the rocky hill. The moment they gained the height of the hill he saw the cannons directly in front of them.

Rifle volleys from Yankees hidden behind boulders and trees spat lead at the advancing Confederates. The cavalry surged doggedly, weaving in and out of stubby trees and bushes. Joseph leaped his mare over a tall bush and landed full in between two cannons just as each of them roared grapeshot.

Jerking his horse to a swift stop, he brought his saber down on the shoulder of an artilleryman. The man crumpled, blood spilling from the wound. He turned his horse and saw others of his company in amongst the four cannons, firing their rifles point blank into the Union soldiers. Sigel's Yankees fought back with ferocity, some grabbing at the cavalrymen to pull them from their mounts.

Yankees fell, but so did Confederates. Smoke became a low-slung cloud.

In the swirling melee of smoke, rushing horses, and men, Joseph discovered his steed had danced directly in front of the bore of a third cannon. He punched his spurs in the mare's side. She reared, and he slid off. He landed on his feet, bumping a Union artilleryman who stood stock still, seemingly engrossed in some matter in the sky. Joseph could not waste a moment to discern the man's blank stare.

With the reins in his hand, he lurched for the saddle, but missed.

His mare backed from him, hooves planted, its body directly in front of the cannon. Joseph pulled the reins with all his strength, but the mare resisted, fear blazing in her eyes.

Just then the cannon belched grapeshot, tearing through the horse and the scraps of iron spreading out, wounding several Confederates. Joseph watched the destroyed horse collapse, torn almost in two. Then he was clubbing a Yankee with his revolver in the back, totally unaware that he had drawn the gun. The burly soldier had Joseph about the waist in a death hold and would have crushed Joseph's ribs had he not bashed the man's skull hard enough to hear the crack. The man collapsed.

Smoke became so dense, Joseph stood in a fog. In a few seconds, the cloud rose, and he raced headlong away from the cannons.

More Yankees sprang out from behind rocks in flanking positions to the Confederates, firing without pity. So many bullets whistled by Joseph's ears that they sounded like a flock of nighthawks. One bullet tore across his shoulder, ripping fabric and slicing his skin.

"Joseph!" Someone called his name. He looked up. Ebie sat astride his mount. "Get on the back o' my ass!"

Joseph raced through milling horses and wounded men and leapt up behind Ebie. They dashed down the incline, eluding the enveloping fire and shell.

Joseph heard Colonel Lane and the two captains yelling, "Retreat!"

He was never so glad as when he and Ebie reached the road from whence they had begun.

The Confederate cavalry gathered in a broad huddle around Colonel Lane. Then more cannon fire whistled over their heads and exploded, sending hot metal down on them.

The troop scattered in a reckless sprint farther down the road.

Joseph held an immediate realization. He knew the battle had only just begun. All he could think was *What next? What could be worse?*

Several miles to the south, astride her horse, riding bareback, Sara heard the resonating clatter of battle, but could only wonder at its portent.

FIFTY-SIX

∞

HOWEVER LONG AND HARD THE ROAD

MARCH 6, 1862, 11 PM
NEAR LEETOWN, MISSOURI

Late that night, the Guard camped among the trees, and the byway was unfettered by marching men. Sara took to the thoroughfare that was lit by a necklace of campfires lining the entirety of it. She noticed slaves in attendance to officers and a handful of washer women, all of whom looked worn to a miserable despondency. *Why did they not stay behind?*

She answered her own question. *Perhaps for the same reason I'm here. To be present for the ones they love.*

She discovered she was riding in the columns of Price's Missouri Guard. She had no idea where McCulloch's brigades had gone.

Continuing along the road lined with the bivouacked men, she had called out, "Third Texas!" over and over, hoping a soldier would come forward, but none did. She considered that, because of her deafness, she had passed the regiment, sleeping deeper in the woods.

Then the halted wagons and cannons barred her course, so she took to plying her way through the thickets parallel to the army.

The snowfall ceased, and the dismal clouds drifted away. The wind picked up.

By the time the light of the fires dwindled to specks in the distance, her entire being was so exhausted she continued in a hazy reality under the bare moon's glow. Driving herself farther, long into the night, she realized she had gone athwart of the road. Her attempts to retrace her direction found only a thin hunting path. She continued upon it. "All paths eventually come to a road," she mumbled. *In the morning, the army must pass by me. In the daylight, I'll see Joseph.*

At one point, she spied a string of campfires extending through the forest and determined to stop there to gain warmth. She knew that were she to stop without benefit of a fire, she might freeze to death. *These Confederates will let me rest by their fire.*

Drawing closer, she beheld not gray uniforms and homespun, but cobalt-jacketed men standing outside pale tents. She turned Esther around and regained the path, slogging deeper into the ice-laden forest.

Near the midnight hour, she spied the light of a fireplace glimmering in the frosted window panes of a house. She rode Esther into a barren, snow-covered field and eased the horse over a fallen fence rail.

Weary beyond her ability to reason, her eyes beheld the house shrinking and expanding, the hallucination widening as she drew closer.

She felt sliced thin, numb and stupid, and her un-splinted leg throbbed with every beat of her heart. The house looked so inviting, at least a windbreak from the cold.

When she alighted Esther, a most amiable man, who introduced himself as Mr. Foster, strode off the porch. He invited her to spend the night with his family. "Heard you comin' a long way off. I'm a light sleeper. Welcome to our home," he said. His wife scatted the children from a bed and insisted she use it. In addition, the man led Esther to his barn.

By late morning, Sara awoke to the clanking of pots, the whispered commands of Mrs. Foster, and the giggles of the children. She dressed as quickly as she could, drank real coffee, and ate biscuits sweetened with honey for breakfast. She had not realized her hearing, though mixed with a buzzing reverberation, was returning. Her thinking, however, was muddled. Following breakfast, she wandered to the barn and combed and brushed Esther.

The sun was leaning on noon while Sara sat near Esther in the barn, lost in her thoughts, looking out the open wide door at placid white fields. A thin sheet of fog extended a few feet above the snowclad ground. *At least the snowstorm has ended.*

She sat on a rail in farmer Foster's barn, her ears popping like firecrackers. Despite lying in a cozy bed, she had tossed all night with horrid dreams.

Then, a whooshing ocean sound replaced the popping in her ears.

Her right leg still throbbed some. Holding it tight against Esther's sides for the previous long day's bareback ride brought a considerable ache. She glanced over at her horse, covered with a wool blanket. *I've ne'er treated you so well, Esther.*

Esther, her head buried in a bucket of grain, snorted. Sara jumped. She heard the snort.

The crashing tide in her ears had suddenly ceased. Instead, she recognized the nuances of sounds in the farmer's barn. A bird in the rafters tweeted a merry tune. A mouse scurried along the floor. Sara stood down from the rail. She heard her own footsteps on the hay-strewn ground. She coughed, and she heard that. She whistled lightly and laughed to identify the cheery melody.

Footsteps came closer, and a bucket swinging. The world was suddenly more alive. Even the smells of the dirt and oaty, musty smell of the horses and the urine-drenched hay seemed more pronounced. She took to spinning like a top despite her sore leg. When the farmer came through the rear door, he found Sara perched atop the wheel of the farmer's wagon, whooping to beat the band. "I can hear! I can hear!"

"Well, you seemed to be able to hear me fine last night," Mr. Foster, a quizzical look on his face, said. "What's different now?"

Sara remembered that, though muffled, she *had* heard his words the night before, as well as his wife and children. She had been so dogged tired, she was unaware. "Oh, Mr. Foster, I was deaf for weeks. Praise God. My prayers were answered."

"They're always answered, child." Mr. Foster set about cracking ice on the top of the horses' water buckets with an ax blade, and pitchforked hay into each stall.

Sara listened to every tidbit of sound. "What a fine noise that is!"

"You were too weary for me to ask last night. I must inquire what a young lady such as yourself was doing out in a bitter night," Mr. Foster said.

At that moment, a rhythmic roll sounded barely perceptible. Sara knew it immediately. Thousands of soldiers were marching, and thousands of horses were trotting. She limped outside the barn and witnessed a wide, gray ribbon of soldiers, flags glittering red and blue in the sun — General McCulloch's army. "There they are! I shall find Joseph at last."

The army of cavalry followed by infantry were traveling east along a road north of where she stood. They were no longer on the Telegraph Road.

Sara tugged Mr. Foster by the arm. She pointed. "What road is that?"

"Just the Ford Road, and..." He stopped, suddenly aware of the thousands of soldiers less than a quarter of a mile away. "By the jumping Moses! Look at the size of that army."

"The Ford Road? Not the Telegraph?"

"No, Sara, the Telegraph Road runs south of here a few miles below Leetown, then turns north toward Elkhorn Tavern. Is who you're lookin' for in that army?"

Sara's smile beamed. "Yes, my fiancé."

In silence, the two watched the fluttering flags, the horses, and the men, their clothes a rainbow of brown, light blue, mustard, and gray. The clatter of armaments, tread of feet, and hoof beats blended into a steady rumble.

"Joseph must be among them! Mr. Foster, may I borrow a saddle, please? I'll bring it back."

She followed the farmer where he kept saddle and tack. He helped her get Esther ready to ride. While he pulled the cinch strap tight, she flung on her heavy cape.

Then, a more urgent sound exploded to the rear of the barn, an intense racket rushing toward them. She looked out the barn door. Hundreds of blue-coated cavalry, their Iowa and Missouri regimental flags spanking in the wind, raced out of the woods, and in but a few minutes set a line in the Foster's field and parallel with the Confederates. Men began unlimbering cannon and caisson.

Of a sudden, Union cavalry on foot, leading their horses, were spilling out of the woods at a run.

Not one hundred paces in front of her, a Union colonel on a dancing steed was pointing and directing more and more soldiers out into the field. A courier galloped to him, shouting, "Colonel Osterhhaus, Colonel Bussey's cavalry and cannons are positioned. Should we attack?"

The colonel, his face abounding with a long, bushy mustache, looked through binoculars. He nodded, and the courier raced away toward the battery that was aimed at the Confederates.

Sara's heart plunged. She had once before seen Union troops surprise an unsuspecting Confederate army. This moment was too much like a repeat of one she had been part of months before at Wilson Creek. This time, she knew she had no time to warn the Confederates. The battle was upon them. *Dear God, please don't let Joseph be killed.*

FIFTY-SEVEN

WAR TAKES THE BLOOD OF MEN AND THE TEARS OF WOMEN

MARCH 7, 1862, 11:30 AM
FORD ROAD NORTH OF LEETOWN, ARKANSAS

Newly appointed Captain Paul McGavin rode alongside General McCulloch and his aide, Colonel Armstrong. Paul, though tired from only three hours of sleep, enjoyed the warming sun. Melting ice dripped from the trees alongside the road. McCulloch's division marched on Ford Road and in the barren fields beside it.

Paul was glad for the clear day, the sunshine sparkling on the fresh snow. Though the weather was brisk, he did not feel chilled. Colonel Armstrong was bundled in his heavy coat; General McCulloch wore only his dove-gray corduroy jacket and seemed oblivious to the temperature. He chewed on a cigar and sometimes straightened the rifle strapped over his shoulder. He wore no epaulets, no regalia of a typical general. His trousers were not gray, but light blue.

Paul thought he looked more like a common citizen than a general. He had come to know General McCulloch, the "deadshot ranger" that his men affectionately called him, as a friend.

In the previous night's meeting, Paul had offered an idea to the generals to avoid assaulting Curtis's Federal army straight on. He informed them Curtis's army had wheeled around and was digging in at the bluffs above Sugar Creek, facing what they thought would be an attack by Van Dorn's army from the west. Paul's excellent description of the Bentonville detour road that rounded the Large Mountain had found favor with not only McCulloch, but with Generals Price and Van Dorn.

On a forced night march, General Van Dorn was leading Price's weary army north around the mountain to arrive squarely behind Curtis' troops and block the Union's vital supply line. They would circle the mountain, pass through the village of Tanyard, and end up at Elkhorn Tavern. McCulloch's division, lined up behind Price's troops, turned right onto the Ford Road along the southern front of Large Mountain. They would join quickly with his counterpart's division. The force would be larger than the Union army and astride the supply line.

The plan seemed ingenious, and Paul did not mind that General Van Dorn took credit for the bold move. He had momentarily shaken the thoughts of the loss of his brother, Ben, and felt confident in the forthcoming battle. The sweet, deaf, café girl still haunted his thoughts. Sara.

"Colonel Armstrong," General McCulloch asked, "which regiments are riding before us?"

"If I recall sir, we ordered them thus — directly in front of us are McIntosh's brigade, the Sixth Texas cavalry, then in front of them, the Ninth Texas, the Eleventh Texas, the First Arkansas and First Texas. The Third Texas are in the front."

"Very good. Greer's a good man to have in the lead. How are Hebert's men doing?

"Hebert's Brigade seems in high spirits, but we've lost perhaps a thousand men by the wayside. This march has been exhausting."

"Such is war's nature. How are General Pike's Cherokees, Choctaw, and Creek Indians doing?"

"Well enough, sir, for an untrained rabble."

"They've not had enough time to train properly," Paul interjected. "I spoke with General Pike last night. He feels fortunate to have them come this far. It has cost a fortune to enlist their number."

"Albert Pike's a good man," General McCulloch said. "If anyone can train those Indians, he can."

"Did you see he's wearing Indian clothes?" Paul said. "He calls it his Sioux suit. Buckskin shirt, fringed leggings, moccasins. He's proud of it."

General McCulloch nodded.

"However," Colonel Armstrong stated flatly, "I'm not sure our Confederate army needs soldiers carrying tomahawks and scalping knives. It's not civil."

"We shall see." General McCulloch doused his cigar against his palm and flung the stub away.

All of a sudden, a number of soldiers broke rank and pointed to the field. Soon, all heads were turned. Paul saw the blue-coated cavalry lining up in the field. Among them, three cannons were aimed at the Confederates.

The first cannon shot whistled a mere second before it exploded above McIntosh's cavalry, sending burning canister balls down on man and horse. Two more blasts shrieked and blew apart in the trees. Several soldiers fell, wounded or dead. Horses went down. The clamor scattered the column. Frenzied horses darted like thistle down blown by the wind, the riders striving to settle the animals. Many riders were pitched to the ground. A few horses bolted fifty yards before being reined to a stop.

General McCulloch was automatic and methodical in his orders. He spoke to his couriers, and they rode away to pass the orders up and down the line in uniformity.

More cannon fire blazed. Rifle fire pierced the air. A bullet zipped by Paul's ear.

Despite the initial surprise, General McCulloch engendered calm. "Re-form the line. Wheel about right," he commanded. The soldiers turned their horses into position, despite the intense firing from the Union position.

"You there," he said to a courier, "tell Pike to send his Cherokees after those cavalry hiding in the woods to the right."

"Yes, sir." The man saluted and rode toward General Pike.

Paul had not even seen the Yankees, barely visible and forming in the belt of trees. He felt amazement for how the general so quickly sized up the situation.

Colonel Armstrong, General McCulloch, and Paul trained their spyglasses on the Federal artillery battery stationed outside the edge of a small woods in the snowy field. A farmhouse and barn stood to the left of the field pieces. The Union cavalry was dismounted in a line on either side.

"I see three cannon." Paul lowered his spyglass. "To the right of the cannon, I see an Iowa cavalry flag."

"Yes, and more than a few hundred cavalry to the left," General McCulloch added. "Maybe a vanguard of Curtis' army, or a misplaced troop trying to gain some glory. I think a few of our regiments can sweep them away." He began scribbling orders for his subordinates and handed them to several mounted couriers.

In two minutes, the Texan and Arkansan mounted infantry of McIntosh's brigade had formed their line and drawn forth rifle and sword. "You may advance, Colonel," General McCulloch said calmly to the nearest officer. Then, in what seemed to Paul like an afterthought, the general said, "Have the men yell like Comanche warriors."

All down the line, the order passed. "Yell like Comanches!"

Three thousand cavalry trotted out several yards, and then broke into a full gallop at the small Union force. Canister blasted over their heads, too high to inflict damage. The soldiers, their rifles aimed while they rode, let out a horrific, yipping war cry. The bellowing and hollering did not abate until they collided with the Union soldiers.

The Yankee gunners were hurriedly attempting to limber the guns, but fell under the sword. The remaining cavalry scattered like ants on a mound, horse and man barreling into each other in the smothering smoke.

Sara mounted Esther at the first cannon blast. She galloped west. *If I can circle around this field and into those trees yonder, I can reach Joseph.* Her thoughts were jumbled. Find Joseph? Save Joseph? Run and hide?

Her heart unchecked by fear, to be this close to her love, she would not be restrained. Her anger rose, for in re-gaining her hearing, all she heard now was the rancor of battle.

Glancing right, she saw the mass of Confederate cavalry charging the Union line. She gained a strip of tightly packed trees and could see elements of more Confederates that were stretching their line on the Ford Road.

She rode a short distance into the trees, often looking out at the smoke-filled battlefield.

Rounding some dense bushes, she almost collided into a company of dismounted Union cavalry. Many soldiers were crouched, others were tying their mounts to thin trees. She saw a soldier holding a blue flag, hanging limp, the word "Iowa" showing.

Several soldiers turned surprised eyes toward her. In that instant, the moment somehow frozen, as Esther was skidding to a stop, a horde of the Cherokees burst through the trees and surged upon the unsuspecting Iowans. The Iowans turned and began firing their Springfields, and the entire forest filled with pungent smoke and was inundated with men bound up in each other, struggling, clubbing, stabbing, screaming.

Esther reared. A warrior in a bright blue turban rushed underneath the beast's flailing legs with his hatchet raised, bearing down on an Iowan.

The two men met like a great clapping, instantly grappling with each other's arms. The Iowan held fast to the Cherokee's hatchet arm. He punched the Indian repeatedly in the stomach. The Indian collapsed. The Iowan gathered his rifle from the ground, raised it, and brought the butt down on his assailant's head. In that second, a bullet pierced the Iowan's neck, and blood spurted out while he sank, clutching his wound.

Sara turned her mare and waded through the crowded trees. Looking back, she saw a buckskin clad Cherokee pull out his knife and carve a piece of scalp from the dead Iowan's head. He raised the piece high, pumped his arms and yelled in a high-pitched chant.

The Iowans were racing through the trees behind Sara. Their horses, no longer tethered to the trees, bolted in all directions, screaming. The animals were like embers flying from a fire when a log is thrown upon it. They smashed into trees and barreled down men. Sara had never imagined such havoc.

She was pinned in the ever-tightening tongs of battle.

Joseph, riding with the Third Texas to the far left of the battle, was astonished by the cannon fire behind him. Colonel Greer's regiment turned their horses, almost as a well-oiled clockwork, toward the commotion. Joseph suddenly could gather no spit in his mouth. He fumbled for his canteen and took a long drink.

He had been preparing himself for a big fight, but was expecting it later in the afternoon. He knew enough of the plan to join with General Price's army at the tavern everyone spoke of, the one with the large elk horns nailed near the roof.

With dense foliage blocking his sight, he could see nothing.

Colonel Greer grabbed a private's sleeve. "Go see the matter. Hurry!" The soldier raced toward the commotion.

The cannonading and rifle fire sounded furious. After a few minutes, a strange noise grew. A great hollering, both throaty and shrill, exploded beyond the trees, and it blended with the thunder of a cavalry charge.

The courier returned and handed the colonel a note. "It's from General McCulloch."

Colonel Greer opened the paper. "Men, we are to proceed up to this small knoll." He pointed past them to a tree-covered hill. "And maintain the left flank." He raised his hands and rolled his eyes.

The echoes of a great collision of men and weapon sounded near, then far, then near again. Joseph wondered what was happening. Again, a strong memory sprung to his mind, one of being in a battle formation. He stood beside Workman. They wore the gray uniform with a blue tint, but other soldiers down the line wore blue. His confusion from the day before about the remembered letter he had kept in his pocket long ago flooded his mind.

He had tried not to think on it, but the evidence was there. Was he truly a Confederate or was he a Union soldier?

He would not be allowed to dwell on his thoughts or ferret a solution, for the entire regiment turned and hastened up the small mount. Atop it, he reached a spot where, when leaning to the side, he could see the battle raging in the farm field. Hundreds of blue coats were racing in disarray past the farmhouse, south into the woods, surrounded by fleeing rider-less horses.

The Confederate cavalry milled about three cannons, celebrating. They were soon joined by Indians, some on foot, some on horseback. The whooping and hollering continued for quite a time. Joseph glanced at his colonel a few yards down the line. He was shaking his head in disgust. He dismounted and stood kicking the snowy dirt.

While the Confederate cavalry were regrouping, more Union soldiers appeared in the fields farther south and began a heated firing. Hebert's soldiers came marching rapidly up the road and fell in behind the small hill by Greer's regiment and in front of it.

Everything Joseph saw seemed deliberate and almost emotionless: soldiers lining up, being ordered to fire, or charge, or retreat.

Joseph began questioning why he was fighting. Elements of his memory that had rushed into his mind over the last two days had left him perfunctorily baffled. He began considering sneaking away. He was becoming more and more assured that he was fighting for the wrong army.

When this battle's over, I'll find a way to escape.

FIFTY-EIGHT

◌

HEARKEN TO THE BATTLE RAGING

MARCH 7, 1862, 11 AM
ELKHORN TAVERN

B en awoke from a nap in his bed, surrounded by Union soldiers, sick or injured to some degree, on mats on the floor. He knew the sound of cannons, but was unsure of the source of the firing. The injured and sick soldiers arose, leaning on their elbows or standing. Each man listened.

"What's happening?" a soldier asked.

Ben did not want to join in a discussion with the Yankees who shared the room. He hobbled onto the upper porch, his splint pinching at every step. He swept a layer of snow from the rail and leaned against it.

Cyntha appeared from her upstairs family room, followed by Polly and her children. The muffled cannonading continued.

"It's off to the West," Ben said.

Anthony arrived on the upstairs porch, followed by Jeanette and Clara, worried expressions on their faces. "Are they practicing firing the cannons?" Anthony asked.

Ben hunched his shoulders. "I don't know. Sounds too much of a hurry to be practice."

Silence.

"There, it's stopped," Jeanette said. "The noon meal is almost ready."

"Yes," Cyntha replied. "We are fortunate that there has been no shortage of food since the army stops here and shares with us."

"Yeah," Ben said sarcastically, "the Yanks got plenty of food they stole from us Southerners and never paid a dime for any of it. Don't thank the Yanks, thank the good people of the South that raised it." Ben immediately felt remorse for his comment in front of Cyntha.

None of the group responded. The Union soldiers went back to their mats. The Coxes, Atkinsons, and Cyntha trod downstairs, leaving Ben to his own disappointing thoughts. He looked out at the white, serried fields and the three roads that met at the tavern. Each road was lined with wagons laden with boxes and sacks of food stuffs and armaments. "Too many wagons. Makes me sick to see 'em."

A handful of tents sat on the snow-covered ground, a larger one for use as a hospital. Dozens of muleskinners milled about campfires, smoking pipes, or cooking their noon meal. A handful of Union cavalry huddled by their horses, keeping their own company. He heard soldiers telling brag stories on the porch below. "I can't believe it, I'm surrounded by an army of sorry bluecoats."

"Probably ain't more'n fifty." Reynolds had stolen up behind him.

Ben turned. "Hey, Reynolds. I guess you're right, but I sure wish my leg would heal faster, so I could get away from here."

"And how would you do that without a horse, my young Texan?'

"I'm a Texan all right, but I grew up in these parts before we moved to Texas. If I fetched one of them Union horses, I'd find my way to freedom. Where you live, old man?"

"I was owned by two different families in Tennessee before Miss Cyntha and her husband bought me and gi' me my freedom. Now I live in Iowa with Miss Cyntha, keepin' the farm runnin'."

"Well, you're a head smarter than any colored I ever met. And besides...." Ben stopped short. The sound of massed rifle fire and more cannon fire came from the same direction as before.

Then Ben looked past Reynolds. Heading from the South up the Telegraph Road, hundreds of Union soldiers came at a trot. Several mule-drawn cannons and caissons hurried along behind them. "Wonder where they're headed?"

Reynolds saw the army. "Looks like they be comin' towards us."

A new clamoring sprang from the opposite direction. A small troop of Confederate cavalry launched up the Bentonville Detour Road. They galloped to a halt beside the wagons, pulled revolvers and shot at the muleskinners and at the Union cavalry. Bullets flew in all directions. Ben and Reynolds ducked.

The Confederate arrival was such a surprise, the Union cavalrymen barely had time to grab their rifles before the Confederates rode back the way they had come.

They raced away about a quarter of a mile before they halted and entered the trees. Standing on the upper porch, Ben could see them blending into the woods, and a handful of gray-clad infantry rushed to take positions with them, their rifles raised.

"Advanced scouting party. The Confederates are coming!" he whispered.

He looked again to the South. More and more Union soldiers raced toward the tavern.

He had the sudden realization that a battle was going to commence right below where he stood. "It's like the compass got shattered. The Yanks are comin' from the South, the Confederates from the North."

He hurried back into the room where the Yankees who could walk were trying to crowd down the stairway, carrying their brogans. Despite his splinted leg, he maneuvered past them and met Cyntha at the bottom of the stairs. The Cox family was gathering a few keepsakes and hurrying out the back door. Anthony, Jeanette, and Clara followed them. Ben looked at Cyntha. She stared with a worried expression out a front window. He put his arm around her and coaxed her out the back door.

Outside, blue-coated soldiers were already filling the yard while the wagon drivers tried to move their wagons. Officers yelled. Squads of men rushed through the tavern and into the yard and spread out along the roads. To Ben, the entire yard had been painted blue.

Immediately, firing commenced between the Confederates and Federals. Ben and Cyntha arrived at the outside doors to the root cellar just as Anthony pulled them open. The women and children were hurried into the narrow storage cellar by Joe Cox.

Ben and Anthony came last and pulled the doors shut. Above them, they heard the rush of many boots. The children, Elias and Franklin Cox, and Clara Atkinson crouched, holding hands to their ears, while Polly and Jeanette tried to comfort them.

The crack between the two cellar doors allowed a sliver of light into the gloomy abode.

"Oh, my Heavens!" Cyntha exclaimed. "What is happening?"

"My dear sister," Anthony said calmly. "We are at war, and the battle has come here."

"Where is Reynolds?"

"He stayed upstairs to care for the sick ones that can't move."

Cyntha attempted to rush out the cellar doors, but Anthony gripped her arms.

"I must save Reynolds!" she exclaimed.

"He's on his own now," Anthony said. "In a way, we all are."

"Perhaps we should pray," Jeanette offered. She swept her black locks from her eyes where tears had brimmed.

Of one accord, the little troop, except Ben, bowed their heads and whispered prayers.

Suddenly, the firing stopped.

Ben stood nearest the door, lifting it a small amount to peer out. He had not prayed with the others, but he had engendered a plan. He knew the Confederate advance patrol had departed, but soon, a Rebel army would be coming down that road. *Hope there's enough of 'em to whip these sorry invaders. If the opportunity comes, this is where I escape.*

Cyntha stepped up beside him and whispered, "Don't do what you're thinking."

"And why not?" he whispered back.

"Because I need you."

Ben looked over his shoulder at her. "What for?"

She drew up close to him, her warm lips at his ear. "I need you to escort me to the Fox sisters up north. Reynolds can't stay with me the whole way to New York."

Ben turned his head. "New York? I'll think about it."

"Please, Ben, I need to set my husband's soul to rest so I can move on with my life."

He wondered if Anthony's family or the Coxes heard her, but her pleading bit at his conscience.

Cyntha pulled him around by his arm and once more put her hand on his chest over his heart. "Please."

"If any of us survive the battle comin', I'll think about it." He turned again to peek out the slightly open cellar door. Gunfire began intensifying. He felt his heart racing, but he knew it was not because of the fighting outside.

FIFTY-NINE

⌘

THERE IS NO SUCH THING AS AN ACCIDENT. IT IS FATE MISNAMED.

— NAPOLEON BONAPARTE

MARCH 7, 1862, 1 PM
THE FORD ROAD NORTH OF LEETOWN, ARKANSAS

Occasional cannonballs launched by new Union artillery over the woods behind Mr. Foster's farm exploded in the field where the victorious Confederates and Cherokees milled. The soldiers scampered back to the Ford Road and began reforming their regiments. The Cherokees panicked and raced away for more than a mile.

Paul watched in astonishment. He had never witnessed a full-scale battle before, and the disjointedness of it amazed him.

He rode alongside General McCulloch in and out of the trees behind Ford Road. They stopped, and Paul waited while Generals McCulloch and McIntosh and Colonel Hebert, still on their horses, bent their heads together in planning. At length, Colonel Hebert and General McIntosh rode back to their brigades to await further orders.

Hebert's division was trotting along the Ford Road to take position on the left flank of the division. McIntosh's mounted brigade had largely backed up into the cover of the trees to await orders for the next charge.

Colonel Armstrong was watching through his binoculars the patches of blue-clad soldiers sprinkling out into the far woods beyond the farm. General McCulloch rode up to him and tapped him on the arm. "You best retreat some into the trees, Colonel. A sharpshooter could pick you off, especially on that light gray horse of yours.

"Yes, sir." Colonel Armstrong backed his horse behind a large oak then leaned around, binoculars up. He spoke over his shoulder. "It's hard to tell their strength, General McCulloch, with the woods covering. I'd estimate maybe a thousand. There's a battery firing from beyond the woods. I see the smoke, but can't tell the number. Maybe eight or nine pieces."

"Our artillery is almost prepared," General McCulloch said. "They'll be returning fire shortly. That'll drive them back."

Paul looked to his left where the Confederate batteries were unlimbering. He turned to Colonel Armstrong. "Do they look to be reinforced?"

"Hard to say. Those blue devils are fast. They seem to be hurrying, but in no real battle formation."

A cannonball landed, exploding several yards in front of the three, tossing up fire and dirt, a smattering of the dirt landing on them.

"What are your orders, General?" Colonel Armstrong calmly brushed the dirt from his sleeves.

"Let's wait a moment. This little delaying force may not be worth our time. I may leave a small regiment and a battery here to keep 'em entertained while we move to join Van Dorn at the tavern. Just hold here."

"Yes, sir."

"Captain McGavin, ride with me a way west. Let's take a reconnoiter, get a better idea of what we're facing."

"I'm right with you, sir," Paul pulled his hat lower. A new chilling breeze had picked up.

The two trotted their horses in a gentle zig-zag through the trees. When they came upon mounted officers, General McCulloch admonished each one to keep cover lest a sharpshooter find his mark.

Despite the snowfall, many of the trees still held to their brown and smoky gray leaves from autumn. Paul listened to the crackle of the leaves under their horses' hooves, a sort of soothing symphony despite the erratic cannon fire.

Again, the face of Sara drifted into his mind. He touched the small silver jewelry box in his shirt pocket and smiled.

He had something to remember her by, but he worried. *I hope she's still alive.* He wished that McCulloch's army would quickly dispatch this wayward group of Yankees, and the battle be over. He stopped himself from hoping the soldier for whom she searched would die. *Not that.*

He deigned to search for Sara the moment the battle was over.

After a jaunt of about fifteen hundred yards, General McCulloch and Paul had passed the Foster farm and the entirety of the army in a wide half circle and entered a thicket of scrabbly bushes that marked the end of the woods. Two tall trees abutted the woods.

Occasional firing popped and snapped to their left. The batteries of the two armies blasted at each other in occasional salvos. No Union or Confederates were in sight. They were alone.

"I believe we've ridden as much as we need," General McCulloch broke Paul's thoughts. "We're far enough from their advance elements that we can take a good long look down their flank."

"Yes, sir."

The two cantered their horses into a narrow clearing a few feet past the bush enfilade. General McCulloch pointed. "Paul, climb that tall tree and tell me what you see. Tie your horse at the bottom."

In less than a minute, Paul stood on his saddle, and was scrambling up the tall, bare elm, its gray branches stretching like witch's fingers into the sky. He found a notch between two limbs and propped himself there. He brought up his spyglass and began scanning the field.

"I think I'll ride a little bit over here to take a look, too." General McCulloch trotted his big, white stallion into the clearing between Paul's elm tree and another shorter tree.

"The Yanks are building force," Paul called down. "Looks like several regiments at least. More soldiers coming up the road behind those woods."

"You're a good man, McGavin. Best I've got." General McCulloch held up his spyglass and began surveying the field, looking mostly to his right.

"Wait a minute. Wait a minute. Look out!" Paul's call over his shoulder was urgent. "General McCulloch, there's a line of Yank skirmishers, maybe a company's worth just beyond that rail fence only a couple hundred yards in front of us. You best take...."

Paul saw the thirty odd puffs of smoke from the skirmisher position before the crack of the rifles.

He turned his head in time to see General McCulloch knocked backward by the bullet and saw the blood spirt out the man's back as the general tumbled from his horse. The white stallion fled.

Then a bullet hit Paul square in his chest, knocking him from the tree. He plummeted, bouncing off his horse and landing in a pile of snow-laden brown and gray leaves. Raising his head, pain surged across his chest and back, and he wondered if this was when he was to die. He drew his hand across his whole chest and felt no blood. He looked down and saw no blood. He forced himself to relax. *Why am I not dead? Don't let me die, Lord.* He realized from within the deepest part of his being that he wanted to live for one overarching reason. *I can't die without seeing Sara.* The pain was so intense, he drifted into a restless unconsciousness.

The two bodies lay in the cold, barren field, unnoticed for over an hour.

SIXTY

∽

TO ASSAIL THE IMPASSIBLE WALL

March 7, 1862, 3 pm
A Bluff Overlooking Washington, DC

Lucas peered through his binoculars at the muddy slop of a city, Washington. Even the cobbled streets were mired in a thick layer of sludge. The entirety of the capital's buildings appeared bathed in soot and filth, dismal gray and black.

Hundreds of chimneys poured smoke into the foul air. Lucas recognized several chimneys were for newly built foundries for the tools of war. In the middle of several streets, wagons and horses skirted large fires that spilled even more black smoke into the sky.

Numerous soldiers stood clumped like blue bushes, warming themselves near the fires while other infantryman hastened on mucky paths among tents packed tight in every available space. The tents extended out of the city north and west for miles. A train sat puffing on a railroad siding, and a second one glided across the Potomac River Bridge.

In sloppy fields, squads of men marched back and forth. In other fields, soldiers labored at duties from digging latrines to constructing crude timber cabin walls around tents. Several expansive tents bore the yellow hospital flag.

On the outer reaches of the town, great embankments for forts had been raised, and crews of soldiers, townsfolk, and freemen toiled at pitching up dirt for new fort walls. In front of the walls, spiked barricades strewed across land that used to be meadows. Throughout the barricades, pickets on horseback waited, spaced every fifty yards.

A great scramble of noises rose from the city to where Workman and Lucas stood on a low bluff.

Workman gave a low whistle. "Must be a hundred thousand men down there."

Lucas, his face now with a dense, full beard, lifted his trumpet to his ear. "Say again."

"That's quite an army them Yanks got down there. What'd you suppose they mean to do with that many men?"

"I imagine they mean to attack Richmond. You've read the papers. General McClellan has been training this army for months. I believe, however, that if my plan works, we will see an end to this war, and this army will never march."

"I agree. Say, I see the Capitol building." Workman pointed. "Never seen it before. Looks like they're workin' on it. Lots of scaffolding. And look there!" He pointed. "The White House. You reckon Lincoln's in there?"

"I would wager he is. But he doesn't stay cooped up all the time. He goes out to view the army or to make a speech. We just have to find out when. Then either you, with your skilled marksmanship, will kill him from a distance, or I will kill him at close quarters.

"But first, we must get into the city, find living arrangements, and endeavor carefully to infiltrate the White House itself, or at least find someone who can inform us of his calendar in advance. In any case, we need to act with due hast, but not without caution."

"He'll have guards around him, won't he?"

"Yes, Workman, he will. But with you wearing the new Yankee uniform that you stole, you will appear as perfectly normal as any other soldier passing on the street. I will wear my old uniform. It still fits. We must not draw attention to ourselves, so I have a plan to explain our detachment from a regiment."

"We done traveled many hundred miles to get here. Illinois, Ohio, Kentucky, Pennsylvania and Maryland. We met a lot of kind people. Thank God for that one couple that let us stay in their cabin during that long snow."

"They let us stay a month."

The two silently perused the strident movements of the throngs of men in the Union camp.

Workman had agreed with Lucas's plan to assassinate President Lincoln, and thus bring an end to the war.

One life for many, Workman thought. He felt no ambivalence at the correctness of the task before them, only wariness of stealing back into the midst of the Union army which he had only months before abandoned. If he was found out, he would be shot as a traitor. He pursed his lips through his mustache. His back felt better, but it worried him occasionally.

Lucas felt called to this task. This was a chore of duty, and the most magnanimous thing he could do for his country. He believed himself a true patriot. He hated Lincoln and the war his election had engendered. He had seen enough bloodshed, read about even more, and this stroke of callousness would surely bring about its end. He was adamant that their effort would bring about the best conclusion for all. If Lincoln was dead, the North would sue for peace.

Deeper down, he felt an immense remorse. Most of his family was dead. His friend, Abram, was gone. He knew he would never see Sara again. His farm was a memory, and he felt himself growing very old. What use was he anymore? *The country will be healed by this one act*, he thought. *If I die, so be it. I am no longer alive anyway.*

He pulled from his pocket the compass Julia Dent Grant had given him. He looked at it until the needle settled. "Hmm. Not an army from the south, but two Southerners riding into Washington from the north to change the course of the war."

WHAT DO YOU THINK WILL HAPPEN IN THE THIRD BOOK OF THE TRILOGY?

If there is one important lesson in life — things don't always turn out as expected. Which questions do you think will be answered in the final book of the series? To tide you over until the next book, I've included a portion of a chapter from the third book in the trilogy on the following pages.

1. What if Sara and Cyntha meet? What if Joseph arrives at Elkhorn Tavern?
2. Will Ben escape or will he help Cyntha go to New York? Will Paul meet his brother? In this life or the next?
3. Did you give up on Abram being just a side story? Don't. He plays an intricate role.
4. How will Julia Dent Grant behave when bound up in war with her husband Ulysses Grant?
5. And Reynolds will be the bravest of all by doing what?
6. Constance Carver and Reverend Felder are caught in a snow storm. Is there a future for them?
7. The notorious Fox sisters are drawing closer and closer to Cyntha. What part will they and John Coincoin play?
8. Joseph is regaining his memory. Will he remember Cyntha? If so, what choices will he make?
9. What will Colonel Greer do? General McIntosh, Colonel Hebert — what will they all do? Is General Curtis up for the battle?
10. I can tell you that the battle of Pea Ridge, or Elkhorn Tavern, will end. But what will be the impact on the characters?
11. Finally, will Lucas's plan to assassinate President Lincoln succeed? And who knows what Dred Workman will do?
12. What plot twists can you imagine?

All the characters converge in many different ways. The third book begins in the middle of battle. The adventure intensifies with more action, more battle, more heart-rending romance, and plot twists. The passion, the longing, the struggle to live.

Sign up NOW for occasional updates on the third book of the trilogy at curtlocklearauthor.com.

PASSAGE FROM THE
THIRD BOOK IN THE TRILOGY

Paul McGavin lay on his back in a shallow pile of snow-frosted, brown leaves. When he became conscious, the first thing he realized was that he was shivering and that he lay on frigid ground. His breathing was strained, his chest felt burdened as if clamped with metal bands. He had no idea where he was or what he had been doing. Casting his eyes back, he saw blue sky and the bleak, scraggly tops of trees, mostly barren of leaves.

Drifting back into a half dream state, he found himself at the Texas creek where his brother, Asa, had ordered him to chase the fleeing horse herd, leaving his brothers and friends to fight the Comanches, and he could not help them. That dream blended into another incident — at Fort Smith — the shootout with the slave bounty hunters.

He awoke flinching, sure that the bounty hunters' bullets were flying at him. Gathering his senses, he slowed his breathing, aware of the reality of his lying amid snow and dead leaves.

His left eye was blurry with a pinkish film. He raised his left hand to his eye to wipe it and felt intense pain in the arm and in the middle of his back, like he had been lying across a railroad tie. He rubbed his bleary eye, and then his forehead and felt a profuse wetness. He brought his hand before his eyes. The palm was covered in blood. Have I been shot? He knew that head wounds bled much out of proportion to the actual wound. He gingerly touched his forehead again at a deep gash and surmised that the wound was not from a bullet.

Fierce cannonading, which had been stilled when he first awoke, spouted loud, echoing booms, followed by intense shrieks, the cannonballs slicing the sky.

Paul sat upright. I'm in a battle.

His thoughts remained muddled. How long have I been out?

Twisting a little, a throbbing pain rose in his chest like he had been slugged with the butt of a rifle. He lay down again and put fingers to his chest where the ache was. He felt a metal square box in the shirt pocket, and he recalled that Sara had given him the small, silver, jewelry case outside of General McCulloch's headquarters on that snowbound night. The night she put her hand to his cheek. Probably that box was the most valuable thing she owned. He felt a surge of ardent interest in the striking, young woman, not just because of her comely appearance, but something intriguing about her charisma and depth of character.

He tugged the box from the pocket and peered at it. It was smashed flat, and a bullet, a Minie ball, was lodged in it. The awareness that he actually had been shot, and that Sara's little gift had saved his life gradually sank in. "Thank you, Sara. Thank you, God."

Paul heard a horse snort and the clip clop of hooves. He turned his sore neck to his left and saw his mare just a few feet away, still tied to the tree he had climbed. He looked up at the leafless elm and saw his binoculars hanging from a bare branch. He remembered then that he had been up in the tree observing the Yankees when he saw the line of skirmishers firing.

One of their shots had hit him. He tumbled down, landed on the back of his horse, which broke his fall and gave the ache to his back, and he rolled a few feet away. *Lucky, I'm not worm meat.*

He bent his neck to his right. Immediately, he saw General McCulloch's body almost covered with the abundant leaves that flitted about in a stiff breeze. Off in the distance, the general's white stallion grazed placidly. Taking a deep breath, he stuck the bent jewelry case in his pocket, then struggled to his feet, clutching his bruised chest. He wiped his bloody hand on his pants and tore the tail of his shirt into a strip and bound his head wound.

A few bullets thudded into the trees beside him. He ducked; and then, half crawling, half walking bent over, he made his way to General McCulloch's body.

Subscribe to Curt's blog at www.curtlocklearauthor.com
Follow Curt on Twitter @CurtLock

If you would like for Curt to speak to your group,
please contact him at Curt@curtlocklearauthor.com

Download your complimentary MP3 album at
www.reverbnation.com/splinteredsongsofthecivilwar